The Boy with Blue Trousers

CAROL JONES

HEAD
ZEUS

First published in the UK in 2019 by Head of Zeus Ltd
This paperback edition published in the UK in 2019 by Head of Zeus Ltd

This is a work of fiction. All characters, organizations,
and events portrayed in this novel are either products of
the author's imagination or are used fictitiously.

9 7 5 3 2 4 6 8

A catalogue record for this book is available from
the British Library.

ISBN (PB): 9781786699879
ISBN (E): 9781786699848

Typeset by NewGen

Printed and bound in Great Britain by
CPI Group (UK) Ltd, Croydon CR0 4YY

Head of Zeus Ltd
First Floor East
5–8 Hardwick Street
London EC1R 4RG
WWW.HEADOFZEUS.COM

The Boy with Blue Trousers

Born in Brisbane, Australia, Carol Jones taught English and drama at secondary schools before working as an editor of children's magazines. She is the author of several young adult novels as well as children's non-fiction. Her novel *The Concubine's Child* was published by Head of Zeus in 2018.

ALSO BY CAROL JONES

The Concubine's Child

For Vincent

The handcart was almost too heavy to lift. It bumped and wobbled around mullock heaps, skirting gaping holes, threatening to spill its cargo onto the pockmarked earth. Steadying the cart, the youth braced for the descent into the gully. In the distance, campfires flickered like fireflies amongst the tents, whilst ahead the bush beckoned.

Dark. Silent. Secluded enough to hide a secret forever.

The gully's banks were ridged with erosion where an army of miners had been at work, shovelling and sluicing with water dragged up from the creek. Makeshift plank bridges spanned the depleted creek as it trickled through the diggings. The gully wasn't deep but its banks were steep. The handcart was heavy and its load uneven. One false step and the cart would escape, hurtling over uneven ground to fling its contents into the water.

The youth paused, searching the night sky. But the skies of this southern land had never offered any heavenly guidance. They were alien, just as the land was alien. Wild and brown, populated by outlandish creatures and unfathomable men. Dry and dusty, with grey-leaved trees that shed bark in long, curling ribbons. A land that resisted order and thrived on chaos.

Although his arms were hard from the backbreaking work of mining gold, he started down the slope uneasily, taking one stuttering step then another, his blue cotton trousers hemmed with dust. But the cart dragged him forward, intent on yanking him from his feet. Gathering speed, it rumbled over a ridge of earth before becoming briefly airborne so that its contents shifted, sliding sideways, threatening to topple cart and youth in an untidy heap. Straining every muscle, he twisted his forearms, battling the dead weight of cart and cargo. Then, in a semi-crouch, he used the power of his legs to halt the runaway cart.

Breathing hard, he rested halfway down the gully's bank, the cart stable for the moment. But its contents had moved so that one blue-clad leg dangled over the edge, the foot bare and covered with scratches. He grabbed the leg by the ankle to place it back where it belonged, finding the flesh still warm, its heat sending a jolt through his arm.

Cradling the leg, he felt a dense mass fill his throat, as if everything that had happened in the past year was rising up to choke him. His gaze lingered on the figure curled up in the cart – arms crossed haphazardly over chest, a single braid draped about the neck – and he felt hot tears well. How had it come to this? How had they found themselves so far from the ordered groves and rice paddies of the mighty Pearl River? Why had the gods of the Celestial Kingdom abandoned them? And how had they come to hate each other so?

They had been friends of a sort once.

1

Pearl River Delta, China, 1856

Already that day Little Cat had picked three baskets of mulberry leaves and reeled three *taels* of silk. One weary arm cranked the reel, while the other managed the complex task of transforming simmering cocoons into a single continuous thread. Yet no matter how nimble her fingers, or how sharp her eyes, her hand still grew raw plucking spent cocoons from boiling water, while her eyes strained from teasing out the gossamer fibres. Silkworms were ugly, insatiable beasts. Their silk was a hefty burden for a girl of seventeen. And she had done more than enough for one day.

That decision made, she reeled the last silk from the cocoons, removed the pot from the stove and doused the coals. She set aside the basket of cocoon husks to feed the fish and stood stretching tired limbs. Outside in the small courtyard, sunlight leaked through clouds, turning the air warm and sticky. She was lucky that the worn, gummed silk of her tunic did not cling to her body like damp cotton. It was said that river mud and persimmon juice made it waterproof. It also made for an arduous process of mashing, dyeing, smearing and drying so that the outer side of the fabric was glazed black to repel water while the inner side turned a matt, muddy brown. No wonder Ma hadn't made her a new set in so long.

Second Brother would be finished at the fishponds. Perhaps he was even now down by the riverbank, plunging his feet in the cooling waters as minnows darted about on the sandy bottom. She too was in urgent need of a wade in the river. Her feet were feeling particularly warm from proximity to the charcoal stove, and her forehead was dotted with sweat from the steam. She walked to the edge of the veranda, listening for signs of activity elsewhere in the house. But there was silence from the kitchen and only the low rumble of snores erupting from Grandfather's room. Her mother must have already set out to the mulberry grove for the evening harvest. Her father would be paddling back from market. Elder Brother would be tending the newly hatched worms in the worm house, chopping leaves and sorting the dead from the living. If she was quick, Little Cat could be down by the riverbank before anyone had a chance to forbid it.

She stepped out from the shelter of the veranda and faced the door to the alley. High brick walls surrounded her on all sides, crowned by a roof of curving clay tiles. Behind her, three main rooms faced south, protected by the veranda from the summer sun. One room faced west, another east, while a wall the height of two men enclosed the small courtyard to the south. Sometimes, when she had been trapped too long inside, she imagined the baked earthen bricks crumbling to dust and blowing away, or melting to mud from summer's torrential rains. But then her entire family would be left with nowhere to sleep and only she would be safe in the girls' house with her friends. What kind of unfilial daughter was she to think such selfish thoughts?

'Little Cat!'

Her breath caught in her throat as her mother's voice echoed faintly up the alley between rows of houses. She could tell that her mother wasn't happy. She considered answering, like a good daughter would, but then Ma would expect her to trudge out to the mulberry grove and spend the last hours of daylight picking leaves for ungrateful worms. If she were a paragon of filial piety like the sons and daughters in the *shan-shu* stories, she would defy robbers to pick mulberries for her mother. She would wrestle tigers to save her father. But she wasn't. Anyway, she would only be defying worms, not robbers or tigers, so it hardly counted as heroic. She might as well not bother. She thought of all the other things she could be doing – trading punches with her brother down by the river, listening to gossip in the girls' house, even daydreaming under the *nammu* trees – and she began searching for somewhere to hide. Ma had the nose of a moon bear and could sniff out any hiding place in the house.

'Little Cat! Where are you?' Her mother's voice rose higher as she scolded so that she sounded like a discordant *erhu*. 'I told you to come pick leaves when you finished the last basket of cocoons.'

A few moments more and it would be too late; her mother would arrive in the courtyard with her sharp eyes and the trusty bamboo stick she used for scaring away snakes. Yet the house was so small that there was only one place where she could be sure to escape her mother's notice, one place where Ma had never thought to look. One place no one would be stupid enough to hide.

She scooted over to the well and dangled her legs over the edge. The well wasn't wide, scarcely one arm's span in diameter. The last time she had hidden here she was ten years old and her father was chasing her with a rush broom for trying to pee standing up like her brothers.

'Little Cat!'

Hesitating for only a moment, she leaned forward to grab the rope that was tethered to the ground and slithered inside, supporting her bodyweight with her arms. She had strong arms from picking and reeling and lifting stone training weights with her brother. Still, it was a tighter squeeze than she remembered and all that was keeping her from falling was an ageing length of rope. Perhaps this wasn't such a clever idea, after all. She almost regretted her decision, for there was scarcely room to brace her toes against the slimy bricks and she could hardly bend her knees. She inched further down, scraping her shoulders against the rough masonry until her head was an arm's length below the rim. Then wedging her back against one side and her feet in the cracks between bricks on the other, she held on for her life.

'Where is that body itchy girl?'

Hearing her mother so near, she shimmied down a little further and held her breath. There was always the danger of a stray giggle to give her away, or a loud splash if she put a foot wrong. The well was shallow but she didn't want to find out just how shallow, for she might get a nasty surprise. She listened as her mother upturned baskets and searched under beds, disturbing Grandfather so that he woke with a snort. She clattered from room to room, muttering curses before finally giving up and stomping across the courtyard and back into the alley with a heartfelt, 'That girl will be the death of me yet.'

Although her toes and legs were screaming at her to release them, Little Cat counted one hundred breaths, not daring to move, for her mother was as tricky as she was nosy. When she felt safe enough to look up, she discovered that the clouds had dispersed, opening a circle of sky above her head, a circle of perfect blue that was suddenly blocked by a dark silhouette. She braced her shoulders for a beating, at the very least a tongue-lashing.

'One day you're going to fall in and then we won't find you till you stink up the well and spoil the water like a dead rat.'

'Oh, it's you, Goh Go. Help me out. My toes are falling off.' She sighed in relief at the sound of Second Brother's voice. She wasn't bothered that he likened her to a dead rat, for he had called her worse many times.

'How long have you been down there?' he asked as he stretched out a hand to help her.

'Long enough.' She wormed her way upwards, bracing her back against the well wall and pulling herself up the rope. Then she adjusted her feet and repeated the process until she was close enough to grasp one of his hands. Between the two of them they hauled her up and over the lip of the well and onto the dusty ground.

'It wasn't so tight last time,' she said, as she picked herself up from the dirt and dabbed at the dirty marks on her tunic.

'*Fai mui*. You eat too much rice. Girls should bend like a willow branch.'

'Maybe inside girls with golden lilies for feet and hands like magnolia petals.' Not girls like her who laboured in rice paddies or mulberry groves. Their hands were scraped and brown from the sun. Their feet walked many *li* each day. Their toes hadn't been broken and curled under like hooves so that they swayed when they walked. How she would hate to be one of those inside girls, forbidden to visit temples with her friends or enjoy the visiting opera troupes. Perhaps their golden lilies might fetch their parents a higher bride price but she would rather chop her feet off altogether. At least they would no longer hurt.

Her twin was staring at her tunic with a smug smile and a glint of laughter in his eyes. 'Ma won't be happy.

You tore your tunic, little sister. Double punishment for you.' These days it was always 'double punishment' never 'double happiness' for her. These days she was always in trouble for one thing or another while Goh Go was the dutiful son.

'Where is Ma?' She twisted her head over one shoulder in a futile effort to assess the damage to her tunic. Perhaps she could repair the tear before her mother noticed it was there. Then again, she wasn't very handy with a needle. Her stitches straggled more untidily than pigeon footprints.

'Probably out harvesting leaves by now. I passed her on the way here.'

It wasn't fair. Why was she always the guilty one? Why didn't her mother ask Goh Go to help, since she passed him on her way to the grove? Why did her twin get to rest when he finished shovelling shit to the fish, yet she had more chores to do? He was only thirty minutes her elder but it might as well have been thirty years.

'You could have helped her,' she said through gritted teeth. She felt like shouting but that was another thing she was chastised for regularly.

'Picking mulberry leaves is for women and children,' laughed her brother. 'Hauling nets is men's work.'

Ever since their father began training him to maintain the ponds and repair the dykes, Goh Go had adopted a superior attitude. Once, they had done everything together – picked leaves, fed worms, planted the winter vegetables – but increasingly he took every opportunity to remind

9

her of their differences. To show off his muscles and his place in the world. To separate himself from her. As if he couldn't wait for her to be sent away. To be sent to live in another village with a stranger. To become part of another family. To become someone else. To un-twin her.

'It doesn't take brains to haul a net. That's why it's called men's work,' she said, and punched him in the stomach before he could deflect her hand.

'Don't start something you can't finish,' he responded with a sidekick to her shin. She grunted with the impact, knowing she would find a bruise there tomorrow. She had grown so much this last year that her trousers barely reached her calves. Ma was sure to notice the bruise and interrogate her. Yet another thing to get her into trouble.

Goh Go removed his bamboo hat and flung it to the ground, baring his shaved scalp to the sun. Then he secured his queue around the top of his head and they faced off, feet hip-width apart and pointing slightly inward, as they had done so many times in the past. Her brother grinned and brought his hands into a fighting stance. He held his left arm close to the body, elbow bent, in the subduing hand position, the other rolling through a series of familiar motions. She joined him so that their arms appeared to twirl around one another as they searched for an opening in the other's defence.

'You've been practising without me,' he said, and she couldn't decide whether he said it with approval or otherwise, for his narrowed eyes registered nothing but opportunism.

'I have too much time on my hands and you are always too busy,' she said with a laugh, and feinted an attack. But that laugh turned to a grunt as he deflected her attack with a winged arm and jabbed her chin hard with his other fist.

'That hurt!' she said, rubbing her chin reproachfully.

'It was meant to. You wonder why I rarely spar with you any more? Someone needs to teach you to stop fighting or no one will marry you. How will our parents find a family willing to take a daughter-in-law who is always fighting and arguing?'

'I don't need anyone to marry me.' Her words were scornful but her feelings were hurt. She wished hurt feelings were as easy to ignore as a scraped knee or a sore chin.

'Sooner or later you have to grow up, Little Cat. You have to stop behaving like a boy. You have to stop fighting and become a woman.'

But it was her twin who had taught her to fight. It was he who practised on her the arts he learned with the other boys. It was he who bought the martial arts manuals and pored over them with her in the mat shed behind the worm house. It was he who mastered the techniques of kung fu by beating up his sister. And now he wanted her to stop? She didn't want to stop.

She fought the urge to cry by renewing her attack. Claws out, teeth bared... like the fierce little cat of her nickname.

2

Most days Young Wu found reason to wander down the alley next to the Mo house. He told himself it happened to be situated along his route to the temple, or that it was the most convenient alley to reach the ferry poled by his cousin, Ferryman Wu. But the truth was that he liked to keep an eye on the Mo twins. This afternoon he was returning home from supervising the silk reelers at his clan's silk filature. As usual, his route followed the path along the river before making a turn through the village. Sandy Bottom Village was a three-surname village of some two hundred families. Situated on a bend in the river, its alleys wound between houses, skirted around banyan trees and traversed irrigation channels. Several of these alleys led to a paved road where the lineage temples and the Wu clan hall were sited. Others came to abrupt dead ends in a ruse designed to hinder any bandit or warlord who chose the village as prey.

It had taken centuries for Wu's ancestors to tame the river at Sandy Bottom Village. They had dug the fishponds, formed the dykes and planted the raised earth, so that from a distance the floodplain twinkled with water, and the land was lushly green with rank after rank of truncated mulberry trees, all arranged in the four-water-six land system. The entire area was criss-crossed with paths that meandered through field and village, yet Young Wu's journey always took him past one particular house, little different to any other whitewashed, mud-brick, clay-tiled house in the district. Except for one thing, or things. The Mo twins. Mo Wing Yong or Ah Yong and his sister Mo Lin Fa, better known as Little Cat.

The many layers of his cloth-soled shoes allowed him to tread softly along the dirt alley, stopping unnoticed at the entrance to the courtyard. Sometimes the only occupants were chickens. Sometimes Grandfather Mo could be seen, squatting on a low stool mending nets or weaving a raincoat from straw. If he was early, he might catch Little Cat and her mother reeling silk thread on the veranda and then he would continue on his way. But if he happened upon the twins alone, he would enter.

'Young Wu!' shouted Mo Wing Yong, catching sight of him in the doorway. The Wu clan accounted for more than five hundred souls in Sandy Bottom Village, by far the most numerous and prosperous lineage. But despite their multitude, everyone knew Wu Hoi Sing as Young Wu, son of Big Wu, who was headman of the village, and the Wu clan elder.

Unfortunately, Ah Yong had momentarily taken his eyes from his sister's hands to greet him. He watched as the girl exploited her brother's moment of inattention by pivoting on one leg and swinging the other in a high kick to the side of his head so that he reeled back from the blow. Yet his friend didn't seem unduly upset at the kick. He screwed up his face, before shaking his head to fling away the pain.

'Need some help teaching her a lesson, Ah Yong?' Young Wu laughed, folding his arms over his chest and leaning back against the wall, legs crossed at the ankles. He knew his comment was guaranteed to annoy Little Cat. Since she was so easily annoyed.

As expected, she threw him a withering glance before returning her attention to her brother. He felt a pang of something that may have been disappointment. He had expected more from her, a stinging riposte or, at the very least, an invitation to argue. The twins were his age mates and he had been keeping an eye on them for as long as he could remember. He supposed it had begun when they were ten and the twins stood up for him against Bully Yee – the biggest, meanest boy in the village – who had taken to calling him Maggot Wu. He didn't know why the boy taunted him in this way. Perhaps because it was the lowest thing he could think to call the headman's son. Or perhaps he really thought Young Wu was as loathsome as a maggot. In any case, he had found himself eating dirt with Bully Yee's big foot on his neck until the Mo twins threw themselves at his attacker. Ah Yong pummelled at the bully's back while Little Cat hung from his neck like a troublesome child.

They had all earned a beating that day, or to be precise, two beatings. One from Bully Yee, and another from their parents for fighting. Big Wu did not approve of pointless fighting, especially when his son lost. He did approve of purposeful fighting however, for bandits were a perennial problem in the region. Just last month he and the other elders had conceived a plan to build watchtowers in the village. His father believed the situation was only going to worsen, with the long-haired Taiping rebels warring with the Imperial Army, the foreigners creeping further and further up the Pearl River, and warlords taking advantage of the whole mess to grab for power.

Anyway, after the incident with Bully Yee, he had taken to trailing the Mo boy through the mulberry groves, sitting next to him in the clan hall at their lessons, or joining him under the banyan tree by the river when the monks came to teach them kung fu. He didn't mind admitting that he admired Yong's strength and agility. And there was something strange and exciting about the idea that his friend had shared a womb with his sister. With a girl. He couldn't imagine sharing a womb with one of his sisters. His two elder sisters would suck all the nourishment from the space and his younger sister would drive him away with her wriggling. He often wondered if some of Yong's maleness had rubbed off on Little Cat in the womb, for she didn't behave like other girls he knew. But if that were true, why hadn't some of her femaleness rubbed off on her brother? It was a mystery he was yet to solve.

Mo Wing Yong was his friend. Lin Fa, however, was generally an annoyance. Or so he complained to her brother. A loud, tall girl who popped up where she wasn't wanted, and spoke up when she wasn't invited. She wandered barefoot where she willed. She didn't seem to care that her pigtails were straggly or her trousers muddy, so unlike his own sisters. Not one of them would ever kick her brother in the head.

'It doesn't matter,' Ah Yong said now in response to his offer of help. He didn't glance up as he answered, focusing all his attention upon his sister, resetting his position, one elbow tucked loosely to his side. The girl was a hand shorter than her brother, and her limbs lacked his muscular bulk, but Wu knew from experience that she struck with the speed of a spitting cat.

'Why are you fighting a girl anyway? She should be wrestling laundry down at the riverbank, not fighting her betters.' He tried again to provoke a response.

'Tongue and teeth will fight each other sometimes,' Ah Yong muttered absently as he blocked his sister's next strike with a receiving hand.

'Tongue and teeth should work together,' Young Wu said, quite reasonably he thought. Even his Elder Sister, who was known for being bossy, would not think of upsetting family harmony like Little Cat.

'Tongue and teeth should learn to shut up!' she hissed, finally losing her temper.

'Little girls should learn to mind their manners.'

'Little boys should keep their opinions and their penises in their pants.'

Luckily, the last comment was too vulgar and disrespectful to be ignored. A curt reprimand was called for at the very least. Instead he found himself pushing off from the wall and kicking away his shoes, a tingling of anticipation twitching his arms.

'Want to show me how?' he offered, as he bent over to roll his trousers higher, and then coiled his queue around his neck. He knew that fighting a girl was unbecoming. He knew that she was goading him, but despite knowing these facts he felt a sense of urgency, as if he must teach her a lesson. Must subdue those long slender limbs, tangle those whirling arms, and flip her to the ground with a twisting leg. She was only a girl but he wanted to crush her. To make her—

'Lin Fa, that is enough!' Ah Yong shouted, capturing both his sister's wrists and holding them so tightly that she could not wrench them from his grasp. 'And you, Ah Sing, stop teasing my sister. She's too stupid to know when to stop and you should know better. You've had plenty of practice with three sisters.' He glanced angrily from Young Wu to his struggling twin.

'If she doesn't want to fight, she shouldn't pull the tiger's tail,' he said with a shrug.

'Who said I don't want to fight?'

'I did, little sister. You think you could win a real fight against either of us? I'm just toying with you.'

From where he stood, Young Wu saw how she struggled to free her wrists, twisting her arms so far that she was in danger of dislocating a shoulder to escape. She narrowed her eyes, flicking venom-filled glances from one youth to the other as her brother watched impassively.

'Let me free, Goh Go, and I'll show him not to mess with the tiger,' she hissed.

'Daaih Lou was right. I should never have let you train with me in the first place. But who listens to their older brother?' Ah Yong said, shaking his head before suddenly releasing her and stepping back. 'It has put all the wrong ideas in your head. Girls shouldn't fight.'

She was breathing hard. Young Wu couldn't help noticing how her chest rose and fell beneath her tunic, how she held her spine rigid with anger, and how red marks like manacles had formed about her wrists. He wanted to hold her close until her resistance melted away. He wanted to soothe her so that she purred rather than hissed. But he spoke none of this nonsense. Men did not speak of such things, not even to their wives.

'Your mother should have bound her feet when she could and then she would not be able to fight,' he said instead, with a conspiratorial glance at his friend. 'Now it is too late. She is *chang gai po*.' Like a chicken she would continue fighting long after she had lost her head.

'It's not true that girls shouldn't fight,' Little Cat shouted. 'One way or another, girls always have to fight.'

'Huh!'

'Teacher Fang invented the White Crane style by observing cranes. Wing Chun learned kung fu so that she could escape a bandit who would force her to marry him. Sometimes girls have no choice. Sometimes fighting is the only way to be free.'

She spat the words but the fight had gone out of her for the moment. Her arms hung loosely at her sides and her breathing slowed. She looked down at the ground rather than challenging them further. Her pigtails caressed the curve of her bowed neck like two ropes of silk. Young Wu knew he should be pleased that she ceased provoking him. This was as it should be, as the sage Confucius advised. Yet he was disappointed.

He strove to be a man of *yee*, a righteous man like his father, yet Little Cat brought out the brute in him. He was drawn to her and repelled at the same time. How could a man be gentle and good if a woman would not listen and obey?

'No one is free,' he said, pointing out the obvious. 'We all have obligations.'

She stood so still that he felt regret form like a pebble in his gut. There was something compelling about the fizz of blood in his veins that her hostility incited. His desire to fight her warred with his desire for righteous action. He did not want to let it go.

'Except perhaps a hermit,' he forced himself to croak.

'Of course a boy would say that,' she muttered, not raising her eyes from her feet, bare and narrow with long toes that clawed into the dust of the courtyard.

'One day you may find, little sister,' pronounced her brother, 'that the price of freedom is too high... even for you.'

Young Wu nodded, recognising this truth. He was the son of Big Wu. He had obligations to his father and the Wu ancestors going back fifty generations. He had to set an example. He had to relinquish vain desires.

3

Robetown, South Australia, 1856

That morning, the autumn sun had beckoned cheerfully, tempting Violet into a sprigged muslin day dress, which had cost the extortionate sum of two pounds six shillings the previous summer. Muslin may not have been the most prudent choice for a walk upon the beach, but how could she have predicted that a cold breeze would spring up from the bay, setting it to flapping, and turning all her labour with the curling iron to straw? The wind was playing havoc with her bonnet too, while twisted ropes of kelp twined about her boots and rimed the hem of her dress in salt. And all her vanity had been for naught, since the only people to see her were the children.

Perhaps an hour of arithmetic would have been advisable after all, despite the children's hankering for adventure, for they had been plodding along the beach for a good half-hour and still the sand stretched ahead for miles. Violet didn't fancy the walk back to town with sand whipping her face, yet neither did a climb over the dunes appeal, with the sword-like grass and prickly heath that dragged at her skirt and scratched her ankles. Not to mention all the nasty, biting things. But at least the walk would be shorter. It occurred to her that every decision in this disagreeable country became a choice between two evils.

Beside her, Alice picked her way through the seaweed, stooping every now and then to examine the chalky backbone of a cuttlefish or toss a flat stone out to sea, whilst James played chicken with the creeping waves. Violet bent to pick up one of the cuttlebones, dusting the sand from her glove with the other hand. 'Did you know, children, that this shell is the backbone of a creature with ten arms called a cuttlefish?'

'Mrs Smith feeds it to her parakeet,' said Alice, snapping the cuttlebone in two. 'It isn't very strong for a bone.'

'I believe its lightness helps the creature stay afloat. And the cuttlefish has the remarkable ability to change colour too.'

'I should like to see that,' said James, distracted from his game momentarily.

'Have you seen one change colour, Miss Hartley?' asked Alice.

'No, but I have read about it in Mr Darwin's book. My previous employers were fortunate to possess an extensive library.' But she did not want to think about her previous employer or his walls of books. She had travelled to the ends of the earth to escape those memories. 'Well, I think we have had enough Nature for one day,' she announced.

'Just a little longer,' Alice pleaded.

'Your nose is pink already, Alice. Your poor mama will have conniptions when she sees you.' The girl was unlikely to risk upsetting her mother since they were all familiar with Mrs Wallace's conniptions. Her brother, however, was made of sterner stuff and would not be dissuaded from his expedition by the threat of a ruined complexion or a tearful mama.

'Cook has promised seed cake,' said Violet, sidestepping the carcass of a large crab.

Food was her customary bribe with eight-year-old boys, but this morning seed cake appeared to have lost its attraction too, for James remained deaf to her pleas. Rather, he poked industriously at the dead crab with a stick of driftwood so that its insides oozed forth in yellowish slime, while Alice looked on in scientific fascination. Violet was considering resorting to sterner measures when he shouted suddenly, 'Look, a steamer!' abandoning the crab and pointing out to sea.

Indeed, a ship was steaming into the bay from the north, coming from the port of Adelaide, no doubt. Sailing low and dark in the water, with twin masts and a single funnel belching smoke, it seemed vaguely familiar.

'It's the *Burra Burra*,' he declared, 'on its way to Melbourne.'

'The *Burra Burra*,' Violet repeated with a shiver. Had it been a mere three months since she found herself ensconced below its decks with six girls bound for service in the South Australian bush, a pianoforte, numerous bolts of cloth, several crates of tea, a barrel of pitch and assorted plumbing fixtures? Already it seemed like an age since she had stepped onto the rickety jetty in Robetown, to be met by Mr Wallace. Following upon the interminable voyage from Gravesend, she had never been happier to find herself with solid earth beneath her feet.

Since the voyage from England, she had discovered a new respect for sailors, something she hadn't appreciated when her father was alive. As a child she was more interested in his tales of strange lands and the even stranger creatures he met than the dangers of his journeying. But on her voyage out she experienced the rigours of a sailor's life for the first time. The sun had burned so hot that it melted the pitch upon the deck. She had it from the mate that the beef had been three years in the barrel. The water was so tainted she could not drink it without a splash of vinegar and the butter had turned to a rancid oil. Perhaps she was lucky she had been too seasick to eat anything other than stale biscuits, so hard she had to break them with a hammer. Her single consolation for these privations had been the inches she shed from her waist. To think that this had been her father's lot for his twenty years at sea.

Violet closed her eyes on further thoughts of her father or her journey. She wasn't one to dwell upon unhappy circumstances. Unhappiness was too debilitating for a young woman of uncertain means and indeterminate family. It was liable to show upon her face in a less than attractive manner and lend an unappealing quality to her voice, a consequence she could ill afford under present circumstances. No, she was determined to make the best of her situation, such as it was, as a poorly paid governess in this rural backwater at the veritable ends of the earth. Well, at least until she could arrange a more congenial situation, one more suited to her talents. For an inventive young woman, that should not prove too difficult.

'If we return now we may be in time to see the *Burra Burra* dock,' she said, pleased at this sudden inspiration. James considered her suggestion for a moment, but the beach still offered too many attractions to lure him away quite so easily.

'And perhaps we might find some gull eggs in the dunes,' she offered. Gull eggs were sure to be alluring to an energetic boy.

'Can I take my stick?'

'Why not.' The dunes were riddled with the burrows of mutton-birds, but Violet was confident she could contrive not to find any of the poor innocent creatures or their eggs.

'And if we meet some bushrangers I shall protect you,' he said, beating at the air with his stick.

'There are no bushrangers in South Australia,' said Alice, who had a sharp way with facts. She had not learned to dissemble in the face of male certainty as yet, something Violet had been forced to learn at quite a young age.

'Then perhaps we shall drum some up, just for James,' Violet said with a wink.

Whether for the sake of seed cake or expediency, Alice acquiesced and they set off across the dunes, the boy kicking up sand while his sister berated him. Violet left her to it. Chastising children was exhausting and to be avoided wherever possible.

The road into Robetown lay on the other side of the dunes. More of a track than a road, most of its traffic comprised the bullock drays that brought wool and wheat from the pastoral runs to the port, drovers herding cattle, and local residents on horseback. On summer nights, thousands of large, brown mutton-birds descended upon the dunes in noisy flocks, heading back to their burrows after a day of fishing far out to sea. At dusk, other small, furry creatures emerged from the dunes to scurry about; dark-visaged wallabies bounding for the marshy ground further inland, and plump grey wombats waddling through the heath searching for roots and leaves. Even for a habitué of drawing rooms, it was difficult to avoid nature in these parts.

From the top of the dune, she gazed out across an expanse of flat country to a string of shallow lakes in the south. It was all so flat and dreary that come winter, the entire area would become a swamp. While to the north, the land stretched away in a series of scrub- and grass-covered hummocks, with a small peak rising in the distance. However, even before she looked northwards, the rumble of hooves and wheels alerted her to the approach of a bullock dray from that direction, as it followed the track through the sand hills. Its driver walked beside a team of twelve bullocks. A black and white dog dodged in and out of the animals' legs, nipping at their heels, while a riderless horse plodded along behind.

Bullock drays were a common sight in the port of Robe as they queued to load their cargo onto the steamers and cutters that plied the coastal route, so she did not pay it much heed. But the children were distracted from their search for gull eggs. They watched the approach of the dray, the driver cracking his whip above his head once when the animals appeared to stall.

'It's Mr Thomas,' said Alice.

'Who is Mr Thomas?'

'He plies the bullock route from Victoria.'

'That is a long way indeed,' said Violet, who had begged some maps of the local territory from the children's father for their geography lessons.

'Mama says he has a sheep station near the Grampians, but he'll be lucky to keep it if he doesn't make some improvements soon. She says he is quite genteel for a dirty, rough bullocky.'

Violet suspected that Mrs Wallace had said no such thing in her daughter's hearing. The children's mother was nothing if not a paragon of propriety. 'It isn't ladylike to listen in on another person's conversation,' she reprimanded dutifully, although privately she had found that listening at doors was the only way to discover anything useful.

'I like him. He tells funny stories,' shouted James, above the racket. The bullock dray was almost upon them now, the combined noise of hooves, wheels, whip and wind drowning out their voices. She could just make out the details of its driver who was almost dwarfed by his bullocks: lean and average height, with a tanned face and thick moustache. A cabbage tree hat rested on the back of his head and he wore a brown twill shirt and moleskin trousers.

'Does Mr Thomas have a Mrs Thomas?' she asked, glancing speculatively at the approaching dray.

'I do not think so,' said Alice. 'He has probably never met a lady as pretty as you, Miss Hartley.'

Mr Thomas did not appear to have noticed their presence as yet. All his concentration was reserved for the uneven track and the great beasts hauling the dray. But Violet had her ways of attracting notice when she deemed it opportune, and now seemed the perfect moment to become acquainted with the almost genteel bullocky with some means and no wife. Through no fault of her own she was marooned in Robetown for the foreseeable future so any promising introduction was worth pursuing. Alice thought her pretty, but Violet was pragmatic enough to realise that any prettiness she possessed would fade soon enough. Already she was at risk of that dreaded epithet bestowed upon every woman above five and twenty years, and unlike her peers she did not have a mama to arrange matters for her, nor a papa to provide even the most modest of incomes. She must depend upon her native wit to secure her future. Love, she had recently discovered, would not procure even a new pair of gloves.

'Quick, children, run!' she shouted above the sound of gusting wind. 'There's a snake in the grass!'

With a squeal, Alice set off at a run through the heath down the dune, but James hesitated, stick in hand, as if he might investigate. Grabbing his hand, she did not give him a chance, propelling him down the slope, her hooped petticoat bouncing about her legs as she ran. She gave him a little push and flung her body forward to land delicately in the dunes.

'Woo there, Bruiser! Woo there, Taffy!' shouted a voice not very far away.

She lay where she landed, waiting until the racket of bullock and dray dulled to a snorting shuffle before raising herself upon one elbow and letting her wide pagoda sleeve float back to expose the delicate bones of her wrist. With a toss of her head, she shook her bonnet so that it fell to her shoulders, revealing disordered blonde locks framing a heart-shaped face, and adding honey-toned highlights to her creamy skin. She opened her eyes to their widest – she had once been told that her eyes were the exact hue of aquamarines – and bit her lips to rosy plumpness. Lying on her side, with her waist curved to its tiniest, her view through the low vegetation showed that the bullocks were taking the opportunity to rest, sinking to the ground with their legs folded beneath them. Of the driver there was no sign.

'Are you all right, Miss Hartley?' Alice called from the safety of the track.

'I believe so. Don't move, children. Take care for the snake.'

She heard a rustle and looked up to find a pair of solid legs planted in the sand beside her. The bullocky was certainly fast on his feet, sprinting to her side so quickly that she did not see him coming. She looked up to find him gazing at her in concern. He seemed taller from this angle, his trousers slung low on his hips and held up by a belt of plaited leather. He bent towards her, extending a hand sprinkled with dark hair, his eyes disturbingly black.

'Thank you.' She clasped the hand in her free one and allowed him to pull her to her feet.

'Can you walk?' he asked with a slight Welsh lilt, examining her boots rather than her face, a unique occurrence in Violet's experience. Usually a man was drawn to her 'swanlike neck' or 'fine eyes'.

'I'm not sure.' She took a tentative step and winced. 'I may have twisted my ankle. I was in too much haste getting the children away from the snake.'

'What kind of snake was it, Miss Hartley?' called James, who was fascinated by anything clawed or fanged.

'A brown one,' she said. Surely snakes came in brown.

'Good thing you ran then. The brown's a bad-tempered blighter.' The bullocky grimaced, revealing a surprisingly good set of teeth. 'Deadly too.'

She was about to extend the conversation into a discussion on the nature of the Australian snake, which she felt certain must be of interest to a man of his profession, but she realised that he was no longer looking at her boots or her face. Indeed, he had taken to stomping about in a very peculiar fashion.

'What on earth are you doing Mr...?'

'Thomas. Lewis Thomas,' he muttered, eyes to the ground. Strangely, he did not appear to have noticed her honey-blonde tresses either. 'I'm ensuring the damned snake does not show its face again.'

'Violet Hartley. The Wallace children's governess.'

He ceased his pacing to take her hand. 'I'd heard Mrs Wallace was advertising in the London papers. The colonies not good enough for her?'

'I expect it was a matter of quantity rather than quality.'

For the first time he looked her in the eye with a curious glance. 'Robetown is something of a backwater for a Londoner.'

'Well, a lady must eat. And there are other necessities.' She replaced her bonnet upon her head, tying the long silk ribbons with a flourish.

'Of course, what lady can survive without her bonnets?' he laughed. 'But this is a harsh land for a woman alone.'

'Every land is harsh for a woman alone. But one does one's best.'

'Miss Hartley is teaching us French,' announced Alice. '*Parlez-vous Français, Monsieur Thomas?*'

'Very nicely done, *chérie*. Your vowels were quite French,' Violet complimented her pupil.

'I'm hungry,' James called from the track, suddenly

31

remembering his stomach, now that their expedition had been interrupted.

'We might have to put you up on the dray then. Since Miss Hartley cannot walk far on that ankle. If you don't mind riding along with the wool,' Thomas said to the boy.

'I don't mind.'

Alice looked as if she might be about to say that she did indeed mind riding with a load of smelly wool, but Violet forestalled her. 'Thank you, Mr Thomas. Alice is such a kind girl, I'm sure she won't mind.'

Thomas supported her as she limped towards the dray where the bullocks waited patiently. He gave a leg-up to James, who clambered happily onto the single row of bales at the front of the dray. Behind him, the load tottered three bales high. Then he placed his hands at Alice's waist and lifted her, light as a kitten, next to the boy. Once the children were settled, he looked at Violet with a lift of one thick dark brow. 'Miss Hartley?'

'My ankle,' she shrugged, with an apologetic smile.

'Those petticoats aren't made for climbing either, I'll wager.' The solid feel of his hands upon her waist was all too brief as he swung her onto the bales. 'All settled?'

When the children answered in the affirmative he took up his whip once more, waving it in a signal to the bullocks. 'Get up there, Bruiser! Get up there, Taffy!' he shouted to the lead pair. Once all twelve bullocks had risen to their feet he commanded them to walk forward. The dog took this as its cue to resume the job of harrying the rear animals.

32

'I didn't see any snake,' Alice informed Violet as the team set off at a lumbering pace towards Robetown.

'That's the thing about a snake in the grass, Alice. It's usually too late once you see it coming.'

4

As the bullock dray rumbled past the ramshackle White Horse Cellar, Violet settled herself to enjoy the view from her perch upon the hay bales. Reputedly, the proprietor of that establishment wore earrings, although she was yet to have the pleasure of his acquaintance. Nor had she met his sister, who was renowned throughout the district for her baked fish. They proceeded up Victoria Street, passing scattered stores and dwellings. Some were sturdy edifices built of the local limestone with proper iron roofs. Others were low-ceilinged hovels, slapped together with slabs of bark for walls, stringybark shingles and calico ceilings. Robetown was so far from the ordered streets of Piccadilly that sometimes Violet felt she had descended into a kind of Danté-ish purgatory from which only the purest of souls would emerge unscathed. And that would not be her, she warranted.

The children squabbled contentedly as they drew closer to home while Violet amused herself studying the figure of the bullocky as he flicked the tip of his lash in the air to coax a bullock to order. She pictured him garbed in a green cutaway jacket that would draw attention to his broad shoulders, and a crimson satin cravat to enhance his complexion. He wouldn't look out of place in Lady Palmerston's drawing room. She might have enjoyed engaging in a light flirtation if several tons of animal had not interposed. But perhaps it would be safer not to distract him.

'Why do you drive bullocks rather than horses, Mr Thomas?' called James, who had no such compunction. He was examining the animals closely as they rode upon the dray.

The bullocky answered companionably as he strode alongside, 'For one thing, they are cheaper than horse.'

'My father could give you a good price on some horse. He breeds them, you know.'

'I do know that. Thank you, James. You are as shrewd as your father, I see,' he answered in the manner of one man of business to another.

'Papa is teaching me.'

Alice had been giving the matter some thought of her own. 'A team of horse would be more handsome,' she said.

'Not to another bullock,' said Violet, and Alice giggled.

'Horses are sensitive creatures,' explained Thomas. 'A single working horse may be faster and stronger than a single bullock, but a team of bullocks is steadier. A team of horses cannot go where a team of bullocks will go, for the bullock has cleft hooves so he does not become bogged. He can handle a flooded river, a treacherous hill or a sea of mud. His feed is cheap, he does not require shoes, and he will not turn up his nose at a home-made yoke.'

'Sturdy, inexpensive and utilitarian, not unlike serviceable cloth,' said Violet, who much preferred silk.

'Much like their master!' laughed Thomas, with a friendly slap on the rump for one recalcitrant beast. The man was not as full of himself as some with less to recommend them.

A half-hour later they came to the Royal Circle where tomorrow the bullockies would queue their teams, while waiting to load their wool onto the *Burra Burra*. Here the dunes were low enough to give a view over the tussocked grasses to the beach, the jetty and the long sweep of the bay. Close to shore stood Mr Ormerod's wool store, and beyond it lay the government jetty, where a most curious event was occurring.

'Woo there, Bruiser! Woo there, Taffy!' Thomas called once more, and the team came to a lumbering halt near to the water's edge. He called the dog to heel and wandered back to stand alongside his passengers, whip held loosely in his hand.

'Now there's a sight I never expected to see,' he said, as they all stared out towards the jetty.

'Who are they?' asked Alice.

'Can we run down to the jetty?' asked James.

'Certainly not!' said Violet.

The *Burra Burra* was docked at the furthest reach of the jetty, where the water was deeper. Its passengers were in the midst of disembarking. Dressed for the most part in wide blue trousers and loose tunics, they trotted in single file along the narrow pier to shore. Most wore shallow, conical hats, and balanced poles with baskets at either end upon their shoulders. From Violet's vantage point on the shore, they looked to be fine-boned and slight of stature with swarthy complexions, very different from the usual run of pale Irish, Scottish and English immigrants arriving on these shores. And nothing like the Germans. Perhaps the strangest thing about them was that they all bore a single plait hanging down their backs almost to their waists.

They could have been a party of oddly dressed young women, but even from this distance she could tell that they were men. There was something about the breadth of their shoulders and the narrowness of their hips that spoke of that sex. Despite the loose garments, Violet knew a man when she saw one, even one as alien as these pigtailed fellows.

'Looks like the Celestials are taking a shortcut,' Thomas observed.

'But it must be hundreds of miles to the goldfields from here. Why would they trek so far when they could sail on to Port Phillip?'

'Since the Victorian government imposed a ten-pound tax on all Chinamen arriving in Port Phillip they've been landing in Adelaide and walking to Ballarat. Robe is considerably closer.'

He gazed at the rickety jetty where the long line of men traipsed towards them, carrying their worldly goods upon their shoulders. 'There's talk of them dropping like flies along the route, poor blighters. Can't find water in the dry. Can't find the route in the wet.'

The novelty of the event was too much for James, who had wriggled towards the edge of his bale and leapt to the ground while Violet's attention was focused on her conversation with the bullocky. Already he was scampering towards the first of the blue-clad men who was even now gaining the shore.

'James, come back here!' she shouted to the heedless boy.

She slid to the ground and was about to take a step before Alice hissed, 'But Miss Hartley... your ankle!'

'Of course, my ankle.' She threw the child a grateful glance.

'I'll retrieve the boy,' said Thomas, setting off at an easy lope to collar James before he could reach the approaching Chinamen.

'That was nicely done, _chérie_. I thank you,' she whispered while the bullocky was out of their hearing. It seemed that she and Alice were to be friends.

'Your ankle must be very painful.' Alice regarded her with a question in her eyes.

'I expect it must. A lady must have a few tricks up her sleeve, even one as pretty as you,' Violet answered her silent question.

By the time Thomas returned with James, to deposit him upon the bales once more, Alice was still beaming.

'You may sit between Alice and me for the remainder of the journey,' Violet told James, determined to keep him in place this time.

'You should consider yourself lucky to sit between two such beautiful ladies,' said Thomas.

Violet acknowledged the compliment with a gracious nod. 'Speaking of luck, I expect those men will need someone to guide them to the goldfields.'

'I expect they will.'

'Will you be heading that way upon your return?' She could not resist a smile at his good fortune. She could do the arithmetic as well as anyone when required, and there looked to be a hundred men trotting along that jetty. She wondered how much each would be willing to pay to reach his El Dorado.

'Where there is one gold digger, there are bound to be more.' He raised a speculative eyebrow at the trail of men snaking along the jetty.

'What's a gold digger?' asked James, gazing from one adult to the other.

'It's someone looking to make his fortune,' she said. 'Someone following his destiny.'

Someone willing to do whatever he must to get what he desired. And that would be anyone who wished to better his lot. Including a blue-trousered Celestial braving a strange new land far from the Middle Flowery Kingdom.

Or indeed a muslin-clad governess, half a world away from London.

5

Pearl River Delta, China, 1856

With only three weeks to go before the Seven Sisters Festival, the preparations were an explosion of colour amidst the grey plaster walls and tamped earth floor of the girls' house. Seven suits of brightly coloured paper clothing hung upon one wall. Seven miniature wooden chairs were set out ready to receive any of the Seven Sisters who deigned to visit from heaven, and the girls were at work embroidering seven pairs of tiny silk shoes as offerings.

Sitting cross-legged on wooden beds, they chatted as they plied their needles by candlelight. The festival was the highlight of the year for unmarried girls in the village and they all made monthly contributions to the girls' association that planned the event. But this evening Little Cat could not get excited about those plans. She was still thinking about the words of her twin and the Wu boy earlier that afternoon. Her twin's words had wounded her more than the bruise colouring her shin. She was thinking so hard that she jabbed her needle through the soft pad of her finger, inadvertently sewing her finger to the silk before she realised. Little Cat was tough. She didn't cry out, for the pain would fade. The smudge, however, was a different matter. She frowned as she considered her handiwork. Her shoes had never been pretty but now they were marred by an ugly brown stain. She tried spitting on the bloody mark but that only made it worse. So did blotting it with the hem of her tunic. She couldn't offend the Empress of Heaven by offering Weaver Girl or one of the Empress's six other granddaughters blood-spotted shoes.

'Little Cat needs all the help she can get from Weaver Girl,' laughed her friend Siu Wan, noticing her dilemma. Weaver Girl was the youngest and most romantic of the heavenly sisters.

She wasn't offended by Siu Wan's laughter. Her friend didn't have a mean bone in her body. In fact, her prettiest feature was her laughing mahogany eyes. Those eyes were so sharp and her hands so steady that she had won the village needle-threading competition three years running. She could thread silk through a seven-eyed needle with only the barest sliver of moonlight to guide her hand. Unlike Little Cat, she didn't need any heavenly help from Weaver Girl.

'It's all right for you; your embroidery skills are legend. But I've been cursed with fat fingers,' Little Cat said, throwing an envious glance at her friend's slim hands, graced with the classical beauty of tender bamboo shoots.

'Your fingers aren't the problem. It's your brain that doesn't pay attention to what your fingers are doing,' Ming Ju said, glancing over at Little Cat's handiwork with a frown. 'How will you sew sturdy clothes for your husband if you're always daydreaming?'

Ming Ju was the eldest of the girls in the house and clearly disturbed at the thought of this future husband's poorly tailored trousers. She had been betrothed for almost a year and considered herself an expert on all things matrimonial, including some rather surprising information she had gleaned from her elder sister. Information that she delighted in passing on to the other girls as they huddled beneath their blankets at night, alternately intrigued and repelled. For who knew that a man might want to touch that part of a woman's body? Little Cat still wasn't convinced that Ming's sister was telling the truth.

'From what your sister says, it's not my sewing he'll be interested in,' Little Cat said, and the other girls giggled.

'Sometimes a man wants to eat you down there,' pronounced Mei Ying in a knowing voice. Young Wu's sister was only fourteen and the youngest girl in the house, except with two older sisters and an indulgent mother she sometimes acted more worldly even than her elders.

'What would you know?' asked Ming.

'Second Sister told me.'

'Don't pay any attention to her, Ming. She just wants to be a crane among the chickens.'

'But it's true,' whined Mei Ying.

'I'm not letting my husband eat me down there even if the rice bucket is empty and the larder is bare,' said Siu Wan, in such a serious tone that they all fell about laughing again.

At night, as they slept jumbled together, they often speculated about their future husbands, a speculation tinged with fear at the prospect of going to live with their new husband's family, perhaps far away, further than they had ever travelled before. Perhaps as far as two or three days' walk from their village, for only the luckiest girls found suitable husbands of a different surname in their natal villages. Sometimes Little Cat thought that choosing the right mother-in-law might be a more reliable predictor of future happiness than choosing the right husband, since the mother-in-law would have the ordering of her new daughter. A girl could only hope that her parents wouldn't be hoodwinked by a wily matchmaker into arranging a marriage with a wastrel, a pauper, or a man with a cruel mother. A mean mother-in-law would ensure a lifetime of misery.

'You had better pray to Weaver Girl for a forgiving husband if you don't improve your sewing skills,' Ming insisted when the laughter died down. She was such a stickler for doing the right thing. She knew more of the *pao chuan* stories and songs than any of them.

But they all knew by heart the story of Weaver Girl and Cowherd, the star-crossed lovers of the Seven Sisters Festival. The two bright stars separated by the starry river of the Milky Way. Their love was remembered each year by girls across the land. According to legend, Cowherd discovered Weaver Girl and her heavenly sisters swimming naked in a lake. Unknown to him, they were the granddaughters of the Empress of Heaven. When he snatched their clothes as a jest, Weaver Girl, as the youngest sister, was delegated to negotiate their return. Unsurprisingly, Cowherd fell in love, as boys are bound to do with pretty, naked girls, and asked her to become his wife. She agreed and the pair lived contentedly together until the Empress of Heaven grew annoyed at her granddaughter's neglect of her weaving duties and insisted she return to heaven. Cowherd tried to follow her but the Empress foiled his attempt by separating the two lovers with a river of silvery stars, allowing them a single conjugal visit once a year on the seventh day of the seventh month.

Secretly, Little Cat thought there was something to be said for this arrangement, because apart from a little weaving, Weaver Girl could do what she liked the rest of the time without a husband or mother-in-law to order her around. But the other girls in the house got all choked up every time the story was told.

The girls' house was one of three in the village and unlike the lineage temples it didn't matter what surname a girl held – whether Wu, Mo or Yee – she might be invited to join if she had friends or relatives staying there. Each night the girls returned to the house after taking their evening meals with their families. Sometimes one of the bride-daughters, who lived with her parents before moving permanently to her husband's village, might stay with them for a night or two. Sometimes one of the sworn spinsters might come back to visit old friends, but mostly it was just the girls supervising themselves.

Siu Wan was Little Cat's closest friend in the house. Her perpetual smile made Little Cat less cranky, while Siu Wan always said that Little Cat made her braver. With her friend by her side, she felt brave enough to walk outdoors during the Hungry Ghost Festival. She would even venture into the woods at the foot of the mountain, unfazed by the thought of giant centipedes or spiders as big as birds.

'It's not so bad. I can fix it for you,' she said now, eyeing the spoiled shoe. 'See how the stain is shaped like a peony.'

Little Cat squinted, turning her head first one way then the other, trying to imagine the stain as a flower, but no matter the angle, it still looked like a sad brown smudge. 'If you say so,' she said doubtfully, handing over the shoe and watching as her friend's needle darted in and out of the silk, transforming the dirty mark into a bright pink peony. 'You'll make someone a fine wife one day, if your skill with a needle is anything to judge by,' she told her with a smile.

'You're making fun of me.'

'No, I'm not. Well, maybe a little. You will make someone a fine wife one day but not because of your embroidery skills. Because of your patience and kindness.'

A flush of red coloured the tips of Siu Wan's ears and she stared even more closely at her sewing as Little Cat continued, 'If we have to marry, I wish we could marry brothers and then it wouldn't matter so much if we have to live in another village, because we could go together. You could marry the older, more sensible brother and I could have the wild younger one. And then Mother-in-law would treat you kindly because she was too busy scolding me to notice if you threw away a few grains of rice or forgot to feed the chickens. Each year we could return to Sandy Bottom Village together for our New Year visits and we wouldn't have to be dragged kicking and screaming back to our mothers-in-law when the visit was over. And if you were with me, I wouldn't mind so much if Ma admired Elder Brother's new wife's cooking skills, or praised her filial piety in front of me.'

She didn't notice at first that Wan's needle had grown still, for she was too caught up in her vision of marital bliss, until her friend interrupted her to ask, 'Is Ah Keong to be married?'

'What? No. Not yet.'

'But there is talk of it?'

'None that I've heard. Then again, Ma doesn't tell me anything. Elder Brother could be betrothed to the Emperor's daughter and I would be the last to know,' she said with a shrug.

'Your parents could betroth you to the son of a butcher and you would be the last to know,' laughed Ming. 'Parents don't tell their children anything until the deed is done. That way the children can't cause trouble.'

'If my parents betrothed me to someone without telling me I would run away. I would comb up my hair and become a sworn spinster like Second Aunt. Or I would run away to the mountains and become a nun. A Shaolin nun with fighting sticks and a sword,' Little Cat said, warming to her theme. She was quite taken with the idea of a sword and proceeded to practise a few swipes at her friends' heads with an invisible sword.

'But by the time you discovered what they'd done it would be too late. The bride gifts would be arriving, the sedan chair would be at your door and you would be barricaded in your room with no escape.' Ming Ju tossed another fried bean in her mouth and chewed thoughtfully, taking great delight in this scenario.

'Little Cat could escape from anywhere,' Siu Wan shouted suddenly, throwing down the slipper she was working on and waving her needle at Ming like her own tiny sword. 'She is the best climber in the village. And besides, her father would not do that. He would not betroth his son... I mean his daughter... without discussing it with her first.'

Every girl in the room turned to stare at their normally quiet friend. The last time Little Cat heard her shout was when a bat flew out from the stand of wild banana trees at the village edge and blundered into her hair.

She screamed because she thought a banana ghost was attacking her. Anyone would have done the same. But for the most part she never raised her voice above a murmur.

'Would your mother betroth you without your know-ledge, Ah Wan?' asked Mei Ying, a wide-mouthed smile making apples of her cheeks. Little Cat wondered what she was up to. As the spoiled youngest daughter in her family she was accustomed to stirring trouble wherever she went.

'What do you mean, Mei Mei?' she asked on her friend's behalf.

'I mean, would her parents discuss their choice of husband with her before they made the arrangements?' Mei Ying looked pleased with herself now that she had captured their attention.

'I think so,' Siu Wan said softly.

'Or would they make sure that the matchmaker came to the house while you were out?'

'I don't think they would do that.'

'Hmm. Then I suppose there's nothing to be concerned about.'

Little Cat relinquished her phantom sword to sit on the bed closest to the door, the one occupied by Mei Ying. Wriggling her bottom, she squeezed into the space between the girl and the door saying, 'What is it that you think you know?'

'Nothing important,' Mei Ying said, laughing behind her hand.

'Nothing?' said Little Cat, pinching her on the arm.

'Ow! What are you doing? I'll tell my brother.'

'Only babies let their brothers fight their battles for them,' Little Cat said, pinching her again, this time to the tender part of her inner thigh. 'Anyway, I could throw your brother to the dirt with my eyes closed.'

Mei Ying yelped, looking to the other girls for reinforcements but they would not meet her eye. They all wanted to discover what she thought she knew.

'Stop trying to be important, Mei Mei, and tell us what you know,' ordered Ming.

'Well, if you really want to know... yesterday as I was on my way to visit my aunt to play with her new baby, I saw a visitor arrive at Siu Wan's house. A middle-aged woman in a skirt and jacket. A woman with eyes that roamed over everything and a frozen-mouthed smile.' Mei Ying paused, raising her chin and tilting her head before adding, 'A stranger.'

Strangers were rare in Sandy Bottom Village, especially ones who arrived in long skirts and jackets where everyone else wore trousers. Visitors were usually known; married women returning to visit their natal families, pedlars and itinerant tradesmen advertising their wares, or local dignitaries attending to official business. As for strangers, the arrival of a visiting opera troupe would always be greeted with excitement, the incursion of bandits with fear. Other than that, the arrival of a stranger usually heralded a betrothal. All her friends knew and feared the arrival of a stranger at their door. In fact, they relied upon each other as spies, for parents often sent their daughters on errands when a matchmaker came calling or betrothal gifts arrived.

If Siu Wan's ears had flushed red before, now her entire face paled beneath its tan. 'Ma sent me to pick wild lychee yesterday. I was gone all morning.'

'Perhaps the visitor came on another matter,' Little Cat suggested, trying to reassure her. But her words were in vain. She watched as a tear rolled down her friend's cheek and dripped onto the shiny silk slipper, now lying forgotten in her lap.

'They sent her away and a stranger just happened to turn up on the same day? If a wind comes from an empty cave, it does not come from nowhere,' Ming confirmed with a nod. 'It looks like your mother has someone in mind for you. We must hope she has found you a pleasant fellow from a good family with a kind mother.'

Siu Wan's shoulders shook as the words emerged from her mouth in a series of gulping sobs. 'I want to choose my own husband.'

Coming from obedient, dutiful Siu Wan, these words surprised them all. Girls did not expect to choose their husbands. At best, their parents might consult them and perhaps allow the young couple to meet before arrangements were finalised. At worst, they would be informed on their wedding day. But neither girls nor boys chose their future partners. Marriage was a family affair, not a love affair. The other girls might expect such rebellious talk from Little Cat, but not Siu Wan.

Little Cat rose from her seat next to the younger girl and flopped down on the bed next to her friend, placing her head on Siu Wan's lap so that she could peer up into her face.

'You're crying a river on my face, Wan,' she said, trying to cheer her up. 'Your mother wouldn't arrange a match without talking to you.'

'You don't understand,' Siu Wan inhaled between sobs. 'My father has already sold one plot of land to pay for Elder Brother's wedding, and I have three more brothers.' She didn't say that her parents needed the money a generous bride gift would bring them, for that would reap shame upon her family. But this fact was understood.

Lifting her hand, Little Cat wiped away the tears that rolled down her friend's face. She didn't know what to say. She didn't know how to make it better.

'We must all do our part for our families,' said Ming.

'You could comb up your hair and take your spinster's vows,' Little Cat suggested. 'You could earn money to help your family that way.'

'I'm not like you. I want to have a husband. I want to have babies. But I don't want any old husband. Besides, Ma would never hear of it.' Her sobs had subsided now but her eyes were still clouded with tears, her face shrouded by a curtain of long black hair that tickled Little Cat's nose.

'We will just have to ask Weaver Girl for help then,' Little Cat said. Perhaps heavenly help would do the trick.

6

Robetown, South Australia, 1856

'Almost there!' Thomas called as they approached the turn to Noorla. On the far side of the lake, the house gleamed as raw and new as its owners' wealth.

'Won't Mama be surprised to see us arrive on Mr Thomas's bullock dray?' James turned to her with a wide grin. The boy's enthusiasm was infectious, if somewhat exhausting, and she was sorry to disappoint him but his mama would not be surprised at all. Violet did not intend her to see them with the bullocky. That would entail an inquisition she would rather avoid.

'Mr Thomas will not wish to churn the approach to the house with his company of bullocks,' she said. 'I'm sure I can hobble the last yards with some assistance from you and Alice.'

The Wallace residence stood all alone on the banks of Lake Butler, its high gabled roof, octagonal bay windows and coloured fanlights setting it apart from the more modest houses closer to town. It had been built with the proceeds of Mr Wallace's sheep and cattle station; plus his bark-stripping, horse-rearing and leather-tanning enterprises, for her employer was a man of many and varied interests, she had discovered upon her arrival. He had established the Craigie run in the earliest days of the Guichen Bay District, when land could be gotten for the claiming of it, a five-pound per annum fee to the Crown, plus a halfpenny per sheep, a penny halfpenny per head of cattle, and threepence a horse. The original inhabitants had no say in the acquiring of it, for she supposed the land was not empty when the Wallaces arrived.

Craigie was situated about twenty miles from Robetown. Violet had only resided there for a fortnight thus far. She found it difficult to imagine the children's mother driving a mob of recalcitrant sheep and cattle a thousand miles over hill and dale. Nor could she envisage her sleeping beneath bullock drays, or swimming horses across flooded rivers, but the Wallaces had indeed settled there after driving three thousand head of sheep and cattle overland from Botany Bay. She could not reconcile that doughty pioneer with the woman she had come to know. But perhaps these ordeals had broken, rather than toughened her. Perhaps these deprivations had hollowed her out, rather than built her up. They had certainly ruined her complexion, for although she was not yet forty, she wore her life upon her face for all to see, poor woman.

No doubt the death of two infants to the scarlet fever

had also contributed to Mrs Wallace's fragility and Violet tried to remain sympathetic. But faced with her constant nagging about the smallest of oversights, she was ashamed to admit that she did not always succeed. And if she sometimes neglected the boy's Latin for a half-hour of ghost stories or a game of blind-man's buff, who could blame her? Certainly not James, who detested his volume of *The Eton Latin Grammar* as vehemently as she did.

By the time she had thanked their rescuer and was limping up the drive flanked by the two children, Violet was beginning to regret their excursion. They had been gone rather a long time, and she conceded that Mrs Wallace might be concerned.

'It may be best not to mention the bullocks to your mother, children. It would only cause her worry,' she said as they approached the porticoed entrance. When James looked as if he might argue the point, she added, 'And she may ban further such excursions. You would not want that, would you?'

'No, miss. Mr Thomas said that he would teach me how to work his dog if I stayed put upon the bales until we reached home,' said James with a slow nod of agreement.

'And I'm sure Mr Thomas is a man of his word.'

The children's mother greeted them at the door, her cap somewhat awry. Unfortunately, she had got herself into quite a state while they were gone. She was breathing hard, her gaunt chest puffing in and out beneath the dull brown cambric of her bodice. The woman could do so much more with herself, given a little advice and some small expense. Having recent knowledge of the London fashions, Violet had offered to assist with her wardrobe, but her advice had been declined.

'Miss Hartley! Where have you been? I sent Billy out looking for you!' Billy did all the outdoor work, now that the younger men had run off to the goldfields.

'We went for a walk along the beach, Mama,' Alice reported helpfully. Violet winced, for their mother frowned upon anything beyond the margins of her rigorously drawn-up schedule. She was inclined to refer to Violet's excursions privately as irresponsible rather than educational.

'A Nature walk, Alice. We have been on a Nature walk. The biological sciences are an important component of the rounded child's education, don't you find, Mrs Wallace?'

'I don't think—'

'We saw some Celestials,' said James.

'What are you talking about, James?' his mama asked, distracted from her inquisition.

'With pigtails. Coming along the jetty.'

'Miss Hartley says they have come all the way from China,' said Alice. 'I should like to sail to China one day. May I, Mama?'

Mrs Wallace looked from one child to the other, her mouth slightly agape, recalibrating her attack. 'Why were you at the jetty?'

'They have landed in Guichen Bay, it seems. On their way to the goldfields,' Violet explained, ignoring her implied criticism.

'Who has landed in Guichen Bay?' interposed a deeper voice as Mr Wallace appeared in the foyer from the rear of the house, still wearing his riding boots. She had thought he was to be at Craigie for the next month, supervising the construction of a dam. Meanwhile, his wife devoted less and less time to the station, preferring to live in town. A fact of which Violet was most grateful or she and the children would be ensconced at Craigie too with the flies, the heat and the snakes. Not to mention the interminable diet of tea and mutton.

'Papa!' the children chorused, flinging themselves into his arms.

'You smell of horse, Papa,' said Alice. 'And sweat.'

Despite having attained the age of five and forty, Mr Wallace remained a fine figure. He had the upright posture of a man of action and a charming suggestion of grey at his temples, but she suspected that these qualities went unappreciated by his wife. Mrs Wallace wrinkled her nose at the sweat staining his blue serge shirt and the perspiration glowing upon his tanned forehead.

'Good afternoon, Mr Wallace,' Violet said with a welcoming smile.

'Good afternoon, Miss Hartley.' He returned her greeting with a nod, before turning to his wife and adding, 'Good afternoon, Eliza.'

'What are you doing here, William? I thought you were to be at Craigie for the month.'

'Can't a man miss his family, my dear?'

'Of course you may,' said Mrs Wallace with a thin-lipped smile, 'only I thought you were needed on the station. You always say that the men can't be trusted to wipe their... to wield a shovel if you're not there to supervise.'

'Papa, can you take us to see the Celestials?' asked James, leaning against his father's legs and looking up. 'They are here in Robetown. A thousand of them at least.'

'Perhaps not quite a thousand.' James tended to run out of numbers beyond fifty and took to guesswork.

'If Miss Hartley can spare you from your lessons. What say you, Miss Hartley? Can you release two naughty children from their algebra for the afternoon to spend some time with their papa?' He threw an arm about each of his children's shoulders but reserved his gaze for their governess.

'Can Miss Hartley come with us, Papa?' asked Alice.

'If she has nothing better to do. She can give us a geography lesson about China on the way. But perhaps she would rather have an hour to herself?'

'Not at all. I'm sure it will prove educational.'

'We shall take the gig then, if Miss Hartley does not mind James sitting upon her knee, and Alice can squeeze between we two.'

'Cannot Alice sit upon Miss Hartley's knee?' said James.

'Alice is twelve and a young lady now, James. She is too big to sit upon a knee.'

Throughout this conversation, Violet noticed Mrs Wallace's smile becoming tighter and tighter until her mouth seemed to disappear altogether as her eyes narrowed to two flinty shards.

'Papa has had a long ride, children, and needs to rest,' she said, taking each child by the hand and depositing those hands in Violet's. 'Miss Hartley will help you wash before luncheon.'

Her hands now free, she reached out towards Violet's sprigged bodice and for a moment Violet thought she would shove her towards the stairs. But then, appearing to think better of it, she made a little shooing motion instead and retrieved her thin smile. 'Cook has made seed cake,' she muttered with a shake of her head, as if casting off unwelcome thoughts. 'Run along now.'

It did not take long for the Wallace party to discover the whereabouts of the new arrivals. They had set up camp on the flat over the rise from the Banks family's tiny bark-slab cottage. Mr Wallace drew the gig to a halt and lifted the children down, before holding Violet's hand slightly longer than necessary while helping her alight. Perhaps a hundred of the Celestials had gathered on the scrubby flat and were engaged in erecting shelters. Violet watched as a group of men stretched a length of canvas over a pole, supported at each end by a pair of crossed bamboo sticks. Others were establishing cooking fires in hollowed-out nests of earth. One group had set themselves apart from the others and she recognised the Government Resident wandering amongst them, from his customary pea jacket. Most of the newcomers had removed their strange hats, for the wind was still blustery, and she saw that apart from a single braid, the front and sides of their scalps were shaved so that their heads gleamed like boiled eggs. The whole encampment appeared most strange, and she wondered how Robe and its citizens must seem to the Celestials.

'Look, Miss Hartley, there's Mr Thomas!' said Alice, pointing to a spot fifty yards distant where the bullocky was involved in an animated conversation with one of the Chinamen. Their discussion contained few words, being made up mostly of gestures. Thomas kept pointing to himself and spreading his arms as if to encompass the entire contingent of Chinamen. Then he would point to the east, presumably towards the diggings.

'You've met Thomas?' asked her employer, giving Violet a sideways look.

'This morning. I twisted my ankle upon our walk and he was kind enough to drive us back to the house.'

'Do you know, Papa, he has names for each of his bullocks?' asked James.

'Yes, I do know that, James. All the bullockies name their beasts.'

'Can we not name our cattle, Papa? James and I can make a list,' said Alice.

'It would need to be a very big list, Alice, for we have three thousand head of cattle and ten thousand sheep, most of them looking remarkably similar.'

'I don't mind, Papa. I have a big imagination.'

Throughout this exchange, Mr Wallace had been leading his children towards the bullocky, who towered over his partner in conversation: a thin man, with a lined brown face and greying pigtail. As they approached, Thomas extended his hand to the other, and they shook upon whatever agreement had been reached, before the Chinaman bowed quickly three times and returned to his fellow travellers.

'G'day, Thomas,' said Wallace, extending his hand.

'G'day, Mr Wallace,' he nodded, 'Miss Hartley, children.' The two men shook hands and stood silently staring out at the encampment for a few moments before sharing a slow shake of the head.

'Have you ever seen the like?' asked Wallace.

'Never thought to see such a thing in Robetown,' said Thomas, 'though I've passed a few parties on the road.'

'You and the headman have come to a satisfactory arrangement, I take it?' Wallace eyed the bullocky shrewdly, one man of business in silent understanding with another.

'They need a guide to the diggings and I'm returning to the Grampians in a few days. I can take them further on.'

Thomas nodded, a satisfied smile subtracting years from his face so that Violet caught a glimpse of the boy he had been not so very long ago.

'Where there is one party of Chinamen, there are bound to be more, I'll wager,' said Wallace.

'I suspect you're right.'

Violet could not restrain the words that suddenly burst forth. 'So you'll be returning to Guichen Bay?'

'As soon as I can.'

'What's Brewer doing with that lot over there?' said Wallace, indicating the Government Resident amidst the small group of men set apart from the others.

'Apparently there's some sickness amongst the arrivals. Brewer is sorting them out now. His wife is getting up a party of ladies to help with their nursing.'

'Miss Hartley could help, Papa. She is very good at looking after people,' said Alice, and Violet had to stifle a sudden intake of breath. 'She nursed me through the chicken pox and I haven't a single scar to show for it.'

Both men turned to consider Violet, who was wrestling her face into a bland smile.

'What do you think, Miss Hartley,' asked Wallace, ruffling his daughter's hair, 'since your services have been so generously volunteered?'

'Well, I… I'm not sure Mrs Wallace could spare me. And there may be danger of contagion to the children.'

'Mama won't mind.' Alice slid her hand into Violet's and looked up expectantly. 'Everyone helps out around here.'

'Perhaps Miss Hartley is accustomed to nursing children, not adults,' said Thomas, casting her a sympathetic glance. 'These men are unknown to her.'

'But Mrs Brewer is helping so it must be safe.'

Violet resisted an urge to throttle the girl but did not remove her hand. She doubted she possessed will or strength enough to tend these men. She had put all that behind her after her mother died.

'Do not pester Miss Hartley, Alice,' chided Wallace so that his daughter's face crumpled.

'No, it's an excellent suggestion. I should have thought of it myself. Of course I would be pleased to help Mrs Brewer and the other ladies. If Mrs Wallace agrees,' said Violet. She could only hope that her employer would veto anything that might endanger her children in even a small way, although she had already discovered that the town's residents were a self-sufficient lot who all lent a hand when needed.

'That's that, then,' said Wallace.

With the matter agreed, the two men proceeded to talk sheep, Wallace going so far as to seek Thomas's opinion on the efficacy of various solutions of tobacco wash in the treatment of scab, while Violet entertained the children with a game of Taboo, the letter 's' being taboo.

'Where might you find a bird, James?' asked Alice, grinning with pleasure at her question.

'In the sky!'

'Sky has an "s",' said Alice.

'No, look up at the sky!' James said raising his arm.

They all turned to look where the boy was pointing. Dancing a jig high above the tents was a giant golden fish, its red tail like a fiery comet against the grey sky.

'Now there's a fish out of water,' Wallace said with a grin, and ruffled his son's hair.

7

Pearl River Delta, China, 1856

Little Cat eyed a plate of sweet lotus root, wondering if she could fit one more morsel in her swollen belly. She had probably eaten more than all Seven Sisters combined that evening, despite the dishes loaded with fruit and sweets to tempt their heavenly guests; pink- and green-tinted peanuts, toasted sesame seeds, red date soup and other tasty offerings. Seven dishes of each delicacy were laid out on a table decorated with seven kinds of flowers, seven shiny combs and hair-binding threads in seven colours. By comparison, the tables set with food for human consumption looked sparse so late in the evening, since the humans had more earthly stomachs to fill.

The Wu clan hall was the largest of the three lineage temples in the village and the site of all major celebrations and the boys' schooling. Tonight it glowed with lanterns and echoed with the sound of celebrating villagers. Little Cat was just deciding there remained a small, lotus-root- shaped hole in her stomach when Elder Brother appeared at her shoulder.

'Have you seen Siu Wan?'

Recently he had sprouted the beginnings of a beard and something edible was clinging to his straggling whiskers. She avoided staring in case she laughed, for there was nothing Elder Brother hated more than being laughed at, especially by his little sister. Wing Keong was the tallest of the Mo siblings and 'always strong', as his name suggested, yet sometimes his dignity was more fragile than an ageing scholar's.

'Not since we prayed for Weaver Girl's blessing,' she said, keeping her eyes fixed upon a spot above his left ear. She thought about the ceremony earlier that evening, before the arrival of the other villagers at the hall. The ceremony before the ceremony. The secret one known only to girls. With their hands clasped and heads bowed, all the unmarried girls in the village had stood in a circle while Ming Ju, the eldest, led them in chanting prayers to the Seven Sisters. She called on Weaver Girl to find them kind and loving husbands and prayed that she and Cowherd would be reunited in heaven. Siu Wan had been particularly fervent in her prayers, almost crushing Little Cat's hand as they chanted. But she said none of this to her brother.

Some years, if the eldest girl was born with 'fairy bones' and could speak to the spirit world, the girls might fall into a trance, arms quivering, legs trembling, and occasionally one of them might collapse unconscious to the ground. She had experienced this only once, the year the second Wu daughter led the incantations and the brick-maker's daughter swooned, lying on the floor in a faint until someone popped a salted plum in her mouth and she woke up coughing. Little Cat's hands and feet had been cold and numb for ages afterwards.

But she didn't mention any of this to her brother either. 'Isn't she here?' was all she asked.

She didn't like to admit that she had been too busy eating and enjoying herself to notice her friend's absence. She had noticed that Siu Wan was quieter than usual these last few weeks, yet no matter how she tried to cheer her friend up, she pretended there was nothing wrong.

Elder Brother shook his head. 'No one has seen her since the flower drum songs started.' He did not say that he was worried, but she saw it in his fierce eyes and the stiff set of his shoulders and suddenly many things became clear. Aiya! She was supposed to be clever, like her namesake. How then had she been so blind to something right beneath her whiskers? Siu Wan had said that she didn't want any other man because she had already found love, but none of the girls could prise a name from her lips, even after torture by tickling. Now Little Cat suspected whom that love might be and she was shocked. Perhaps she hadn't picked up on the clues because she didn't expect her serious elder brother to be in love. He seemed more concerned with silkworms than girls. How wrong could she be?

'Let's get Second Brother and search for her.'

*

After splitting up, the three Mo siblings scoured the village, which was strangely empty on this festival night when most of the population was celebrating at the Wu ancestral hall. Only the most ancient of grandmothers and grandfathers, and those too ill too attend, had stayed at home. Even the babies had joined the celebrations in their mothers' arms, so that Little Cat wandered alone through the deserted alleys, accompanied only by the distant sounds of celebration. At first she suspected she might find Siu Wan at the girls' house, nursing her sadness in silence. But the only occupant was the cat they fed on titbits swiped from family tables, and he was napping, oblivious, in the middle of Ming Ju's bed. So after checking her friend's home and the Yee lineage temple, she re-joined her brothers at their appointed meeting place, under the banyan trees by the village gate.

Lit only by moon and stars, the stone archway loomed over her waiting brothers. Her twin was watching patiently as Elder Brother paced up and down, a frown marring his normally placid face.

'I can't find her anywhere,' she said, eyeing him with concern.

'Daaih Lou combed the mulberry groves near the village and I checked her family's wormhouse. Nothing but a bunch of hungry worms,' said her twin, 'and not as many as expected, come to think of it.'

The Mo twins exchanged glances. Had disease struck

the Yee worms? Or hadn't they kept back enough cocoons for hatching this season? Neither possibility made for a promising return on their mulberry leaves... unless of course they had sold yet another plot of land. But speculation was beside the point, with Siu Wan missing and Elder Brother looking ready to explode.

'What if the Long-hairs snuck into the village while everyone was celebrating?' he said, ceasing his pacing for a moment. 'What if she has been snatched away? I would never forgive myself.'

Everyone knew that the Long-hairs kidnapped girls to service their unspeakable needs. They also stole youths to fill their ranks of rebels and bandits. But her twin gripped his brother's shoulder and led him over to a stone bench beneath the banyan trees, urging him to sit, saying, 'Every dog in the place would bark if bandits entered the village, Daaih Lou. We would have heard something.'

'You're right. But if bandits didn't take her... where is she?' He sank his head in his hands, covering his face.

Little Cat met her twin's eyes again, relaying a silent message. She wondered if he knew more than she did, if their brother had confided in him. 'Siu Wan is upset that her parents are secretly arranging a match for her,' she ventured.

'There's nothing secret about it. By now the whole village knows that a matchmaker has been called in,' Elder Brother sighed.

'Have you spoken to our parents?' her twin asked.

'Father knows Siu Wan and I are... fond of each other. He has broached the matter with her father, but it's no use. Yee has received a good offer. A much greater bride gift than we can afford. Plus her mother thinks it best that she marry out of the village so...'

So... both her brother and her friend were doomed to unhappiness, unless they could find a way to change their elders' minds, and in her experience elders' minds were less malleable than a slab of granite.

'I promised her I would find a way to fix things, but now she has disappeared and I don't know where to find her.'

She glanced up at the faded decorations above the gate, where a river of blue wound through a painted village, just as their own river cradled Sandy Bottom Village in one of its bends. Except, with the recent summer rains, their river no longer meandered gently around the village. Its waters swelled to the very brim of its banks, threatening to overflow onto the path. One misplaced step could sweep away the unwary.

She cleared her throat before uttering the words she suspected none of them wanted to hear. 'If she wasn't feeling well, perhaps she wandered down to the river to get some peace and quiet. Perhaps she fell asleep under the willow trees. That is all.'

'We've searched everywhere else,' said her twin, his hand still resting reassuringly upon his brother's shoulder.

Little Cat did not mention the thought that crept upon her like a winter shadow. They had all heard the stories of girls who donned their finest clothes, roped each other's hands together and in the darkest hours of the night, threw themselves into rivers. Surely Siu Wan would not do that? Yet despite her reticence, her brothers turned as one and set out at a brisk pace in the direction of the river, so that she had to run to keep up.

All three were breathing hard by the time they reached the riverbank at the edge of the village, where houses gave way to mulberry bushes. Ahead, Little Cat could see a stand of willow trees silhouetted in the moonlight. The willows grew on a mound that formed a low cliff at the river's edge. Here the river bottom shelved steeply, creating a deep pool where people came to fish for carp, shaded by the curtain of drooping branches.

'I think I see her,' she said, pointing in the direction of the willows, where a slight figure stood far too close to the cliff edge. 'Best not to surprise her.'

'What is she doing? I promised her I would find a way for us to be together,' Elder Brother murmured, before striding out so that his two siblings could only hurry to catch him up.

As they drew closer, Siu Wan sensed their approach. She turned her head in their direction without moving her feet. Her face appeared waxen in the moonlight and devoid of all recognition.

'Wait! Wait for me!' Elder Brother called as he kicked off his straw slippers and raced towards her, Little Cat and Second Brother doing their best to keep up with him. But the girl under the willow trees paid him no heed. She turned back to face the river, stepped out from the cliff top in one graceful leap and dropped like a stone into the water.

Little Cat's heart plummeted with her, but there was no time to blame herself for not taking her friend's misery seriously enough, for being too caught up in her own concerns to realise what she was planning. A moment later, Siu Wan reappeared, bobbing up and down in the swollen river. She flailed about, arms beating futilely at the water so that Little Cat wasn't sure whether she struggled to stay afloat or to propel herself beneath the dark surface. Whatever her intent, she was in imminent danger of going under permanently.

'Daaih Lou! We must go where the river takes her,' she shouted, changing course and heading directly for the lapping waters, downstream from where Siu Wan had entered the river, trusting that her friend would be borne along by the current for at least a little longer. If ever the Seven Sisters heeded her prayers, it needed to be now. 'I don't care about husbands,' she bargained as she ran, 'but please save my friend.'

At least her brothers listened, turning to sprint across the path, over the lip of the grassy bank and splash straight into the river where sandy bottom gave way to churning water. The fact that neither of them could swim didn't seem to enter their heads. They were too busy living up to the names their father had bestowed upon them, always strong and always brave. Except sometimes it was better to be smart rather than strong or brave.

She jumped in after them, sand sucking at her feet as she called, 'Goh Go, take my hand! Take Daaih Lou's hand in your other one!' If she could just brace herself here where the river was at its most shallow, perhaps her brothers could strike out far enough to reach Siu Wan as she was carried past by the current.

She closed her eyes, whispering, 'Please, Weaver Girl, take pity on two young lovers.'

She felt her hand swallowed by her twin's fierce grip then, opening her eyes once more, she watched as he stretched out his long arms to capture Elder Brother's hand before his feet no longer scraped the bottom. All the while, she waded forward, cold water swirling around her waist, searching the river for the small, bedraggled bundle that was her friend, and begging Weaver Girl's aid.

Amidst the noisy celebrations, Young Wu felt suddenly alone. It was an uncomfortable feeling. All around him, his friends and neighbours were enjoying themselves, yet he might as well have been standing by himself in the middle of the clan hall. One minute he was assuring his great-uncle's widow – whose only son had sailed for Gold Mountain three years earlier and had not been heard from since – that he would come and mend her roof, and the next he just knew that Ah Yong and his twin had disappeared from the hall.

How he knew he wasn't sure, but as his skin prickled all over, he realised that all evening he had been aware of their presence. Until he wasn't. Not surprising with Ah Yong – for he was a head taller than most of the others – yet he always sensed where his friend's twin was too. And now both twins were gone. He told himself there was no reason other than this uneasiness, to leave the celebrations and wander through the village looking for them. And when he heard a female cry drifting from the direction of the river, there was no other cause for alarm, other than concern for his friends. There was no reason for the swift surge of panic in his blood. And the tight feeling in his chest was simply too much fatty goose. Nevertheless, he followed the cry to the riverbank.

At first he wasn't sure what he was witnessing when he arrived. Figures moved through the water, like a sinuous worm in the moonlight. He blinked, trying to get a fix on the sight, for admittedly he did not see so well in the distance, especially at night. Through narrowed eyes the vision appeared for all the world like a human chain, snaking through the churning waters of the swollen river.

'I can't go any further!' he heard Little Cat's voice gurgling above the rush of wind and water.

'Let me go!' shouted her brother. 'I can't reach her!'

A pale shape drifted towards the chain. It was less than two body-lengths distant, but it might as well have been an ocean.

'I can't, Daaih Lou! We will lose you too,' he heard Ah Yong shout.

As he watched the furthest figure struggle to be free of the chain, understanding dawned. The Mo siblings were trying to save someone being dragged downstream by the current. Little Cat was their anchor, but she was being towed out of her depth by the power of the river and the desperation of her eldest brother to reach whoever was drowning. In a moment either the river or Ah Keong would have their way and Little Cat and both her brothers would join the drowned. Stolen from this life – his life – by the river.

He had barely completed this thought when he found himself knee deep in water, splashing towards Little Cat, deeper and deeper until the river was lapping at his chest. He grabbed her hand, dug his toes into the sand, and shoved her out into the stream.

'Go!'

Almost immediately his arm strained as he struggled to stand firm while the river surged around him. He watched Ah Keong flail forward, as the body drifted a mere hand's-breadth away from him. So close, yet not nearly close enough. His heart hammering, Young Wu released his toes, bobbing for a moment in the water, before touching the bottom again, the river forming a cold collar around his neck. He hoped it would be enough.

'I have her!' shouted Ah Keong.

There was no time for celebration. Wu felt himself being dragged forward by the current and the pull of the Mo siblings. Digging in his heels, he edged backwards. His arm was being ripped from its socket and he felt Little Cat slipping from his grasp. He held tighter, crushing the bones of her hand as he fought the river's current and the dragging weight of the human chain that would haul them all to their doom. Sliding through wet sand, he inched backwards, defying the river's might. One small step. Then another. Until the water no longer threatened to engulf him.

Instead it flowed around him, like any other island stranded in its midst.

8

They sprawled on the riverbank, laid out like a row of fish to dry. For several minutes no one spoke. Perhaps their words, like their hearts, were too waterlogged. Little Cat snuck a look at Siu Wan from beneath wet lashes. Her friend lay face down on the grass; head supported by her arms, tendrils of hair snaking down her back like riverweed. Sodden clothing clung to her slender limbs. Elder Brother lay beside her, barely a finger's-width separating them, as if he dared not hold her, yet could not bear to be separated.

When a tremor quivered through Siu Wan's body, he reached an arm across her shoulders, to quell the motion with the pressure of his hand. Little Cat didn't know whether her friend shivered from cold, or the enormity of her escape. For escape it had to be. She could not deny that Siu Wan had thrown herself into the river, for she had seen it with her own eyes, but surely she hadn't been in her right mind when she stepped off that cliff. In her misery, she had forgotten herself.

If she had been in her right mind, then she had chosen a watery death over family, friends and future. This was something that Little Cat couldn't understand. Surely there was always a way forward? Surely, no matter how grim the beckoning future, there was a way to make it bearable. To find purpose. She couldn't believe that her friend had lost all courage. And the thought that made her saddest of all was that Siu Wan had been bereft of hope, and she hadn't even noticed.

'Good thing it's a hot night, or we might catch cold.' Young Wu's voice rippled into the silence like a flat stone in a pond. She had forgotten about him for a moment too, forgotten that he had appeared at her back, just as the river seemed likely to drag them all to their deaths.

'Thank the gods,' she spluttered, 'that we do not sneeze.' She might have thanked him if he weren't so annoying. He was probably too foolish to realise the danger they had faced. Why else would he wade neck deep into a swiftly flowing river at night? And what was he doing down by the river when the festival was on the other side of the village? He should have been listening to flower drum songs and scoffing roast goose with his Wu cousins. Instead he had waded into trouble alongside the Mo siblings.

Sometimes she felt like each time she turned around he was there, trailing after her brother like a starving dog. In any case, her reply silenced him. As for the rest of them, Little Cat fancied that no one knew what to say. How could words mend her friend's despair or her brother's heart? What use were words in the face of duty? Their elders had ordained their lives. So they lay on the riverbank, staring up at the night sky and contemplating their narrow escape in silence. If only the Sky God could beam help down from the heavens.

After a long while, Second Brother heaved himself up to sit cross-legged saying, 'Siu Wan is well now, Daaih Lou?'

'She is very cold.'

Perhaps he longed to hold Siu Wan in his arms and warm her shivering body with his own, but with others watching, he dare not.

'I can warm her,' said Little Cat, sliding closer to her friend's other side and pressing up against her. Although Siu Wan had been immersed in the river only fractionally longer than she, her skin was icy, as if the river had drained all *qi* from her body. 'Come back to us,' she whispered as she rubbed her friend's skin briskly, trying to generate heat.

Gradually, warmth returned to her body and her shoulders began quaking as she sobbed quietly, her head still cradled upon her forearms.

'I'm here,' said Elder Brother. 'I'll always be here.'

'But I won't be here with you,' said Siu Wan, her words muffled by tears and grass. 'I'll be far away in some other man's house. I can't bear it, Ah Keong. I can't bear to live without you. I would rather be dead.'

'You don't mean that!' said Little Cat, terribly afraid, given the circumstances, that she did. It was hard to believe that her big brother, who rarely said more than two words at a time, inspired all this emotion. Who anyone would think had nothing on his mind but the care and feeding of silkworms or whether there would be fish again for dinner. How had he inspired such devotion in the prettiest girl in the village?

'And how will *I* live if you're dead?' His voice teetered on the verge of anger but Little Cat wasn't sure with whom – Siu Wan, their parents, or the entire world. She couldn't blame him for any of those.

Momentarily Siu Wan ceased sobbing and sat up to stare at him. With her long wet hair and pale bloodless face, she could have been a water spirit, intent on dragging them all down into the river's depths. But she wasn't. She was only Yee Siu Wan. Her friend. She was only a lost girl.

'How would *I* go on, knowing that I couldn't save you?' Elder Brother added.

'I didn't think of that.'

'Should I throw myself in the river too? Or should I hang myself from the willow branch that dangles above your watery grave?'

Little Cat suspected that the willow wouldn't bear her brother's weight, but the sentiment was certainly solid. She could feel tears pricking at the back of her eyes and a lump swelling in her throat. She hadn't known her brother had such poetry in him.

'Is that what you want?' he asked.

'Never.'

'Then we will find another way.'

As they spoke, the two had somehow sidled closer so that they sat with hips touching. Elder Brother curled his arm around Siu Wan's back, his head bowed, so that his straggly chin rested upon her shoulder, his nose breathing in her wet hair. They looked hopelessly sad, yet desperately happy at the same time. If love could make you this muddled, thought Little Cat, it was better avoided.

'Betrothals can be broken.' Young Wu startled them, his voice jarring the night air. 'Excuses can be made. The priest might find that the happy couple's birthdays are incompatible. That the marriage would be inauspicious.'

It was true that this sometimes happened, although the family reneging on the betrothal would have to compensate the offended party. Handsomely, of course.

'The wedding will be several years away yet. Anything could happen between now and then,' he added, nodding with the pomposity of a fifth-ranked scholar.

'Anything… such as what?' asked Second Brother.

'Such as a more attractive offer.'

Silence descended once more as they digested this piece of information. A more attractive offer? How could Elder Brother make a better offer when Yee had already rejected the Mo family's best offer?

Elder Brother lifted his head from Siu Wan's shoulder, sitting to attention. 'We don't have the funds to make a better offer.' His voice was heavy as a drum above the soft slap of the river.

'We could find the funds,' said Second Brother, springing to his feet in a burst of enthusiasm. 'We could find them on New Gold Mountain.'

New Gold Mountain. Little Cat inhaled the words. A faraway land. A land of untold riches known only through tales brought back by travellers. A land of strange people and even stranger animals, where the white ghosts ruled, and the animals nursed their babies in pouches like a woman cradling a babe in a sling upon her chest. Little Cat had seen a drawing of one of these creatures, standing upright on its long tail and powerful hind legs. If the animals carried their young like people, what other wonders might be found there?

She sat up too, drenched clothing and damp spirits forgotten as she fixed her eyes on her twin. What did he have in mind? Once, she and her twin had been almost like one person. She always knew what he was thinking. But the time was long gone when they spent days plucking pests from the mulberry bushes, competing to see who could collect the most bugs. Or raced each other through narrow alleys to see who could reach the river first. He did not share his secrets with her any more. Just as he rarely invited her to train with him. He had abandoned her in spirit, if not in flesh.

'It is said there is wealth for the taking. That the rivers run with gold and lumps of it can be plucked from the ground,' he continued.

'"Marry your daughter to the Gold Mountain guest. When his ship comes home he will bring a fortune."' She chanted the words to the popular song, but Elder Brother glared her to silence.

'Like it was said there was work to be found in the south seas, so that the poor and the foolish were lured into slavery,' he said. 'Waa! If it were true, everyone would be crossing the seas.'

'But this time it is true, Daaih Lou! I have seen it for myself when we took the fish to market. A man there was showing a souvenir from his journey, a nugget he had washed from a river. It gleamed on his palm, a pebble of pure gold. And the gold wasn't his only prize. He had brought back enough money to build a two-storey house for his parents, refurbish the lineage temple, and open a dry-goods store.'

They were all silent for a moment, entranced by this stranger's good fortune. It was too dark for Little Cat to see her twin's expression but she read his excitement in every muscle of his stance. He stood poised on his toes, as if ready to embark on adventure that very instant.

Elder Brother tightened the arm that girded his beloved's waist. 'Even if it were true, how can I leave our family? I am the eldest son. Our father and mother depend upon me. They would never let me go.'

'I could go,' said Second Brother, 'and the Mo elders could be persuaded to guarantee money for my passage.'

Little Cat glared in her twin's direction. How long had he been hatching this plot? Waiting for the right opportunity to raise it. Without breathing a word to her.

Young Wu cleared his throat, saying, 'It is true that

my father sent Ferryman Wu and his brother to the Gold Mountain when we were children, remember.'

Was he in on this secret plan of her brother's? Had they hatched this plot together? Wu's father was the most powerful man in the village, the head of his lineage, and one day, his son would inherit his role – if the old man ever decided to die. He had already survived a bout of typhoid and a drunken fall from a donkey.

'That is true. And I also remember that his brother never returned home,' Elder Brother reminded them. 'He died in an opium den on old Gold Mountain, so they say.'

But Little Cat also remembered that day when Ferryman Wu returned from Gold Mountain, sauntering through the village gate in a brand new suit of clothes of the finest silk. She remembered how she and the other children had followed him from the gate to the door of his parents' house, chanting questions about where he had been and what treasures he had brought home (with not a little curiosity about any treats he might care to share). It turned out that he had returned with a lot of stories but not so much treasure.

Now there was a New Gold Mountain, thousands of *li* to the south, rather than the east. There were new adventures and new opportunities for those who dared to claim them.

'I could go with you, Goh Go.' The words emerged from her mouth before she had time to censor them. Her brothers could be so dismissive of her ideas that she usually planned them well in advance, issuing her thoughts a few scraps at a time. Second Brother had developed a special look, which he reserved particularly for her suggestions – a frown and a smile that combined to make him appear constipated.

Still, she had their attention now, though she could not make out their expressions in the dark. She could only hear the scorn in their voices.

'Women don't leave our shores!' said Elder Brother.

'Waa! Girls can't go to the Gold Mountain, Old or New!' said her twin.

'No one would send you!' said Young Wu.

'Why wouldn't they send me? I am strong. I am brave. I am clever. I can fight. And I can work day and night.'

Her question was greeted with a chorus of laughter. 'That is no answer!' she snarled.

'Your question doesn't deserve an answer,' said Elder Brother, shaking his head in disbelief. 'One girl crowded into a stinking ship's hold with hundreds of men? One girl sharing a leaky tent in a strange new world with a dozen men? One girl from the Middle Kingdom, alone in the land of the outside barbarians? How could my parents have sprouted such a melon head?'

Her twin was kinder but equally dismissive. 'You are eighteen now, little sister. Our parents will be talking to the matchmaker soon. You cannot go to the New Gold Mountain.'

She could see that they would never let her cross the seas. She would be lucky to go further than the next

84

village. And then she would be tied to her new husband's hearth, and her growing brood of children, and then grandchildren, until the day she died. And even then her spirit would likely be shackled to her husband's ancestral altar. She would have no adventure. She would find no fortune.

'But I want to help Daaih Lou too,' she said, not knowing how to express what she really wanted. Not even to herself. It was beyond her imagining.

'I might know a way.' Young Wu thrust out his chin and set his hands on his hips. 'Not for this girl to go to New Gold Mountain. That is clearly absurd. But to help earn money for the Mo family,' he clarified.

'How could this be done?' asked Elder Brother, turning to face him.

Wu appeared to take a moment to savour their anticipation before saying, 'The Wu clan needs more silk reelers for our new silk filature. We have brought five treadle-machines down from the north. The market for silk is growing so fast that we cannot find enough skilled reelers amongst the Wu women and my father pays his workers well.'

So... her twin could sail across the world to dig up a future on New Gold Mountain. And she could trudge through the mulberry groves each day to spin a future at the Wu filature. It wasn't exactly a glittering prospect and yet... perhaps she was being offered an opportunity. A path that diverged from the future set before her like a bowl of cold rice. Who knew what it might bring? Perhaps this was not something she should fight. Perhaps she should trust in the *tao* and allow opportunity to show her the way.

The *tao* and the intolerable Young Wu.

9

The silkworms had an entire house to themselves. It nestled in the midst of the Mo family mulberry groves, almost two *li* from the village, where the worms would not be discomforted by the sounds and smells of human life. Unlike Little Cat, whose daily chore it was to collect the night soil to feed the fish, the silkworms were too delicate for such odours. Although with only eighteen days from egg to cocoon, their lives were bittersweet. They would eat and eat and eat. Then they would spin their cocoons and die. Little Cat supposed she should be glad that eating wasn't her only pleasure.

Day and night for the eight months of the breeding season, Elder Brother catered to the worms' needs. He chopped fresh leaves and cleaned the baskets of silkworm dirt and dry leaf litter, saving it for the fish. And when the worms were at their largest and most ravenous, he stayed awake feeding them every two hours throughout the night. For all her complaints about picking leaves and reeling silk, Little Cat did not envy him these tasks.

She might be subject to her mother's whims, but Elder Brother was a slave to worms.

He was cutting up leaves when she arrived. Wide shallow baskets crammed the open shelves that lined the walls of the wormhouse. The baskets teemed with small white worms, gnawing their way through mounds of tender, chopped leaves. Their chomping resounded like the smacking of a thousand pairs of tiny lips.

'Are you good, Daaih Lou?' she asked as she entered the cool, airy shed.

'Not bad,' he shrugged, not looking up from the swiftly moving chopper. 'Ah Yong will be here with Father soon. Then we shall see.'

A powerful odour of fish announced her father and brother's arrival. They appeared in the doorway of the wormhouse, their faces still shaded by wide-brimmed hats, trousers rolled to the knee from their labours in the silt-laden bottoms of the fishponds. In the shadowed interior, Little Cat had to look twice to tell them apart for Second Brother was almost a twin to their father. Both sported a thick brush of hair, a wide-mouthed grin, and long fish-shaped eyes that flashed in the light. Their faces were tanned to a shining dark brown from working outdoors: pruning mulberry bushes, caring for fish and poling the leaves to market along the region's web of creeks and canals.

Elder Brother, however, was half a head taller again,

and more like their mother in appearance, if not in character. His face was longer with a cherry mouth and wide, oval eyes. He always looked as if he was deep in thought, even when he was only deciding if the next batch of eggs were ready to be hatched. Little Cat had the same long face and bouncy hair as her mother and elder brother, but wore her father's wide smile and quick eyes. When they were young, she had been taller than her twin but he had outpaced her several years ago, much to his delight and constant reminders. Now the top of her head was level with his eyebrows.

'Little Cat, what are you doing here this late?' asked her father.

'Elder Brother had a task for me, Ba.'

Her father looked at her sceptically, for they all knew she had a thousand excuses for avoiding extra tasks.

'Have you seen Mr Yee lately?' she asked absently, while studying the nearest basket of worms with great interest.

'I see him every day, daughter, as you well know, since his fields are next to ours.'

'Mm. I wonder then if he has spoken to you of his daughter's betrothal.'

Their father glanced at each of his children in turn, his mouth fixed in a hard, straight line, except for the slight quirk at the corner. 'So... you have confided in your brother and sister then, Ah Keong.'

'I have, Ba.'

None of them had told of Siu Wan's desperate act on

the night of the Seven Sisters Festival. And Elder Brother did not mention it now. It would remain the siblings' secret, except for Young Wu, who dogged her brother like a shadow, learning all their secrets. Sometimes she caught the strangest expression on his face, as if his eyes warred with his mouth, his eyes conveying one message while his mouth spoke another. He was a strange fish, that boy.

'And Siu Wan has confided in our sister,' Elder Brother continued, glancing in her direction.

'Mmm, I expect you hope I can do something about that. I feel for you, son, I know what it is like to be married to a woman you have not chosen,' he said, then hurriedly added, 'But it has turned out well for me and it will for you too.'

'Daaih Lou is very sad, Ba,' she ventured, summoning a pathetic look, one that she had been practising for days.

'That may be so but I have already spoken with the girl's father and we could not come to an agreement. This situation has not changed. The Yee family haven't prospered recently. Yee has made some foolish decisions and taken on too much debt. Now he has sold his last plot of land to the Wu lineage and must lease it back. He needs cash, ropes of cash.'

Little Cat had a sudden image of Mr Yee weighed down by jingling strings of the square-holed coins known as cash, all looped in a noose around his neck.

'Ah Yong has a plan for acquiring cash,' said Elder Brother.

'Waa! Cash is not so easy to acquire, boy. You cannot pluck it from trees or dig it up from fields.'

'You can on New Gold Mountain.'

Their father turned to stare at Second Brother who until now had remained silent. 'What kind of unfilial children have I raised? You think I do not see what is happening here?'

Little Cat felt an elbow to her ribs and looked up to find Elder Brother making faces at her, his eyebrows waggling meaningfully.

'As always, we respect your wishes,' he said. He placed his palms together – the signal for Little Cat and Second Brother to follow him – and the three siblings bowed to their father the requisite three times.

'Some other, more gullible fathers would be reassured by this gesture, Ah Keong.'

'Honourable Father, we only wish to set before you a possibility.'

'A possibility, is it?'

'It is. Only a possibility,' nodded Second Brother.

'And you, daughter, are you part of this possibility? You have your nose in everything, it seems.'

'If you think it possible, Ba, then it is possible I may be part of this possibility,' Little Cat said, keeping her face blank, except for an excited twitch at the corner of her mouth which could not be tamed.

'So… what is this possibility?'

'I would ask the Mo elders to sponsor me to seek our fortune on New Gold Mountain. To find enough gold so that Siu Wan's betrothal might be set aside and she and my brother could be married.'

'And you, daughter? You expect to go with him?' Ba asked, an expression of horror widening his eyes.

'If you allow—' she began excitedly, only to be quelled by a swift kick in the shins from Elder Brother.

'Certainly not. There are no women from the Middle Flowery Kingdom on New Gold Mountain,' said her twin. 'The idea is ridiculous.'

For a moment, Little Cat thought that her brothers would betray her and leave her out of their plans. She began devising subtle and suitable reprisals, with various scenarios involving dead fish.

'But,' he continued after some thought, 'our sister also has a possibility to help Daaih Lou.'

Little Cat forgot herself long enough to flash a grin at her twin before settling her face back into solemn repose. Her father would be swayed by good sense rather than feeling. 'The new Wu filature needs more silk reelers. They will pay three times what I can earn reeling silk at home,' she said.

Her father closed his eyes and shook his head several times slowly before asking with a sigh, 'Then who would help your mother?'

Little Cat was ready for this question, having argued silently to herself half the night in preparation. 'Mui Mui wants to learn from our mother.' Indeed, her twelve-year-old cousin had squealed in delight at the suggestion. Their aunt had died of a snakebite three years ago and her daughter had no one to teach her the art of reeling silk.

'Your mother will not like it. She will make us all suffer.'

Little Cat bowed her head in apology.

'And what about you, Ah Yong? Who do you think your mother will blame if you cross the seas to the land of the foreign devils and are lost to us? She will curse me for the rest of our days.'

'You will not lose me.'

'And what if you return with a blue-eyed ghost child and present him as my grandson? Like that pale-haired boy we saw on market day? What would the ancestors say? What would your mother say?'

'I will return with nothing but gold. I promise this.'

Their father clasped his hands behind his back, strode to the door, and stepped out into the long evening shadows, cast by row upon row of neatly pruned mulberry bushes. They stretched like a marching army to the horizon, where distant mountains encircled the plain. The sun glimmered low upon the mountains, shading the hills a deep purple. Little Cat watched as her father lifted his face to the sky, considering possibilities. Like her brothers, she waited in silence for his decision. There was nothing more she could say. She could only offer up a silent prayer to Weaver Girl that his answer would be the one for which they all longed.

10

Robetown, South Australia, 1856

Several days after her first visit to the Chinese camp, Violet arrived at the entrance to the makeshift hospital in a rustle of silk. Slipping beneath the canvas shelter, she was met by a wall of serviceable wool in the persons of Mrs Brewer, the Resident's wife, and another lady, who stood with their backs to her tending a patient. Neither woman appeared to have heard her above the sound of the man's whimpering.

'It would help if we knew what he is saying,' said Mrs Brewer, who Violet recognised from her excursions about town. 'I would ask the headman to interpret but I'm embarrassed to admit that I cannot tell him from the others when they are largely dressed the same.'

'Lewis Thomas seems to have befriended the man.'

'Then perhaps I shall seek out Mr Thomas, or judging from his distress, this poor fellow is like to die.'

'Luckily, we don't need to ask what ails most of them. What comes out of their buttocks tells us,' said the other lady.

'Margaret!' Mrs Brewer said with a giggle.

'Well, it's true, Eleanor. They are either vomiting from one end or excreting from the other. But this one... there's some fever but...' A slight wobble of bonnets told Violet that the women were shaking their heads in dismay over the man's symptoms.

'And he's amazingly loud for one so ill.'

'Good morning, ladies.' Violet announced her presence, so that the bonnets turned as one in her direction, revealing two women of middle years, one plump, the other thin, their greying hair parted at the centre and pulled into tight buns. At the sight of Violet they stifled any further giggling to present a united front of matronly competence.

'Miss Hartley, isn't it? Mr Wallace told us to expect you,' said Mrs Brewer, examining Violet's costume with a raised eyebrow. 'I hope you've brought an apron with you.'

Violet nodded. 'I'm ready to roll up my sleeves.' In fact, she had purposely left off her fine linen undersleeves that morning, well aware of the nature of the work to come. Although not without a sigh of regret, for her purple taffeta did not look half so well without them.

'You must call me Eleanor, my dear, since we are to work together. And here is my great friend, Mrs Margaret MacDonald.'

'How do you do, Mrs MacDonald,' said Violet, extending a gloved hand. 'Please do call me Violet.'

'Forgive me, dear, but are you certain that you're prepared for this work?' Mrs Brewer's scepticism was camouflaged by a kindly smile. 'You're young and the work won't be pleasant.'

'Don't worry, ma'am, I can assure you that I have nursed all the usual childhood illnesses, including, on several occasions, far too much bread and butter pudding, and some unfortunate instances of diarrhoea.' Violet punctuated her list of qualifications with a conspiratorial smile.

'I'm sure you know your remedies, but these are grown men we're treating. Strangers, whose customs we cannot always understand.'

'I've encountered my share of unpleasantness before, and the men are ill and in need of care. We are all the same in that.'

'Well then, if you're certain, I expect you'll do nicely.'

'And beggars can't be choosers,' said Mrs MacDonald.

'Some of the ladies are reluctant to tend the Celestials,' Mrs Brewer added by way of explanation. 'They worry about catching some unknown disease or other. But from what I've experienced so far, it is just the usual shipboard ailments. And we've all seen those before. Dysentery, catarrhus, constipation, malnourishment...' She paused to check Violet's reaction. 'Our most pressing worry is the possibility of typhoid fever, although Dr Penny assures me that none of these men are afflicted.'

Typhoid fever. Mrs Wallace would not be impressed. She had only agreed to Violet volunteering under pressure from her husband and daughter.

'So we must be especially careful not to contaminate the water,' Mrs Brewer continued, noticing Violet's glance at the jug and ewer sitting on a nearby stool.

'There's been talk in London that the sewers running into the Thames are to blame for much of the city's illness,' said Violet. In fact, her previous employer, the earl's daughter, had become so particular about water that she would not drink anything other than tea or wine – preferably wine – and consequently blamed all of London's ills upon the Band of Hope and their temperance brethren.

'Yes, we've read the reports.'

'But none of this helps us fathom what is wrong with this fellow,' said Mrs MacDonald, indicating the moaning man.

'He has none of the usual symptoms?'

The man in question lay upon a stretcher made from rough-hewn branches and a length of hessian. He tossed his head from side to side, whether in delirium or pain, Violet could not say, for the ragged sounds issuing from his throat were as impenetrable to her as the cries of a raucous gull. '*Ngah… ngah… ngah*,' was the nearest she could approximate the sounds.

'May I?' asked Violet. Approaching the stretcher, she crouched low over the man so that curling locks of gold escaped her bonnet. His eyes widened and he reached out a hand as if to touch Violet's hair. '*Si…*' he breathed, his mouth agape. Had the man never seen a blonde-haired woman? she wondered. But before she could ponder this thought further, she was struck by the sight of his open mouth and the foul stench issuing from it. At the rear of his mouth a swollen mass enveloped one of his molars, a pea-sized eruption oozing pus. The tooth surrounded by this evil matter was blackened with decay and the gum flamed an angry red. No wonder the poor man squawked so loudly.

Standing with not a little relief, she fanned her face with a gloved hand, and turned to face the other women. 'I think I may know what the trouble is,' she said. 'I think this man may be suffering toothache.'

'*Ngah… ngah…*' The Chinaman resumed his refrain and Violet wondered whether he had been telling them what ailed him all the while.

'Quite bad toothache from the sound of him.'

Alongside Violet, Mrs Brewer leaned forward as if to inspect his mouth for herself but Violet placed a gentle hand upon her arm with a warning smile. 'I would not recommend it without a dose of the strongest cologne.'

'Well, my dear, welcome to the team,' said Mrs Brewer. 'Let's put you to work then and hope you don't regret it. And we had better send for Dr Penny to extract that tooth or we shall all be deaf by tomorrow.'

Violet exited the tent, worn out from traipsing to and from the creek and lifting men too ill to move weak limbs. Being younger than her fellow nurses, she had volunteered to do most of the heavy work. What had she been thinking? Her back ached, her neck hurt and her corset was chafing her ribcage, yet she could not contain a smile. Mrs Brewer said that she hoped Violet would be free tomorrow for another few hours and Mrs MacDonald had deigned to enquire after her recipe for peppermint water. It had been a long time since Violet basked in matronly approval, and not at all since she had grown to womanhood. It was an unexpected feeling.

Around her the Chinese camp seemed as busy as Covent Garden market, with blue-clad men going about the business of cooking, washing and scouring the locality for food and firewood, all the while shouting to each other in their indecipherable language. A few heads turned to stare as Violet threaded her way through the camp, but most kept their eyes to the ground, not wishing to cause inadvertent offence, she warranted. She wondered what it would be like to arrive in a foreign country, not knowing what small act might be considered offensive by its inhabitants. What habitual custom might be thought rude, if not abhorrent.

'Miss Hartley, how goes the nursing?'

Thomas appeared from behind her, his voice sending ripples of surprise along the skin of her arms, and she realised that she was yet to set her sleeves to rights. Her hair too was a sticky mess, she was still wearing her apron, and the hem of her gown was crusted with mud. Damn the man, a lady liked a little warning. There was a world of difference between artful *déshabillé* and slovenliness.

'Very well, thank you, Mr Thomas. As you can see, my ankle is fully recovered.'

'And you don't appear too much the worse for wear.'

'A lady never admits to wear,' she said, a smile twitching her lips, 'but I will admit to tiredness. I'm afraid I don't have quite the robust constitution of a bullock driver.'

'For which we gentlemen can all be thankful.' He grinned so that the late afternoon sun caught a flash of white teeth. 'I was surprised that you volunteered to nurse the Chinamen. You appear too... ah... delicate for such work.'

'Appearances can be deceptive. And volunteer is not the word I would have chosen,' she laughed.

'Alice did throw you to the wolves. But I'm sure Mrs Brewer is grateful for your help.'

'Yes, she is. And I am happy to help,' she said, surprised to find that it was true.

There was silence between them for a few moments before Violet broke it by saying, 'I suppose you'll be leaving soon?'

'As soon as the Celestials are rested. Their legs won't take them far after so long at sea, but they're keen to reach the goldfields. They seem to think that gold is there for the taking.' He scratched his head so that his hat slipped back, revealing thick tufts of black hair curling upon his forehead.

'I hope they won't be disappointed.'

'I have no doubt they'll be disappointed. But they're industrious fellows, and will soon set to work digging it up.'

'And what of you... you're not tempted to join them? It seems half the country is looking to strike gold.' She was surprised to find she was holding her breath, waiting for his answer.

'Not me, Miss Hartley. I'm not a gambling man. I'd rather invest in hard work and land.' He held her eyes a moment longer than courtesy dictated. 'Gold can be a fickle mistress.'

Ten minutes later, she was still pondering his words as she set out once more for Noorla, footsore and weary, but with her heart floating light in her chest. Despite her tiredness, it had been a good day. Perhaps there were opportunities here if one was prepared to take a risk. Perhaps she could make a life here, at least for the present. Mr Thomas might believe that gold was an uncertain mistress, but Violet knew from experience that Love was far more fickle.

Gold, however, might just make for the perfect marriage.

11

Pearl River Delta, China, 1856

Young Wu was whistling as he arrived at the Wu lineage silk filature. Pausing a short distance from the open door, he inspected the building as he did every morning, from its beaten earth floor to its clay-tiled roof, admiring its construction. His father would have been content with thatch, but he had argued for tiles, as thatch would foul the fine silk fibres and lower their quality. From the outset he had been building for the future.

'What are you smiling about, Goh Go?'

'Uh? I wasn't smiling,' he said, frowning down at his third sister, Mei Ying, who accompanied him to the filature most mornings, at the order of his mother who didn't like her youngest wandering the fields alone with her nose for trouble.

'Your lips were turned up at the corners.'

'I was stretching my face,' he said with a shrug. 'Don't you stretch your face in the mornings?'

'My face is fine. It doesn't need stretching,' she said, giggling behind her sleeve.

He stretched his face once more to prove his point before continuing on to the filature. Although its establishment had been his father's idea, the clan elders had agreed that the son should supervise. 'See how much damage you can do,' if he recalled his father's words correctly. The venture was small, with only ten basins so far, but Young Wu had plans for expansion. One day he hoped that the Wu filature would purchase all but a fraction of the cocoons grown in Sandy Bottom Village and perhaps from as far away as Small Mountain Mo village at the foot of the distant purple hills. News from Kwangchow was that the silkworms faraway in the West were diseased. In the land known as Faat Gwok the worms were dying, and the outside barbarians were hungry for silk from the Middle Kingdom.

'Little Cat is starting here today,' announced his sister, peering up at him closely. 'Perhaps I will be the one to teach her how to work the treadle. She will not like that.'

'Ga Jie will teach her how to work the treadle. She is eldest.'

Mei Ying screwed up her nose saying, 'But our cousin is also the fastest. If she teaches Little Cat it will slow down production. It won't matter if I stop reeling for a day.'

He wasn't sure whether his sister was more interested in showing up Little Cat or taking a day off from reeling, but he wasn't about to go along with her plan. She had too many plans for a girl of fifteen and was far too attached to them. Neither his mother nor his elder sisters had succeeded in curtailing Mei Mei's plans. Girls needed to learn early to 'eat bitterness', for if they didn't they would become unhappy wives with even unhappier husbands. Unfortunately, his mother had indulged his youngest sister too much, in his opinion, and as her elder brother, it was his duty to rectify the matter. Their father was too busy with clan business to pay much attention to his younger daughter. And once she was married she would no longer be his problem. Unfortunately, Big Wu reserved most of his notice for his son.

'If you teach her she will learn poorly,' he pronounced. 'That is all I have to say.'

The clack of treadles and whirr of cogs announced that most of the girls were already at work, and the large room steamed with the basins of simmering cocoons. In setting up the filature, the Wu clan had imported five cumbersome treadle machines from the north. Young Wu had travelled to Kwangchow himself to take delivery of the machines, along with a man who would reassemble them and instruct the reelers in their use. For it was men who most often operated these silk reeling machines in the north, a fact that Young Wu found astonishing. How could men, with their large, clumsy hands, spin gossamer fine silk? Little Cat would be the first of his reelers who wasn't a Wu. The first girl who wasn't a relative.

Ga Jie was seated in the airiest position closest to the open door where she would benefit from any stray breeze. Her younger sister assisted her by adding and subtracting cocoons to the simmering basin and keeping the charcoal stove burning. His cousin was twenty-five years old, long past the age when a woman should be married and gone to live in her husband's village, but she remained steadfastly single. There was nothing wrong with her that he could see; she had four sound limbs, her face was clear of birthmarks and she wasn't at all feeble minded, yet she had combed up her own hair and remained a spinster. These *sou hei* were becoming more numerous in the surrounding villages. In fact, the practice was turning into something of a fashion, to the horror of the clan elders and all right-minded men. For how would men get wives if women refused to marry? And what would they do if this aberrant behaviour became an epidemic? Young Wu blamed the parents for not raising more filial children. Such a thing would not be countenanced in his father's house.

A cough sounded behind him and he turned to see Little Cat standing in the entrance, bouncing up and down on her toes as if to spring away at any moment. Her hair hung in a shiny black rope to her waist and Young Wu had a sudden impulse to reach out, tug her towards him and make her stop bouncing. Her bounciness distracted him from the introduction he had rehearsed all evening. Her hair distracted him too. He wondered whether it would feel soft as the skeins of silk draped like curtains about the filature. He wondered if her skin would be as smooth to the touch as it looked.

'Good. You are here. Come this way.' He schooled his

features into the stern expression required of a supervisor of the illustrious Wu clan's filature, pulling his shoulders back to stand even taller than usual. The Mos were a tall family and the top of Little Cat's head reached to his hairline. He wanted her to look up to him. He wanted her to admire this splendid thing that he, Young Wu, scion of the Wu clan, had created.

'It smells like wet dog in here,' she said, wrinkling her nose at the damp animal smell rising from pan after pan of simmering cocoons.

'You would do well to get used to it.' He ushered her to the treadle where his elder cousin sat, expertly plying her chopsticks with one hand and guiding the silk filaments with the other, while her foot pedalled rhythmically. 'Ga Jie will teach you how to operate the treadle.' He referred to his cousin by her relationship name rather than her given name, for Little Cat knew that already, just as she knew everyone in the village.

'Good morning, Ah Wei,' she greeted the older girl, before tipping her head to one side with a frown and saying to him, 'But I already know how to reel silk. I am the fastest reeler of silk in the girls' house.'

It occurred to him then that nothing with Little Cat was ever straightforward. If you expected her to be amenable, she became hard and uncompromising and tried to kick your shins. But when you expected her to be hard, she confounded you by showing her softer side, revealing a girl who hugged her friends and rescued them from fast-flowing rivers. He never knew which girl he would meet on any given day. She was nothing like his sisters. He always knew what to expect from them.

Folding his arms across his chest, he said, 'As you see, we have a new and faster way of reeling, which my father desires you to learn.' Aiya! Why did he have to go and mention his father? As if Big Wu's words carried weight where his own were feeble puffs of air. 'I have transported these machines all the way from Shanghai. On one of these machines, a skilled reeler can spin twelve *taels* of silk each day.'

He paused for her exclamation of surprise, but he waited in vain. For now, rather than bouncing on her toes, she began tapping one foot impatiently, stirring up dust that lifted in the breeze to hover near his cousin's machine.

'Stop that tapping!' he ordered. 'You will dirty the silk.'

'Stopped,' she said, mirroring him by folding her arms across her chest and standing rigid as a stone lion guarding a temple. 'Except how will I pedal this machine without tapping my foot?'

There was little doubt that the silk filature was a house of Wu. Under its tiled roof, Wu girls surrounded Little Cat. She felt them at her back, with the tappety-tap-tap of feet on treadles. She spied them from the corner of her eye, with the whirr of hands spinning reels. And she heard the eldest of them at her shoulder, issuing reminders and corrections and the occasional exclamation of dismay.

'Wah, you do not do it this way. See how you have the fibres all tangled. You must twist them just so.' The older girl reached around her to adjust her hand as it fed silk filaments through the guide to the reel.

She breathed Wu air. And all the time, she was conscious of that boy pacing the floor, sticking his nose into everyone's business. He had grown taller this last year and his shoulders had filled out so that they strained at the seams of his tunic. He must have called on the barber that morning too, for his chin and the front and sides of his scalp shone smooth and pale, his long queue hanging past his waist and tied with a twist of cotton. She wondered how that hair would look, set free of its braid. But only rebel longhairs and bandits wore their hair loose – in defiance of the Qing emperors – and only Taoist priests were allowed their topknots. All other men complied with the edicts of the Qing.

The boy walked with a swagger, in a wide-legged gait. She wondered whether this was intentional, designed to take up more than his share of space, just as his lineage took up more than their share of land in Sandy Bottom Village. So many of the villagers had sold their land to the Wus in times of trouble and were forced to lease it back. Or perhaps he had grown accustomed to claiming space in a house full of sisters. It hadn't escaped her notice that Young Wu had become conscious of his own importance of late. Yet strangely, although they were age mates, he still trailed after her twin. Perhaps that was it. Perhaps he merely searched for a brother, someone with whom he could share an allegiance, a boy he could look up to. Goh Go was the nearest thing he could find.

'Does he always swagger up and down like that?' she asked her instructor, when he stepped outside briefly to answer a call of nature.

'Most days he sticks his head around the door a few times but that is all,' the older girl said, narrowing her eyes suspiciously at Little Cat.

'He preens like a tomcat for Little Cat,' said Mei Ying.

'You are talking nonsense, Mei Mei. Only last month he challenged me to a fight.'

Mei Ying shrugged. 'That is one way of getting close to a spitting cat, I suppose.'

All the Wu girls giggled at this remark, with Ah Wei's little sister laughing so hard that she almost knocked over the basin of bubbling cocoons, yelping as she righted the hot pan with her bare hand.

'You don't know what you are talking about. Why would your pious brother be interested in a girl who... who...' she spluttered, suddenly lost for words. With a girl who... what? What kind of girl was she, exactly? Sometimes she no longer knew. The only thing she knew for sure was that she didn't want the same life as her friend Siu Wan and most of the other girls in the village. She dreamed of a different life.

'A girl who acts like a boy?' Mei Ying finished her question for her, looking around with a smug smile.

'I do not act like a boy!'

Why would the girl say such a thing? Just because

Little Cat had breasts like cherries rather than apples, didn't mean she wasn't as much girl as any of them. Wu's little sister was being her usual troublemaking self.

'Be quiet, Mei Mei!' hissed Ah Wei. 'I can hear him returning.'

When Young Wu swaggered through the door once more, all the Wu girls were sitting with heads lowered, eyes cemented to the interminable strands of spinning silk. Only Little Cat was motionless, her hands curled into fists upon her lap, as she glowered in the direction of the doorway.

'What?' he asked, halted in his tracks by the flush of anger on her face.

'Nothing. We are all good little Wu girls here.'

12

Little Cat sat with the other girls on the veranda of their house, braiding each other's hair before heading to the mulberry groves to prepare the trees for the coming winter. Even without the aid of a calendar they could feel winter on its way. Already the mornings were crisp, and in the wormhouses paper sheets of eggs had been put into storage until autumn. Siu Wan finished twisting Little Cat's hair into a single braid, tying it with a length of red silk purchased from a pedlar only last week. Then she turned around so that her friend could return the favour.

'I think I might comb up my hair and become a sworn spinster like Ah Wei. Then I would answer to no man,' Little Cat said, checking to see the other girls' reactions.

'But who will look after your spirit tablet if you become a *sor hei*? Who will burn incense for you when you are dead?' Siu Wan was so horrified at this idea that she jerked her pigtail right out of her friend's hand, her mouth wide with shock. 'Who will rend their clothes at your funeral?'

'Perhaps I will adopt a poor orphan to be my heir.'

'Perhaps you won't have to worry. Perhaps no man will have you,' Mei Mei said with a cheeky laugh.

'And maybe *you* won't be laughing when your husband wants to jab you down there after you've just pushed out his first son,' Little Cat replied, indicating Mei Mei's lap. 'One month off from baby-making won't seem like very long then.'

The girls' laughter was interrupted by a voice calling from the alley. 'Is anyone there?'

At first she thought it was Elder Brother come to effect his usual morning ruse of pretending to collect her so that he could speak with Siu Wan. She whispered to her friend to answer the door so the lovers would have a few moments to themselves. But when she returned to the veranda it wasn't Elder Brother following her. It was Young Wu.

'Daaih Lou, what are you doing here?' said Mei Mei. 'Boys aren't allowed in the girls' house.'

Young Wu halted in the middle of the sky well and stood with his fists resting on his hips. 'I think you are all safe from me,' he said.

Little Cat wasn't sure whether he meant this as insult or reassurance.

'And I think we can take care of ourselves,' she said, not bothering to get up from where she sat on a low stool. She expected him to return the jibe in some way and was almost disappointed when he merely smiled saying, 'I come with a message.'

'Does Ma want something?' asked Mei Mei.

'The message is for Little Cat.'

Everyone turned to stare at her. Who would be sending her a message from the Wu household? Any official business would be conducted through her father. And anything unofficial would be most unusual. She barely knew Mrs Wu. The elder Wu sisters had married and left the village years before. Big Wu barely knew her, and like most girls, she preferred it that way. An unwelcome thought buzzed about her head like an opportunistic mosquito. Was she about to lose her job at the filature already? Was Big Wu unhappy with her work? Or was his son the unhappy one? Perhaps that was why he had merely smiled at her rudeness.

Little Cat wasn't rude as a matter of policy. There were actually people in the village who found her quite pleasant. But there was something in Young Wu's manner that set her hackles to rise. She wanted to spit and claw and urinate on his bedding. The superior way he stood with his hands on his hips irritated her. The way he swaggered through the village as if he owned it rankled like a splinter in her foot. The way he made pronouncements rather than conversation set her teeth on edge. Actually, so many things about him made her crazy. And that smug smile almost drove her to punch him.

Why then did her heart skip a beat at the thought that he wanted to be rid of her?

'Which one of you Wus has a message for me?' she said, finding her voice – smaller than she would have liked.

'My father wishes to speak with you.'

That gave her pause. Big Wu was the headman of the village. The Emperor counted on him to collect the grain tax, repair the riverbanks and keep up the Imperial roads. The village counted on him to maintain the alleys, the temples, and guard the crops. He gave permission for fairs and markets and travelling theatre troupes. He decided where wells could be dug, temples could be built, and people could be buried. He decided which rule breakers should be punished and how. Big Wu was the most important personage in the village. What could he possibly want with her?

Nothing good, she suspected.

'I'll ask Daaih Lou to come with me.' Her older brother would know better what to say to the headman. He would be a bulwark in any storm.

'No need to take him from his worms.'

'Perhaps I should get my father.'

'There's no need for that…yet,' said Young Wu. He smiled again and Little Cat grew more worried. The smile seemed to hold either promise… or threat. She could not be sure which.

'Come along then.' He swivelled on his heel, strutting across the sky well and turning into the alley without a backward look.

Expecting her to follow.

'And he doesn't like to be kept waiting.'

13

The Residence of Recommended Man Wu sat on the high side of the village, beyond the clan hall, looking down towards the river. There was no danger of flooding up here. In years when the river rose higher than usual, and water seeped into the alleys and sky wells of the village, Big Wu kept his feet and his rice dry. Everyone in the village knew what the sign outside his house said, even if they could not read, for the title of Recommended Man was awarded to few. It was the mark of a scholar. Yet it was rumoured that Wu had not sat the provincial examination at all. He was too busy overseeing clan and family to devote the necessary years to study. Instead he had paid a noted scholar to sit the tests for him. But since even failure at the Imperial examinations brought honour to one's ancestors, no one in Sandy Bottom Village condemned him for cheating on the infamous eight-legged-essay. No one would dare.

Once the Wu residence had comprised only the customary three bays, but with prosperity, Wu had added a second house and larger courtyard to the rear. All this Little Cat knew by reputation only, for until now she had never ventured beyond the two towering timber doors that barred the front entrance. Her father said that when the doors first arrived on a bamboo raft, up the river from Kwangchow, they were taller than the wall and Big Wu had to add three more rows of bricks to accommodate them. Today the doors were guarded by the fading remnants of two fierce red door gods, pasted there last New Year, and a banner suspended alongside, proclaiming the old saying that even she could recognise: 'The five good fortunes have arrived at the door.' She wasn't so sure.

As Young Wu stepped over the high doorsill and marched into the small front courtyard, she paused to twitch her sleeves straight and take a fortifying breath, before following after him. The first thing she noticed was that the courtyard was paved with grey flagstones, unlike the usual dusty sky wells of the village houses. It was surrounded by rooms on all four sides, with soaring timber columns, like a row of mighty trees, supporting the veranda. Gatekeeper Wu, a distant cousin of Wu's deceased father, limped from a room by the entrance and regarded her suspiciously through his one good eye, the other roaming the courtyard disconcertingly.

'Master says to take the girl through to the second courtyard,' he announced importantly, and slammed the doors with a reverberating boom behind them.

If Young Wu was surprised that she was ordered through to the family's private quarters he did not show it in her presence, ordering her to 'Come!' in his usual peremptory manner. Meanwhile, her stomach curdled as if she had feasted on rotten clams. As a child, going unnoticed by Big Wu had become a skill practised by virtuous and naughty alike. If the headman became familiar with your name it could mean only one thing. Trouble. One of her father's Mo cousins had become so distressed after an interview with Big Wu that she hanged herself from a camphor tree beside her family's wormhouse and it had been cursed with dying worms ever since. At least, that was the story told late at night in the girls' house when they wanted to scare each other with ghostly tales. But that girl had died before Little Cat was born, so who knew the real truth of the story. All she knew was that a visit to the residence of Recommended Man Wu was not to be recommended.

She followed Young Wu's broad back across the courtyard, over the granite paved veranda, through the reception hall lined with rosewood chairs and the ebony altar limned in gold, and into a second, larger courtyard shaded in summer by a peach tree. Here, shiny-leaved kumquat bushes and azaleas flourished in ceramic urns, and the veranda was hung with red silk lanterns. At Little Cat's house, the only decorative object was her mother's dowry vase of blue and white porcelain, and that was marred by a long crack where Little Cat had used it as a stool when she was six.

'My father will be in his study.'

Although the outer walls of Wu's house were rendered

earthen brick like the rest of the village, the inside walls were fashioned from timber panels, carved into an intricate cracked ice lattice and pasted with rice paper to keep out draughts. Most of the doors to the family's private quarters were thrown open to allow light and air to enter, but one corner held a room, which was shut up, tight. This was the room to which she was led.

'Is that you, Hoi Sing?' A brisk voice responded to Young Wu's knock.

'It is. I have brought Mo Lin Fa.'

'You took your time.'

Little Cat hesitated in the doorway behind Young Wu. Did he expect her to kneel and kowtow? Was head-knocking in order? Was she here to beg forgiveness? Or had she done something unforgivable? Perhaps she had discarded one too many cocoons in error. Or snapped one too many filaments of silk through less than perfect concentration. Was the headman about to turn her out when she had barely begun to help Elder Brother earn his bride gift? She did not want to prostrate herself like a kowtow worm, but nor did she wish to anger him. In the end she decided upon the *wanfu*, cupping her hands together loosely at chest height, and shaking them up and down three times as she bowed. She hoped it would be sufficient.

'This worthless son apologises for his tardiness,' said Young Wu, dropping to his knees and knocking his head on the floor. It was strange to see this boy – usually puffed up like a bullfrog – make himself so small. But he appeared to take it as a matter of course. 'Here is the girl Lin Fa, known as Little Cat. The one we have spoken about,' he added, rising once more to his feet.

'Good morning, Wise Master,' she said, while staring at the embroidered panel decorating the hem of the headman's sleeves, for that seemed a safer option than looking at his face. She might find something there she did not know how to handle. An uncomfortable thought.

'Ah Sing, you are to take these documents to Wu Village under the Mountain and give them to the clan elder,' he said, handing his son two scrolls tied with ribbon.

'But that is almost a day's walk, Ba.'

Little Cat risked an upward glance as father and son spoke. She had never set foot in a room full of such shiny new furniture. A large cupboard dominated one wall, gold writing emblazoned on the black panels of the doors. A tall open-shelved cabinet was filled with numerous vases, ornaments and a few scattered books. There were several more carved rosewood chairs, a rattan bed for the enjoyment of a pipe of opium, a large blue and white urn for storing scrolls and an ornate desk where Big Wu sat looking up at his son through narrowed eyes.

'Then you had better start now if you wish to be home before the moon sets. I will deal with this girl.'

She did not like the sound of that. Nor did she like the way his gaze lingered on her as he ordered his son about. His eyelids drooped low with age and his eyebrows sprouted wayward grey hairs that seemed to writhe at her like snakes as he spoke. A black silk cap covered his shaved scalp and his greying queue draped whip-like in a tight braid over one shoulder. On the desk before him, his tools lay ready: an abacus, a bamboo backscratcher, an ink stone and paper, a wooden stand holding several calligraphy brushes, and a solid soapstone seal curled in the shape of a crouching tiger. She eyed them apprehensively, unsure whether she was about to be chastised by word, deed, coin or letter. None of which appealed.

Young Wu graced her with one cursory glance before nodding at his father. He took a step backwards and bowed once, saying, 'I will depart now then, honourable father. The old man at the gate will see you home, Little Cat.'

'I know the way.'

He stepped through the door and out onto the veranda. Despite herself, Little Cat looked after him longingly. For years, she had wished him gone, resenting the way he preened for her brother's attention. Now she would do almost anything to have him remain. She did not relish being left alone in this room with its old-man smell of ink and opium and hair pomade. Left alone with Big Wu's mean eyes and stern voice.

She parted her lips but no sound emerged. Begging him to stay would incur a debt – if only of friendship – and she could not risk that. In any case, he would not disobey his father. He was nothing if not a dutiful son.

'And close the door after you. Too many flapping ears out there listening to conversations that don't concern them.'

After a moment's hesitation, Young Wu crossed the courtyard once more, arms swinging, without a backward glance. When he had departed, his father leaned back in his chair to consider her. He scowled as his gaze travelled from the top of her already untidy braid to her bare feet, filmed in dust. Big Wu's scowl was another of his tools, calculated to strike fear into villagers young and old. She folded her hands and waited to be told how she had offended.

'So… you have been reeling silk for my son at our filature.'

'I have, Wise Master.'

'My son has told me about you.'

What had Young Wu told him? This did not sound good.

'I wanted to get a good look at you. You've grown up. Tall, like your brothers. A bit gangly for my taste, but not without charm.' He folded his hands inside his wide sleeves.

She did not know whether he expected thanks for his words, so she kept silent.

'Has your father arranged a match for you yet?'

'He has not informed me of any match.'

'Of course, with the money he owes the Wu lineage for that second plot he farms beyond the wormhouse, he won't have much cash to spare for any dowry. And there's your two brothers to provide with bride gifts too.'

She bowed her head in silence. Not to hide her shame… but her anger.

'You don't have anything to say about that? My son tells me that for a girl you usually have more than enough to say.'

'No, Wise Master,' she said through gritted teeth.

Surprising her with his swiftness, he pushed back his chair and swept towards her. She flinched, but he only strode past, opened the door and shouted, 'Old Man! Where are you?'

Soon enough, the gatekeeper appeared on the veranda. 'What is it, Wise Master?'

'I have important matters to discuss with this girl. I am not to be disturbed until I call.'

Once the gatekeeper had shuffled back across the courtyard, he did not return to his chair, as she hoped. After closing the door, he took two steps towards her so that she could smell his morning breath of salted fish upon her face. Her legs wobbled like silken tofu as she resisted the urge to back away. Why had he really brought her here? Perhaps her mother was right. Perhaps her unmaidenly ways had brought shame upon the Mo family and he was so offended that, rather than send for her father, he had chosen to berate her personally.

She closed her eyes, readying herself to accept his chastisement. Surely a lecture from the headman must hurt less than one of her mother's scoldings, usually accompanied by a whack with a rush broom? She must bow her head and accept this shame. She must promise to behave as a good daughter of Sandy Bottom Village. To speak quietly and keep her opinions to herself. To dress modestly and never roll her trousers to the knee again. She must answer humbly and accept punishment gratefully. That was what she told herself as she waited for him to speak.

Except Little Cat did not always heed her own advice.

'My son has told me *all* about you.'

'He has, Wise Master?'

'He has told me that you fight with your brother.'

'Ai... only training.'

'That you roll your trousers to your knees and display your legs for anyone to see.'

'Ai... I don't recall.'

'That you twist and turn and dance like a crane,' he said, peering at her legs. 'Is this true?'

'I spar with my brother sometimes.'

'Show me these kicking legs then... that I may judge for myself.'

Reaching out with his long yellow nails, he picked up the bamboo backscratcher that rested on his desk and waved it in her direction. She eyed it warily as he taunted her with the tiny, clawed hand and bent to roll up her trousers as instructed.

'Are they knees? They look more like shins to me. Up! Up!' he said, poking at her thigh with the stick.

She did not like the threatening way he pointed at her. She liked the poking even less. 'I can ask Second Brother to demonstrate the kung fu for you, Wise Master,' she suggested.

'No need. Up!'

She did not like the way obedience made her squirm, as if it were peeling away something more than the hem of her trousers. 'My father can fetch him from the fields.'

'No need, girl. We will conclude this business between ourselves.'

Big Wu might be the biggest man in the village, but he wasn't her father. She did not owe him obedience. She would never burn incense for his soul. And he certainly had no care for hers. All thoughts of Elder Brother and the bride gift fled. Any thoughts of Siu Wan's future happiness were forgotten too. All she knew was a profound desire to be gone from here.

'And if you please me I may have an offer for your father,' he said.

There was no doubting his meaning and he wasn't talking about reeling silk. This wasn't the first time a man had made lewd suggestions to her. But it was the first time she had felt fear. She didn't like that feeling either. Silently she made her decision before the 'offer' was even disclosed. She would never please him in that way, no matter the consequences. She would never let those old man hands touch her. She would fight to the death before she submitted. She unrolled the faded black trousers to her ankles, and stood to confront him.

'My father isn't interested in your offers and neither am I.'

'Your interest is of no concern and do not be so sure about your father.'

'You are old,' she said, her disgust evident in her voice.

'Do not anger me, girl.'

'I want to go home.' She backed away, coming up against the edge of the desk.

'Not so fast, my little wildcat.'

Two steps, and he grasped her breast with one hand as he thrust the tiny bamboo claw between her legs. 'Don't worry. Your father will be grateful. Who knows? I may give him back his land…'

She stood stunned into immobility as he slid the claw back and forth between her legs, grating against her pubic bone. She wanted to cry out but her tongue swelled in her mouth, filling it with silence.

'I've been thinking of taking a concubine for some time. The Old Woman Inside is getting long in the tooth. You might do nicely. Once you're trained,' he laughed.

She shifted an arm to make the sawing weapon stop, but her limbs moved as if through deep water. Before she could grasp the backscratcher, he released it, pinioning both arms behind her back and thrusting his body against her so that the desk gouged her spine.

'I'll show you how to fight, little girl.'

He shackled both wrists with one of his large hands and wrenched her arms higher behind her back, while the other yellow-clawed hand smothered nose and mouth, forcing back her head.

'Open your legs,' he hissed, fishy breath oozing between his fingers and seeping into her nose, so that she gagged upon his words.

She wanted to resist but her limbs had become wooden.

Her senses wadded in cotton. Soon she could not fix on any notion at all. Each thought drifted across her mind like a shadow.

'Do I have to do everything for myself?'

His hand relinquished its hold upon her face to fumble beneath her tunic. Long nails dug into the soft flesh of her stomach as they fiddled with the cord tied about her trousers.

'I have a gift for you. One you'll like.'

She stared up at the wooden battens of the ceiling, noting how the rafters were carved in a twisting mass of vines. Flowers floated amongst the leaves. Fist forced her legs apart.

'A woman needs a man. Not a boy.'

Dust motes drifted in the light filtering through the papered wall.

'Why should I pay for a worthless peasant girl, anyway? It does not even have proper breasts.'

She felt sharp teeth at her breast and heard a moan of loss emerge from somewhere close.

'Your father owes me. Everyone owes me,' he said, releasing her breast to laugh even harder.

Outside in the courtyard, she heard a woman's voice calling for her husband. Gatekeeper Wu shouted in reply. Closer to hand a grunting sound, like a pig snuffling at the forest floor. A vague ache in her shoulders. Pain in her yielding neck. Roughness. A shadow of thought flitting across her conscious mind.

She tried to capture it.

'Let me go.' She choked out the words, her throat shuttered, her mouth dry.

Clawing at her breasts, hard and sharp. 'I never relinquish what is mine.'

'Let me go,' she rasped, dragging up her head.

'Now it begs.' Fingers digging into raw flesh. 'Beg again. I like it.'

She gathered her scattered thoughts. Searched them out, drew them together, and mustered every last shred of her will. Then when a useful idea presented itself, she threw her head forward and smacked her forehead into the bridge of Big Wu's nose. Fracturing his concentration. And his nose.

He cried out, reeling in pain, and released her wrists in shock. There was no time for thought, but now her fighting instincts had returned. She lifted her right leg and stomped her heel hard on the frail bones of his foot. Then as he curled inward on his agony, she sought the prize that lay waiting upon the desk.

Her searching hand met cool stone. Grasping the heavy seal, she swung her arm high, bringing it down upon his head with a crack. Pouncing tiger.

He dropped to the floor and she stood over his body, quivering. She had to be sure. Then her mother could never again accuse her of leaving a task unfinished.

14

Robetown, South Australia, 1856

They had been outside in what was loosely termed the garden for barely a half-hour and already Violet's curls were limp upon her cheeks and a mosquito had feasted upon her décolletage. Today was only a taste of the hot weather to come and already the thick stone walls of the schoolroom were beginning to appeal. Violet wondered how she was going to make it through an entire summer in this heat. How odd to be longing for a cold, wet London winter.

'Why does James get to stand so close to the peg?' Alice complained, a frown etched between her brows. The heat appeared to be affecting her too, normally so good tempered.

'Because your arms are longer than his. You can throw further.'

'But he is wearing trousers and I a dress. That is an advantage too.'

The girl was right. Unlike her brother's jacket and

trousers, her clothing was designed to hamper movement. And now that the summer was almost upon them, the layers of petticoat her mama insisted upon were particularly odious for an athletic child like Alice, and quite unsuitable for the climate. Violet could not argue with her logic so she did not try. Instead, she leaned closer and whispered in her ear, 'But you have a much better eye than your brother, *chérie*. Your aim is true.'

Alice held her gaze for a moment, before relenting with a gracious nod. 'That is quite right, Miss Hartley. James is at a disadvantage due to his size. I shall let him have a full yard's handicap.'

'Very generous. I commend you. Isn't that kind of your sister, James? To let you throw the quoits from closer in?'

The boy did not reply and she realised that he had been very quiet throughout the entire conversation, which was not at all like him. Usually he was positively bubbling over with interjections. He was also very competitive by nature, yet now he did not appear to be paying any attention to their game. He stood looking across the lawn into the distance, apparently lost in his thoughts, a quoit dangling from one hand. If Violet had been artistically inclined she would have made a study of the sturdy, tow-haired boy silhouetted against the silvery lake, the endless scrub and the infinite sky.

She wondered what had stolen the boy's attention from their game. Beyond the lawn lay the lake, and beyond the lake lay the town. Noorla sat all by itself amongst the ti-tree scrub, separated from the rocky shore by a thin strip of land. Sometimes she imagined a ship being driven onto those rocks, its timbers smashed to splinters, its crew and passengers cast adrift into the night. Castaways, not unlike her.

'James?' she said, coming to place a hand upon his shoulder when he did not respond. 'Are you unwell?'

'Don't bother about him, Miss Hartley. Mama says he cannot keep his mind upon one thing for longer than two minutes.'

'Do you want to go inside?'

The word 'inside' was enough to wake him from his dream for he answered, 'Mr Thomas is returned.'

His words set her to scanning their surroundings, searching for the unmistakable form of the bullock driver, but Thomas was nowhere in sight. It had been three months since she last saw him. He had returned to Robetown, his dray laden with wool bales, before departing with yet another party of Chinese bound for the goldfields. She could not deny that her thoughts had drifted his way every now and then in the interim. And now he was back.

'Where?' she asked, hoping excitement wasn't evident in her voice. Alice had a sensitive ear for a girl who had only just turned thirteen.

'On the circle. With his bullocks. See?' said James, pointing across Lake Butler to the low rise of the Royal Circle where several bullock teams waited with their loads.

'How can you tell Mr Thomas from the other

bullockies?' scoffed Alice. 'They are all the size of ants from here.'

'His team are all Herefords,' said James and Violet looked at him quizzically. 'All red and white.'

'Of course.' Now that she thought about it, he was correct. Thomas's bullocks had been all of one breed, with their shaggy white faces and chests, reddish-brown coats and long horns that protruded almost horizontally from their heads.

'Perhaps we could pay him a visit,' she suggested lightly. 'It's only a short walk around the lake to the Circle. We could all do with the exercise.'

For once James did not leap at the chance of absconding from Noorla. 'My throat hurts,' he said with the puzzled expression of a child accustomed to robust good health.

'A spoonful of honey on our return shall fix it.'

Alice was looking sceptically heavenward, where a bank of dark cloud threatened from the south. 'There's a great deal of cloud.'

'You're not afraid of a few drops of rain, are you?'

'But what about Mama? You told her we were to play a game of quoits on the lawn.' The girl peered at her, aware that Violet and her mother did not always see eye-to-eye on the children's educational needs.

'We will be back before she notices we have gone.'

'But what if she asks me what we did this afternoon?'

'You must learn to be a little more flexible, Alice. The world is weighted against a young woman as it is. I'm surprised your mama has not taught you this.'

As Alice held her gaze, Violet observed the thoughts flitting across her face with its unfortunate scattering of freckles, neat nose and clear blue eyes. She may as well have been speaking them aloud. Disagreement. Doubt. Followed by a subtle wavering. The girl really was an open book. Violet often wished that her own mother had lived long enough to teach her the skills a woman needed. Instead, her father had scraped together the funds to send her to a minor school for young ladies where she learned such useful skills as embroidery, French and flower arranging while he sailed the seven seas. How French and embroidery were supposed to help a penniless girl get on in this world was a mystery to Violet. They had not helped her fend off the advances of wealthy, entitled men. Nor had they taught her how to charm a gentleman into appreciating her point of view. She had had to learn those talents through trial and error. And they had certainly been of no use when her previous employer decided to turn her out of the house without a reference and then spread malicious lies about her to half the matrons of London.

So, Alice would do well to learn from Violet while she was able.

'But is it not a lie to say we were somewhere we were not?' said Alice, still mulling over Violet's advice.

'No, my dear, it is merely a slight tweak to the facts. One that is more convenient for everyone concerned. For example… are you not bored confined to the lawn with six loops of rope and a wooden peg for your only amusement?'

'Yes.'

'Do you wish to walk over to the Circle and visit with Mr Thomas and his bullock team?'

'I do. Mr Thomas promised to teach me how to work his dog,' croaked James, holding his throat ostentatiously now. 'Papa would be pleased if I could train his sheepdogs.'

'I suppose so,' said Alice. 'I like Mr Thomas.'

'I think we can agree that we all like Mr Thomas,' said Violet. 'But what would happen should your mama find that out? He is not exactly your mama's class of person.'

Alice sighed, glancing up at her mother's bedroom where the curtains were already closed at three o'clock in the afternoon. 'Mama wouldn't be pleased. And we would all be in trouble.'

'So if she were to ask what you did this afternoon, it would suit everyone if you left out the part about visiting with Mr Thomas and only mentioned playing at quoits upon the lawn, would it not?'

'I suppose you are right, Miss Hartley. It would be in all our interests.'

'Well then, let's set out before the weather turns on us.' The weather or Mrs Wallace. She did not know which would prove more hostile.

Violet was glad she had thought to wear her blue plaid that morning for not only was it quite becoming, any unforeseen dampness would not show under the arms after a spot of exertion on this warm afternoon. They set out at a brisk pace along the track to town, with the lake lapping at reeds to their right, and the ocean crashing to shore beyond the sandhills to their left. If James lagged behind somewhat, Violet did not make too much of it. Perhaps the lad *was* feeling a bit peaky, but he would be right as rain after a bracing walk and some dinner. Violet resolved to fix the boy a potion of hot water, honey and rosewater upon their return. That always did the trick.

Noorla was only a ten-minute walk from the Circle so it wasn't long before they were within hallooing distance. The bullocks rested with their limbs curled beneath their bodies, waiting patiently while their drivers stood in a group smoking and chatting. Mr Thomas noticed their approach and raised a hand in greeting, before leaving his fellow bullockies to their conversation and walking towards them. Violet quickened her step.

'Hello, Mr Thomas. This is a surprise. I didn't expect to see you for some time.' She did not mention that the last three months had dragged worse than the unseasonably wet winter.

'A pleasant one I hope, Miss Hartley.'

'Indeed. James has been telling us you promised him a lesson in canine management.'

'I did. Although I doubt I called it that.'

'That was very kind of you.'

'And I expect he has come to hold me to it. The lad has a long memory.' He whistled softly and the dog appeared at his heel, a border collie, James had revealed recently. 'This is Ruby. Lie down, Ruby.'

The dog settled obediently on her haunches, her gaze alternating between her master and the bullocks. She wriggled her hindquarters as if she could not wait to nip at the heels of another bullock.

'The first trick is to teach her to stay still. It's her nature to be restless.'

'Can I try?' asked James, his eyes lighting up for a moment.

'Why don't you and Alice take Ruby down by the lake and practise?' said Violet.

Thomas released the dog with a gesture and she trotted happily after the children, tail wagging.

'Have you had Ruby long?'

'About six years. Since I took up my run. Trained her myself from a pup.'

'She must be good company on the road.'

'And on the farm. Ruby works with bullocks and sheep.'

'But how do you tend your sheep while you're travelling?' she asked. 'Are there not dangers to the flock?'

'I employ shepherds. Carting wool and wheat is a sideline until I build up stock.'

'You do not suffer loneliness spending so much time alone?' she asked.

'I have Ruby. It can be hard and lonely work for a shepherd, or a bullock driver, without a dog. And sometimes I am fortunate to converse with the most congenial of strangers.'

In her entire life, Violet had not been alone for longer

than a few hours. What might it be like to be alone in the bush for days, a dog one's only companion? Yet being alone wasn't a prerequisite for loneliness. One could be alone in a house full of people. One could find oneself alone, lying abed with a lover. One could find oneself alone in the midst of a conversation. Not with this man, though. He gave their conversation his full attention, just as he did his team of bullocks and his dog. She suspected that whatever he undertook, he would give it his all. Lewis Thomas would not be a man of half-measures, a man who declared undying love one day and abandoned his lover to her fate the next.

'Do you have a background in farming, Mr Thomas?' she asked.

'I have a background in many things,' he said with his slow grin. When he smiled, the light seemed to dance across his dark eyes like the gleam of polished onyx.

'Including sheep?' she said, with a nod towards the lakeshore where the children were throwing sticks for Ruby. A light rain had begun to fall but Violet determined to ignore it, and hope it went away.

'You could say that. My family farmed for generations in Wales.'

'But you're a long way from the hills of Wales.'

'New hills. New possibilities.'

She waited, but he said no more.

'And what of your history? From where does the Hartley family hail?'

'Oh, we are not very interesting,' she said with a shrug.

'My father was a navy man. My mother died when I was a child. And now he has gone too. So I must make my living where I can.'

'I wonder that you didn't seek a position closer to home. Robetown is a long way from London.'

'We do what we must to make our fortunes. Perhaps, I too am seeking new possibilities.' She shivered a little, becoming aware that the rain was setting in, dampening the sleeves of her bodice and wetting her face. 'I'd better get the children home before the rain gets any heavier.'

Turning to the lakeshore, she saw Alice now petting the dog, but no sign of James. That boy was always running off. Chasing birds, following the small native rodents to their hide holes. In search of adventure. But how could he have disappeared in the blink of an eye? She scoured the scene more closely, scanning the scrub, the reeds, the choppy expanse of water, until she noticed a small, dark shape lying beside a clump of bulrushes at the water's edge.

'Oh my God. It's James.'

Picking up her skirts she hurried towards the lakeshore, calling out to Alice as she ran. It wasn't very far – perhaps one hundred yards – but hampered by her billowing petticoats, tight corset and fashionable boots, it seemed to take forever. By the time she reached James's small form, Thomas had caught up with her. He scooped up the boy in one movement, holding him in his arms and looking down with a worried frown.

'What's wrong with James?' asked Alice, coming to

stand at Violet's side, the dog following at her heels. 'I thought he had returned to you.'

Violet put a hand to the boy's forehead to find it hot and clammy. His eyes were closed, lashes fluttering as his eyes moved restlessly beneath their lids. His face was flushed and tendrils of hair stuck to his cheeks, whether by rain or fever, she could not tell. Seeing him lying forlornly in Thomas's arms, she felt a pang of guilt, a tiny stab to her conscience, but she shook it off. If there was one thing she had learned in her short but eventful life, it was that regretting mistakes was futile. It did not undo them. It only made the going forward more arduous.

'James is ill,' she said to Alice. 'We had better get him home to Noorla. Quickly.'

Before the rain worsened his fever. Before Mrs Wallace discovered that her children and their governess were no longer playing at quoits in the garden and had in fact embarked upon a poorly timed expedition to chaos.

15

Pearl River Delta, China, 1856

The path to Wu Village under the Mountain was long and winding. The Emperor expected landowners great and small to provide land and upkeep for village roads. Who could blame them if they obliged by providing narrow scraps of land at the borders of their plots so that their neighbours had to furnish the other half. Unfortunately this meant that the roads floundered between mulberry grove and rice paddy, fishpond and vegetable garden like a headless chicken. Young Wu did not blame the landowners for begrudging their land – not when it could be put to more profitable use – but it made his journey frustratingly slow. Especially when he wished to be finished as soon as possible so that he could return to Sandy Bottom Village.

He could not shake the feeling that he was needed. It nagged at him like the angry patch of skin behind his knee, which flared up every time his father grew displeased with him. He kept seeing Little Cat's face, as she stood before his father, pale where she was usually tanned, expressionless where she was more often annoyed. There were those who made a habit of disrespect – discontented men who were always complaining to the magistrates, long-haired louts who fomented rebellion – but most of the village viewed his father with healthy respect. This was only natural, since the Wu lineage owned three-quarters of the surrounding land. But it did not explain Little Cat's face. He could not escape the feeling that something had gone awry this morning. Yet what could he do? His father had ordered him to deliver these documents and he could not disobey.

By mid-morning he had reached the neighbouring village. He paused to make an offering at the Earth God's shrine outside the village gate, then wandered through crooked alleys to await the ferry by the riverbank. There were few bridges in the district and many rivers. Everyone relied upon ferrymen to pole them from one bank to the other. Like most ferries in the district, this one was constructed from thick poles of bamboo lashed together to form a wide-bottomed boat, which was fashioned to carry people, produce and livestock.

Most of his fellow travellers were about the business of agriculture, burdened with baskets and barrels of vegetables, fish or mulberry leaves. One boy carried a load of chopped wood, while another laboured under a stem of bananas. Men and boys alike were garbed in cotton trousers and tunics in faded shades of *lam cho* blue, rolled to the knee. He was the only one wearing shoes.

Before he had taken ten steps the reason became apparent. With winter almost upon them the river was low, before the coming of the rains, so that waiting passengers had to navigate an expanse of mud to reach the ferry. He wasn't too concerned. Planks of wood had been laid helpfully in a line leading to the river's edge, and unlike his fellow passengers, he was weighed down by little more than his misgivings and two paper scrolls. Besides, he had practised the art of kung fu since he first grew out of his divided trousers. He thought little of balancing upon one foot to aim a sidekick with the other. Scaling a wall or leaping a ditch did not faze him. Balancing upon a narrow plank to cross a muddy river flat should have been a trifle.

He stepped out, keen to score a place on the ferry before he was squeezed between a barrel of fish and a bad-tempered donkey. However, several steps in he realised that the plank's usefulness was deceptive. While the trail of planks suggested a jetty of sorts, in fact his path floated upon a sea of mud. And like any sea, it was subject to turbulence. He sensed the heavy-footed pedlar – yoked beneath twin baskets brimming with sweet potato – who stepped onto the plank behind him. As the plank wallowed deeper into the mud it rocked from side to side. And the pedlar, deciding that the mud was a more predictable option for himself and his wares, abruptly abandoned the plank to wade into the mud. Caught in mid-stride, Young Wu wobbled as he tried to recapture his balance. Despite all his years of kung fu, despite his lithe and athletic frame, he was pitched to the side by the yawing plank.

He landed on his hands and knees, deep in the mire, to a chorus of laughter from his fellow passengers. Any entertainment was appreciated to break the tedium of waiting for the ferry. And the fact that Young Wu's shoes, crisp new tunic and rolled documents proclaimed him a landlord no doubt made it doubly amusing. Averting his face from their mirth, he collected the scattered scrolls now smeared in grime, and struggled to stand. His hands sank into the mud as he levered himself up, but with a little explosive power he pushed to his feet. He could feel the mud spattered upon his cheeks, see it plastered to his sleeves in thick grey cuffs.

Ignoring his audience, he straightened his spine, pulled back his shoulders, and righted his dignity. He set off for the ferry with a determined gait, except for the fact that he had to prise each foot from the wet earth. It sucked and slurped at his feet so that his swagger slowed to a shamble. On another day he might have been angry at this embarrassment but as he lumbered towards the river, his thoughts churned in confusion. His father had ordered him to Wu Village under the Mountain and he rarely disputed his father's will. That way lay the turbulence of family disharmony. That way lay shame. From the age of five, he had learned to recite the Sixteen Maxims of the Kangxi Emperor. He had been trained by the whiplash of his father's tongue. For if a son did not obey his father, then a wife need not obey her husband.

A servant need not obey his master. A subject need not obey his Emperor.

That way lay chaos.

Yet he could not help feeling that the gods were sending him a message. He could not help feeling that his life was about to change. And as he stared down at the swallowing mud, he realised that Grandfather Earth was telling him to turn back.

16

Little Cat did not know that a heart could beat so fast. It drummed at her ribs like a woodpecker so that she thought it must burst through her chest. She waited, tucked inside a large basket that smelled of cabbage, peeking out through the bamboo strips and praying to Weaver Girl that she would not be discovered. She waited until she heard Gatekeeper Wu shuffle across the courtyard then crawled from her hiding place, flitting like a shadow from one veranda post to another until she reached the gates.

They loomed, twice her height, barred by a narrow iron latch. All she had to do was lift the latch, open the doors and step over the sill. Yet she hesitated. What would happen when the old gatekeeper finally braved his master's ire and investigated why he had not shouted for his dinner? Perhaps if she called for help, if she explained that she had feared for her life, they might bring her before the county magistrate and she could plead her cause. Then the magistrate would decide upon her punishment. If she were lucky he might choose only the second of the Five Punishments, a beating with heavy bamboo. At least there was a chance she might escape execution.

Then she thought of Big Wu, lying on the floor of his study, mired in his own blood, and she realised that she would not live to face a magistrate. The Wus would hunt her down. They would string her up. They would put her in a pig crate, weighed down by rocks, and throw her in the river. Young Wu would not rest until she was caught. He was his father's son. And his father would see her in Hell.

Perhaps that was where she belonged for her crime. Perhaps she was destined to spend eternity wandering the Ten Courts of Hell, cut into pieces, deep-fried in oil and ground to a bloody pulp. But since the prospect of being drowned in a pig crate was a lot more immediate than the tortures of Hell, she lifted the latch, heaved open the doors and ran. She ran down the hill, past the Wu clan hall, over the irrigation ditch, through the alleys and along the river until she reached the Mo family fishponds, panting for her life. She did not care if she was seen, that would come later.

She ran to her brother. The boy who had shared her mother's womb. The boy she grew up wanting to be. The boy she learned to fight alongside. The boy she always trusted to guard her back. If she imagined that she might endanger him, she thrust that thought aside. Never for a moment did she fear that he would turn her away. He was her twin. He was her other half.

At least he had been until he became a man.

She found him stripped to the waist, trousers rolled to the knee, shovelling silt from the bottom of the pond. He did not look like a man who was about to set out on the journey of a lifetime to New Gold Mountain, who despite his promises might never return to his home.

'Goh Go.' The words shivered in her throat, almost unrecognisable as her voice.

'Little Cat? What's wrong?' he asked, staring up at her in alarm.

She stood several feet above him on the raised bank of the dyke, where mulberry groves stretched behind her in row upon row towards the horizon. Where fishponds and dykes had long ago carved order out of the chaos of torrential rains and surging rivers. Where an ancient emperor's edict had brought order to the turbulence of village life. And she knew that her world would never be the same again either. She had become a harbinger of chaos.

'Is that blood?'

For the first time she noticed her clothes. The faded black of her *sam fu* was spattered with rusty marks. She held hands to her face that were smeared crimson.

'It's not mine... I have done something.'

She curled her hand into a fist. She could still feel the heft of stone. Sealing Big Wu's fate.

'Done what?'

What was it she had done really? She had defied a clan elder. She had protected herself.

'I think I have killed Big Wu.'

He blinked and shook his head, as if he could not believe what she was saying.

'What?'

'I hit him over the head.' She did not tell him how many times. But in the moment she had not counted.

'Where?'

Was it her imagination, or did he back away? The muddy water rippled around him, but it could have just been fish.

'Up at the Wu house. In his study. He's not moving.'

'What were you doing up at Big Wu's house?' He clutched at detail as if to make fact disappear. She wished she could do the same, roll back time so that she had never trailed behind Young Wu to the house of the Recommended Man. Never ignored her misgivings and trusted him.

'His son, your friend, brought me there. I don't know why. But Big Wu sent him away. And when we were alone he attacked me and I...' She gagged at the memory. 'I fought back.'

Her brother stood knee deep in the pond, considering her words. She waited for him to splash towards her, place his hands upon her shoulders and tell her that everything would be all right. That together they would fix this. She waited for him to help her from the ground where he had tossed her during one of their sparring sessions. To brush stones from her knees where she had fallen from a tree they climbed. She waited for him to denounce the headman, to curse Wu and his ancestors to the thousandth generation.

'I warned you to stop fighting. I warned you that it would bring trouble.' His words hit her like a blow to the stomach. 'The Wu lineage owns half our father's land.'

'You think I invited him to attack me? It is the Wus who have brought trouble upon me.' Young Wu who had lured her into his father's lair. Big Wu, who had tried to take the only thing that was hers. 'They think they own everyone and everything!'

'They do own everyone and everything! And if not them, then others like them. We can only accept this. Accept who we are.'

But who was she? She was daughter and sister. Her mother would have her be wife and mother. Big Wu would make her his concubine. Yet why couldn't she be a scholar, or a warrior or a pedlar of trinkets? Why couldn't she decide who she was and who she would become? She could comb up her hair like Ah Wei and vow to remain a spinster. She could be a woman, yet not a woman. Owe no obedience to husband or son. She could escape.

Her brother sighed, spearing his wooden shovel into the mud and clambering up the bank to stand several steps away. She wondered if, eighteen years ago, they had faced off like this, or if they had nestled close as a single babe in their mother's womb, limbs entwined. She wondered what might have been if they had both been boys. Or girls.

'You killed a man, little sister. There is no escaping that.'

'They will come for me.'

'I know.'

'You are leaving for New Gold Mountain and I don't know what to do without you.'

'There is only one thing to do. Go to the mat shed and wait until I come for you.'

She slipped into the mat shed behind the wormhouse, hoping that Elder Brother would not notice her presence. If he discovered her, he would feel it his duty to tell their father, for he always did have an iron rod up his backside. And who knew what would happen then? Even now, the Wus might be searching for her, descending upon their house, questioning her mother, interrogating her grandfather. The fewer people who knew her whereabouts, the safer she and they would be.

She hid between rows of silkworm mats, the bamboo frames lining the room like expectant skeletons. Taller than a man, each frame awaited its crop of fat worms to be slotted into place, spinning their lives away. But this late in the year, the mat shed was silent and empty, apart from the ragged sound of her breathing. Rush mats formed the walls of the shed, so that in the sparse light her hands appeared to be covered in dark smudges. She clasped them together to stop them shaking, but nothing could halt her thoughts.

She didn't know how long she waited for Second Brother but she never doubted that he would come. He was her other half. She was *yin* to his *yang*. And despite his efforts to deny it, to turn her into a traditional wife and perfect sister, a part of her would always be *yang* to his *yin*. They were twins and he would never abandon her.

Bare feet did not announce their presence, so when she saw the tall shape silhouetted in the entry she shrank back into the shadows in surprise. The Mo boys weren't the only broad-shouldered, long, lean men in the village. Young Wu came close to them in height, and fancied himself broader.

'Little Cat!' hissed the intruder as he strode further into the hut so that she could make out his features. Long leaf-shaped eyes darted about the room, searching for her.

'I'm here,' she said, stepping out from between the rows of empty mats.

'Come.'

He didn't wait for her agreement, but turned and stepped back outside. She followed him into the late morning sunlight that streamed through low-lying clouds.

'It looks like rain.'

'Good. Harder to track us.'

'Where are we going?' she asked, realising the answer as soon as she spoke, for his *ta'am* rested on the ground nearby, the two large baskets attached to their carrying pole. Second Brother had devoted an entire day to scouring the local thickets for a stout pole that would last the distance, however long that might prove to be. However far the pole might need to travel. The baskets contained half his body weight in provisions, all carefully assembled for the journey to New Gold Mountain. A new life was packed in readiness for his departure.

Two pairs of blue cotton trousers and two blue tunics. One padded jacket and trousers, for protection in the unknown winters that lay ahead. Woven hemp sandals. A cotton quilt lined with wadded silk, new-made by their mother and bestowed with a grudging *hou wahn*. A straw sleeping mat rolled up and tucked inside the quilt. A wooden block for a pillow. Rice bowls, chopsticks, spoons, cups and a wok. A well-thumbed phrase book of the foreigners' mysterious language, wrapped in gummed silk to keep it dry. And a paltry few slivers of silver for trade.

'Here, put this on,' he said, handing her a bamboo hat that was sitting atop one of the baskets. 'Tonight we will do a better job of disguising you.'

Before she could ask him what he meant, he had hoisted up pole and baskets, twisting his body until the weight settled comfortably between his shoulders.

'Hurry, we must leave now.'

'When will we be back?'

He looked into her eyes then, and the hard planes of his face softened almost imperceptibly.

'You will never be back, Little Cat.'

17

Robetown, South Australia, 1856

By the time they reached Noorla's doorstep, water was streaming down their faces in rivulets, their skirts hung wet and cumbersome upon their bodies and even Alice's pantalets clung to her legs beneath her skirt. Although James remained limp in Thomas's arms, the bullocky appeared to notice neither his weight nor the rain. His shirtsleeves were plastered to his forearms so that she could see the lean strength beneath.

'Thank you, I can take him now.'

He opened his mouth, perhaps about to offer to carry James upstairs, but Violet's eyes pleaded with him to desist. 'I am stronger than I look.'

He nodded in silent understanding. 'Let me know how the boy gets on,' he said, depositing him gently in her arms. Then tipping his dripping cabbage-tree hat in farewell, he turned back to town once more. As Alice opened the door for her to carry James inside she watched him stride away. She hoped it would not be the last time she saw him.

But the boy was heavier than she had anticipated, and the stairs proved an additional hurdle. By the time she reached the door to his room, her arms were quaking with the effort and she was breathing hard. She lowered him to the bed, where he lay pale and unmoving, so unlike the jack-in-the-box boy she had come to know. While Alice drew back the bedcovers, she removed his short jacket and trousers, then struggled to thrust his flaccid limbs into his nightshirt. Throughout this procedure he did not stir. He may as well have been a corpse.

'Is James going to be all right?' asked Alice, when they finally had him snug beneath the covers.

'He will be putting beetles down your back again in no time.'

'Shall I go and tell Mama?'

'Of course. As soon as you have changed out of your wet clothes. But, Alice, your mama may be angry if she discovers we let James visit with Mr Thomas. We wouldn't want that, would we?'

'No, we wouldn't,' Alice agreed with a frown, perhaps remembering the kerfuffle over their last adventure, when her mother took to her bed with a headache for two days when she could not find them for an hour or two. 'But it was you who wished to visit with Mr Thomas.'

'I believe it was James who wanted Mr Thomas to show him how to train a dog.' For a moment the girl looked as if she might debate the matter but Violet added, 'Your brother needs us now.'

Alice gazed down at her little brother, lying prone in his bed. Perhaps in that moment, she remembered that despite being annoying, he was her only sibling and her mother was unlikely to produce more.

'When you're better, I'll play at bullockies with you in the garden,' she promised her silent brother. 'You can be the bullock driver and Miss Hartley and I will be the bullocks.' Bending towards him, she stretched out her hand as if to brush a lock of sticky hair from his forehead. But Violet intercepted her by enfolding that hand in her own.

'Best not get too close. Your mama won't want both her children ill with the *grippe*. And James will need your prayers.' She forced a smile. Clearly the boy was very sick. She suspected that he would need more than prayers in the coming days.

She hoped the doctor would not be too far from home.

Mrs Wallace sat by her son's bedside, bathing his forehead in cool water. James's illness seemed to have jolted her from her usual, jittery state and roused her into action. With her hair pulled back in a tight bun beneath a plain white bonnet, and a long apron tied about her waist, for the first time Violet caught a glimpse of the plucky squatter's wife she must once have been. Her fear was written in the grooves upon her forehead and the wild look in her eyes, but did not show in her steady hands and calm demeanour. She had already applied a medicinal plaster to his chest and dosed him with poppy syrup.

From her place by the open window, Violet looked out over the track from town, hoping to catch sight of Dr Penny upon his chestnut horse. Mrs Wallace had sent Billy to fetch him as soon as she laid eyes upon her son. From that moment, she had hardly spared a word for Violet, other than to issue instructions. She uttered no rebuke or lecture when told that the children had been caught in the rain while playing at quoits. She did not question why the governess had failed to notice earlier that her charge was ill. Violet's story was met with nothing more reproachful than a hard stare. A reckoning was yet to come.

The weather had set in for the afternoon so that sea and sky merged in a dull grey, the lake's surface rippled in the watery light, while the land was hazed in a curtain of steady rain. The world had turned to water. But through the rain, she spied the tiny figure of a man upon a horse, plodding along the track between ocean and lake. She watched him draw closer, gradually discerning the bulky shape of panniers and a small valise strapped to the saddle behind the rider. Even from this distance she knew the outline of the town's small, sturdy doctor.

'He is coming!' With her words, a breath of wind ruffled the lace curtains, as if the room itself breathed a sigh of relief.

But any relief was short-lived. An interminable hour later, the doctor was once more packing his equipment into his valise as James lay listless upon his bed. Apart from an occasional bout of coughing, the boy had barely stirred, even when the doctor bled him.

'Perhaps it is only a severe cold,' Mrs Wallace suggested, her eyes fixed to her son's pale face, 'and he will be himself again in a day or two.' Violet would have admired her optimism if she believed it, but there was a hopeless note to the woman's voice. She was, after all, a woman who had buried two babes.

'We can only hope, dear lady,' said Dr Penny. 'But the boy's condition is worrisome. We should know more tomorrow when the symptoms resolve themselves further. At this point it could be any of a number of maladies. Until then, we must keep a close eye on him. I can ask Mrs Ling to help you nurse him.'

Mrs Ling was well-regarded as a home nurse in the district and to Violet's way of thinking, probably a good deal more experienced in the management of umpteen maladies than the boy's mama.

'Thank you, doctor, but Miss Hartley and I will manage,' said Mrs Wallace and Violet suppressed a sigh.

Dr Penny returned his leeches to their small pewter case, saying, 'I've given him a little calomel and bled him to remove any bad humours. The fever is tolerable but try to keep him cool. It's his throat that concerns me most. A poultice of grated carrot and turnip may help. You can have your cook make one up.'

With each new bout of coughing, Violet expected James to wake, demanding a cup of ginger beer in his wheedling, boyish manner. But throughout the doctor's examination he remained too lethargic to open his eyes, as if they were gummed down by the weight of his illness.

The doctor finished packing his valise and stood, a smile too tenuous to inspire confidence flashing briefly through his beard. 'I'll return in the morning to see how he's getting on then,' he said, patting the mother's shoulder.

When Violet returned from seeing the good doctor upon his way, Alice was sitting on the landing outside her brother's room, workbasket at her side, plying knitting needles.

'I'm knitting James a scarf. Do you think he will like it, Miss Hartley?'

'I'm sure he will love it.'

'I'm trying very hard not to drop my stitches. I haven't got very far but already there is a mistake... see?' She held up the piece to show Violet a ragged hole at the bottom of the knitting.

'Would you like me to unravel and fix it?' The poor girl had got her stitches into such disarray that the only way to repair it was to begin again.

'Yes, please,' said Alice, handing her the needles.

Violet inspected the floor for signs of dust before taking a seat next to Alice. She slipped the needles from their woollen loops and began carefully unravelling the uneven stitches as Alice looked on. When she reached the bottom of the hole she inserted a needle once more.

'Will you rewind the wool for me, please, Alice? If we work together, we shall have the job done before you know it.'

'Is James going to die?'

'Whatever gave you such an idea?'

'He looks very sick.'

'It is probably just a bad case of the *grippe* and he will be up and about in a day or two, annoying you once more. James cannot die,' Violet promised. 'Your mama will not allow it.'

It was a long night, sitting turnabout at James's bedside with his mama, listening to his cough turn to a bark that racked his robust, little boy's chest. By dawn, when Violet struggled from sleep to relieve her employer once more, the lad's neck had swollen to bull-like proportions so that his head did not look to belong any more to his body. Mrs Wallace went to her bed, eliciting a promise from Violet that she would wake her if anything changed.

Overnight the boy's lips had also developed a dry flaky appearance, as if he had been too long in the sun, and his breathing grew even more laboured. Violet thought to spoon a few drops of ginger beer into his mouth – the boy had such a sweet tooth – but the liquid caught in his throat, dribbling forth from the corner of his mouth in a bubble of beery saliva. For a moment, in the dim lamplight, she could have sworn she saw a froth of crimson fleck his lips and she imagined that James was coughing up what remained of his lungs. His painful bark took her back to that low-ceilinged cottage where the curtains were always drawn against the sunlight, and the birdsong was drowned by the sound of her mother's cough. There had been no money for a nurse and her father was still at sea, but a twelve-year-old learns quickly. A twelve-year-old grows up in no time, when circumstances demand.

She wiped the saliva from the boy's mouth, feeling a tug at her heart. She had promised Alice that her brother would recover, but she saw that she may have misspoken. Were his lungs even now turning to mush? Was his throat choking him of air? Squeezing the life from him? He coughed again and an invisible hand clutched her throat too. She realised that it was more than fear of rebuke that she felt. More than fear for Miss Violet Hartley's welfare. She was afraid that they might lose that wilful little boy.

When the doctor arrived soon after breakfast she had never been more relieved. Surely they could rely upon his qualifications. The man had doctored sailors and soldiers and been in the Maori War. Surely he had seen illness in its myriad variations and would know what to do about a small boy who could barely catch a breath. She woke Mrs Wallace, who did not wait to dress but rushed to her son's bedside in nightgown and wrapper. Together they watched the doctor probe and prod the boy, waiting in silence for his pronouncement.

'The boy has developed a malignant throat,' he said,

and Violet could tell by his tone that this news was not good. 'Come, take a look.' He beckoned for Mrs Wallace to approach the bed and Violet peered over her shoulder. Holding James's mouth open with a steel instrument, he gestured for them to look inside.

'You can see that a membrane has developed around the child's tonsils, restricting his breathing.'

Wrapped around James's tonsils was a thick, grey mass, growing like a fungus in the back of his throat. Violet put a hand to her neck, suddenly conscious of a desire to swallow.

'There are surgeons who advocate the removal of the membrane but in my opinion, and in the opinion of several medical men I respect, this will only lead to pain and bleeding in the patient. I do not recommend it.' He paused, to allow time for his words to be taken in. 'I will make up a mixture of cayenne and vinegar, which seems to have some efficacy in these cases.'

'But he will recover, won't he, doctor?'

'Ah, dear lady... I believe that his recovery will depend upon his constitution... and the will of our Lord.'

'M-my James is a strong boy. He has never suffered more than a cold. He loves nothing more than to be... to be... outdoors,' Mrs Wallace stammered, on the verge of tears.

'Well, that is certainly a good sign. Most adults and many children do recover from a putrid throat. But, Mrs Wallace...'

'Yes?'

'You may want to send word to your husband.'

Violet rushed to her employer's side for the woman looked likely to swoon. But Mrs Wallace brushed her aside, saying, 'You may leave now, Miss Hartley. You have done enough for one day.'

The shadow of death loomed in the boy's brightly coloured room and Violet wasn't sorry be elsewhere. She felt sad and anxious for James, she did. She wished with all her heart that he might be saved. But when that familiar voice of guilt nagged to be heard, she blocked her ears to it. Guilt was a futile emotion and she had resolved to be done with it years ago. It had not brought her mother back, no matter how loud and long she blamed herself for not being clever enough, or good enough to save her.

If Dr Penny could not cure James of illness, Violet's guilt stood no chance.

18

Pearl River Delta, China, 1856

The ominous feeling in the pit of his stomach hadn't abated by the time Young Wu reached the entrance to his father's compound. The doors were flung open against the walls, concealing the peeling remains of last spring's Door Gods and the snarling dragon doorknockers. Yet the sign declaring to all that they were entering the presence of Recommended Man Wu remained visible. He paused at the entrance, wondering why the house had been left so unguarded. Only the high doorsill barred his way, a barrier to any uninvited ghosts, a wall to keep the family's luck inside, but not much use in keeping out human intruders.

No one had noticed his arrival. Their old gatekeeper was probably out and about upon some errand. His mother was likely in the kitchen preparing the evening meal with Little Sweetie, a distant Wu cousin whom his father had purchased as bondmaid in a favour to her impoverished parents. His younger sister would be returning from the silk filature, or off gallivanting with a friend, since he wasn't there to supervise. And if his father weren't down at the clan hall with his cronies, solving the problems of the Empire, he would be safely ensconced in his study.

He stepped over the sill, passed by the gatekeeper's room to his left and entered the front courtyard. It was that hour between day and night where the shadows crept towards evening, yet the courtyard was still hazed in a dusky light. A cold breeze had sprung up from nowhere, rustling the paper lanterns and cooling the lingering sweat from his long walk. It circled around him, playing with his hair and raising chicken skin on his arms. And in the quiet of the empty courtyard he heard it keening through the empty rooms of his father's house. His bare scalp tightened in the cold and he shivered with the coming of night.

Now that he was home, the terrible feeling that had followed him all the way from the ferry did not fade. If anything it grew worse, as if his stomach gnawed upon itself, one moment empty, the other full to bursting. He had not felt like this since the day Bully Yee pushed him to the ground and made him eat dirt. The day that his father denounced him as a weak and worthless son, unfit to be named Wu. On that day, it had been Ah Yong who saved him by clapping him on the back and telling him it had been a good fight. That it did not matter if Bully Yee won or their fathers punished them. They had put up a good fight and that was all that mattered.

Not to Big Wu.

But all that had been long ago. He was a man now and he must swallow his fears, listen to his instinct and if necessary, brave his father's wrath.

His cloth shoes whispered upon the flagstones as he strode across the courtyard and stepped into the main hall where the sacred lamp flickered upon the altar. From here he could see through to the second courtyard where not a soul stirred. There was only the wind, moaning even louder now as a fresh gust blew through the main hall and extinguished the sacred lamp. He did not stop to think about this lamp that burned day and night, the light of the Tao that was never allowed to die. He followed the sound of the wind across the void to his father's study where the moaning was loudest. Even the closed door could not muffle the sound. It rose in a high-pitched wail before fading to a prolonged sigh. A brief respite then the wailing began again.

If the wind's voice sounded like a woman, Young Wu did not acknowledge it. For if he did, it would suggest a lack of trust in the father to whom he owed his existence. He dared not imagine a girl crying or broken in his father's study, a girl whom he had abandoned. He did not want to expose what lay behind that door for then he would have to act upon it. Yet he must.

He reached for the door pull, a brass ring attached to a bat of good fortune, its wings outstretched like a butterfly. The moaning was almost ear-splitting now, rising to such a pitch that he thought surely the entire village must hear it. Opening the door, he put one foot over the sill and then the other, his eyes momentarily closed. When he opened them it was his mother he first saw. She knelt on the rug rending her clothes and tearing at her hair, a wild keening issuing from her throat. Then he noticed his father lying on the floor beside her, his robe hitched up to show his bony ankles. Young Wu could not understand why his father did not remonstrate with his mother. If she talked too much while serving his dinner he would throw his bowl to the ground in disgust. Yet now he lay face down and silent, as his wife wailed louder than a cat in season.

'Ma... Ma... be quiet,' he hissed. 'Ba is sleeping.'

If he didn't instantly calculate the sum of the clues set before him, who could blame him? What son expects to enter his father's study and discover him murdered? Find his mother keening over a bloody corpse? That was the knowledge these moments finally brought to him. His mother's grief, his father's still form, the discarded seal lying upon his disordered robe, his greying queue matted red, the seeping blood staining the rug. Added together, these facts resulted as surely as the tallying of an abacus, in a single explanation.

One minute the only movement in the house was the rattling of the wind through empty courtyards, the only sound was the wailing of his mother; and the next moment, Gatekeeper Wu was hobbling into the family's inner sanctum with what seemed like the entire Wu contingent trailing behind him.

'Aiya! Aiya! Who did this?'

'Where is the murderer?'

'Who has killed Wu?'

The angry voices bled into each other so that Young Wu could not separate them. He felt like the entire clan had come to accuse him of being a bad son. How else could this have come to pass?

'What shall we do, Master?' the old man said, pulling at the hem of his tunic. 'What shall we do?'

'My father is dead, Old Man. He cannot tell us now.'

'You must tell us what to do. You must find the murderer.'

Suddenly his mother ceased moaning and spoke to him. 'You must avenge your father's murder or his *po* will not rest.' He waited for her to say more, to reveal some truth that he might grasp. Something that might help him understand. But with these few words she resumed her wailing, bowing repeatedly over the lifeless form of her husband.

'It's true,' said his Second Uncle, shouting to be heard above the din. 'Your father's *po* will not rest in his grave. It will become a ghost to haunt the living. Look at all this blood! Even his *hun* may not remain in its tablet.'

Young Wu watched as a ripple of horror passed through the assembled Wus. Third Aunty actually looked up at the peach tree as if to discover his father's *po* hovering in its leafless branches. But there was nothing there, only the annoying breeze that had plagued him since he first returned home.

'There aren't enough offerings in the world to ease his journey in the underworld if you do not avenge his death,' said Third Uncle, to which the gathering of Wus nodded as one. Young Wu wondered if the ancestors gathered, silent and invisible, for he felt the weight of their judgement upon him too.

'The girl did it,' said the old man, his good eye fixed upon Young Wu's face. 'She was the only one here. No one else passed through the gate. I will attest to that.'

'The girl was alone with him. This is true,' cried his mother, interrupting her bowing briefly. 'He ordered us not to disturb him.'

The gathering nodded in understanding, for you did not disturb Big Wu if ordered not to.

'You must find her and take her to the *yamen* so the magistrate can deliver justice,' announced Third Aunty, who was a great believer in the Emperor to bring order.

'That old woman is talking nonsense. You must find the murderer and deliver justice yourself!' said Second Uncle. 'Only then will your father's *po* sleep.'

'Ya! How will your father face the Courts of Hell while his murderer runs free?' said Third Uncle, shaking his fist for emphasis. 'He will be the joke of the underworld. All the demons of Hell will be laughing at him.'

Faced with this barrage of advice, Young Wu was yet

to find his voice. Both his father's younger brothers were glaring at him, expecting him to set things to rights, but his tongue was glued in place, as if by a mouthful of sticky rice. How could he set his father's death to rights when it was his father who ordered their house, who lavished punishment and doled out praise? It was the father who sat in judgement in Sandy Bottom Village. Not the son.

'The girl cannot have gone far, Master,' said the old gatekeeper. 'I don't know how she escaped without my notice.'

'Perhaps she is still here!' said Second Uncle. 'Let's search the building. She cannot escape us all! And when we catch her, Young Wu will deliver justice!'

'Justice! Justice!' shouted the Wus. 'Young Wu will deliver justice!'

He tried not to picture the form this justice would take. He tried not to imagine Little Cat thrust into a pig crate and thrown in the river. He shut his eyes to the vision of her body jerking on a rope, long bare legs kicking air.

'The gate was wide open when I arrived,' he said finally. 'She will not be here any longer. Are you sure no one else entered, Old Man? Perhaps when you went to relieve yourself?'

'The doors were closed and latched when I left. When I returned they were open. That's when I went and knocked on the old master's door.'

The Wus gathered in a circle around him, waiting. Everyone in the village knew him as Young Wu, son of Big Wu, who was headman of the village and the Wu clan elder. Everyone expected him to take action. For who amongst them could rest easy if a ghost was on the loose, especially one with a temper?

'Second Aunty will lead the women and search the girls' house for any sign of Little Cat. I will speak to the Mo family.' He stood with his legs apart and his hands akimbo, trying to find the strength to do what was needed, to do his duty as a son. He was eighteen and he was a man. And yet… he had not been a man for so very long. He was not practised in its ways. And murder had not come to Sandy Bottom Village since he was a small boy and Bully Yee's father killed his mother by striking her in the face with an iron cooking pot.

'And then what, Master?' asked the old man.

'And then… and then we shall see.' He knew they expected him to vow vengeance upon the perpetrator but he could not bring himself to do it. Not yet. Not until he had to.

19

The Mo family conveyance was more raft than boat and needed a steady hand to keep it afloat. Their father had built it when newly married – five giant bamboo poles lashed together, each a hand's width in diameter – and it had done good service for their family, ferrying mulberry leaves and hanks of silk to market and returning laden with rice and tea. Second Brother scampered along the raft like an otter but it took Little Cat most of the morning to find her river legs, for the narrow raft tilted dangerously with any jerky movement. By midday she was wielding the long bamboo pole as expertly as her brother.

They kept to the canals and creeks, avoiding the busy river traffic where they might be more easily discovered. Her twin was accustomed to poling the raft along these waterways from his many trips to market with their father. But by late afternoon, when they had passed through the market town and were deep inside the watery maze of Sun Dak county, he decided that travelling on foot would be faster.

They rounded a bend in the creek and joined a wide shallow waterway where fishermen worked huge nets hung from flimsy bamboo frames. Others fished from rafts with shiny-feathered cormorants that rested on the boats with wings outstretched to dry. The birds were trained to dive for fish and return the catch to their masters. Little Cat wondered whether the birds would be so obliging if their necks had not been snared to stop them swallowing all but the smallest of prey.

Second Brother guided the raft to the bank where a stand of trees concealed them from the inhabitants of a nearby village. Little Cat stepped lightly to the bank, trying not to capsize the raft, as her twin dug his pole deep into the river mud to hold it steady. Once she was on dry land he handed her one basket at a time, before disembarking and hauling the raft up behind him.

'How will we return the raft to our father?' she asked.

Her brother did not look up from the business of securing the raft.

'Goh Go?'

'We won't.'

There was no need to say more. She knew a pang of guilt then for she hadn't thought about returning the raft once during the many hours of their journey. Her head had been too full of thoughts of capture to consider the repercussions of their hasty departure. She had not spared a thought for her father, who would lose the boat that saved him regular long walks to market hauling heavy baskets.

'I'm sorry. One day I will get him a new raft. When we have made our fortunes on New Gold Mountain.'

'Will you also get back his land?'

'What do you mean?'

'The Wus are certain to take back our lease now,' he said, looking up from his business with baskets and boat to face her. His wide mouth was set in a grim line that matched the frown scratching his forehead. 'Now that a Mo daughter has murdered the Wu clan elder.'

'I did not—' she began, but he cut her off before she could deny the word 'murder'.

'I doubt they will see it that way.'

Was it murder to defend your honour, even your life? Big Wu had put his bony hands upon her. He had cleaved at her sex with his bamboo claw. Should she have stood frozen like a frightened rabbit and let him have his way? Even as she grappled with these thoughts, another image teased at the edges of her memory. One she could not quite catch. It flitted away just as she snatched at its meaning.

'Wing Chun defended herself,' she said. She did not know how to explain her reasoning to her brother so she invoked the name of the renowned female warrior as her shield.

'Wing Chun is a myth. You see what happens when girls learn to fight?'

'What?'

He shrugged, as if that said it all. 'A man knows how to fight without killing. Women always take things too far. You should have cried out.'

But who was there to listen? Big Wu had sent them all away: the gatekeeper, who surely knew what was afoot, his wife, who did not want to know. Young Wu, who had turned away from her, who had abandoned her.

'You could have pleaded with him.'

She could not bring herself to tell him that fear had stolen her voice. She could still feel the dry hard lump of it clogging her throat. 'When has Big Wu listened to anyone?' she said instead. 'Did he listen to our father's cousin?'

'Aiya! That old story. Can the flames stop the moth throwing itself at them? Ba says his cousin was always disturbed.'

It seemed to her that Fate had a history of disturbing girls. But she did not say this to her brother either, for he wouldn't understand. He stood with his back to the river, his shoulders yoked beneath the weight of his baskets. The last rays of sun lit one side of his face, the other was in darkness.

'Well, we must ride the tiger now,' he said, staring out at the craggy peaks lining the horizon. Beyond the hills lay the city of Kwangchow and the mighty Pearl River. He did not glance back the way they had come, to the village where their family had lived for twenty-three generations. He spoke no regret of leaving home without even a prayer of leave-taking to the ancestors, but she saw it in his eyes.

'Come. Let's find somewhere to rest. And then we must make some changes.'

*

The Mo twins squatted beneath a bower of osmanthus trees eating a hasty meal of hard rice cakes and dried fish. Although the nights were growing colder, they dared not light a fire to warm aching limbs or boil water for tea. Even now the Wus might be sniffing out their trail.

The river lapped at the bank below, its far side shrouded in evening gloom. And around them the heady scent of osmanthus flowers merged with the stink of river mud and dried fish to give Little Cat a headache. Or perhaps it was merely the weight of her pigtail dragging at her scalp. So much had happened in the last twelve hours that her thoughts were as muddled as her tangled braid. Perhaps if she laid her head on the grass and closed her eyes, when she awoke everything would be different. She would be back in the girls' house gossiping with her friends and dreaming of warrior nuns.

'No time for sleeping. We must travel through the night.'

'I was only resting my eyes.' It wasn't only her head that ached. Her entire body felt heavy, so that she must order her limbs to obey. And her monthly bleeding must be arriving early because her trousers were spotted with blood.

After rummaging in one of his baskets, Second Brother's hand emerged with a knife. He waved it in her direction, the blade catching a stray gleam of moonlight. For the first time since she had appeared at the fishpond that morning, he smiled. It wasn't an encouraging sight.

'What's that for?'

'Camouflage.'

He shuffled towards her on his knees, a glint in his eyes. The last time he had given her that look was just before he executed a sidekick to her shin. She sprang to her feet, landing in fighting stance, her hands already poised for attack. This was a strange time to be sparring but perhaps he wanted to keep her on her toes. Anything might happen on their journey.

'You think I am playing with you? I am done playing, little sister.' He stood without urgency, straightening to his full height, slightly taller but in other ways almost her mirror image. Broad-shouldered, long-legged, with a thick mane of hair that reached to his waist.

'Undo your pigtail.' When she didn't move he added, 'You want to fight like a man. You want to go adventuring. Then you must look like a man.'

He was right, of course. She could not continue as she was. She had never heard of a girl venturing across the seas to New Gold Mountain. And although she wore the same *samfu* as any village boy, and walked upon the same tough-soled feet, her hair declared her sex. Her mother longed for the day when the eldest Mo aunty would braid her daughter's hair into a married woman's bun and send her off in a sedan chair to her husband's home. It would signify the end of her girlhood and the beginning of her new life as a grown woman. But Little Cat now dreamed of combing up her hair and becoming *sor hei*, a self-combed woman. She would vow to remain celibate for the rest of her life. She would do away with the need for a man. She would be a grown woman, but make choices like a man. She would comb up her hair into a bun, make her offerings to the gods and celebrate with a banquet. Then all her friends and family would give her lucky red packets.

That was her dream.

'Men don't cry, little sister,' said her brother, an expression of disgust on his face.

She wiped away tears with the back of her hand and promised herself that she would not cry again. She would face this new future – whatever it might bring – like a woman. Like a warrior. She untied the ribbon that fastened her pigtail and ran her fingers through her hair, unravelling each braided strand so that it hung down her back like a skein of reeled silk.

'Go ahead. But try not to make me bleed.'

Her twin clutched a fistful of hair from the top of her scalp and handed it to her.

'Hold this out of the way.'

Then he took the knife and slashed at the remainder, slicing as close to her scalp as possible around the circumference of her head so that one single pitiful hank remained.

'When we get to Kwangchow you can visit a barber. This will do for now.'

He stooped to gather the discarded hair and took it down to the water's edge where he released it into the river, jettisoning any clue to their presence. In the darkness she could not see where it floated. She did not know which way the river would take it or where it would end up. Just as she did not know where this journey would take her. All she could do was follow it to its end.

She lifted a hand and traced it over her prickly scalp. Then she gathered the remaining hank and began braiding it into the tight queue of a man.

20

The trail of Wu men wound up the alley, their torches casting shadows across pitiless faces. The wind ruffled their clothes and whipped their hair, adding to the tension as they pressed close to his heels, their hands itching for vengeance, their voices barely restrained to a sullen murmur. The Wus were under siege and someone must pay.

He knew as soon as he stepped through the gate that the Mo family had heard the news. The last of the daylight had faded and only a single oil lamp and the flickering torches lit the courtyard but they were lined up along the veranda as if waiting for an execution. He wondered how much they knew. Whether they knew that their daughter had bludgeoned his father with his seal, so that he died in a pool of his own blood. What were they hiding behind those pale, anxious faces? His father said that everyone was hiding something.

Ah Keong looked up expectantly as he entered, but Young Wu did not meet his eyes. He couldn't afford to give any hint of silent contract or promise. On this of all days, he must be his father's son. Hard and uncompromising, merciless and unforgiving.

'The thunder is loud yet little rain falls.' He heard his father's laughing voice in his head, shaming him still, even though he was dead.

One by one the family approached and bowed, even the old grandfather, leaning on his cane.

'We have heard that your father has passed,' said Mo, shaking his head, his face grim. 'It's too sudden.'

'We hope that you will restrain your grief,' said the grandfather.

'Do not be too sad,' said the wife.

'Whatever we can do to help,' said Ah Keong, clapping him on the shoulder.

'Where is Ah Yong?' he asked, ignoring their condolences. If Little Cat were in trouble she would seek her twin first.

'He didn't tell you?' The father shrugged, as if it was of little import. 'He left a day early. It's a long way to New Gold Mountain.'

'You know my brother. He isn't one for farewells. Too afraid of blubbing like a girl.' Ah Keong laughed, but it did not ring true.

Young Wu lifted his chin and crossed his arms over his chest, in imitation of his father. He wished he wore a robe to cover his trembling legs. It had been a long day and he had been walking for most of it. 'And where is your sister?'

'She isn't here.'

'Little Cat was the last person to see my father. No one has seen her since. I took her there myself this morning.' He did not speak of her crime but the horde at the gate spoke for him.

'I saw her,' announced the wife. 'At noon. I sent her to gather wood in the scrub by the river, but she hasn't returned. I was about to ask Ah Keong to go looking for her.' She caught his eyes and held them in a vice of truth.

'We are very worried,' said Mo. 'There is talk of bandits in the hills.'

There was always talk of bandits in the hills. Bandits were responsible for every stolen pig and missing chicken in the village.

'Perhaps the same bandit who killed your father has kidnapped my sister.' Ah Keong aimed a worried frown in the direction of the huddle by the gate.

'There was no bandit!' shouted Second Uncle, shooting a vicious glance at the Mos. 'Little Cat killed Big Wu.'

'Little Cat killed Big Wu!' echoed the mob.

'My granddaughter wouldn't hurt a fly,' croaked the old man, waving his cane at them.

Young Wu put up his hand for silence and one by one the cries of rage faded to a mutter. He looked at his hand in surprise as if it held some magic power. 'It is I who have the power,' his father's voice whispered in his ear.

'You can search the house but she isn't here,' said Ah Keong. 'As my mother said, she went to gather firewood.'

At this, the woman set up a loud, keening cry. 'Aiya! What has happened to my daughter? What if she is dead like your father?'

'Why aren't you out searching for my daughter's kidnapper,' it was Mo's turn to shake his fist at the mob, 'instead of accusing an innocent girl? My daughter did not do this thing. She could not!'

But Young Wu knew in his heart that Little Cat could do this thing. He knew she had the rage and the strength. She had the courage to strike, unlike his father's son.

'I will search the house… alone,' he told his uncles and cousins. 'Wait here and do not let anyone leave.'

It did not take long to search the few rooms and when he was done his heart lifted a little at the reprieve. Wherever Little Cat was, she wasn't here. He would not have to stand in judgement tonight. He would not have to kill anyone tonight. Yet just as he was about to take his leave there was a commotion at the gate as a group of his youngest cousins squeezed through the crowd shouting gleefully in their high, childish voices, 'Mo's boat is gone! Little Cat has taken Mo's boat! Little Cat has run away! Can we help you hunt her down?'

He glared the boys to silence, summoning his sternest expression and hoping his uncles would not contradict him. 'There will be no hunting down. Not tonight. It is too dark. And I must help my father's *po* to its rest,' he commanded. 'We will begin tomorrow.'

By the time Young Wu returned home a white banner was hanging from the gate, announcing to all that there had been a death in the house. Reputedly, the banner would also dissuade his father's *po* from wandering. But since everyone in the village already knew of the death and his father could never be dissuaded from anything, there was probably little point.

During a brief lull in the wailing while his mother and sisters ate their dinner, he carried the body to the main hall with the help of his cousins, placing incense and offerings within reach. Little Sweetie had already covered the altar with a cloth, for the gods might be offended by the presence of the corpse. Now it was his task as eldest and only son to wash his father's body. Wiping a lifetime of impurities from those rigid limbs.

He dressed in a suit of mourning clothes that was kept at hand for emergencies, donning the coarse white tunic and trousers and layering over these a length of hemp cloth with a hole cut for his head. Luckily, his father's coffin lay in readiness in the storeroom. Big Wu had ordered it on his fiftieth birthday, along with suitable *shou yi* – the many layers of elaborate clothing that would form his shroud – enough to see him through to heaven and proclaim to all the many generations of descendants who would ensure his posterity.

But first the body must be cleansed.

'You must go to the stream to draw water for the ritual washing,' his Second Aunty advised as he approached the well in the front courtyard toting his wooden buckets.

'It's permissible to draw water from a well, so long as the appropriate offering is made to the guardian spirit,' argued Third Aunty, patting her matron's bun authoritatively with a satisfied expression.

'How can you draw heavenly water from a well? It must be taken from a stream or river. Especially in the case of unnatural death.' Second Aunty gave her sister-in-law a venomous look. There was nothing unusual in this, for the two women were like snake and mongoose. He wasn't sure which was snake and which mongoose, so he trod warily around both of them. He waited while they argued over the correct procedure for obtaining the heavenly water necessary for the ritual washing of the body. Second Uncle's wife believed that she was an authority on all rituals, while Third Uncle's wife was a staunch believer in the opposite of anything her sister-in-law proposed.

'But why is stream water more heavenly than well water? They both come from the gods,' Third Aunty appealed to the gathered aunts, uncles and distant cousins. The house was already straining its walls with relatives, and his elder sisters and their husbands were yet to arrive. Death was a time for families to close ranks, and in the case of Big Wu, this included most of the village.

'Because that is the way it has always been done!' Second Aunty was growing shrill now. She tugged at her husband's arm but he ignored her, not wanting to get into an unseemly fight with his brother. Last time that happened they didn't speak to each other for three years.

'That is what it advises in the Book of Rites,' she continued. 'Do you want Brother-in-law's *po* to wander the village causing chaos? Do you want him to become a hungry ghost searching for a body to replace his own?'

Of course, there was nothing Third Aunty could say to this. For one thing, she could not read. Neither could Second Aunty, but that was beside the point. None of the assembled relatives wanted his father's *po* wandering Sandy Bottom Village looking for a replacement. He might choose one of them. That was the thing about ghosts: they were unpredictable. They did not abide by the rules of gods or humans. They made their own rules. Just because his father was murdered didn't mean his ghost would seek his murderer to replace him. He could just as easily choose one of his relatives. Therefore, his relatives must do everything in their power to placate him.

Second Uncle pointed to Young Wu's buckets saying, 'It will take more than a bucket of water to appease my brother's *po*, no matter how heavenly. It will take more than paper money and plates of noodles to feed his hunger.'

He knew that his uncle was disappointed in him. He wanted to tell him to be silent but he had used up all his authority at the Mos' house. Now he had nothing left but habit. Habit would not do for long. He would have to devise something else soon or he would lose all control over events and then his father would be deeply disappointed in him. The fact that he was dead was irrelevant.

Just then his mother and sisters renewed their keening, the cries issuing from the rear courtyard and drifting through the main hall to ring in the ears of the assembled mourners. Although empty, the buckets dragged at his shoulders as if they brimmed with 'heavenly' water. He knew what his uncles expected. And yet, part of him could not accept that Little Cat was responsible for his father's death. She might be capable of killing, but what possible reason could she have? Had she angered his father so greatly that he struck her and she struck back, accidentally, killing him? This was the only explanation he would allow himself. Then again, despite the old gatekeeper's denials, a bandit may indeed have climbed over the wall and killed his father. Perhaps, as Mo suggested, that same bandit held Little Cat hostage, even now. Abusing her. He imagined her struggling to free herself. Her legs and arms held down as she was set upon by a band of Long-hairs. Her sweet breasts crushed by greedy hands...

Was Little Cat murderer or victim?

A small moan escaped his throat, like a counterpoint to the wailing of women. His father was dead and the girl he... the girl might be his murderer, or his fellow victim. He did not know which of these would be worse. That Little Cat had his father's blood on her hands, or that she lay bleeding and captive in the distant hills. Either way, as his father's son, tomorrow he would be expected to take action.

His mother had fallen into a restless sleep in her room. His younger sister had returned to the girls' house, too frightened to stay in a place where her father's *po* might ambush her in the night, even though Mei Ying was usually the first to scoff at spirits. Meanwhile, Young Wu kept vigil over his father's body in the main hall.

He could not say that the old man looked peaceful, despite being surrounded by his favourite possessions and outfitted with pearls in hand and mouth, precious enough to bribe the Hell judges should the need arise. Big Wu looked as he had always looked... superior. His flaring nostrils and thick untamed brows were as menacing as ever. For a moment, Young Wu was relieved that his father was gone, before quickly thrusting that unfilial sentiment aside.

'Don't leave us,' he moaned, as any dutiful son would.

The longevity lamp flickered by his father's head as the wind prowled through the empty rooms of the house. He was so tired that his eyelids drooped. His legs were leaden from the long walk and his head still ached from the day's turmoil. If he could only lay his head down... if he could only sleep for a while.

He jerked awake, his chin bobbing on his chest. He didn't know how long he had slept but the wind had dropped, leaving the air heavy as an invisible blanket, and the sweet floral scent of opium teased his nostrils in the still air. Perhaps the old gatekeeper had ducked out for a smoke during all the fuss over his father's body. But he would have gone to bed by now for the moon cast vague shadows over a silent courtyard.

Young Wu was stretching his legs, shaking the stiffness from his limbs, when he felt someone enter the hall from his family's private quarters. He didn't actually hear anyone. It was more a disturbance in the air. He could have turned towards the new arrival but he didn't; the hairs on his neck warned against it. So it was out of the corner of his eye that he glimpsed the arrival of his father's *po* on the other side of the room. For what else could this bloody apparition be? This shadowy figure, with the blurred outline? It was too dark to tell if the *po* had the tiny mouth reputed of ghosts, but he caught a wisp of blood-soaked robes as the ghost floated across the room to his right, a jagged wound like a red flower on its pale skull. He had washed that wound only hours previously, scrubbing at the dried blood to drive away impurities. He knew the truth of what he was seeing now.

'Is it you, Honoured Father?' he asked, unsure of the appropriate greeting for a ghost.

'Who else would it be? Who else has been bludgeoned to death in his own house?'

It was him.

'Shouldn't you be on your way to the Pure Land by now?' Just as he would in life, Young Wu appealed to his father's vanity. Few souls were judged moral enough to go straight to the Pure Land. Only the most pious and exemplary escaped the arduous passage through the Ten Courts of Hell.

'I see the vultures are circling,' said his father's *po*, ignoring his question.

'The vultures?'

'All your uncles and aunts and their snot-nosed sons, hoping for a share of the loot.'

'I'm sure they're only expressing their sorrow,' he said, trying to placate the *po* before it escaped the house to run rampant through the village, causing who knew what kind of mayhem.

'And you, boy? How do you express your sorrow? How do you fulfil your filial duty? By bleating like a sheep over my corpse? By smoking up the house with Hell money? How is that going to help me down there in the underworld while my killer roams free?' His father's voice reverberated in his head, setting it to thumping again.

'I don't know, Honoured Father.'

'You don't know? You don't know? You are unfit to be called Wu!' the *po* thundered, surely loud enough to wake his mother. 'How could I be so unlucky to have this donkey for a son?'

'Please forgive this worthless son.' Young Wu fell to his knees, knocking his poor head on the ground, fixing his eyes to the floor.

'You must hunt down this girl, whose hands have bathed in my blood,' the *po* thundered.

'I will, Father.'

'You must bring her to justice.'

'I will, Father.'

'Until then, my *po* cannot rest in its grave. My *hun* will not lie docilely in its tablet, handing out boons to my snivelling descendants.'

'I will, Honoured Father. I swear I will avenge you.'

'And, boy…'

'Father?'

'Do not expect any favours from me!'

'I won't, Father. I will follow the Mo girl to the ends of the earth. I will kill her in the name of the Wu lineage. I will have your vengeance.'

His vow was met by silence. Only after the silence had extended for a thousand heartbeats did he dare to look up. The hall was empty. His father's *po* had gone, leaving behind nothing but the stench of death.

21

Kwangchow, China, 1856

They approached the city from the wide, wet plains of the south, traversing a patchwork of rice fields, creeks and islands. At first Little Cat had to rub her eyes, unsure if the vision was real, for the city spread out before her like a dream, far greater than anything she had imagined. North of the city reared a range of mountains, white clouds floating upon their shoulders, while the Pearl River wound to west and east in a mighty bow. Little Cat had never seen such a large expanse of water, as if all the rivers of China had joined together on their journey to the sea. Pagodas and temples jutted skywards, soaring above the roofs of the city, the whole encircled by a wall, taller than the banyan trees guarding Sandy Bottom Village.

They scrambled aboard a laden ferry to cross the river, dodging junks and sampans of every size and description: barges laden with tea and rice, long flat boats belching steam, sea-going junks embellished with dragons, the entire flotilla dwarfed by a war junk with wing-like sails and a hull huge as a gaping mouth. In places the watercraft were so tightly packed they made a city unto themselves with people clambering over boats to get from one place to the next. The whole business of the world appeared to be taking place upon this water-city: buying, selling, cooking, eating, washing, sleeping, fighting and other more private activities from the look of the brightly coloured boats bearing painted ladies with fingernails as long as chopsticks.

The city was so broad there were sixteen gates along the wall's circumference, so they were told. They entered through the Bamboo Gate in the south-west corner of the city. Here the great wall loomed over them, blocks of red stone forming its base, with grey bricks above. Elsewhere it was covered in a cloak of lush vegetation, and as they passed through they discovered that it was also many *chi* thick. The hordes of people were equally astounding, thronging the twisting alleys that wound between a maze of warehouses, shops and the walled gardens of the rich. In the face of these masses, she began to feel more like the tiniest minnow than a girl of eighteen summers. Of small importance in this river of humanity.

'Aiya! Watch where you're going.' She had been so busy looking around that she ran straight into Second Brother, slapping him in the middle of his shoulder blades with the *ta'am*. Stupidly, she had insisted on taking her turn carrying it, since she would have to acquire her own load soon. This meant that for the last two days, her neck and shoulders groaned in protest, every time she moved.

'You're the one who stopped in the middle of the road!'

She followed his gaze upwards to discover an enormous pagoda towering above them. She counted nine storeys. Once it might have been the pride of the city but now its brickwork was crumbling and saplings were sprouting from its walls. Yet her twin was staring at it open mouthed. Perhaps she wasn't the only one who was overwhelmed by the size of this city.

'Come on. We must hurry to find the agent and organise your passage before it is dark,' he said, all business once more.

'Don't walk so fast then or I'll lose you in the crowd.'

'Give me the *ta'am*, and hold onto my tunic if you're worried.'

'What makes you think I'm worried?'

They ventured deeper into the heart of the city, passing through narrow streets cluttered with a forest of banners outside shops selling anything Little Cat could imagine needing and many other items she could not. Hats and mats, bowls and brooms, clay puppets and herbal remedies, even a dentist stall where rows of human teeth hung like a curtain at the entrance. Amidst all this confusion of goods, hawkers wandered, spruiking their wares. She almost squealed as an old man burdened with a bamboo pole brushed against her, for the pole was loaded with a string of dead rats. She hoped he was advertising his services as a rat catcher, and not selling dinner. Two men beating a gong marched by carrying a flag with writing. When she asked Second Brother what it said, he replied, 'They are searching for a stolen child. A little girl.'

She clutched the hem of her brother's tunic. It would be so easy to lose yourself in this tumult.

They passed the entrance to a shop where a man sat on the ground outside with a heavy wooden board locked about his neck, so broad that he could not reach his head, nor see his feet. It also meant that he could neither eat nor drink so long as he was collared in this fashion.

'Chang Ho Lee. Stole two chickens from his neighbour. Twenty days in the *cangue*.' Second Brother read the sign that was pasted to the board.

'If they punish a petty thief in this manner, what will they do to... to someone like me?' She could hardly breathe the words.

'Best not to find out.'

After much searching, they found the shipping agent's place of business in the south-east section of the new city. It was situated in a tall, narrow building backing onto a canal. Several villagers were already waiting when they arrived, squatting in a line in the alley outside, surrounded by their worldly goods packed into identical bamboo baskets. Little Cat recognised some of the dialects being spoken but others were too different from her own to make much sense out of them. When it was finally their turn, a servant ushered them into a room on the ground floor where a robed and hatted man with a drooping moustache sat behind a scuffed desk, hundreds of scrolls filling the shelves that lined the walls.

Little Cat followed Second Brother's example as he bowed to the agent, who did not look up from his paperwork.

'What are your names?'

'We are the Mo brothers from Sandy Bottom Village, Wise Master.'

'Sandy Bottom... let me see... the Mo clan,' he said, consulting the paper before him, which was crammed with row after row of tiny writing.

'Passage for New Gold Mountain,' Second Brother added.

'I can see that... but your clan has guaranteed passage for only one Mo brother.'

Little Cat kept her head bowed and her lips closed as the agent peered up at them. She did not want him to inspect her too closely, for fear he found something awry. And her twin had told her to resist commenting on anything, for her new-found manly voice was not yet manly enough. Second Brother cleared his throat before providing the explanation they had rehearsed during the long hours of the journey.

'Our parents decided that two Mo brothers would be better than one. Our mother is a simple woman, Wise Master, and was concerned for my younger brother's safety. Our father decided to send me along as companion.'

'Then your father should have obtained a guarantee from your clan for you as well.'

'Our village elders will be happy to guarantee my passage. The Mo brothers are hard workers. You'll see, we will repay the cost of our passage in no time. And then there is your one-third share of the gold we find as well. We will make it worth your while.'

'That may be. But I have no record of it here.' He stabbed a long-nailed finger at his ledger. 'Do you have anything else of value to guarantee your passage? Gold? A land title? Perhaps a younger sister as a bond?'

'No.' Little Cat held her breath as the agent flicked a glance in her direction.

'Well then, your clan has not negotiated this with my broker. I can send only one Mo brother without further guarantee. I have already outlaid money for provisions,' he counted out his costs on his fingers as he spoke, 'equipment and passage. You will need money for the fees imposed by the government of New Gold Mountain. Who will repay me all that silver if you abscond?'

'I give you my word.'

'But I need the word of your clan. They will be responsible for your debt if you abscond... or die. Life is full of dangers.'

As Second Brother argued with the shipping agent, Little Cat grew sicker and sicker until she thought she might vomit all over the broker's rug. She would be left alone here in the sprawling city of Kwangchow while her twin boarded a ship for New Gold Mountain. She would be left to fend for herself on these noisy, crowded streets where beggars haunted the doorways like skeletons.

For she could not return home. Worse awaited her in Sandy Bottom Village.

Becoming tired of the discussion, the agent brushed them aside saying, 'One Mo brother will board a junk at dawn that will take him to Hong Kong. He will wait there in the barracoons until his ship for New Gold Mountain sails. The second Mo brother is not my concern.'

They followed the agent's servant through the Wing Hing Gate to the banks of the Pearl River where the low tide exposed the mud flats and beyond them the floating city of the boat dwellers.

'The master's junk will leave from the government wharf,' the man said, pointing a short distance upstream. 'For a few coins you can find a bed with the boat dwellers.' He pointed downstream towards the flotilla of sampans crawling with the grey-garbed boat dwellers wearing their strange bowl-shaped hats.

Once he had left, Second Brother did not give her a chance to speak. He turned in the direction the servant had indicated saying, 'Come, let's find where the junk will leave before we decide what to do.'

They picked their way along firm ground at the river's edge, avoiding the mud flats. This narrow strip of land between the city wall and the river was populated with houses, merchants' *hongs*, temples, even one of the barbarians' strange temples with the cross. Still bearing the *ta'am*, Little Cat struggled to keep up with her brother who strode along the narrow alleys as if chased by a demon. She trailed after him as he stalked towards a barren area between two rows of buildings, her eyes focused on the uneven ground that was scattered with large vessels of unbaked pottery, so that she did not at first notice what lay ahead. When she finally lifted her eyes to take in her surroundings, she was met with a sight far worse than any nightmare.

The first thing she saw was a cage made of bamboo poles, taller than a man and wider at the bottom than the top, where a man's head protruded. It appeared that his head bore the entire weight of his body, his feet dangling through the bottom of the cage. Two wooden crosses, fixed at an angle, stood nearby, blood staining the rough timbers and fraying ropes that had tied down prisoners. She knew without being told what these crosses were for. *Lingchi.* The death of a thousand cuts. Reserved for the execution of the worst criminals, the traitors and long-haired rebels who offended the Emperor, the unfilial killers who murdered their parents and employers. The Emperor and his magistrates had been on a rampage lately, reputedly executing all the men of one village for siding with the long-haired Taiping rebels.

Closing her eyes, she tried to force down the rising panic that threatened to overwhelm her. But rather than calming her, in her blindness, she tripped over an unexpected rock, falling to her knees so that the baskets tipped sideways, spilling their precious supplies. She was fumbling around on the ground, trying to collect them when her hand found something curved and smooth.

She realised then that it wasn't a rock that had tripped her up. It was the shallow bowl of a human skull.

'Now look what you've done!' Second Brother fumed, returning to her side to set the baskets to rights, his eyes fixed on her alone. 'There's no money to replace these if they're lost.'

Could he not see what was before them? Could he not see the pile of human heads dumped in a pen by the wall?

'Why don't you carry them then? Since they are your supplies and it is your passage!' She spat out the words that had been on her tongue since the conversation with the agent. 'In fact, why don't you leave me now, since you will be off in the morning anyway? I will manage.'

'Is that what you think?' He sat back on his heels, tea, rice and salted duck forgotten as he stared at her. 'That I would leave you here alone?'

'What else should I think? There is only one passage and two of us.'

Shaking his head, he took the baskets and carrying pole from her hands and shouldered them himself. She could not decipher the expression on his face. His lips were clamped tight, turned down at the corners, and his eyes looked lost. Was he angry with her or with the agent? Was he afraid for her or for himself? He closed his eyes for a moment, drawing a deep breath, before opening them to a view of something far away. He looked beyond this field of death to something only he could see. And then she knew that what she was seeing on his face was resignation. Resignation tinged with fear.

'You are shooting arrows from the mouth if you cannot see what is before you. And I don't mean these unlucky fellows.' He pointed to the pile of gruesome heads.

He was right. Of course he would not leave her alone in the city with the Wu clan hunting her. Of course he would not leave her to risk this execution ground. He was her twin. He was her big brother. He would send her as far away as possible to a land where she would at least have a chance of survival.

'I had a dream too, Lin Fa.'

She could not remember the last time he had called her by her given name. She was always Little Cat, Mui Mui, Trouble.

'It's not too late. You could return home. You could ask the Mo elders to back you. There will be other ships.' She spoke these words to encourage him, but she also spoke to allay her guilt.

'But they have already backed me. If I ask twice they will know you have taken my place.'

'They will know anyway, Goh Go.' It wouldn't take them long to figure out that she had gone with her twin. Where else would she go? She was a young woman alone. She was a fugitive. Her only other option would be to sell herself, and she had already killed a man to avoid that fate. Her one hope now was to lose herself in this river of humanity and trust that her ship sailed soon.

He considered her words, nodding agreement. 'Then I will return to Sandy Bottom, for our father will need me. Elder Brother will need me. The clan will not back me twice. Not with the Wus pressuring them. And if the Wus take back our land, Ba will need my help to survive.'

Little Cat looked down at the bloodstained ground. She could not meet his eyes but she heard the uneasiness in his voice. It lingered in the spaces between words and caught on the thoughts left unsaid.

'There is chaos coming, Mui Mui. The Long-hairs and their Heavenly Kingdom are here to stay. So are the foreign barbarians. The Emperor taxes us to starvation to keep them out, and the foreigners will stop at nothing to grab more. I see nothing but chaos and famine ahead.'

Despite closed eyes she saw again the ragged beggars squatting in the street, the shreds of skin like banners waving from wooden crosses.

'We have been lucky so far, lucky to have the silkworms, but if the Wus take half our land, our family will need me even more.'

As they would need Little Cat to find her luck on New Gold Mountain. She must do everything in her power to repay the debt to the agent and send money home to her family. She could not regret killing Big Wu because she had done it in self-defence. If she hadn't fought back, he would have taken more than her honour. He would have stolen her belief in her own strength. But in saving herself, she had injured her family. She had threatened their futures. Because of her actions, the situation had now gone beyond helping Elder Brother to earn a bride gift. If she were captured or killed, or failed in her quest, her parents and her brothers would pay dearly.

They would lose the last of their land and be driven into servitude. The weight of this debt rested heavier on her shoulders than any two baskets ever could.

She was still kneeling in the dirt at her brother's feet. From now on she must learn to be a man in more than her borrowed clothes, a man like her twin, who was strong and brave. A man who had sacrificed his dreams for others. For her.

'You can count on me, Goh Go,' she said, touching her forehead to the bloodstained earth.

22

They had been on the water since dawn, he and the old man. Ostensibly, the old man accompanied him as servant, but mostly Young Wu worked the pole while the old man proffered advice on how to do it better. Apparently, in his youth the gatekeeper had owned the swiftest raft on the river; his strength and speed with a pole was the talk of three villages. His skill with the worms was also legendary. As was his capacity for holding his liquor. Plus he was known as a man to avoid in a fight. Only bad luck and old age had brought him to the Wu residence where Big Wu, in his benevolence, had employed him as gatekeeper. If nothing else, the boat trip reminded Young Wu why he always avoided being caught alone with the old man. He could talk your ears off with his stories.

'It's quicker to follow the river, Wise Master,' the old man advised, as Young Wu turned the raft into one of the many creeks that threaded the region.

Young Wu knew the Mo twins better than anyone. Ah Yong would keep to the backwaters, even if it took a little longer to reach his destination. He would do everything in his power not to be found, especially if Little Cat were aboard his raft.

'The Mo boy will not keep to the river. We might catch him up.'

'Wah! You will not catch him up. That boy is bigger, stronger and faster than you.' It did not occur to the old man that he cast slurs upon his new master. He merely spoke the truth.

'Then we might find proof that Little Cat is with him. We don't know this for sure yet.'

The old man fixed him with one eye saying, 'We know this, Wise Master. Where else would the girl go?'

Yet even with the weight of the Wu clan and his father's *po* urging him to vengeance, he hesitated. He had his father's word that Little Cat had killed him. But what if he had dreamed the encounter with his father's ghost? He had been so tired after his long walk and the events that followed. What if his uncertainties had manifested in a dream? What if his awe of his father had permeated even his sleep… Little Cat might even now be in danger. And no one was doing a thing to rescue her. This is what he told himself as he stubbornly poled the raft along the silt-bottomed creeks and canals that Ah Yong would have taken en route to market, and from there to the great city of Kwangchow.

*

Who would have thought that old squinty eye had such a sharp gaze? But perhaps that's what came from having eyes pointing in different directions; they covered twice as much ground. In any case, one minute Young Wu was cursing the raft, the creek and anyone who had ever built a boat, for his aching arms and back, and the next the old man was shouting and waving them towards the bank. They had left the canal and entered a broad expanse of shallow river where the banks sloped gently down to the water. The old man was pointing to a spot beneath a grove of trees where a raft had been hauled up above the watermark and partially concealed beneath some bushes.

'Aiya! Do you not see it?' he shouted. 'I'd know that raft anywhere. The Mos never could build a boat.'

Young Wu eased the raft towards the bank, holding it steady while the old man clambered to solid ground, then he followed after him.

'It looks like any other raft to me.'

'See the way the bamboo is lashed together,' said the old man, shaking his head so that the wattles of his neck wobbled. 'What kind of excuse for a knot is that?'

Young Wu studied the ground near the raft, noticing the muddle of footprints in the wet earth. They were fresh. Not more than a day old.

'It is possible this is the Mo boat,' he said.

'It is certain that this is the Mo boat,' said the old man, who had never demonstrated this level of obstinacy when Big Wu was alive.

'He would not dare,' reminded his father's voice, 'for I was always right.'

Although it was early winter, the sun beat down upon Young Wu's bare chest and arms where he had removed his tunic to better pole the raft. He was strong, with the lean hard muscles of a youth who liked to run and jump and spar. Yet Ah Yong was taller, broader and stronger. Braver, if history was anything to go by. If he were taking his sister to safety, he would do everything in his power to protect her.

Young Wu brushed an arm across his forehead, wiping away sweat. He had left his mother and uncles to carry out the necessary rituals to lay his father to rest while he set out upon this journey to find his father's killer. He wore the white clothes of mourning, yet he did not feel sad. He felt burdened. Hounded. As if the weight of his clan's future had been foisted upon him. Secretly, he did not know whether he was man enough to carry it.

And then there was Little Cat.

He stood at the water's edge and tried not to listen to his father's voice. 'Only the most unfilial of sons would not avenge his father's death. Only the most cowardly.' And that was when he saw it, a scrap of red cloth lying discarded beneath the trees. Just like the length of red silk that had fastened Little Cat's pigtail on the morning when he had led her to his father.

'They must have taken to the road, Wise Master,' said the old man, perhaps afraid that he had gone too far.

'Then I suppose we had best follow them.'

If the city was nothing new to Young Wu, he expected the gatekeeper to be awestruck, at least for a short while. But the old man confounded him by confronting the imposing walls and soaring pagodas with a nonchalant, 'I see the foreigners' *hongs* have burnt down again.' They had reached the outskirts of the city and from where they stood on the opposite bank, had an excellent view of the riverside land the Emperor had allocated the white ghosts. It had been destroyed by fire for the third time a year earlier and the foreigners were temporarily encamped elsewhere.

Apparently the old man had been a great traveller in his day too.

The city lived up to its reputation, however, over the next two days as Young Wu and his doughty servant scoured the streets, searching for the Mos' shipping agent. It seemed that the whole world did business in these narrow alleys – acrobats rolling barrels on their feet, barbers shaving customers' heads, bears dancing for the amusement of passers-by, men carrying lending libraries in boxes upon their shoulders. Anything and everything could be found on the streets of Kwangchow. Except for the one agent who had arranged Ah Yong's passage.

'If you don't mind me saying, Wise Master…' the old man began.

'But I do mind.'

'We should have put the squeeze on Old Mo when

we had the chance.' He mimed a throat-squeezing action with his crooked elbow. 'He would have crowed like a cock and saved us this trouble.'

The Mo clan elder had denied knowing which agent had arranged Ah Yong's passage, saying a broker had organised all. And the broker was not due back in Sandy Bottom Village until the following month.

'Old Mo is eighty if he's a day. He could have died.'

The old man shrugged. 'I'm just saying.'

'Here it is,' said Young Wu as they arrived at the door of yet another agent's place of business. As with the others, a line of villagers squatted in the alley outside, waiting their turn. It seemed as if half the population of Kwangtung was sailing to New Gold Mountain. But Young Wu did not wait. A Wu did not wait. The gatekeeper slipped a few coins to the agent's servant and they were ushered inside.

'Name and village.'

A well-fed fellow of his father's age sat with a ledger open before him, a reminder of that morning's breakfast clinging to his long drooping moustaches. He did not look up. As with his previous enquiries, Young Wu took a peremptory rather than obsequious tone in order to establish his credentials.

'Are you the agent for the Mo lineage of Sandy Bottom Village?' he asked, with a perfunctory nod in lieu of a bow.

The agent looked up, taking in Young Wu's tattered mourning garb and unkempt hair, which gave away little of his status. He had neither washed nor shaved since his father's death, it being obligatory during these first days of mourning. As a first-grade mourner, he would theoretically mourn for three years. Although, in practice, one year plus a day either side added up to three.

'Don't tell me we have another Mo looking for passage.' The agent put down his writing brush with an exasperated sigh. 'I told the last fellow and his brother that I could not sponsor them both without further guarantee from the Mo lineage.'

The agent continued with his catalogue of complaints, whining about who would pay whom and who would renege on whom while Young Wu stood before him in shock. So, they had finally found him, the agent they had hunted for two days. Young Wu felt his shoulders sag, but whether in relief or dismay, he couldn't be sure.

'I have cash,' he pronounced, interrupting the flow of complaints. 'I do not need guarantees. I do need to know which ship they are bound for so that I can join my cousins on their journey to New Gold Mountain.'

The agent consulted his ledger. 'I have Mo listed for passage on the *Phaeton*. It's due to sail any day now. But only one of the Mo brothers is sailing. They could not offer any guarantee for the other.'

It took a moment for the man's words to penetrate. Two pieces of information to process. Brothers? But of course, a woman could not travel to New Gold Mountain. Little Cat could not venture across the southern seas… not unless she disguised herself as a man. He imagined her tall, lithe frame clothed in the blue tunic and trousers of the working man. Apart from her hair, she would not look out of place. Not with her long stride and no-nonsense attitude. She would pass for a young man, barely growing into his height. And then there was the second piece of information he gleaned from the agent's words. Only one Mo brother was travelling. Did this mean that Ah Yong would leave Little Cat behind? Or would he sacrifice his place for his fugitive sister's escape? There was no doubt in his mind which choice his friend would make.

'Do you wish to arrange passage?' The agent was growing impatient. Time was money.

'How many *taels* of silver for passage to New Gold Mountain on the *Phaeton*?' he asked, rolling the strange sounding word on his tongue.

'Passage for two, Wise Master,' said the old man, tugging at his tunic. 'Your venerable mother would curse me to the end of my days if I let you go alone.'

Young Wu turned his head briefly to consider the gatekeeper, who beseeched him with one eye while the other roved the room. He had no intention of actually sailing to New Gold Mountain. He would capture Little Cat long before her ship departed. Still, anything could happen between now and then. The gatekeeper was old. He might be more burden than help. He would certainly prove annoying. Then again… he could do with someone to watch his back, even a toothless old tiger like the gatekeeper.

'Passage for two,' he nodded.

'Well then, two silver *taels* for each of you. But you will need to purchase supplies and pay licence fees once you arrive. And I cannot guarantee passage on the *Phaeton*. By the time you arrive in Hong Kong, that ship may have already sailed.'

23

Hong Kong, 1856

She woke, scratching, to the usual stink of hundreds of bodies crowded into a dark vermin-infested shed. Many of the occupants were still sleeping so she hurried to the latrine before they awoke, squatting over the pit with her tunic pulled low to hide her secret. Sometimes she had to hold on long after she was squirming in discomfort, to get a little privacy. Once, she could wait no longer and risked a trip to the latrine in full view of three others, standing with her hips thrust forward, tunic draping her thighs, and aiming outwards, hoping she would not spray her trousers too badly. The situation could only worsen on the journey to New Gold Mountain so she had better get used to it.

She had been here on the island of Hong Kong five days now, waiting for her ship to sail, holed up in barracks provided by the shipping agents. The little food she was given would be tossed to the pigs back home. Meanwhile, the waiting men were encouraged to while away the days gambling and smoking opium, sinking deeper and deeper into debt. She had barely seen anything outside the barracks, except for that first day when the junk sailed into a peaceful green harbour, the barbarians' strange buildings skirting the water's edge and climbing the slopes of the peak that watched over the town. In Kwangchow she had seen only a few of the tall, pale-skinned barbarians with their hairy faces and big noses. Here they were everywhere. Even the women, with their outlandish robes that wrapped the upper body like a parcel, yet belled out around their legs like a Manchu tent. She suspected they must wear baskets beneath their gowns. Either that or they had very fat legs.

There was barely enough room to spread out her sleeping mat and each time she left her possessions unguarded to visit the latrine she would return terrified that something would be stolen. She wished Goh Go was here. She wished she had someone guarding her back. But she was alone. She had left her brother back at the government wharf when she clambered aboard the junk for the journey down the Pearl River. He had not waved in farewell. He had merely stood silently, following her with his eyes, his figure growing smaller and smaller as the junk drew away, until he dwindled to a speck and disappeared. What if she never saw him again?

By the time she returned to her mat, the barracks was stirring. She sensed a new excitement amongst some of her fellow residents. The question was, which ship was ready to sail? Some of the men had been waiting for weeks while their intended vessels were repaired and provisioned in readiness for the sailing season to New Gold Mountain.

'What is happening?' she asked Big Nose, the tall, gangling youth from Kwangchow who slept on the mat beside her.

'The *Phaeton* sails on the next tide. The emigration officer has issued his certificate. We must pack our belongings and be ready to leave at the sound of the gong.'

They trotted in single file along the road the outside barbarians had named after their queen, balancing their *ta'am* upon their shoulders. The foreign buildings squatted like huge stone blocks along the waterfront. Altogether Little Cat estimated that the line of men would total half the male population of her village. How would they manage, crammed below decks for the long journey to New Gold Mountain? And how would she manage to keep her secret? She had trained her voice to a new manly register during the days since they left Sandy Bottom Village. She modelled her new swagger upon Young Wu, her hips thrust forward, legs slightly apart, arms akimbo. Except since she was carrying more than half her body weight balanced precariously in two baskets, her swagger was more akin to a lurch.

The *Phaeton* sat at anchor half a *li* from shore, where they were ferried by the boat dwellers, who plied the harbour as they did in Kwangchow. As they paddled closer to the ship, she realised how large it was compared to the junk that had brought her down the Pearl River. Three masts rose like tree trunks from the deck, festooned with so many ropes that she could not begin to fathom what they might be for. The deck was long and low to the water so that she imagined the ship skipping across the waves, or being swamped by them.

She clambered up the rope ladder behind Big Nose, then waited as her baskets and pole were hauled up after her. Standing in his shadow as they waited for the rest of the company to board, she stared out at the town, encircled by sea and mountains, knowing that this might be her last sight of the Middle Flowery Land. Soon they would be herded below deck where they would live in semi-darkness for the next two or three moons, before arriving on the shores of an unknown land far to the south. This thought threatened to bring tears to her eyes but she squeezed the lids tight and fought them back. She could not afford to draw attention to herself. She needed to blend in, to become just another boy in blue trousers bound for New Gold Mountain.

She was startled out of her reverie by Big Nose saying, 'You don't have to stick with me. I know no one likes me.'

It was the first time since she said goodbye to Second Brother at the government wharf that anyone had made a personal remark to her. Most of her fellow emigrants travelled with friends or family from their villages. Most of them had trekked from the rice-growing districts of See Yap where they spoke a different dialect. Even those from the silk districts of Sam Yap, like Little Cat, embarked on the long journey in groups. Few travelled alone. And both the See Yap and Sam Yap groups had elected their own leaders to smooth their passage upon the long and difficult journey to the goldfields, while the shipping agent appointed a headman to negotiate with the foreigners.

'What do you mean?' she asked Big Nose. She had not spared a thought for her mat neighbour, who she knew hailed from Kwangchow. She had been too busy staying alive to wonder why he kept to himself.

'Isn't it plain as the nose on my face?' he asked, tapping a finger to the side of his nose.

She studied his face, noting for the first time the sharp bone structure and the long, crooked bridge of his nose. In the dim shadows of the barracks his queue had seemed like any other, but this morning, she saw that his hair glinted red in the sun and his eyes were a light elm brown.

He nodded at her realisation. 'I am mixed breed. My mother was a boat woman. My father was… who knows,' he shrugged, 'and now she is dead and I'm alone. There is nothing left for me in the city.'

So… he was an outcast thrice over. Once because all land dwellers looked down upon the boat people. Twice because his mother had probably been a saltwater girl, going with the foreigners for money. And thrice because his father was a foreigner, a ghost man. Now his mother was dead and he was left alone in the great city. It seemed that Little Cat wasn't the only person aboard ship who was fleeing. She wasn't the only one who was different; the only one who travelled alone. Although she was probably the only one who had done murder.

'There is nothing left in my village for me either,' she said, with the briefest hint of a smile, allowing the smallest chink in her armour to show.

'Then perhaps we can be alone together. I am named Su Ching Yih. But everyone calls me Big Nose.'

'And I am named Mo Wing Yong. But everyone calls me...' What would everyone call her now? Now that she had thrown off the mantle of Little Cat to become... 'Strong Arm,' she announced with a bow.

'Strong Arm, eh?' he said, looking dubiously at thin wrists poking out from the sleeves of her tunic. 'We will see about that.'

So... she would be called Strong Arm. And somehow or other she would find the strength to match her new name. For only strength would keep fear and regret at bay. Only strength would redeem her family's future.

Young Wu had been cursing the wind for two days. It teased them mercilessly, bowing out the sails then flattening the battens into an open fan. For a while it seemed they would be trapped on the Pearl River in this creaking old junk forever, never to reach Hong Kong. The vessel thronged with landless farmers and unemployed city dwellers, all looking to make their fortunes on New Gold Mountain. Or at least redeem their debts and rescue their families from servitude. The old gatekeeper had made plenty of friends, sipping tea, smoking his pipe and playing at dominoes with this motley group of emigrants. Apparently, another of the skills gained on his travels was a familiarity with many dialects. Gatekeeper Wu was glad of a new audience to regale with his stories, leaving Young Wu largely alone to stew over his situation.

He had left off mourning garb once they departed Kwangchow, mindful of not drawing attention to himself. Little Cat would be alert to pursuit and he did not want to make her job easier by standing out in his dirty, ragged white garments. His father would surely forgive him this breach of etiquette, given the importance of his mission. At least, that was what he told himself. The truth was, the mourning clothes were a constant reminder of his father's demand for vengeance, a reminder he could do without. Already, he was haunted day and night by the image of his father lying in a pool of his own blood, and a vision of his friend's twin standing over him, a bloodstained stone seal in her hand. A girl he had once dreamed...

'Master!' called the old man. 'Look!'

He roused from his regrets to see the old man pointing eastwards. That morning the junk had finally sailed out of the Pearl River Estuary and into the South China Sea before entering a passage between what looked like two islands rising steeply from the sea. Now he saw that they were sailing through another passage where ships and boats were dotted upon the waters of a wide harbour. To one side of the harbour, foreign-looking buildings populated the shoreline. They also climbed the slopes of a mountain peak that loomed over this island that the Emperor had ceded to the barbarians to placate them. It appeared they had arrived in Hong Kong.

The junk docked next to a row of white stone buildings and a gangplank was lowered to the wharf. The shipping agent's representative soon appeared to herd the new arrivals, with their baskets and poles, to a barracks where they would await the ship that would take them across the southern seas. But Young Wu wasn't prepared to wait without question while his quarry escaped. He didn't plan to sit on this forsaken island any longer than he had to. He certainly didn't plan to travel to New Gold Mountain. He would find the girl, avenge his father and then he would go home. He would be a boy no longer. He would do his duty. He would be a man. He would become his father's son. Why then did he feel this hollow ache in his stomach? As if part of him was missing.

It wasn't difficult to grease the palm of the agent's representative to find out where the *Phaeton* lay at anchor. Information had its price, like everything else.

'*Phaeton*, you say?' the man answered, putting his hand to his forehead to shade it from the noonday sun and staring out to the harbour. 'There.' He pointed.

Young Wu followed the line of the pointing arm out across the water, where a three-masted ship headed for the harbour entrance, sails billowing. Even from here he could see the specks of blue scattered about its decks.

'Too late to catch it now,' said the man, with a grin.

Young Wu's shoulders sagged beneath the weight of his *ta'am*. He felt bereft, as if his past and his future sailed with it. Who was he if his mission remained unaccomplished?

'Was there something you needed aboard?' asked the agent's representative, noticing his despair.

Something he needed? Only his life. His future. Now there was only one way to reclaim it. He must join this horde of emigrants from the Middle Flowery Kingdom and seek his quarry and his fate across the southern seas.

24

Robetown, South Australia, 1857

'Do you think Mama might enjoy a walk upon the beach this morning, Miss Hartley?' Alice asked, looking up from her schoolbooks with a hopeful expression. The two had retreated to the schoolroom to take refuge from her mother's grief in French grammar.

'Why don't you ask her?'

Violet suspected that Alice's mama had determined never to enjoy anything again, but she did not voice this thought to her pupil. The child shouldered enough sadness already.

'It's such a glorious day that a walk must cheer her, mustn't it?' said Alice. She glanced towards the window where the morning sun poked its nose between the curtains. No thanks to the lady of the house, who had ordered all the windows and curtains closed.

'If your mama feels unable, *we* may still take a walk along the beach,' Violet said and was rewarded with a smile. 'We shall look for crabs,' she added, wondering how long it would take Mama to crush the poor girl's spirit.

James had been gone almost three months now but the mirrors were still draped in black. Most days, Mrs Wallace emerged from her room only to issue instructions, or sit sobbing alongside her daughter, ensuring that Alice remained as mournful as she. After the funeral, Mr Wallace had returned to Craigie to see to his cows and sheep. Violet wished that she could escape so easily, but currently she had nowhere else to go and besides, she was loath to leave Alice alone in her grieving mother's care. The poor child went about with the look of a trapped rabbit. And in the face of her mother's grief, even a hint of laughter was quickly schooled into submission.

For two weeks, Violet and Mrs Wallace had sat by James's bedside, wrestling with his illness, as he laboured more valiantly than a dying coal miner to catch his breath. The doctor had come and gone several times and still the boy did not rally. And when he finally appeared to be on the mend – his fever abated, his cough eased – he suddenly took a turn for the worse, his heart racing faster than one of his father's thoroughbreds. James died in his mother's arms at five o'clock of the morning, just as the sun was rising beyond the lake.

Throughout his illness, Violet had done her best to comfort his stricken father, serving him cup after cup of Darjeeling and reading aloud from Mr Dickens' *Hard Times*. But there was little she could do to aid the distraught mother who remained inconsolable. And now

Violet and Alice were trapped with her in this house of death and she could see no hope of immediate escape.

'Miss Hartley, may I speak with you in the drawing room?' said Mrs Wallace, materialising at the door to the schoolroom the following morning, with her daughter disappearing into the woodwork behind her. 'You may wait in your room,' she added, with a stern glance for Alice, who had a haunted look.

This did not bode well.

Violet followed her employer downstairs to the drawing room, arranging herself in a ladder-backed chair facing away from the disquieting new family portrait Mrs Wallace had recently commissioned. The daguerreotype took pride of place on the mantel, housed in a tooled leather case, lined with red velvet and sealed behind brass-mounted glass. Upon entering the drawing room, a guest was obliged to stop and admire it, for it would not be ignored.

Mrs Wallace had called in the artist, who arrived with all haste on the first steamer from Adelaide. Violet had watched him pose the family for the portrait. Mama and Papa sitting on a pair of dining chairs, with Alice and James seated between them. At first glance, the portrait brought a smile to the viewer's face, to see the father with his arm about his beloved daughter's waist, and the dear boy with his head resting gently upon his mother's shoulder. But upon closer inspection, the viewer noticed that there was something not quite *comme-il-faut* about the little family. Something about the boy's eyes was... disconcerting. Unearthly almost. Like the eyes of one of Monsieur Boucher's delightful painted cherubs.

For indeed, the boy's eyes had been added after the event. Ensconced in his studio, bent over his workbench, the artist had taken a fine sable brush and painted them in. Since they would not open of themselves. Since the happy family was an illusion. Not because the family was unhappy (although that was arguable), but because one of its members was in fact... a corpse. Several times a day Violet was confronted by the unhappy portrait and reminded of this truth. Each time she entered the drawing room she experienced an overwhelming desire to pick up the tooled leather case, dash it to the floor and watch as the fragile silver image tarnished in the hostile air.

To the boy's mother the portrait was a way to keep her dead son alive. To Violet, the memento mori spoke only of death and sadness. And Violet had no truck with sadness. Like any illness, sadness was to be wrestled with as valiantly as a malignant throat. So although she sat facing away from the portrait, this did not prevent the uncomfortable feeling that she was being observed from beyond the grave. She could not rid herself of the sensation that those painted eyes watched and judged. Nor could she avoid noticing the scrap of hair pinned to her employer's gaunt chest inside a gold-rimmed brooch. A brown curl sealed behind glass forever.

'Alice and I have been having a chat,' Mrs Wallace

began, her hand straying to the brooch. 'I have decided to send her home to England to complete her education. So your services at Noorla will no longer be required,' she announced abruptly, clutching at the brooch. Violet could see the bones bouncing about beneath the skin like piano keys.

'I wonder if Alice may feel lost so far from home? Particularly given... recent events,' she suggested.

'Given recent events? You mean, the death of my beloved son...'

'Yes. James's sad passing...'

'... given that your neglect killed my son. That and your meddling with the Chinamen.'

For a moment, Violet was dumbstruck. But she had been accused of worse in her time and had faced it down. 'I don't know what you mean,' she protested. 'I nursed poor James far into the night. I... I cooled his fever. I changed the dressing at his throat. I... I did everything I could. And Mr Wallace asked me to nurse the Chinamen.'

'Oh, yes, once the damage was done you became most solicitous, particularly over my husband. And I'm sure Mr Wallace was appreciative of your attentions. As others have been in the past... no doubt,' she said with a smile that exposed her cheeks, sunken with grief.

Violet knew what that smile implied. She had seen it before. Right before the serpent struck.

'But who or what caused the damage? That is the question,' Mrs Wallace continued, uninterested in any response on Violet's part.

'A miasma in the air, a pollution in the water? Who can say?' Violet scrabbled for reasons. 'And then we were caught in the rain while playing at quoits.' Did the woman think to blame her for an act of God? She may have been slightly remiss in not putting James to bed sooner, but she had not struck him down with the illness.

'Quoits? Ah yes, Alice has told me of your excursion. She has told me how my son complained of a sore throat and yet you *insisted* on chasing after that Thomas fellow, that dirty, rough bullocky. You placed your appetites above the welfare of my son.'

'No... Alice is mistaken. The children desired to play with Mr Thomas's dog. And it was only after we arrived that James—'

'Spare me your excuses, Miss Hartley. My daughter was not mistaken and she does not lie. Do not think I haven't heard about your previous... adventures. But I won't sully my son's memory by naming them. Tales of your exploits have reached even here. We're not so much a backwater as you think, and I am not the uncultured colonial you counted upon. I have a wide acquaintance. Even in London.'

'I did not think that at all.'

'If I had known what kind of woman you were earlier, I would never have engaged you. How a woman of your lax morality has the audacity to teach children is beyond me.'

Throughout this speech, Violet watched as a drop of spittle clinging to the corner of her employer's mouth poised to dribble down her chin, while the bony hand flexed rhythmically about the brooch. As if the woman desired to strike her.

'I'm sorry you feel that way,' she said, leaning forward to hold the other woman's gaze. 'I have only ever exercised the utmost care for the children, and respect for you and Mr Wallace.'

'Of course, you would say that. But I am not so easily fooled.'

'And if you are referring to my previous employer, the earl's daughter, she was quite unhinged by her husband's philandering ways. It was my misfortune to find myself under her roof.' Seduced by that husband's smile and his promises. A house of her own. A gig to drive about the town. Yet he hadn't a shilling to his name, she was to discover when it was too late.

It all belonged to the earl.

Mrs Wallace's face remained closed to Violet's explanation. 'Unhinged by the treachery of a woman she had taken into her home and treated with naught but kindness, you mean.'

'I didn't think you the kind of woman who listens to malicious gossip. The kind from which an unmarried woman, such as I, cannot protect herself.'

'Protect herself! It is your employer and her children who need protecting. I will not have you near my daughter any longer! And I certainly will not have you near my husband!' Mrs Wallace was screeching now, the spittle spraying forth from her mouth. Violet knew that she would not listen to reason, would not be dissuaded. Grief had stolen her reason and someone must be made to pay.

She gathered her dignity, saying, 'Then I shall be gone within the week. And I would expect to receive a month's wages in lieu of notice.'

'You shall receive *nothing* from me. Since you have taken everything. And you will be gone by tomorrow or I shall have you thrown onto the street. But you would know all about that, wouldn't you?' She sprang from her chair as if she could not bear to be in Violet's presence a moment longer, then swept from the room dragging her skirts behind her like a thunderous cloud.

Violet was staring into the empty depths of her coin purse when Alice sidled into her room, looking furtively about and twisting her hands in the folds of her black skirt. Her hair had escaped from its plaits and Violet saw that she had been crying.

'You had better not speak with me or your mother will toss me from the house without my valise,' she said, not unkindly, despite the fact that Alice had landed her in this quandary. The poor girl was no match for her mother.

'I didn't mean to get you into trouble. When I asked Mama if she wouldn't like a little walk upon the beach, she began questioning me about where else we had been on our excursions. And then she asked me about that day... the day James became ill.'

'I thought we had agreed on quoits,' said Violet, with a sigh.

'I could not lie to Mama. Not when she has lost so much.'

'I know.'

She still had a daughter though. And Alice still had a mother and a father. That was something to be going on with. Something Mrs Wallace might want to remember before she sent that daughter to the other side of the world where anything might happen to her.

'The truth is dangerous, Alice. I told you this once before. Now it has got you sent away, and me destitute without a roof over my head.'

'I'm sorry.'

'I know you are, *chérie*. But it cannot be helped now. We must both make the best of things.'

Violet had been destitute before. She had been without a roof over her head before. She still had her wits. And her beauty... while it lasted. She would make the best of her situation, for what else could she do? Something would come along. But Alice was of such tender years and little experience. She was to be sent ten thousand miles alone to the other side of the world, poor child, far less prepared for misery and solitude than her governess. Perhaps Violet was the luckier of the two after all.

'I don't want to go to England. I want to stay here with you.' Alice's eyes pleaded with her for comfort and Violet was tempted to gather the child into her arms. But what would be the point? She needed to stand strong in the face of misfortune. She must learn to stand on her own two feet now that she was being sent away. Violet knew the folly of false comfort.

'Your mama has decreed otherwise, Alice. But I shall discover where you are sent and I will write. And in the meantime, I have a gift for you.'

She rummaged in the top drawer of the dresser, retrieving a hefty volume bound in salt-stained green cloth. It had been the last gift from her father. Placing the book in Alice's hands she said, 'Here is my favourite book. It has helped me through many a difficult situation. I want you to have it.'

'*Vanity Fair.*' Alice read the title aloud.

'I'm sorry I cannot stay with you, Alice, but Mr Thackeray's words will have to serve instead. Whenever you are feeling sad or unsure, ask yourself, "What would Becky do?" and she will guide you.'

Clutching the book in one hand, Alice threw herself at Violet, resting her head upon her shoulder. Despite her misgivings, Violet could not help but wrap her arms about the child's waist, stroking her back like the babe in arms that she was.

'There, there... don't cry. You will ruin my gown with your tears.'

25

Guichen Bay, South Australia, 1857

That night it was Strong Arm's turn to sleep on deck. Most of the men from Hong Kong were squeezed head-to-toe between decks, lying upon narrow wooden shelves, arranged one atop another. But the three iron-barred hatches offered little ventilation in the crowded space between decks, so the men were allotted turns sleeping in the open air. At the outset of the voyage, the headman appointed by the company that chartered the ship had organised the two hundred and sixty men into groups. Each had its designated cook and barber, and each group took turns sleeping above deck. Eating and sleeping dictated life on board. Twice a day a drum sounded, and the cooks carried platters of food from the galley down through the hatches to the between decks, struggling to fill the men's stomachs with an unchanging diet of rice, increasingly putrid salt fish and a miserable allowance of pickled cabbage. They counted themselves lucky when the ship called into port and a few mouthfuls of fresh vegetables or pork were added to their rations.

During the day, they were allowed on deck in groups to wash in salt water or take a little exercise, but at night they were locked below decks. For two months, Strong Arm had endured the belching, farting, snoring and groaning of two hundred and sixty men living in close quarters. She had listened to the desperate moans of the opium addicts and tried to ignore the stench of seasickness that had come to permeate the ship's timbers. It was a far cry from the half-hearted bickering of the girls' house in Sandy Bottom Village. But she tried not to think about the village, for she could not afford tears in front of these men. Not if she wished to keep her secret. Already the other men laughed at her self-ascribed nickname.

Aboard ship, the only amusements were endless games of dominoes and cards, interminable bouts of gambling and the fun that could be had from laughing at one another, so she did not blame them for their teasing. In between bouts of seasickness, Big Nose had passed his time trying to teach her the foreigners' language, which he had learned running errands as a boy in Kwangchow, while she had attempted to teach him the basics of kung fu. But the strange words came lumpish and clumsy to her tongue, and Big Nose tangled his limbs into knots.

They had all been whittled away by the voyage. The bones of Big Nose's face had grown so prominent that his nose now protruded like the beak of a goose, and Strong Arm's limbs were so thin they made a lie of her nickname. Beneath the sleeves of her tunic she had lost her muscles and gained the dainty arms of an inside girl, despite her attempts to practise kung fu whenever she was allowed on deck. So as time passed she had to be even more careful to keep her body covered, making her smellier than most since she could not strip off her tunic to douse her body with buckets of cold seawater. She had to train her mind to think like a man, a youth, so that she would not let her secret slip, not even to Big Nose.

Sometimes she thought her journey would go on forever. That she would never reach the promised bounty of New Gold Mountain, nor return to the lush green groves of her home. Her sleep was tormented by images of Big Wu with his bamboo claw, sawing, chopping and stabbing at soft flesh. Wild eyed and bloody, Big Wu's ghost pursued her through her dreams so that she woke dry-mouthed and sweating, horrified by what she had done. She had killed a man.

But not this night. On this night they spread their mats gratefully upon the open deck, staring up at unfamiliar stars, relieved to escape the noise and stench of so many bodies crowded together in the cavernous space beneath them. They were lucky that it was summer in this strange land where the seasons were upside-down, for in winter the journey around the bottom of the world would have set them to shivering on their rush mats with only thin cotton blankets to keep out the chill winds. As it was, the voyage from Hong Kong had been balmy, sailing across the South China Sea to the port of Singapore to take on fresh water and provisions, then through the Sunda Strait of the Spice Islands, and around the west coast of the great southern continent, before turning eastwards along its lower shores.

Once, as they sailed the brilliant blue waters of the west coast, the captain had allowed the entire contingent above deck in relays when a whale surfaced near the ship. The giant beast had spewed spouts of water from a hole upon its head, as it cruised alongside the *Phaeton* for upwards of an hour. Strong Arm had never thought to witness the like, and marvelled that the gods had created such magnificence. She could only dream of what other wonders they might have in store in this new land, and hoped she would be equal to any task set before her. Her family depended upon her success.

These southern waters heaved with the wind, making the below decks particularly foul, so she was glad to sleep above deck. Despite the rolling of the ship, she slept soundly the night through. When she awoke the following morning, she was surprised to see that the *Phaeton* was once more hugging the coast, where a line of dunes edged the shore and an outcrop of rocky islets broke the calm waters of a wide bay. As the ship sailed level with the curve of a long white beach, she sensed a new urgency in the bustle of the crew on watch. They had put away their buckets and paintbrushes and abandoned their sailmakers' needles. Today was not a day for the usual shipboard maintenance. Today, something new was about to happen.

'Where ship now?' she called to a crewman who was hurrying towards the mast, where several others were already scaling the rigging. The unfamiliar foreign words emerged sluggishly from her throat.

'Welcome to ye new home, lad,' said the man, pointing to a spot in the south where a rocky promontory thrust into the sea, wild surf pounding its feet. Atop the cliff, a triangular white pillar rose as if in warning. She did not understand all of the sailor's words but she knew their intent.

'Where Melbourne?' she asked, puzzled by the lack of buildings upon the shore. They had been told that their destination was a booming city with a busy port, made wealthy by the discovery of gold. But all she could see were barren dunes, the distant promontory, the smudge of several modest buildings and what looked to be a lone jetty snaking into the bay.

'Forget Melbourne, lad. This is Robetown, Guichen Bay.'

She turned to Big Nose, a question in her eyes. Perhaps he could decipher the man's meaning. But her friend only stared out at the deserted shore and shrugged.

'How we get to diggings?' he shouted to the sailor who by now was halfway up the mast.

'Why, ye walk, m'friend,' he called down to them. 'Ye walk.'

Strong Arm's earlier cheerfulness evaporated like salt spray upon her skin. Had they come so far to be abandoned in the middle of nowhere? Or like the unsuspecting crickets the children of Sandy Bottom caught and kept in cages, had they been duped into captivity? Were they doomed to spend the rest of their lives labouring as coolies on some rich ghost-man's land far from the Middle Kingdom, like so many others before them? If that were the case, she might never find the money to help Elder Brother and repay her family for the trouble she had brought upon them. She would never repay her debt to Second Brother, who had given up his dream to save her skin, and who even now might be eking out a living on the streets of Kwangchow.

Around her the other men were stirring, alerted by the proximity of land and the sailors clambering in the rigging above their heads. She and Big Nose weren't the only ones to realise that something was afoot, for soon the entire deck was filled with a hubbub of noise. And as the *Phaeton* sailed towards the approaching promontory, the anxious voices of her fellow passengers rose above the flap of sails and swish of the bow wave.

Where were they?

A stiff shore breeze brushed her cheeks as the sun rose higher above the brown flat land that stretched to the horizon. It looked so different to the ordered fields, wide rivers and lush green mountains of her homeland. It appeared wild and barren, and not at all welcoming. Then she noticed that the captain had arrived on the bridge and was standing in earnest conversation with the first mate.

'Ready about!' shouted the mate, his voice echoing

in the wind, and all around him the crew responded to his command by increasing the urgency of their activity. Strong Arm watched as sailors loosened the ropes controlling the sails, so that they flapped about in the breeze. All the while the crew shouted encouragement to each other, as the timbers of the ship creaked and groaned beneath them and the pulleys and winches clanked against the masts.

'Hard aport!' shouted the mate, and the *Phaeton* responded by turning slowly into the breeze, heading straight towards the beach, it seemed to her. But the wind was gusting now, setting the sails to whipping and cracking, and she could feel the ocean clutching at the ship's hull. Unlike the rafts that plied the rivers and creeks of her home, a ship of this size did not turn quickly. And now the *Phaeton* appeared to be labouring in the wind. Instead of completing its turn about, the ship stalled, leaving it stranded like a wounded duck, at the mercy of wind and wave. She felt the deck tip as a huge swell caught the ship's beam and propelled it sideways across the water.

'All hands on deck!' bellowed the mate.

Above their heads, the sails flapped futilely as the ship was carried along by the rising swell and the gusting wind. Somehow the captain had underestimated the power of the surf and the strength of the breeze. She grabbed her friend's arm and fought her way across the tilting deck to a rail where they could hold on, trying to stay out of the way of the shouting, scurrying sailors. Trying not to be lost overboard. She had felt the water's might once before on the moonlit night of the Seven Sisters festival. She did not wish to risk it again.

'Should we go below?' Big Nose suggested above the noise. 'It may be safer.'

'If the ship sinks we will be trapped.'

They clung to the rail as chaos reigned around them, sailors clinging to the rigging as the *Phaeton* was swept up in the swell, beyond control of captain or crew. It slid across the glistening sea until it was brought to a booming, shuddering halt, as if the very fabric of the ship had been torn asunder. From the sound of the crash, Strong Arm felt sure that a hole must be ripped in the ship's hull and water already flooding into the hold. She thought of the men below, the men she had lived cheek by jowl with for two moons. If the ship took on water they would be trapped by the iron-barred hatches that were bolted closed every night. She imagined them struggling to stay afloat in their watery cavern as waves engulfed the *Phaeton*, filling the hold, then the between decks, before dragging the entire ship beneath the waves.

But to free them she would have to release her grip upon the rail to open the hatch, and she did not know what would happen to the ship next. She would have to trust to the whims of fate and the will of the gods. She had already done that once, when she waded into the river to save Siu Wan. She had done it a second time when she left her family behind and boarded the *Phaeton* to sail across the ocean. She did not know whether she had the strength to do so again. What if she was washed overboard? She would be swallowed by the waves that swirled about the listing ship. And who amongst these foreign sailors would jump in to save her? Young Wu had saved her once. Never again.

Then she took a deep breath. In the chaos wrought by the waves, the crew appeared to have forgotten about their human cargo. It was up to her and her countrymen on deck to free them.

'We must open the hatches!' she said to Big Nose, her voice whisked away by the wind. Out of the corner of her eye she saw that one of the other men was also hurrying towards the hatches. Releasing her grasp on the rail, Strong Arm hauled herself hand-over-hand towards the nearest hatch trying not to think about water, waves or indeed the often fickle nature of gods.

26

Violet rose earlier than usual that morning, in order to be gone from the house before her employer stirred. She was so keen to be gone that she had reduced her toilette to a mere fifteen minutes. She considered ignoring Mrs Wallace's ultimatum, for she suspected that old Billy would have neither the will nor strength to haul her bodily down the stairs, but then again, she would not put it past the woman to attempt the deed herself. A wrestling bout with her employer on the Persian rug did not appeal. Although undoubtedly Violet would have won, given the scrawny nature of the other woman's arms.

So she had packed a small valise with a change of attire, leaving her trunk for Billy to deliver when she sent word of new lodgings, and tiptoed from the house just after dawn. She thrust the thought of Alice from her mind. The girl would survive without her, despite her mother, and there was nothing she could do to change the situation. Mrs Wallace had spoken. Violet would write to her when she was settled, in the meantime, Becky Sharp's guidance would have to suffice. Violet's more immediate problem was how to find a new position. Four solitary gold sovereigns clinked at the bottom of her reticule. She had retrieved them from Mr Wallace's hatbox when she knew his wife to be in the kitchen. Violet wasn't a woman to be swindled of her wages, and she doubted that the wealthy grazier would court gossip about town by reporting her to the constabulary or his wife. Mrs Wallace was another story. She could keep her sovereigns.

It was too early to make her way into town without inciting talk amongst the townsfolk – who were grateful for any and every morsel of gossip – so she decided upon a stroll out to the Cape to pass time away from prying eyes and to consider her future… which she had to admit was looking far from rosy. This wasn't the first time she had been dismissed, nor was it the first time she had been left homeless. Like many an unmarried woman, hers was a precarious position. She was employed at the whim of others, subject to their good opinion, vulnerable to their good faith, susceptible to their promises. And others could not always be trusted to keep either their faith or their promises, in her experience.

She listened to the coins clinking in her reticule and considered them scant recompense for her current situation. She had been lured ten thousand miles by the promise of employment and now it had been snatched from under her. And like her previous employer, Mrs Wallace was guaranteed to spread lies about her, so that procuring another position as governess in the colonies might prove difficult. For all her optimism, at this particular moment, Violet was bereft of ideas.

Her thoughts in ferment, she did not realise how far she had walked through the scrub until the sand beneath her feet gave way to rock, and she emerged from the dunes to find herself standing upon the rugged promontory of Cape Dombey. Even on a still day the breeze blew fresh upon the cape; and the ocean churned below the cliffs. Today the wind gusted so ferociously that she dare not venture close to the cliff's edge for fear of being borne away. Her petticoats billowed about her legs like a ship in full sail, so that she had to set down her valise to do her battle with them.

As she struggled to bring some order to her person, she glanced to the south where the coast stretched away in a series of rugged inlets, wild surf pounding the cliffs. At the entrance to these inlets an islet rose from the seabed, the rocks eroded aeon after aeon until they formed an archway, an archway that led only to danger. Ahead of her, at the tip of the cape, the white pyramid of an obelisk towered in warning to any ship unwise enough to venture close. White seabirds with grey wings and feathery black crests like hats nested on the rocky plateau leading out to the obelisk, defying both wind and rain. Yet there was no refuge to be found here for Violet, not from the wind, the churning waters, nor her thoughts. Guichen Bay had proved no haven for her.

So, what to do next? She would have to go somewhere

beyond the reach of Mrs Wallace's vindictive tentacles. Somewhere the grazier's wife was unknown. For there was no going back to London. The earl's daughter would make her life hell the moment she set foot upon those shores. There was small hope of employment there, even if she could find the funds to return, for that shrewish woman had turned the whole of London society against her, and her husband had done nothing to prevent it. He had done nothing to protect Violet or her reputation. His backbone was made of empty promises. His love was as fickle as the wind.

Once again, Violet had only herself to depend upon. 'And only yourself to blame,' whispered a voice in her head, but she determined not to listen to it. Instead, she directed her attention to the sweep of Guichen Bay, pondering the question of how to find cheap yet respectable lodgings to eke out her small store of sovereigns. A ship was approaching from the north, a tall three-master. Not so long ago she would have been surprised to see a ship of this size entering Guichen Bay. Unlike the coastal steamers that plied these waters, the clipper was too large to moor at the town's jetty and would have to weigh anchor in deeper water. But two weeks earlier, to the town's amazed good fortune, the British ship *Land of Cakes* had appeared in the bay out of nowhere – or out of Hong Kong, to be precise – bringing a cargo of Celestials bound for the goldfields. Like those arriving by steamer from Adelaide, the Chinamen were evading the Victorian poll tax. But the *Land of Cakes* had bypassed the port of Adelaide and instead sailed direct to Guichen Bay, enlisting half the town's small population in ferrying the passengers to shore and providing them with provisions. Then the *Cornwall* had followed it just a few days ago.

The approaching ship was even larger, twice as big from the look of it, and totally unprepared for the local conditions. She stood watching as it attempted to tack into the bay but was caught in a swell and swept onto one of the many sandbanks that formed there. Even from her perch a mile away, she could see the ship listing sideways. It would soon be taking on water. The crew would have to get their passengers over the side and into boats swiftly, or the Celestials' voyage would end at the bottom of Guichen Bay.

If she hadn't been so worried about her own situation, she would have felt sorry for them. They had come so far in their quest for riches, like all those who had come before them, the thousands of men and women who had uprooted their lives and descended upon the Victorian diggings from every corner of the world. There were probably numerous children running wild on the diggings at Ballarat, Bendigo and the like. Children of parents who had struck gold. Children whose parents knew nothing of Mrs Wallace or any of her acquaintance. Children who quite possibly had no one to provide a suitable education, or at least an education befitting their parents' new-found fortune. No one to elevate them to their new-won status or teach them the finer points of French grammar, geography and the delights of arithmetic.

Unless, of course, those parents were lucky enough to procure the services of a respected governess. One who had tutored the grandchildren of an earl. A governess with the impeccable credentials of one Miss Violet Hartley.

Perhaps she too could strike gold upon the diggings.

27

The deck swarmed with passengers, the captain's wife and children amongst them. Despite the chaos surrounding her, this fact reassured Strong Arm, for the captain would not let his family drown. Already he and his wife grieved for one of their children who had died of sickness shortly after departing Hong Kong. If the captain believed his vessel were about to sink, surely he would put his remaining family in a longboat and row for shore. Comforted by this thought, she huddled on the foredeck with Big Nose and her fellow countrymen, all hugging the baskets that contained their futures, the only things they had salvaged from between decks. They did their best to stay out of the crew's path as the men rushed to carry out the mate's orders. Meanwhile, the waves swirled about the bow that was pointed shoreward, yet going nowhere.

Some time later, the bosun's whistle piped, shrilly enough to be heard above the commotion. 'Furl sail and square the yards!'

The words were incomprehensible to Strong Arm, but the bosun's meaning became evident as the sailors set to work, shuffling along the rigging, grabbing and punching at the billowing sails before rolling them up and making them secure.

'Let go anchor!' ordered the mate.

The crew seemed so purposeful that for a time she hoped all would be well, that the ship would sit tight until the rising tide could release it from whatever reef or sandbank held it captive. But the ship continued to fill with water, despite the men labouring at the pumps. At one point Big Nose peeked through the hatch, returning to report that there were at least three *chi* of water flooding the between decks and no sign of the sea relenting. But what could they do? Their fate was in the hands of the crew... and the gods. All they could do was wait.

The sun was high overhead by the time the bosun shouted, 'Ready the boats!'

Strong Arm's hopes faded as she recognised the word 'boats'. So... the captain could not save the ship and they were to be put ashore. She watched in dismay as the first boat was lowered into the surf to crash futilely against the ship's hull. When it became apparent that the sea was too wild for the small boat to make shore, the bosun ordered it to be raised once more. She could only stare helplessly at the waves swirling below.

Big Nose nudged her in the ribs with an elbow to get her attention. 'Do we jump?'

'Can you swim?' she asked, looking doubtfully at the surf.

Big Nose nodded. 'Like a fish. I was raised on a boat.'

'I was raised on a mulberry grove.'

Her friend blinked, not knowing what to say to this. Although they were of an age, because of her slight frame, Big Nose was under the impression that Strong Arm was scarcely more than a boy, and she had not disabused him of this notion. Yet despite his greater size and his familiarity with the ways of the big city, he still looked to her for agreement. Perhaps he was so accustomed to being an outsider that he treasured this new friendship all the more, and did not want to jeopardise it.

'Perhaps the gods will look kindly upon me,' Strong Arm added with a shrug. She said it to reassure her friend, so that Big Nose would save himself if the time came to abandon ship. If he tried to save her they would likely both drown. She felt sure that she had already used up the gods' goodwill. That time she had been fortunate, narrowly escaping the water ghosts who reputedly lurked in rivers and seas, waiting to drag the living beneath the surface and steal their bodies. If not for Young Wu arriving on the riverbank, perhaps some other soul might have inhabited her body. But it wasn't the water ghosts who haunted her now. It was the Wus.

She shook her head, trying to rid herself of this

thought. She did not want to think about Young Wu, son of Big Wu. He was the source of all her troubles. Not her saviour. If he had not delivered her to his father's lair, she would not have needed to defend herself. She would not have caused her family so much loss. She would not have the memory of Big Wu to haunt her. She did not want to encourage any more ghosts.

'Do not worry,' said Big Nose, squeezing her shoulder reassuringly, as if reading her thoughts, 'it will not come to that. We haven't journeyed so far to fail now. Somehow we will make it to shore, and then we will find our way to New Gold Mountain, even if we have to walk ten thousand *li*.'

She peered over the side of the ship, where cresting waves frothed white, and towering breakers cascaded towards the beach, and wished she shared her friend's confidence.

By the time Violet reached the jetty, a crowd had gathered. It seemed like the entire population of Robetown was assembled on the beach outside Mr Ormerod's store to watch the foundering ship. Amongst a group of ladies sheltering from the wind beneath a grove of casuarina trees, she spied Mrs Brewer and Mrs MacDonald, clutching at hats and bonnets that threatened to fly from their heads in the next gust. No doubt, they discussed preparations for tending the stricken immigrants, if they should make it ashore. She was about to join them when she noticed Lewis Thomas in conversation with Mr Melville, the harbourmaster. He stood with his back to her but she recognised instantly the curl of that midnight hair upon his collar, and the way the moleskin trousers fitted his thighs. Despite her troubles, her spirits rose and her pulse quickened at the sight of the bullocky. She had not seen him since the day James took sick.

As if he sensed her presence he turned away from the ocean and lifted a hand in acknowledgement. She smiled and waved in return, before heading over to join the other women. As they watched, a boat was lowered over the side. It bobbed in the water for a few moments before smashing against the ship's hull. The ladies' communal intake of breath was loud enough to be heard above the gusting wind.

'The swell is too great,' observed Mrs Brewer.

'The ship may break up before this gale abates long enough to lower the boats,' said Mrs MacDonald.

'The captain should have waited for a pilot,' chided Mrs Ormerod.

'Well, it is too late for that now,' said Mrs Brewer with a tired sigh.

Violet thought she did not sound her usual hearty self. Perhaps she felt the strain of caring for so many sick men. Judging this as good a moment as any to announce her presence, she ventured a few steps closer, saying, 'We can only trust to God's mercy to save those poor men now.'

At first she thought they did not hear her, too deep in their contemplation of the game of life and death being played out before their eyes. Or perhaps the wind spoke too loud, for they did not turn their gaze from the ocean. She said again, 'I shall pray for their deliverance.'

'She would do as well to pray for her own soul.' She heard the hiss of Margaret MacDonald's words above the whistle of the wind.

'I beg pardon,' she said with a frown. Perhaps they spoke of someone else, these women she had worked alongside for months.

'It is too late for prayer,' said the blacksmith's pinch-faced wife. 'The Lord knows a prevaricator when he hears one.'

Not a one of the ladies turned to face her. Their shawls were a wall she could not breach, not without elbowing her way into their midst.

'Mrs Brewer... Eleanor,' she began, 'it is me, Violet. Come to offer aid to those poor lost souls.'

The Resident's wife relented enough to glance her way, though she would not meet her eye. 'As you can see, Miss Hartley, we have more than enough assistance here. We don't need you. Not today.'

'Nor ever,' said Mrs MacDonald.

'You would do better to return to Noorla.'

'It turns out I am no longer needed there either. Mrs Wallace finds she can dispense with my services. But I expect you already knew that.' It occurred to her that they probably knew much more than that. God knows what that horrible woman had told them. What rumours she had gleaned from London. What lies she spread about

Violet's past. 'Please, Eleanor, don't believe everything you hear.'

'No man is safe around her, from what I've heard,' Mrs MacDonald remarked snidely to the gathered matrons, 'not the nobility, or the gentry. She does not discriminate. Not a simple farmer like Mr Wallace... not even a child.'

Violet had heard evil spat from the genteel lips of the earl's daughter on that day she was thrown from her ladyship's house, but Mrs MacDonald's last word hooked her flesh sharper than any thorn.

'I... I did all I could... I...' Her words were whipped away by the wind, as her skirts flapped wildly, beating at her legs. She had thought these women were her friends but she should have known that friendship's veneer was gossamer thin. To add to her confusion, she realised that Mr Thomas had left off his conversation with the harbourmaster and was striding towards her, his expression stern. With all that had happened, she did not know if she could stand firm in the face of this humiliation if he were to turn on her as well. She had been a fool to trust to friendship. When had it ever held true in the past?

'Do not worry, ladies. I shall not trouble *your* husbands,' she said, finding the right words at last.

Thomas reached her side, just as the women's mouths gaped open at this audacity. He slipped a hand beneath her elbow, holding her upright.

'Have a care, Thomas,' said Mrs MacDonald, throwing a flinty-eyed glare at Violet. 'Not all evils announce themselves openly.'

'Do not worry, madam. I know evil when I see it.'

For a moment Violet allowed him to support her weight, surprised by how solid his forearm felt. She expected strength from a man who drove a team of twelve bullocks for his living, but it was more than physical strength she perceived. She was almost tempted to believe that she could rely upon him. And that, of course, would be a grave error.

Pulling back her shoulders, she looked beyond Robe's women and out to sea, where the ship's boat fought to stay afloat in the perilous waters of the bay. 'So, Mr Thomas… what says our harbourmaster?' she asked, swallowing the jagged lump that lodged in her throat.

'Melville says the crew are assembling rafts.' He nodded in the direction of the harbourmaster who had a telescope to his eye and was staring out to sea. 'Meanwhile, we must make our preparations while we wait upon the weather.'

'Do you think the men will be saved?'

'I should think so. Most of them. But there's little you can do here and… you have your own sorrows to contend with. I've heard what happened to the poor lad.'

'He fought so bravely.'

'He was a plucky little fellow.'

'His mother blames me and perhaps she is right to do so. If I hadn't let him play in the rain… if I had not been so selfish…' She fixed her eyes upon the sand, hearing again Mrs Wallace's harsh words of the previous evening, and a tear squeezed from beneath her lashes. She thought of her exile from London a year earlier and the tear rolled down her cheek.

'Don't blame yourself,' said Thomas. 'The boy was likely coming down with the sickness for days and didn't think to tell.'

'I did my best to help him. But she has thrown me from the house. Without notice or wages,' she said, gulping back the tears that tracked through the dried salt spray on her cheeks, 'and she is spreading lies about me to every grazier and professional man's wife in the colony.' She put a hand up to her face to wipe the tears away with her sleeve.

'In the heat of the moment she may have threatened but surely...'

'It is true. You heard how Mrs MacDonald spoke to me. And Mrs Ormerod looked at me as if I was no better than a... a... whore. She has turned them against me, women I thought were my friends. I have to get away. I have to go somewhere beyond the reach of their spite.'

She felt his arm waver beneath hers and waited for him to release her. Just as she had suspected, his arm wasn't as solid as it promised. But then he surprised her by placing his other hand over hers and saying, 'If there's anything I can do to help.'

The word *anything* was as powerful as an aphrodisiac to Violet.

'Well, perhaps. Perhaps there is something. It's a great

deal to ask, I know… but…' she sniffed back the tears that had turned her voice husky, 'perhaps you could take me with you to the goldfields.'

All through the afternoon, the crew laboured at building a raft to launch into the heavy surf as the ship settled even further on its side. Strong Arm watched in growing dismay as the assemblage of empty barrels and planks was lashed together upon the deck. Couldn't they find some bamboo? Surely a sturdy raft of bamboo would ride the waves better than this ramshackle construction. The general consensus amongst her fellow passengers was that the craft would sink before it got anywhere near the shore. They looked on in horror as the crew surveyed their handiwork. Strong Arm thought she would have more chance of surviving if she clung to a barrel and let the waves take her where they would.

'If the raft capsizes, try to grab anything that floats and hang on,' Big Nose advised. 'Do not fight the current.'

'Does that include you?' she said with a laugh. But the sound emerged more like a cough.

'Just try not to drag me under,' Big Nose answered in all seriousness.

'You're a good friend, Big Nose,' she said, and her friend looked down at his bare feet in embarrassment.

But they were in luck. Either that or the gods had taken pity on them. For as the sun went down, the wind finally blew itself out and the bosun once more ordered that the longboats be launched. One by one, the boats were lowered into the sea, the terrified emigrants from the Middle Flowery Kingdom climbed over the side, and their miserable belongings were thrown down to them. If they were lucky, their baskets landed in the boat in one piece. If they weren't, their hopes sank to the bottom of this wild, southern ocean along with all their worldly goods.

Strong Arm was lucky. And as the longboat finally put to shore, she heard the voice of Big Wu rasping in her ear, taunting the worthless little peasant girl from Sandy Bottom Village, and she could not help wondering when her luck would run out.

28

In a small town where everybody knew everybody, the few households offering rooms to respectable lodgers were suddenly full. Violet was reduced to renting a sour-smelling room at the rear of the Bonnie Owl, her sleep accompanied by the unwelcome lullaby of drunken men. But every cloud has a silver lining and since her reputation was already in tatters, there was now little to prevent her going about town as she liked. She set out in the direction of the bullockies' camp on the shores of a small lake where the local graziers had taken to washing their wool before it was shipped abroad. Mr Thomas was encamped there, she had heard, and she was determined to enlist his services in transporting her to the goldfields. So far, he was proving oddly recalcitrant in the matter, mustering all sorts of arguments to do with her comfort and security. Clearly, he knew little about the life led by a young woman of poor fortune yet good taste. She had never been particularly secure. Not since her mother died and her father deposited her in that third-rate school, leaving her to fend for herself, and went sailing in the Americas.

And in this instance, she had decided that comfort could be forsaken temporarily in the service of expediency… and a ride to the goldfields.

This morning she had assembled all her weapons and was congratulating herself on how fetching she must appear as she strolled out in her silk taffeta day dress and beribboned ringlets, when she caught the sound of male voices and the whiff of campfire smoke. Although Dr Penny had organised the great influx of Celestials into various campsites about the town, these voices were speaking English – well, at least an inferior version of it – and she also heard the intermittent barking of their companions. So, patting a few stray hairs into place, she pinched a tad more colour into her cheeks, and sashayed into the clearing where the bullockies had made camp.

As expected, her arrival was met with surprised confusion, and not a little interest, before one of the old timers found his voice, asking, 'How can we help you, miss?'

'Good day to you, sirs, I'm looking for Mr Thomas. Is he here?'

'Over in yon dunes, talking with the Chinaman.' He indicated the direction with a bob of his head. 'Can we offer you a cuppa?' A sooty black tin dangled upon a stick over the fire, no doubt brewing up the unpalatable liquid that passed for tea amongst the bullockies.

'Thank you, but I must decline. Pressing business with Mr Thomas, you see.'

There was nothing for it, she supposed, but to traipse through the dunes, getting all hot and bothered. She could think of more pleasant ways of doing that.

'I believe this grass may be giving me hay fever,' she observed, to no one in particular. Another reason to secure her fortune and be gone from this infernal country.

As she set off once more, through the bush towards the dunes, a chorus of ragged singing followed her from the bullockies' campfire.

'If e'er I go a-wooing
Whate'er may betide
The little town of Robe-town
Shall furnish me a bride.'

Skipping from one rock to the next, Strong Arm stooped beside a rock-pool to harvest a clump of drifting seaweed. With the tang of salt in the air and a fresh onshore breeze fanning her face, it felt good to be alive. Even when she caught her reflection in the pool's surface, for once the image staring back did not startle her. After almost three months, she had grown accustomed to the sight of her roughly shaven head, although she would never grow used to her stink. Despite the urgency of her quest, today she almost felt free. For the first time in her life, she had no one telling her what to do every moment of the day.

She had no one telling her how she must behave or who she must be. She could decide that for herself.

Further down the beach, Big Nose was busy digging for clams. She smiled as she watched him twist his lanky body to and fro, burrowing his feet into the sand. It felt good to have a companion on her journey, and she only wished she could tell him the truth. She wished she could feel as easy in his company as she had sharing secrets with her friend in the girls' house. But she could not risk exposing her identity. And to be honest, she did not want Big Nose to treat her differently, to treat her like a girl. She did not want to listen to the kind of homilies spouted by Young Wu issuing from his lips.

From their campsite next to a small lake on the outskirts of Robetown, she could hear the waves crashing upon the beach. During the day, while the headman negotiated for the tents and mining equipment they would need on their journey, Strong Arm and Big Nose combed the area in search of food. Neither of them could spare their small store of silver for provisions, so they joined their fellow countrymen roaming the lakeside and the beach. Big Nose had grown up on a sampan on the Pearl River. He thought he knew everything there was to know about water, but the wooded lake a stone's throw from the ocean was nothing like the wide expanse of the mighty Pearl River that teemed with vessels of all shapes and sizes. Nothing but birds cruised its surface. Flocks of black swans, along with several types of duck and wading bird, with eels swimming beneath them. She wished Second

Brother had thought to pack a net, for eels made good eating and could be smoked for the journey.

As well as the recognisable, there were also many queer and wondrous creatures inhabiting the scrubby woodland, like the rabbit-sized animal that bristled with spikes and a lizard that flaunted a huge frilled collar. One afternoon, just before dusk, she had surprised a strange bird loping through tall grass with its chicks. The bird's neck and legs were so long that it stood almost as tall as she. It showed no fear either, looking her in the eye, and when she came too close for its liking, fluffing its feathers and hissing angrily. She suspected that its kick would be harder than Second Brother's and she was the one who retreated.

Neither she nor Big Nose had ever seen the ocean before they embarked upon the journey from Kwangchow. Nevertheless, they soon discovered the clam-like shellfish to be had by digging in wet sand, the mussels clinging to rocks in the tidal pools, and several kinds of seaweed that could be spread out to dry in the hot sun. They had been warned that the journey to the diggings might take a month or more, so they would need all the food they could find to sustain them on their journey across a land of alien forest, swiftly flowing rivers and unfamiliar men.

The trek to come might be fraught with danger but for the moment she was safe and she was free. She had survived. And if at night she was haunted by the spectre of Big Wu's bloodied head floating through her dreams, she was comforted by the thought that his son was far away on the opposite side of the world.

Violet caught up with Thomas, standing atop a dune in animated conversation with a Celestial of middle years. The Celestial looked like any other of his countrymen, dressed in a pair of baggy blue trousers and knee-length dress, his face shielded from the sun by a conical straw hat with a wide brim. On his feet he wore a pair of straw slippers and he was flipping backwards through the pages of a small book as they spoke, apparently searching for a word.

'Ah, Miss Hartley, what a surprise to see you here,' said Thomas, with the lift of one dark brow.

'Am I interrupting something important?'

'Mr Low and I have been concluding arrangements for his group's journey to the goldfields. More than two hundred of the fellows. Apparently they've heard of new diggings on Creswick Creek.' He returned his attention to the other man, saying, 'This is Miss Hartley.'

'How do you do, Mr Low.'

She extended her gloved hand but he did not take it, instead bowing and saying, 'Very pleased to meet you, Miss Hartley.'

'Miss Hartley seeks to join our little group.'

Mr Low's eyes widened in horror, before he schooled his expression into placid acceptance. 'Maybe very hard. Walking many days. Too hard for lady.' He paused for a moment then added with a laugh, 'Too hard for Low.'

'But this particular lady is ready for anything, Mr Low.'

The Chinaman's expression was bland but she could see the doubt in his eyes. Nevertheless, he did not speak further of his misgivings. Perhaps he was saving that for a later conversation with the bullocky.

'Talk more later,' he said to Thomas with a nod. 'Goodbye, Miss Hartley.'

When he was gone, she turned to Thomas with a winning smile. 'I wondered if you might have a list of useful equipment I will need for the journey.'

'I haven't agreed to take you. I don't think you understand the hazards of the journey, Miss Hartley.' His gaze raked her from the top of her carefully arranged coiffure to the tips of her highly polished walking boots and to her chagrin it wasn't one of admiration. 'For example, is this your idea of travelling attire?'

Actually, in the past she had found it the perfect arrangement for travelling. The light brown hue of her dress did not show the dust, and she could walk at least a mile or even two a day, in the boots. 'I should think so.'

He shook his head, one corner of his mouth turning down in wry amusement. 'You won't get further than the Stone Hut Inn in those boots. And your dress, pretty as it is, will be in tatters before a week is out.'

She met his words with a warm smile. They might not be encouraging, but at least he appreciated a well turned-out costume when he encountered it. 'I'm sure I can find something in my wardrobe to satisfy you, Mr Thomas. And I can purchase new boots.'

'Your wardrobe isn't my only concern. You will be surrounded by two hundred and sixty Chinamen. Men following customs you have never before encountered. Most of whom won't speak a word of English. You will sleep on hard ground with only the dray for shelter. You will wade across streams and tramp through mud. You will wash in a bucket, if there is water to wash at all. Walk for up to twelve hours a day in the heat of summer. Eat nothing but half-cooked mutton and scorched damper. And you will have to piss behind a bush like everyone else.'

He held her eyes in a vice-like grip. 'And these are only the expected hardships. I may not always be able to protect you and I cannot nursemaid you. We aren't headed for Ballarat either, so I cannot even tell you what to expect at our journey's end.'

'I think you underestimate me, Mr Thomas. I'm tougher than I look.' She had to be, to survive. Better to be predator than prey.

His expression softened momentarily. 'I reckon you are at that, but you don't know what you're in for. Why don't you let me put you on a steamer back to Adelaide?'

'There's nothing for me in Adelaide. Or England. You must know that.' By now she was certain he had heard some, if not all, of Mrs Wallace's slander. She held his eyes, daring him to deny the truth, for she had never been a woman who lowered her eyes. 'My reputation appears to be tarnished beyond restitution.'

He was the one to look away. 'What if we arrive at these new diggings and you're the only woman there?' he said, glancing down at the beach below.

'It seems to me there are women everywhere in this country.' Except perhaps amongst the Celestials. 'And where there are women there are children. And where there are children, there is a sore need for learning. I may start a school.'

'Well, don't say I didn't warn you. And if you cannot keep up... you will be left behind.'

He spoke harshly, but Violet did not believe him for a minute. She had already decided that Lewis Thomas wasn't a man to leave a woman to face danger alone.

'Then we are agreed,' she said, holding out her hand. After a moment he took it, enclosing her lace clad fingers in a powerful grip.

'Against my better judgement.' He pointed to the beach below. 'There are your fellow travellers. And...'

She followed his gaze out over the dozen blue-clad Celestials foraging upon the beach, to the ocean beyond, where a tall clipper was tacking into the bay.

'... here come some more, if I'm not mistaken.'

29

Young Wu gazed at the distant shore, with its long white stretch of beach arcing north, and its rugged cliffs to the south, all bulwarked by a border of scrubby dunes, and wondered if he had been delivered unto Hell. The first the *Yan Hendrick*'s passengers knew of Robetown or Guichen Bay presented itself when the hatches were unbolted and they were ordered up the ladders with their belongings. Shading their eyes with their hands, they emerged onto a deck beaten by the harsh light of a burning sun, to find that the ship had anchored in a small bay. The sight of a half-submerged ship stranded in the middle of the bay did not inspire confidence. Nor did the token jetty and the absence of anything remotely resembling a town. Had he survived two months in the cramped space between decks, alternately vomiting and purging his bowels, to be deposited upon these barren shores? Had he endured sixty days of the old gatekeeper's constant ear-bashing to be dumped in this backwater?

Where was the bustling harbour of Port Phillip? Where was the booming town of Melbourne?

And where… was Little Cat?

'You cannot do anything right.' He heard his father's voice thrum in his head. 'All you had to do was find a simple peasant girl and bring her to justice. You had an entire village of Wus at your back. Yet you could not accomplish even that. How do you think to take my place as a Wu elder?'

But he had travelled to the edge of heaven and the corner of the sea to find her. He had put aside his feelings and yoked himself to duty. Didn't his father realise the sacrifice he had made?

'How can my *po* rest while the girl roams free?'

He had a duty to his father and the Wu ancestors. He could not fail now.

'I think the ship took a wrong turn, Wise Master,' croaked a voice beside him. He looked over his shoulder to find the old man standing next to him, breathing hard, four overflowing baskets at his feet.

'Don't call me "master". You are supposed to be my uncle, remember,' he replied with an irritated frown. 'And don't sneak up on me.'

'Forgive me, Ma—'

'*Jat.* I am your nephew now.'

'This rotten old man keeps forgetting. This old head isn't what it used to be.'

And yet the gatekeeper never forgot a face, or a fact. Indeed, he had a prodigious memory for every conversation he had ever had or overheard, and liked nothing better than to regale those around him with this knowledge.

'Uncle Wu!' shouted the burly Ah Cheng, one of the old man's card-playing cronies. 'What's happening?'

'Those snake-heart agents have landed us here to save on tax,' the old man said with a knowing nod, although how he knew this, Young Wu could only guess. Despite his poor grasp of the barbarians' language, 'Uncle Wu' managed long conversations with the crew whenever he was allowed on deck. He would have them laughing at his antics, and sharing around the fiery liquid they called 'rum'. The headman too had turned out to be an old acquaintance from the gatekeeper's days in Kwangchow. Uncle Wu, it seemed, knew everybody and everybody knew him.

'We have to walk to the goldfields from here,' the old man said to Ah Cheng.

'How far is that?'

'A few hundred *li*.'

'Waa! So far! We borrowed from the agents for passage to Melbourne. Ballarat is only a few days' walk from there,' said Ah Cheng. 'Those agents are nothing but leeches! They would suck blood from a corpse.'

Uncle Wu made his opinion of all snake-heart agents plain with a thick gobbet of spit to the deck. 'They probably stole the tax for themselves.'

If the men were restless upon being told of the long walk ahead, insult was added to injury with the news that they were to pay five shillings a head of the foreigners' money to be ferried to the jetty. Yet more debt to be loaded upon what they already owed the agents. Uncle Wu was one of the most loudly indignant, several times adding to the puddle of saliva pooling on the deck, until Young Wu elbowed him in his skinny ribs and hissed at him not to draw attention to them. If he was going to find and punish Little Cat, he did not want to attract more notice than necessary.

He gazed shoreward to see that several longboats were setting out from the village jetty, rowed by the white ghosts, and the crew was even now preparing to throw lines down to them. One of their fellow passengers was so incensed that he refused to pay and was promptly tossed overboard, baskets and all. This discouraged any more objections, and the ferrying of the passengers was undertaken without further disruption.

By the time the Wus finally clambered up the ladder to the jetty several hours later, their clothing was damp with salt water and their baskets weren't much better. Most of their fellow passengers had already been landed. So once everyone was assembled at the end of the jetty, they formed a line behind the headman, hoisted their *ta'am* upon their shoulders, and began to walk in single file towards the shore. He and his fellow passengers had expected a short journey along a well-travelled road to the city of Ballarat. Now they must once again set out upon a long journey facing unknown hazards. What was their alternative? They had all made their choice when they departed Hong Kong for New Gold Mountain. No matter their sinking hearts and their fear of the road ahead, they had no choice but to trust the headman to make arrangements for the forthcoming trek.

'Ballarat! Ballarat! Ballarat!' someone shouted, and before long the chant was taken up by three hundred voices.

'Ballarat! Ballarat! Ballarat!'

He heard Uncle Wu's voice add to the chorus and wondered what the old man found to be so pleased about. They had been deposited like refuse in a primitive village in the middle of nowhere. They were surrounded by men they could not trust, men who owed no allegiance to the lineage of Wu. Soon they would be at the mercy of men who were not even Han, outside barbarians who did not know the teachings of the sages, and could not be trusted to act in a righteous manner. Yet somewhere in this vast land, concealed amongst these baffling foreigners, was Little Cat. He just had to find her.

Quickening his pace, he pulled out from the line of men. Few gave him a second glance as he jogged towards the front, his baskets bouncing at the ends of his *ta'am*.

'What is it, Ah Sing?' asked the headman when he trotted alongside.

Here he was no longer Young Wu, son of Big Wu, headman of the village and the Wu clan elder. He had become just another anonymous immigrant looking to secure his future with the promise of New Gold Mountain. Perhaps he wouldn't have minded that life, living free from expectation, his only obligation to pay his debts and send money home. Except that he was bound by his vow to his father's ghost. Bound by his duty to his family and the Wu ancestors. Bound to find and kill a girl he had known his entire life. His closest friend's sister. A girl who moved with the speed of a spitting cat and fought with the heart of a lion. A long-limbed girl with dancing eyes and fiery temper…

The headman was staring at him expectantly, his lips pursed with irritation.

'I must find my cousin. My mother's brother asked me to keep watch over him, for he is a reckless lad and took off on his own before his parents could stop him. But I could not buy passage on the same ship.'

'What do you expect me to do about it? The boy could be anywhere.'

Young Wu slipped a hand into the pouch he carried at his waist and withdrew a handful of cash, the copper coins clinking as he deposited them upon the headman's palm. 'My cousin sailed aboard the *Phaeton*. Perhaps you could ask the white ghosts for news of that ship.'

The headman gazed derisively at his palm, and hawked up phlegm. Young Wu added a few more coins to the small mound.

'I will ask. But I promise nothing.'

The jetty ended next to a squat building made of pale stone, where men were busy unloading huge bales from wagons hauled by armies of giant cattle. The building fronted a narrow beach, while on the other side of the jetty he spotted a shallow cave hollowed out of the rocks. And at the foot of the jetty a deputation had gathered to meet them, one man garbed in a long black coat and narrow striped trousers standing to the fore. The man's face sprouted thick tufts of hair fringeing his chin to his ears while leaving his cheeks bare, so that he resembled a monkey. Monkey Man approached the headman of the *Yan Hendrick* and nodded in a perfunctory bow. The headman bowed politely in return.

'Good day to you, sir. Henry Melville, Harbourmaster and Receiver of Wrecks, at your service.'

Young Wu did not comprehend these words but he saw that Monkey Man intended a greeting. There followed a lengthy conversation, in which the Master of the *Yan Hendrick* also joined, once he had been rowed ashore by his bosun. At one point another of the white ghosts was motioned forward and it became apparent that they were to follow him, for the headman shouldered his baskets once more and called for the men to do likewise. They set off along a dirt track, headed towards some scattered buildings.

'Ah Sing!' said the headman, gesturing Young Wu to his side.

'You have news of the *Phaeton*, Senior One?'

The headman nodded. 'Maybe I have heard something.'

'Then it has landed here in this bay?'

'It is a possibility.'

Why did the man speak in mysteries? Did he expect Young Wu to grease his palm with more cash?

'Then may this humble person ask where it is now?' he asked, bowing from the waist, but refraining from the indignity of falling to his knees. He would save that as a last resort.

When the headman's lips remained clamped, Young Wu thought he was going to ignore the question, despite all his grovelling. But then the man turned away from the dusty road and the troupe of monkey-faced foreigners, to stare out to sea. With no wind, the waters shone like glass beneath the clear blue sky. He pointed to the middle of the bay where the tall ship lay broken upon a reef.

'There. There is the *Phaeton*.'

His words ricocheted through Young Wu's body like a sharp stone; scraping at his throat, constricting his lungs, and gouging his heart, before lodging deep in his belly. Little Cat might already be dead. The thought should bring him relief. He should be grateful that his father's ghost would be avenged without him raising a knife. But all he felt was hurt.

'And its passengers?' he managed to ask.

'You did not ask news of passengers. Only of the ship,' the headman replied, his mouth twitching. Perhaps he disliked peering up into Young Wu's youthful face. Perhaps the man disliked Young Wu's swagger, for he could not help being the son of a landlord, no matter how he humbled himself. Or perhaps the headman simply wished to prolong his suffering.

Young Wu reached into his pouch and produced several more coins.

'All aboard survived,' said the headman as the copper clinked into his hand.

A surge of feeling swept through Young Wu's body, leaving him weak-kneed and light-headed. Little Cat was alive.

'Not for long,' his father's ghost reminded him.

30

Strong Arm was finishing the last of her rice when Big Nose reappeared at their cooking fire, a frown lining his forehead. 'Have you seen my rice bowl? It isn't where I left it,' he said.

The rice was scant enough, as much of the supply the immigrants had brought from China was lying in the flooded hold of the *Phaeton*. She and Big Nose had to make do with a pitiful amount, served up with whatever they had in their baskets. In this case, some pickled cabbage and a few specks of salted duck. And now his bowl had gone missing.

'Did you put it down near the well when you went to draw water?'

On this first day of their trek, they had been surprised to discover the well, a round, stone-lined shaft dug by their predecessors, not far from the shores of a wide lake. She wondered why her countrymen had bothered to dig a well so near a lake until she cupped her hands in the lapping waters and brought them to her mouth, only to spit out a mouthful of salt.

They had stopped by the well for their midday meal after a long morning trekking down an uneven track bordered by swamp, before climbing low scrubby hills to see a plain spreading as far as the eye could see. It was the first day of their trek, but she was already tired to her bones after so many weeks at sea. Strong Arm had always prided herself on her strength and was annoyed by her body's betrayal.

'Aiya! I had not finished eating from it. I put it down for one moment only while I got my chopsticks, and when I returned, bowl and rice were both gone.' Big Nose looked so bereft at the loss of his lunch that she had to cover her mouth with her hand to keep from laughing. 'It's nothing to laugh about!' he said, rubbing his empty stomach. Like all of them, he looked skinny. And from the stories he told of his life in Kwangchow, she knew that he had made a bare living running messages for the foreign devils. He had never needed the muscles of labourer, farmer or fisherman.

'I will help you find it,' she said. 'Perhaps someone moved it by mistake. It must be somewhere around here.'

They searched the immediate area, hunting amongst the baskets and poles dotted about on the ground, asking the men of their group if they had seen it. When that proved unsuccessful, they widened their search to include the adjacent cooking fire, where a group of men from a fishing village plied their chopsticks industriously, eating with such gusto that their shoulders appeared to shake. As they ate, she noticed that they snuck looks at the search party.

'There it is!' said Big Nose, pointing to the brawny figure of Fat Lu, who leaned cross-legged against an overflowing basket, shovelling rice into his mouth from a colourful porcelain bowl. 'Give me back my bowl!'

Fat Lu barely looked up from his rice, his eyes sliding over Strong Arm's friend as if he did not exist. 'Did I hear a mouse squeak?' he said.

'That's my bowl, Fat Lu. Give it back.'

'This old thing? It's a bowl like any other.'

'It's my bowl. No other has one like it. I had it from my mother.' Indeed, where most of the men ate from coarse blue and white bowls, Fat Lu ate from a fine porcelain bowl blooming with pink peonies.

'Are you saying that I *stole* your bowl, Big Nose?' Fat Lu swept a conspiratorial glance around the other men from his village, who had all stopped eating and were watching the encounter with interest, although she noted that their shoulders still quivered... with laughter, she suspected.

'It's the only thing I had from my mother,' said Big Nose. 'And now she is gone to the ancestors.' She waited for her friend to accuse the burly fisherman of the theft, but he just stared at the bowl, his shoulders slumped.

'It's Big Nose's bowl,' she said. 'I have seen him eating from it many times.'

'But everyone here has seen me eating from this bowl,'

said Fat Lu, licking his lips as he invited corroboration from his friends.

'This is so,' they replied, nodding obligingly.

'I would not taint my lips upon the bowl of a rotten mixed-egg like him.'

'You lie!' She felt indignation for her friend, rising like steam in a bubbling pot, threatening to blow the lid clear.

'So, now you call me liar and thief!' said Fat Lu, unfolding his ankles to stand with his chunky legs akimbo and arms crossed. Even in this wide-legged stance he stood as tall as she and twice as large in girth.

She took a step towards him, the steam gathering force, but Big Nose held her back with an upraised hand saying, 'Do not let him goad you. It isn't worth it. Remember the old proverb: force tells weak from strong for a moment, but truth tells right from wrong always.'

Fat Lu laughed. 'Which is more precious? Your pretty bowl or your pretty friend?' he asked, striding up to Big Nose and flicking his head with one fat finger.

'So you admit you took it?' said Strong Arm.

'Maybe it's so. Maybe it isn't. The question is, what is he going to do about it?' he said, dashing the bowl to the ground where it shattered upon one of the jagged white rocks strewn about the countryside.

'I... I...' Big Nose stood like an empty husk, searching for an answer to Fat Lu's belligerence. Why didn't he say something? Do something? She felt the bubbling anger inside swell to include her friend. Why did he let Fat Lu bully him without fighting back? Yet how can you find winning words against a bully? Strong Arm had been fending off men like Bully Yee and Fat Lu her entire life. Men like Big Wu. Men who thought their size or their importance gave them leave to take whatever they wanted. To hurt whomever they pleased.

Finding no words powerful enough to combat his tormentor, Big Nose simply dropped to his knees to gather up the broken porcelain. 'It belonged to my mother,' he whispered as he worked.

'You gutless ghost!' Fat Lu spat. He shifted his weight to one leg and struck out with the other, landing a blow to the kneeling youth's right cheek.

Strong Arm could stand by no longer. Despite her friend's silent warning, despite her vow to stay out of trouble, she took off in a flying leap, her legs seeming to run through the air, before kicking out at Fat Lu's belly. The kick propelled him backwards but he recovered more quickly than she expected, to stand legs wide, hands raised in fighting stance. He threw a punch, which she blocked, returning the punch before shifting her weight to one leg and kicking his shin with the other foot.

Fat Lu was angry now. He rained down punches upon her, his meaty fists bringing all the might of his size to bear upon her weakened frame. Instinctively, she knew that he could not be overcome with strength. Only speed and technique could bring him down. She blocked a punch with her forearm, simultaneously striking out with her other hand in a jab to his chest. But still he kept coming. She blocked and jabbed, then stepped back, swivelling on one foot, to upset his balance before aiming a kick with her other leg that toppled him to the ground.

She rested momentarily, catching her breath, waiting to see if he was eager for again. Meanwhile, Big Nose was once again standing, staring at her with his mouth slightly agape. She blinked at him and was about to speak when a blow to the back of her neck caught her off guard. She jerked forward but her reflexes saved her, so that she swivelled once more to resume her fighting stance, facing in the other direction. Three of Fat Lu's cronies were coming for her, toothy grins splitting their faces like snarls. They approached cautiously, conscious of the range of her feet. But she knew that as soon as they gathered their courage they would charge as one.

Bending down, she snatched up a *ta'am* that was lying next to one of the baskets and resumed a fighting stance, side-on to the three men, the staff held before her in both hands. They hesitated at the sight of the weapon, but she knew that their dignity would not let them back down against one lone boy, and sure enough, after a reassuring glance at each other, they charged. The *ta'am* took on a life of its own, blocking blows high and low and striking out at unguarded limbs in a blur of movement.

Out of the corner of her eye she saw Big Nose place his broken bowl on the ground and take a tentative step towards her. She shook her head, warning him away, knowing that he would be more hindrance than help, for then she would have to defend them both.

She took a blow to the cheek and another to the ribs,

noting the pain in an off-hand way, but forcing it to the back of her mind. She needed all her concentration to ward off their attack. If she could only wear them down before they vanquished her. Given enough time she knew she stood no chance against three grown men. Four, if Fat Lu decided to re-enter the fray. She was weakened by the voyage, the long hours trudging along an uneven track beneath a burning sun and her lack of practice. Time alone would wear her down.

Twirling the *ta'am* one-handed, she stepped back, and back once again. They closed on her, thinking she was retreating, and in a blur of speed she thrust the stick at one man's chest, blocked the kick of another, and ducked out of reach of the third man's swinging arm. But now she was squatting as the others recovered, advancing upon her from three sides. She levered herself into a semi-crouch and jumped backwards, trusting there was nothing behind her. She was breathing raggedly. It would not be long now. At the very least she expected to be beaten to a pulp.

A single shot from a gun rent the air, stopping her opponents in their tracks.

'What's going on here? Mr Low! Where are you?'

The ghost man materialised in their midst, spitting fiery words from an angry red mouth. With his bulging eyes, sun-reddened face and short, dark hair plastered to cheeks and forehead, he had the look of a warrior from the opera. Plus he had no qualms about stepping between her and her opponents, brushing aside her stick as if it were nothing more than a stray branch and standing between the combatants, his arms outspread. A black and white dog followed at his heels, its fur bristling, barking as fiercely as its master.

'There's to be no fighting in my camp! Is that clear? No fighting or you are on your own!' he roared, the words emerging too quickly for her to catch a single one. Plus she had no breath to speak, even if she had understood his words. She could only stand before him panting, glad for this respite, however brief.

'Low! Where are you?' he shouted.

She recognised the name of the headman amongst the other unintelligible sounds.

'Low sleep.' Big Nose surprised them all by answering. He surprised Fat Lu and his cronies because they did not know that the skinny boy from Kwangchow spoke the foreigner's language. And he surprised her because she did not know that her meek friend had the courage to speak up. Beneath his tan, his face had taken on a greenish colour.

'Low smoke pipe at midday.'

'Who are you?'

'This humble one is called Su Ching Yih.'

'Well, I cannot call you Su. That's a woman's name, mate.'

'I am known as Big Nose.'

The ghost man stared at her friend for a second, before his face broke into a broad grin. He did not look so ferocious then, even with a full mouth of white teeth gleaming in the midday sun. 'Big Nose it is then. Lewis Thomas is my name.' The man held out a large square hand sprinkled with fine dark hairs. Big Nose shook that hand.

'Now. What's going on? Why are these men fighting?' The man faced them all, the gun resting loosely in his hands. Fat Lu's friends shuffled back a few steps.

'Is mistake, Mr Thomas.' Big Nose glanced at Fat Lu and his friends one by one, urging them to silence. 'My friend,' he indicated Strong Arm with a nod of his head, 'think I am in trouble. He defend me. All mistake. No trouble here.'

'Mistake, eh?' He raked his gaze across them all, man and boy, no doubt noting the cut cheeks and bruises she could already feel on her battered limbs, the damage she had wrought upon the others. His eyes came to rest upon the *ta'am*, which she still held in a tight grip. 'He's just a boy.'

Strong Arm did not know what the bullock driver or her friend was saying. But she did not like that the man's gaze had settled upon her.

'He is sixteen. He is Strong Arm.'

'He's strong, all right. Despite his skinny looks.'

'He is called Strong Arm.'

The man examined her more closely, from her straggling queue to her dirty trousers. She held her breath, praying that he would not see through her disguise. Sometimes she was astounded that she was yet to be exposed. She glared at the man in return, daring him to see the girl beneath the sweat-stained tunic, to detect any trace of beauty in her snarling face.

'Any more fighting and you'll be tossed out. All of you. Savvy? Tell them,' he said, turning once more to Big Nose.

'This man say any more fighting and he will throw us from his party to find our way across this blighted land alone,' Big Nose said in Cantonese, aping the ghost man's commanding tone.

For a moment, Fat Lu looked as if he might speak. But then, perhaps realising that there wasn't much point speaking to a man who did not understand him, with his opponent the only available interpreter, he thought better of it. With one last threatening stare for Strong Arm, he turned and swaggered back to his place by the cooking fire, his cronies following.

'And you two…' the bullock driver said, looking from one to the other, 'gather your things and come with me.' He beckoned her with a wave of his hand. She did not understand his words but she understood the gesture. When she saw him peering at her more closely, she stared at the ground. She had invited his notice by letting her temper get the better of her, but she did not want it. She wanted to go unremarked. Unremarkable. So much for that.

As they collected their belongings from around their cooking fire, and stowed them in their baskets, Big Nose finally spoke. 'It was better to let the matter rest, my friend. Fighting does not always win the war.'

'He kicked you.'

'What is one kick between friends?' Big Nose laughed, rubbing his ribs.

'He would kick you again.'

'Maybe so, but that is in his nature. It wasn't personal. Now we have made an enemy.'

So... she had made another enemy. What was one more? One more enemy to prevent her repaying her debt to Second Brother and her family. One more enemy to prevent her finding the gold to pay for Elder Brother's wedding, to stop her justifying Second Brother's sacrifice. She realised that she had done exactly what her twin had accused her of. She had promised to think before she acted, yet she had let anger goad her into the fray, as always.

Yet what was the alternative? Let Fat Lu do as he pleased?

Their baskets repacked, they shouldered their *ta'am* once more and prepared to join the bullock driver at his wagon. But as they straightened up it became apparent that a crowd of onlookers had gathered to see what the commotion was about. Her eyes roamed over the ranks of curious men. Men she had been locked up with between decks for many weeks. She knew them, but not well. She had kept as much distance as the limited space allowed, for fear of betraying her secret. Now she had made herself the object of their scrutiny.

She looked away, but not before her glance grazed the features of a face she knew well. Square-jawed, heavy-browed, angry brown eyes, floating amongst the sea of blue-garbed, brown-faced men. Even shaded by a straw hat, surrounded by other straw hats, she knew that face. That tall broad-shouldered physique. She risked another sideways look into the midst of the crowd, to be sure she hadn't imagined it, but like a ghost, the figure vanished as soon as she tried to pin it down. Had she imagined it?

'I never relinquish what is mine.'

In her mind, she heard again the rasping voice. She saw the broken head, the blood seeping into the rug, and she knew without a doubt that she was surrounded by enemies. Real or not.

31

Violet soon became accustomed to a life surrounded by the chatter of the road. But for the most part, the Celestials avoided her. She wasn't sure if this was because most of them had never met an Englishwoman before landing in Robe, or whether they believed she was in some way deformed beneath her hooped skirts. Either way, they generally gave her a wide berth. So far that morning, she had managed the odd word with a wan-faced Mr Low, as many words as she could contrive with Thomas, and a few choice words for the bullocks, who produced copious amounts of manure to pepper her path. She had even begun to fear that the dog might turn out a better conversationalist than Thomas, who seemed to be avoiding her. To her disappointment he had directed her to walk behind the dray out of range of his whip, which meant, short of shouting, conversation was limited. This was particularly vexing, because how could a man appreciate her fine figure when she was concealed behind twelve plodding bovines and a laden wagon? Especially when she had risen long before their dawn departure in order to complete her toilette. She might as well be wearing a flour sack for all the notice the man took.

She thought luncheon would be the perfect opportunity to further their acquaintance, despite the lack of privacy, but no sooner had Thomas set two stools beneath the drooping branches of a grey-leaved tree than he was called away to the far side of the camp, his rifle slung over one shoulder. From where she sat, all she could make out was a whirl of tangled bodies and a lot of angry shouting. She gathered from the commotion that an altercation was taking place, which was soon halted by a single shot from Thomas's rifle. Now he had returned, a thunderous expression darkening his face.

'It's worse than herding sheep,' he said, slapping his hat to his thigh.

'Perhaps you could train Ruby to nip at Celestial heels too,' she said, directing a speculative glance at the dog trailing after its master. Men did like their dogs, and it was rather sweet the way Ruby kept returning to the rear of the bullock wagon that morning, as if to check upon her progress. Apparently, Violet had become one of her herd.

'Sometimes I wonder why I got myself into the business of carting humans. Carting wool is so much simpler.' Thomas stared back the way he had come, where the ruckus had subsided. 'Wool does not gamble. It does not imbibe. And it never resorts to fisticuffs.'

'But it does not pay nearly so well either.'

'There is that. Except if the journey doesn't kill them, they'll do each other in,' he said, a sweeping arm indicating the congregation of men once more squatting before their cooking fires. 'You shouldn't have to witness that, Miss Hartley.'

She put her head to one side and glanced up at him from beneath her lashes. 'Now that we are to share a bullock dray, perhaps you could call me Violet. And I could call you Lewis.'

'Violet.' The word rolled off his tongue melodically. She liked the sound of her name caressed by his Welsh lilt. She wanted to hear it again.

'Lewis, I...' she began, but before she could complete her sentence he was distracted by the approach of two Celestials. They were lugging what she presumed were all their worldly goods upon their shoulders. What were they doing here? Thomas had not called the order to resume the march.

'We are here, mister,' said one, barely a man, thin as a reed, although taller than she, taller than many of his compatriots. The other, of a similar height, looked even younger, with the smooth cheeks and coltish limbs of a boy. There was nothing remarkable about the two. There were merely two more blue-clad gold seekers from amongst the Celestial horde. Except on closer inspection, she realised there was something odd about the younger one, some delicacy of eyebrow, some fineness about the lips. Something she could not quite put her finger on, but all the same, decided that she did not like.

'From now on you two will travel with me,' said Thomas.

'Mr Low not happy, mister.'

'I don't care about Mr Low's happiness. Mr Low is too fond of the pipe. Besides, that one…' he said, indicating the boy with a jerk of his head, 'needs keeping out of trouble.'

'Not trouble, mister.'

'How old did you say he was anyway? And what is he doing here on his own?' said Lewis, peering more closely at the boy.

'Old enough. Strong Arm is sixteen, mister.'

'He looks more like fourteen to me.'

'He get money for his family,' the older one explained.

'No doubt.'

The younger boy had been staring at the ground but at the sound of his name, he looked up, and for a second his eyes met the bullocky's. Violet frowned. Then, with a flick of her hair, she placed her hand upon Lewis Thomas's arm to draw his attention back to where it belonged.

'Is there somewhere a lady can find a little privacy, Lewis? It's been a long morning.'

'Follow me,' he said, after a moment. 'Something can be arranged.'

He turned away from the two Chinamen, but not before a final concerned glance at the boy. Violet sighed. That was the problem with good men; they tossed their goodness about indiscriminately. She would have to do something about that. Violet did not like to share, not if it could be helped. There had been little enough in her life that was all her own.

'On second thoughts, Miss Hartley will need someone to look out for her on this journey. An escort, if you will. You two…' he paused, tipping his hat back to get a better look at the two Chinamen, 'can provide it.'

Skirting the perimeter of the gathering, Young Wu and his uncle crept closer to the lake, where a thick growth of rushes sprouted from black mud. A flock of giant birds with bills as long as his arm swam close to the lake's shore. White with black wings, and large pouches beneath their bills, the birds dipped their heads as one beneath the water, hunting for fish. When they emerged, they seemed to sense the foreign presence. One bird stretched out its massive wings, wider than a man is tall, flapped them briefly in warning, before the entire flock sailed further onto the lake. He had never seen a creature like it and looked to the old man to check whether he had also noticed these strange birds. But it was often difficult to tell which way his 'uncle' was looking, with his single wandering eye.

'Very useful, a pouch like that,' said his uncle.

Ducking beneath the twisted boughs of fine-leaved trees, the bark peeling from their trunks in thin white sheets like paper, the men circled back towards the bullocky's camp. Young Wu wanted to discover where Little Cat had gone, but without alerting her to his presence. He was almost sure that she had noticed him earlier amongst the onlookers. Her eyes had slid over the crowd, resting briefly upon him, before looking away. He could only hope that she didn't believe her eyes, that perhaps she would mistake him for an apparition, an embodiment of her guilt. He wasn't ready to confront her yet. That meeting, when and if it came, must be on his terms.

'Pity it didn't work.' The old man's voice rustled beside him, dry as the paper bark.

'What are you talking about now, Old Man?'

'The plan. The plan to get her done by those yokels.'

Had that been his plan? The fishermen had been only too happy to beat up a couple of upstart youths for the price of a caddy of rice. It hadn't been difficult to convince them to start a fight, especially the fat one. But had he planned for them to kill her, or merely rough her up, leaving the killing for him? The fishermen had the brawn, but not the skill to kill Little Cat. She had got out of more scrapes than he could remember. And she never shied away from a fight. The Mo twins had always been like that. Brave. Braver than him. But then again, they did not have the Wu name to live up to. A Wu couldn't afford to act foolishly, no matter how brave.

He closed his eyes, picturing the girl's flying limbs, the taut bow of her torso beneath the ugly blue tunic. The way she had whirled through the air light as a darting swallow. She was thinner than he remembered, more delicate, even posing as a man. From behind the milling crowd he had watched her. Wanted her. He could no longer deny it.

'We will have to do it ourselves,' sighed the old man. 'Or your father's *po* will not rest.'

'I will do it. When I am ready,' he said, leaping over a fallen tree to land several paces distant from his erstwhile uncle.

The old man rested his weight upon the trunk before clambering over. 'It's no easy thing. Killing. Especially a woman.'

'I can do it.'

'She is only a girl. And you are a Wu.'

What did he imply? That Young Wu could overpower her easily? That only a coward would shy away from such a task? Or was he suggesting that it would be an unfair fight? Young Wu shook his head to get the old man's words from his head. He couldn't afford to think about the matter too deeply. That way lay chaos. That way lay the muddy waters of love and hate. From the moment he saw Little Cat again, his thoughts had become mired in confusion, a swamp far more treacherous than the black mud rimming the lake's shore.

'I can do it.'

'A righteous son nourishes his parents in life and in death.'

'I know this, Old Man.'

'And your father was always a greedy one. His ghost will take plenty of feeding. Even as a boy he demanded more than his share. Wanted whatever another had,' said the old man, swatting at a mosquito that had landed on his arm and was digging in for a meal. 'Got it!' he exclaimed gleefully, giving Young Wu a sideways glance.

By now they had circled around the midday camp to a spot a stone's throw from the resting bullocks. Crouching behind a tangle of papery branches, they considered the scene before them. The ghost man stood with his back to them, the ghost woman at his side. Young Wu could not discern the relationship between the two, whether they were husband and wife, or merely fellow travellers. The woman's wide skirts were crushed against the man's leg, their arms almost touching. What this meant, he wasn't sure. The outside barbarians were still a mystery to him. But there was something between them.

Facing them were Little Cat and that mixed-blood coward, Big Nose. These two also stood close, their baskets knocking together. Clearly, they had formed an alliance, although of what sort, he couldn't be sure either. But as the bullock driver spoke to them and Big Nose translated, the two traded glances, both wearing the expressions of startled chickens. Something had set a fox among the hens.

'The girl and her friend have their baskets with them,' whispered Uncle Wu. 'The foreign devil has taken them under his protection.'

'I can see that!'

He hissed the old man to silence. If the foreigner had taken Little Cat under his wing, it would make it that much more difficult for Young Wu to fulfil his vow. But she was a woman masquerading as a man. Sooner or later she would need solitude, and Young Wu would be watching, waiting to strike. What concerned him more was why the bullock driver had decided to protect her. Surely she was just one more man from the Middle Kingdom amongst many. What had the ghost man seen in her? What did he know?

And what did he want?

32

Western District, Victoria, 1857

Nothing could have prepared Violet for the unremitting heat of the road. The sun seared her skin through sleeves and gloves, turning the underside of her dress into a Turkish bath. Yesterday it had got so bad that she was forced to abandon several petticoats. Dust and grit from the road invaded every available crevice of her skin so that she was coated in grime. Even at night, curled up on stony ground beneath the dray, the temperature rarely dropped below unbearable. During the day, Lewis took pity on her and made space for her to ride on the bullock dray, but squeezed between the Celestials' store of mining equipment – the handcarts, cradles, sluices, buckets, shovels and picks they deemed crucial – the ride was so uncomfortable that walking was preferable.

What had she been thinking when she conceived the brilliant idea of joining this trek? A bucketful of gold and a line of suitors could not warrant this torture. At night she dreamed of long cold baths and iced tea. During the day she ached for dark rooms and wet London winters, anything to relieve her parched throat and desiccated skin. What sins had landed her in this hell?

On the second day of the trek the flat and treeless plain had extended in a mindless trudge through barren emptiness. It must have disheartened some of the Celestials because they went so far as to jettison goods they had hauled all the way from China. The track behind them became littered with the wooden blocks they used as pillows, earthenware crocks, iron cooking pots, padded jackets… anything that weighed down the baskets that burdened their shoulders. Although not a one abandoned their opium pipes, she noted.

When the travellers stopped on the second night at the Kangaroo Inn, solid stone walls, chimneys and the promise of a bath lightened her spirits. But the proprietor merely laughed when she asked for a bath to be drawn and pointed to a chipped ewer in a cracked bowl. The same held true two nights later at the Royal Oak in the town of Penola. She was excited at the thought of a township. But upon arrival, weary and footsore, she discovered that the entire settlement consisted of a mere two dozen dwellings of hand-sawn timber, with a few cobbled together from the local rubble. And there was nothing royal about the rough slab hut, with sagging calico ceiling, which did service for an inn. At the time, she consoled herself that Lewis might have time to spend with her but he devoted the entire two days of their stay to gathering supplies for the remainder of the journey.

The interminable diet of mutton and beans was now supplemented by damper, which Lewis had shown her how to cook in the campfire. Violet had never made a loaf of bread in her life but, surprisingly, she was becoming quite accomplished at dousing the flour with beer to get a yeast, kneading and shaping the dough into a flattish cake, then setting it to bake in the ashes once it was risen. She had been sceptical when he first pulled one from the coals to reveal a greyish, ash-coated lump. But upon brushing away the worst of the ash and breaking it open, she found that the loaf was quite palatable.

The Celestials, it turned out, would eat anything. In addition to the smelly black eggs they craved, the dried seaweed, and other unidentifiable stuffs they brought with them, they had taken to bartering for food from the natives. Magpies, lizards, several types of weed and once an entire back portion of a kangaroo, were devoured with gusto.

After leaving Penola, the cavalcade travelled north-east across more flat country covered in open forest where at least there was scattered shade. They wound through mile after mile of twisted white-trunked trees and dry yellow grass, groves of brown stringybark, with squat grass trees sprouting on fire-blackened trunks scattered amongst them. She found this forest quite disconcerting. Despite its open nature, she would not like to wander far from the bullock dray, for by its sameness the forest became a maze.

They were now eight days into their journey from Robe and she was yet to make further progress in her quest to win the affections of Lewis Thomas. She might almost have thought he was avoiding her, except the idea was so ridiculous that she would not countenance it. He was most likely constrained by the presence of so many Chinamen, especially the two youths he had taken under his wing. Violet was determined to rectify matters. If she could win his heart, at least one possible future would be assured. So in the last hours of daylight, as her fellow travellers finally made camp in undulating country by the banks of the Glenelg River, Violet decided to take action. The first thing to be done was to take a bath, since they had finally come to a river. The second thing might prove a little more complicated, but she felt adequate to the task.

There was something to be said for having a Celestial at your beck and call. She summoned Big Nose to her side and explained that she wished Strong Arm to accompany her upon a walk upriver. He was also to ensure that under no circumstances were they to be followed. Then she ignored his protests that the lady might not be safe with only Strong Arm for company, and set off along the river, with the boy trailing behind her. After all, Strong Arm was the one with the kicking feet and flying hands. She felt confident that he would protect her if it came to trouble. Intuition told her that she needed no protection from the boy himself.

The river trickled rather than flowed at this time of

the year, yet there were inviting pools to be found here and there. She glanced behind to ensure that the boy still followed, only to find him looking around furtively, as if frightened.

'Do not concern yourself. They're too afraid of Lewis's rifle to follow us.'

Of course, he did not understand her. Although she suspected he was learning more English by the day.

'Savvy?' she added. 'No man follow.'

The boy followed, but his uneasiness did not lessen. There was a habitual tenseness about him, as if he was wound tighter than a fob watch. She wondered briefly what made him so anxious, then cast off the thought. He was a mere child. How many dark secrets could he have? Fewer than hers, she expected. She returned her focus to the uneven riverside path. It was cooler by the river, shaded by enormous reddish-brown trees with girths two arm-spans around, and huge spreading branches. She longed to immerse herself in a pool beneath their shady arms, to wash the dirt and grime from her body and float free in the river's cool waters.

After a ten-minute walk, they reached a place where a bend in the river had formed a pool enclosed by a cluster of boulders. The pool was protected from view by a grassy bank, several large trees, and the smooth granite boulders. Violet could already feel the cool waters of the river swirling around her.

She motioned for the boy to turn around saying, 'You stay here.' Then she skipped down the bank and proceeded to divest herself of garments. When she had worked her way down to pantalets and chemise she paused, then stepped out of the pantalets too, so that she stood with legs and arms bare, clothed only in the thin cotton shift. She dipped a toe in the shallows, then waded into the pool's centre where the water reached to her waist. Small fish darted out of her way as the silty bottom squelched between her toes. But it wasn't unpleasant. Lowering herself into the pool she fell backwards, to rest half-submerged in the cool waters. She let her hair and chemise float around her, luxuriating in the feeling of freedom. Then in a moment of abandon, she slipped the dripping garment over her head and tossed it to the bank.

She immersed herself once more, the water enveloping her like silk. She relaxed into its embrace, closing her eyes and relishing the tingling cold. Somewhere high above she heard a sudden burst of raucous laughter, as if from a lunatic asylum. She stood to look about her, but apart from the boy there was no one to be seen, nothing but a cream and brown bird sitting upon a nearby branch gazing down at her. Its eyes were slashed with brown stripes that gave it a crazed look. As she watched, it opened its beak and the wild rolling laughter began again, soon joined in chorus by a second bird in the next tree. She sensed that she wasn't the only one observing the birds. The boy's attention was also drawn from his guard duties and he stared, first at the laughing birds and then down at the pool. For a moment his gaze fixed upon her body, before he quickly glanced away.

Not in embarrassment or shame, she realised, simply for fear of being chastised. In his eyes, for that brief moment when he observed her exposed breasts, she saw nothing but mild curiosity. Why didn't it surprise her that she saw no lust in his gaze? The boy was old enough. Either he had no interest in women or...

Well, there was one way to find out. Stepping from the water, she pulled the sodden chemise over her head so that it moulded the curves of her body, and climbed the bank once again.

'Boy!' she called. He turned his head over one shoulder but his feet remained planted.

'Boy! Come here!' She beckoned him with a crooked finger. Reluctantly, he took a few steps in her direction.

'Closer!' He knew what she meant. She could see it in his eyes.

Faced with her intransigence, he shuffled nearer until only a foot or so separated them. His eyes, shaded by their straw hat, were firmly fixed upon the ground, the thick dark lashes fanning his cheeks. The bones of his face were delicately sculpted, the eyebrows winged. The Celestials were not heavily bearded but even so, she could detect no hint of a bristle. Not even a subtle down. Mrs Wallace had more whiskers than this lad.

Swift as a pouncing cat, she reached out to place her hands upon the boy's chest, unsurprised to discover small soft mounds. She grinned, pleased with her powers of discernment, and gave them a quick squeeze. Then she wove her hands through the air, tracing the shape of womanly curves.

'So... you do have secrets?' she laughed. 'Well, I'm sure you have your reasons.'

The girl-boy looked stricken, as well she might, and backed away, her eyes wide and flitting from Violet, to the pool, and the camp ten minutes' walk behind them. The camp full of two hundred and sixty Chinamen.

'No speak,' she hissed. 'No speak.'

'Perhaps.'

For a second, Violet thought the girl might run. But instead, she dropped to her knees and knocked her head upon the ground, not once but thrice. Banging her head so hard that Violet felt certain she must damage her brain.

'Well, I never,' she said, astounded for perhaps the first time in her life.

She bent down, pulling at the girl's arm to haul her to her feet. There really was no need for such a demonstration. It was almost embarrassing. Then in a rare moment of something akin to sympathy, she wrapped her arm around the girl's waist and whispered, 'No speak,' in her ear.

She was little more than a child really. So long as she kept out of Lewis Thomas's way, Strong Arm might become a friend worth having.

'Friends?' she said, holding out a hand.

The girl stared at Violet's hand for an instant before clasping it tentatively in her own. 'Friends,' she repeated, presumably understanding the gesture, if not the word.

33

The clearing was lit by the glimmer of scattered campfires. Violet knelt by one, pouring a mug of tea from the billy, the firelight casting a golden glow over her features and framing her face in a spun silk halo. She put a hand up to her forehead and smoothed away a loose tendril of hair that was in danger of being caught by a stray cinder. On the other side of their campfire, the gesture caught Lewis's attention. He had been poking about with a stick in the coals, but now he looked up, meeting her eye through the flames. He seemed almost jittery this evening. When his hand had brushed hers earlier as he passed her a chunk of mutton, she caught his almost imperceptible intake of breath and was puzzled. Men usually made no secret of what they wanted. Why was he so diffident?

For months, since she had first met him, she hadn't been certain how Lewis felt about her. One minute he seemed charmed, the next wary, at times indifferent. Now she was beginning to suspect that he was repressing desire. Whether he did so out of gentlemanly respect or for want of privacy, she couldn't be sure. But she decided that she had had enough of his reticence. She wanted to get him alone. She wanted some hold over him. She wanted him to be hers. She wasn't sure yet for how long, but certainly until she found someone better. Only then would she feel safe.

'Lewis?'

'Violet?'

'There was something I wanted to show you. Something I discovered on my walk by the river earlier this evening,' she began hesitantly.

'Can it wait until morning? The ground is uneven by the river. I wouldn't want you to be hurt.'

'No. I don't think this can wait until morning. It might have repercussions for the remainder of the journey. It has to do with the men, you see.'

'You sound very mysterious. I suppose we shall have to investigate then.'

'I think it best.'

Violet retraced her footsteps along the riverbank, Lewis by her side. At one point she tripped over a fallen branch in the dark and he gripped her upper arm, his fingers firm upon her flesh. And when a strange cackling growl rent the night she flinched, moving closer to him.

'It's only a possum,' he said. 'It won't hurt you.'

'Are you sure?'

'The dangerous creatures are those you don't hear.'

They continued along the river, their path lit only by

the first glow of starlight, until they came to a tree that soared as high and wide as a church. So large that one could not fail to notice it. Taking his hand for the first time, she led him closer to the tree, so close that her back rested against its gnarled and battered trunk. She drew him towards her, saying, 'Look.'

'I'm looking.'

She could barely make out his features in the dark but she could hear the tension in his voice. With her free hand she lifted her arm above her head, so that her sleeve fell back to reveal her pale inner arm.

'See,' she said. She felt her breath quicken and a delicious warmth spread between her legs. 'See the mark.'

But he wasn't looking at the scarred tree. He couldn't tear his eyes from her. In an instant he had closed the space between them, so that his thighs touched hers, and she was glad for the loss of her petticoats.

'What mark?' he groaned, as he grasped her other wrist, forcing her hard against the tree. She felt his weight along the full length of her body as he pushed against her. She moved slightly, moulding herself better to his shape.

'The Chinaman's mark. Carved into the tree,' she whispered. 'What can it mean?'

For answer, he bent his head, their lips almost meeting. He hesitated, as if seeking her permission, then touched his lips to hers. At first their mouths met, light as the caress of a butterfly's wing, but when she parted her lips he increased the pressure, crushing her mouth to his, until she felt possessed. His hand slid down her arm, releasing it, and she wrapped both arms around him, exploring the hard muscles of his buttocks through rough spun trousers.

'You want me too.' It was a statement, not a question, and needed no answer. All the same, she answered him by unbuckling his woven leather belt, lifting his shirt and running her hands over the warm smooth skin of his back.

'Take off your corset.'

'Can't you feel? I'm not wearing one.' After her swim, she had slipped her dress over her chemise, and donned a single petticoat, wanting to luxuriate a little longer in the feeling of freedom.

He groaned again, and began fumbling with the buttons at the front of her dress. She helped him, longing to feel those rough palms cupping her breasts, sliding down her torso, exploring her most sensitive places. Her entire being quivered with desire and hot tongues of flame licked through her body. He felt her desire, sliding the dress from her shoulders to slip his hands beneath the neckline of her chemise and mould his hands upon her breasts. She shrugged her arms from the sleeves, her breath coming in gasps.

'Don't make me wait,' she whispered.

He released her breasts and she gasped again, missing his hands already. Then he hitched up her skirts, bunching them around her waist as his hands roved beneath, questing gently. Fingers trailed the length of her thigh then teased softly at her most intimate place. She tugged at his trousers to pull them down over the hard muscles of his buttocks and thighs. She wanted to brand his flesh with the imprints of her palms. To draw him even closer until they became one flesh. She pressed him to her so that there was no space left between them and she could feel him hot and hard against her.

'Now,' she said. The word was both command and supplication.

He lifted her from her feet, and imprisoned her against the massive tree, holding her there with his weight suspending her. She wrapped her legs around his body and rode him hard as he thrust inside her. Her hands clawed up his back as he thrust again, and again. She squeezed her thighs and pushed back against the tree, ignoring the rough bark as he drove into her. Faster now, every part of her body focused on the pleasure radiating from her centre. And then as she rode that wave of pleasure to its climax, she held him so tightly that he emitted a low animal sound from his throat as he convulsed in his own climax.

They remained where they were for a few moments, until their breathing slowed, before he released her. Then resting his forehead against her shoulder, his hands spread over the curve of her hips, he murmured, 'What have you done to me? You're a dangerous woman, Violet.'

To her surprise, she realised that she too was in danger, when she had set out to capture him. She sighed, letting her fingers rove his thick black hair. Even now that passion was spent, she longed to feel him inside her, something she had never experienced before. Usually she wanted to escape once the deed was done – she had never been one to bask in useless sentiment – and she wasn't sure that she liked the sensation. If there was one thing that had saved her from despair in her worst moments, it was remaining in control of her emotions. She might not be able to control others but she had always been able to govern herself. Now she had ventured into treacherous waters where she could not see the bottom, nor fathom how to reach shore.

Lewis raised his head, leaning back so that he could stare into her eyes. A sliver of moon had risen above the trees now, casting a blue glow over the forest, and creating deep shadows upon his face. 'Nothing I haven't wanted to do from the moment I met you,' he said.

'You could have fooled me. You barely speak to me.' For a time she had believed he was immune to her charms. Almost.

'I find it difficult to imagine that anyone could fool you. And words are overrated.'

'I like words,' she whispered.

'What would you have me say?'

'That's up to you, isn't it?'

'I…' he faltered. He looked at her quizzically, as if about to say more, then apparently thinking better of it, he stroked her cheek gently.

She wondered what he had been about to say. A declaration of some kind, perhaps? If she had read him truly, a declaration from a man like Lewis would be tantamount to a promise. She wanted that promise. She needed that promise, for without it she still had nothing. With it, she could begin to rebuild. She smiled, silently inviting him to kiss her. He lowered his head to hers, but, just as their lips were about to meet a sharp cry ruptured the night.

'That wasn't another possum, was it?' she asked.

'No. That wasn't a possum. That was a woman.'

34

Strong Arm waited until the sun had long disappeared behind the mighty trees before creeping from the camp. The ghost woman sat by the fire, making sweet couple talk with Thomas, the bullock man. Big Nose had fallen asleep in the tent they shared, and most of their fellow travellers were resting after another gruelling day of walking. She was still shaken by the events earlier that evening. From the moment the white-haired ghost woman had placed her hands upon her breasts, Strong Arm had been consumed by fear. It gnawed at her insides and churned her stomach so that she was sick with it. If the ghost woman exposed her, anything might happen. At the very least, news of a female impostor would travel far and wide, perhaps as far as the Middle Kingdom. As far as Kwangchow.

Perhaps even as far as Sandy Bottom Village.

The Wu lineage had a thousand arms. Arms that might reach all the way to New Gold Mountain. It would not take much for one of those arms to dispatch the vengeance that Big Wu's death demanded. If Young Wu should hear rumour of a woman amongst the gold seekers from the Middle Kingdom, he would suspect that she had escaped to New Gold Mountain along with Second Brother. He would send word to capture her and bring her home. Or... he would hunt her down himself. Perhaps he had already set out.

The thought of Young Wu sent a fresh wave of shivers through her body. The more she thought about him, the more he haunted her, just like his father. Except it was in her sleep that she saw the bloody head of Big Wu floating before her, whereas his son had come to her haunt her daylight hours. She thought about him at odd times; hearing his laugh when Big Nose made a joke; seeing his swagger in Thomas's long stride. Then there was that day when she had spotted his face amongst the crowd of men watching her fight. There had been no sign of him since. Was he a momentary vision, a symbol of her guilt, fear and... And how could he have known which ship she sailed upon, even if he had guessed where she was bound?

Why couldn't she stop thinking about him?

The moon was yet to rise but all she had to do was follow the river. She remembered the bend that cradled the pool, guarded by the great trees and the ring of boulders. She needed to escape the camp full of men, to find a place where she could be alone to think. To calm her trembling body and agitated thoughts before she did something foolish. She needed space to breathe, to cast off her fears and think rationally. And to be honest, seeing the other woman's clean bare flesh had made her long to immerse herself in the cool waters of the river. She had been on the road for so long, first the salt road of the sea, then the parched dusty trek through this alien land in the heat of summer. Splashing her arms with salt water, or dipping her face in well water, only made her feel dirtier. She longed to be truly clean, especially on those days like today when her body chose to remind her that she was a woman. These were the times when keeping her secret was most difficult. She had become practised at sneaking away into the bush when no one was looking.

It did not take long to reach the pool. She clambered down the bank, careful not to trip over any exposed tree root or rock. The moon had risen above the trees now, a sliver of silver amongst a field of stars. Strange stars, that belonged to another world. Standing at the pool's edge, she unbraided the long queue that hung down her back, freeing her dusty locks. One hand rested ruefully upon her bare scalp as she wondered if she would ever be able to regrow it. She scanned her surroundings to check that no one had followed then, hesitating for a solitary heartbeat, she cast off her smelly blue tunic and trousers. She set the soiled loincloth to soak in the shallows before plunging naked into the tingling waters of the river.

She let her body sink so that only her face showed above the surface, legs scraping the squelching at the bottom of the pool, head bent back so that her hair floated around the pale shimmering outline of her body in a black cloud. She closed her eyes, shutting out all thoughts of the Wus, the ghost woman, the past and the future. Water enveloped her ears so that the world around her grew silent. There was only now. She relaxed her limbs, allowing her body to float freely, unencumbered by guilt or debts of money or loyalty. If only she could always feel this freedom.

Suddenly, hands grasped her shoulders in an iron grip, shattering her peace. She cried out instinctively as she felt them touch her, before the hands pressed down upon her shoulders, pushing her entire head beneath the surface of the pool. Taken by surprise, she hadn't time to take a single breath before the water swallowed her. She dug in her heels, trying to find leverage, but they only sank deeper into the soft mud. Arms flailing, she fought to break her head above the surface, but her shoulders were held in a death grip. She twisted and jerked, trying to wrest her shoulders free, all the while fighting not to open her mouth and gasp for the air that her body craved. As her head grew dizzy with the effort and the lack of air, she fought like a wild thing, lashing out with her arms, trying to grab onto whoever was holding her down. She knew an overwhelming desperation to find air. Any way. Anywhere she could. Then, just as the urge to open her mouth became irresistible, the weight on her shoulders was released.

She surfaced gasping, air more imperative than flight or fight. Before she could recover her senses, she was grabbed from behind as strong arms wrapped around her, one at her waist, another collaring her neck and covering her mouth. Coarse fabric pressed against her back. Legs as inflexible as tree trunks restrained hers. A skull pressed hard against her cheekbone. She could not see her captor, but there was no doubt in her mind who held her.

'You killed my father,' he said.

She couldn't answer. What answer did she have that a Wu would accept?

'Slaughtered him like an animal in his own house.'

She tried to bite the hand, but he held her so close that she could only mouth at the palm with her lips.

'Why would you do such a thing, Little Cat? When all my father wanted was to ask you a question?'

But a Wu did not ask. He took.

'Now I have to kill you. My father's *po* has demanded it of me. My family has demanded it of me.'

She felt the hand about her waist slide upwards, grazing one breast as it slid further around her side to hold her even tighter, if that were possible. She bucked and twisted, trying to kick free with every muscle in her body. Not again.

'Before I kill you, I need you to tell me why. I only wanted to help you. Did you hate me so much? I thought you were coming to like me...' He paused for a second before continuing, 'I will let you speak, but the moment you cry out you are dead. Understand?'

She bobbed her head in assent with the fraction of

movement his grip allowed. He relaxed the hand covering her mouth, letting it slide over her chin to her neck where it held her throat in a firm grip.

'Now tell me why?'

Her voice, when she found it, was hoarse, constricted by the hand at her throat. 'Your father tried to force me. He tried to rape me.'

'You lie!'

'I... I... couldn't let him do that so I used what weapons I had.'

'I don't believe you.'

She was conscious of the knuckle of his thumb nudging the underside of her breast where the flesh was softest, as his fingers dug into her ribs. He held her so tight, her legs locked between his, his groin pressing against her hip, that there was no space between them. No room to manoeuvre or attack, and no way to disguise the fact that he wanted her. He wanted to kill her. But he wanted to fuck her too. She knew all about a man's wants from the other girls. For an infinitesimal moment this idea captured her thoughts and she imagined his arms wrapped about her in love, rather than in death. She felt his strong legs entwined with hers and the thought did not repel her. What was she thinking?

Disgusted with herself, she thrust the idea from her mind. She didn't want a man. Any man. She wanted to be a self-combed woman. And if she couldn't, then she would rather live disguised as a man, free to make her own choices. She certainly didn't want this man. He was a

Wu, like his father. He thought he could take whatever he chose, from whomever he wanted. But he wouldn't take her. She wouldn't bow down to the desires of any man. She was her own woman and she would kill... or die first.

'You think I would attack for no reason?' she asked.

She felt him hesitate, his grip relaxed for a fraction of a second, and she squirmed in his arms. But it was no use. In a fair fight she might be able to best him, despite what Second Brother had declared that day by the well, but this was no fair fight. He had ambushed her when her defences were down and now his greater strength would be her doom.

'If you're going to kill me, make it quick.'

'I have no choice,' he murmured. 'You gave me no choice.'

'You think your father gave me a choice?' She felt the pressure at her throat increase and she opened her eyes. She wouldn't go blindly to her death. 'Why don't you look at me as you kill me?' The hand at her throat muffled the words.

'If I look at you I am undone,' he groaned. 'I don't want to kill you, Little Cat, I—'

A shout from the riverbank cut off his words. 'Who's there!'

As swiftly as his hands had captured her, Young Wu relinquished his hold. 'I'll be back,' he hissed in her ear. Then, like a fox surprised at its prey, he turned and trotted across the river, retreating into the darkness of the trees on the opposite bank. Little Cat could do nothing but hunch her shaking body, trying to cover her nakedness with her hands. She didn't have the presence of mind to snatch up her clothes. In any case, it was already too late, for the man was even now crashing down the bank and splashing through the shallows to her side.

'What's happened here? Who attacked you?' asked the bullock man. He hadn't recognised her. Perhaps, if she kept her back to him she could keep her secret yet. 'Who are you?'

She could hear the confusion in his voice as he took in the long wet hair clinging to her naked back, the gentle curve of her waist, the suggestion of plumpness to her buttocks... then the shaved scalp of a man from the Middle Flowery Kingdom. She felt the water ripple as he waded around to her side so that he caught her profile in the light of the wan moon. She turned her head away, but not before a sharp intake of breath told her that he had recognised her.

'Lewis!' a female voice called from the riverbank. 'Who is it?' The white-haired woman approached too.

She heard the splash as he crossed the pool and back. He thrust a piece of clothing at her. It was her tunic. She took it gratefully, quickly pulling it over her head. Then he handed her the trousers, before wading back to the pool's edge. Keeping her head bowed, she followed him, donning her trousers as soon as she reached dry ground.

The Hartley woman had reached them now, scanning the pair in the dim light. 'It's that boy, isn't it? Or should I say... girl?'

'So it seems.'

'What happened to him… her?'

'That I have yet to discover. But one thing is certain…
I will.'

For the first time since Young Wu had pushed her
beneath the cold waters of the river, Strong Arm looked
up. The man gazed at her sternly but not unkindly, from
familiar black eyes. But the woman's pale eyes shone in
the moonlight, like those of a demon escaped from the
courts of Hell. She didn't know why, but this woman
was her enemy. Her lips professed friendship but her eyes
said something completely different. This thought did
not worry her unduly, for the Hartley woman, with her
skinny arms and helpless manner, was too weak to do
her much harm. Young Wu was another story. Somehow
he had discovered her whereabouts and followed her all
the way from the Middle Kingdom. He had hunted her
down like prey, and like prey he would pursue her to
the death. She would never be free of him. No matter
where she ran, no matter where she hid, she would
always be looking over her shoulder. She would struggle
to repay her debt to her family. The Wu family demanded
vengeance and Young Wu would deliver it. Only death
would end his quest.

But did his quest have to end with her death? If *he* were
to die, perhaps his quest would die with him. Then she
could disappear into this vast land, far from the other gold
seekers, far from the eyes of the Wus, and find another
way to help her family. This was an unpredictable land.

There were countless dangers at every turn. Anything might happen to a man far from his home across the seas and no one would ever discover what, or who, had been the cause. Perhaps this story might have an alternative ending after all.

She remembered hands holding her beneath the river, grasping her throat, pinioning her body. Then she thought of other hands. Sharp-nailed and liver-spotted. Clawing at her most vulnerable places, and in her mind they became one. And if a tiny voice sounding a lot like Little Cat whispered in her head, 'But he saved you when the river would have taken you,' she refused to listen.

If she were to live, Young Wu must die.

35

The giant trees towered over him, silhouetted against the vast net of stars. As he fought his way along the riverbank they taunted him with his smallness. He was a Wu and yet he was nothing to these ancient trees. He was nothing to the yellow-eyed creatures watching him from their branches. The girl still lived and he had failed in his duty to his father and the Wu ancestors. Soon the bullock driver would return to camp and prise the story, or a version of it, from her lips and by the time that happened, he and the old man must be gone.

Dry grass scratched his bare ankles and low hanging branches scraped his head as he skirted tree and boulder, breathing hard. He leaped over a fallen tree trunk, and scrambled down the grassy bank to recross the river, one *li* downstream from the place where he had confronted Little Cat. He had to reach camp and make his escape before he was caught. But that didn't mean he must abandon his quest. He and the old man could trail the group from afar, tracking their passage through valleys and forests, across plains and over mountains all the way to the goldfields. Twelve bullocks and two hundred and sixty men did not travel unnoticed. And if he lost the trail, he could follow the signs carved into trees by his predecessors, other men from the Middle Kingdom who had left warnings of wicked landowners who would exploit them, or kind men who might help, who pointed their countrymen towards New Gold Mountain.

He knew where they were headed, a place known as Creswick Creek. The name of the diggings caught in his throat. Little Cat would not escape him a third time.

'She didn't escape. You let her go.' The voice of his father's *po* came to him in the whooping call of an owl. He felt its looming presence in the shadows that closed in around him.

'The bullock driver interrupted me.'

'She was all but dead and you let her live. What kind of son are you?'

He remembered the way Little Cat had thrashed in his grasp as he held her beneath the water, powerless to escape. If he had only kept her there a while longer, she would be dead now. Instead he had succumbed to temptation. He had needed to hear her voice one last time, even if her words were poisoned with hatred. He could not resist the sensation of her body pressed against his. From the moment he had seen her floating naked in the pool, her flesh luminous as a pearl in the moonlight, he had been transfixed by her vulnerability.

A vulnerability he had never seen in her before. He had wanted to hold her. Cradle her. Protect her. Instead he had put cruel hands upon her and sought to take her life. If the bullock man hadn't come he would have squeezed her throat until her body was nothing but an empty shell.

'You could have finished her off even then.' He heard his father's words in the rustling of small creatures and the creak of ancient branches. 'Death comes quickly.'

He almost defended his inaction; Little Cat's words were lodged in his memory, but he could not bring himself to repeat her lie about his father. Big Wu could not have done what she said. His father was a righteous man, an honourable man, a man of *yee*.

'I could. I will,' he promised his father, the words emerging as a ragged gasp as he thrashed through the bush. What else did he have in his life other than his family and his clan?

Little Cat's vulnerability was a lie too, as deceptive as his own pretence at bravery. She had taken a lump of stone and smashed his father's head to splinters of bone. There was nothing vulnerable about her. Somehow he had been seduced by his friendship with her brother and the desires of his body. But he would not make that mistake again. He would not betray his ancestors or his loyalty to the clan a second time. He would prove his mettle to his father's *po*, if it were the last thing he did on this earth.

*

The bullock man sat on a log a small distance from the glowing coals of the campfire. He had roused Big Nose from the tent after cajoling the Hartley woman to her bed beneath the bullock dray. Clearly she did not wish to go, but he had insisted that she needed her rest to be fresh for another day of travelling on the morrow. Now he watched Strong Arm's face as he questioned her friend. There was no hint that he had betrayed her identity to Big Nose in his glance, merely concern. Perhaps she might yet keep part of her secret from her friend.

'I want to know the whole story. Tell the boy he is to leave out nothing.' His voice did not rise above a soft burr but she knew that he was determined to prise the truth from her.

Big Nose was rubbing his eyes, still half asleep. He looked from one to the other bemusedly. 'What happened, Mr Thomas?'

'Your friend here nearly got himself killed. I want to know by whom and why.'

Clearly whatever he was telling Big Nose was a shock, for his eyes widened and his mouth opened slightly. She supposed that learning your friend had been attacked and almost killed might be a shock if you were a man of peace like Big Nose.

'Thomas says you are in grave danger. He asks who is responsible,' he said.

She looked down at the ground, avoiding his eyes. 'No speak,' she whispered in the foreigners' tongue. She did not want to lie to her friend, but her existence was already a lie, a lie she had no intention of admitting. She could only hope that Thomas would not expose her.

'Tell the boy I will keep his secrets, but for the good of the camp I must know who attacked him and why. If this was the work of those bullies he fought earlier, I need to know so that I can put a stop to it.'

Big Nose relayed Thomas's words. 'If you have secrets, he will respect them. And so will I,' he added, with a hurt expression, as if to ask why she hadn't confided in him already. They were friends who had shared the perils of the road, their hopes and fears for the future. 'If you are in danger, you need to say. You are not alone here.'

'Crows everywhere are all black,' she said, making light of the danger. She did not want to tell more lies, yet how could she confess to Big Nose that she had killed a man? He was a person of restraint. He wouldn't understand, especially when she couldn't tell him the whole truth without giving away her identity.

'What did the boy say?'

'He says there are bad people everywhere.'

'Very enlightening. But I want to know about one particular bad person and we are going to sit here until I do.' Thomas folded his arms across his chest and stretched his powerful legs towards the fire. It appeared he was not to be moved.

Big Nose held out a hand as if he might place it upon her shoulder, then thought better of it and let it drop to his side. 'We all have secrets. We've all done things we regret. It's hard for minnows, like us, to survive in this world, where the bigger fish would snatch us up in one gulp.'

But she refused to live her life as a minnow. That was what got her to this land in the first place. If she had remained a minnow, she wouldn't be here. Big Wu would have swallowed her whole. And if not her, then he would have punished her family. He might haunt her dreams but she didn't regret fighting back. And she couldn't regret his death either. She could live with that ghost. The anger still raged inside when she thought about that day in Big Wu's house, and she wanted to lash out at him all over again. The only thing she regretted was the trouble she had caused her family. Perhaps she had become one of the crows now, since death meant so little to her.

'The man who attacked me seeks vengeance for his lineage,' she muttered finally. Big Nose would understand that.

'Why does he seek vengeance?' Big Nose translated Thomas's question after he had relayed her words.

Here was the truth of the matter then. If you put something into words, did that make it true? If you left it unsaid, did that make it false? Could she admit the truth even to herself? And why did Young Wu really seek vengeance? Because he wanted to kill her, or because others demanded her death? Truth wasn't a simple matter.

'He seeks vengeance because I killed his father, Wu, the headman of our village.' The words were a whisper of truth.

Big Nose greeted her explanation with silence, as if he

couldn't quite accept what he was hearing, as if it did not sit with his understanding of reality. He fixed his gaze upon the coals, avoiding her eyes, the red glow turning his familiar craggy face into a thing of shadows. Perhaps he would never look at her in quite the same way again. This thought wrenched something in her heart. She had so few friends now, she couldn't afford to lose him.

Thomas was glancing speculatively from one to the other of them. 'What did the boy say?' he asked, a wry twist to the side of his mouth.

Big Nose cleared his throat. 'He says that he killed that man's father.'

This was enough to unfold the bullock man's arms and bring him to his feet. He stalked towards her, coming to a standstill so close that she caught the scent of his animals upon him. She shuffled back a step.

'He must have had a reason. A boy doesn't kill a grown man without good reason.'

'Thomas asks the reason for this killing.'

'That man's father attacked me first. He was the headman of our village and the Wu clan elder. If I hadn't fought back I would not be here now.' Another partial truth. 'But now this man and his clan hunt me.'

Big Nose nodded, apparently accepting her explanation, but he still did not look at her. He began a short conversation with Thomas, who searched her face as Big Nose spoke the name of Wu, as if he could read her mind. He knew part of her secret, so perhaps he could guess the rest. After all, he must know the ways of men.

'He was tall, this man Wu, and will stand out from the others. We could search the camp for him but I suspect it would be futile. He'll be long gone by now. Tomorrow morning I'll ask your leader to make a headcount and then, at least, we'll know what name he has been using, and if he travels alone. But Strong Arm...'

Her new name sounded strange in the foreigner's tongue, as if he spoke of another person, not the girl Little Cat, or the boy Strong Arm, but someone altogether different. Someone she no longer knew.

'... you must not leave camp alone again. I cannot risk it.'

He had expected to find the old man snoring in their tent but he was awake, squatting by the glowing coals of their campfire, repairing a tear in Young Wu's other trousers. The blue fabric seemed even more coarse and colourless in the dim light, like a puddle of grey. Just like his life.

'Come. We must leave.'

'What has happened?' The old man knew of his mission but did not breathe the word 'kill' aloud, for who knew what ears listened to their conversation in the midst of this camp of tightly packed tents?

'Nothing. Nothing has happened. Something almost happened and that is why we must leave,' he said, grimacing in disgust at his failure, 'before leaving becomes impossible.'

Soft sounds of snoring emanated from beneath the

canvas where their tent mates slept. Leaving might disturb them, but their gear was packed and ready. All they need do was shoulder their *ta'am*, take up their baskets and head off into the night.

The old man hazarded a glance at the surrounding camp. He appeared almost fond, as if it saddened him to leave. 'I will fetch our baskets,' he said, creaking to his feet. 'There is always another opportunity, nephew. You will fulfil your vow.'

'I do not need you to tell me this, Old Man.'

He knew it only too well.

36

From the homestead veranda, Violet looked out over the grass-covered slopes of gently rolling hills and shallow valley, to the blue shadow of the craggy Grampians beyond. Here and there clumps of eucalyptus trees provided shelter for livestock, and shade for the Celestials who were encamped by the creek. Mere weeks earlier, she would have considered the rustic bluestone dwelling primitive, with its galvanised iron roof and undressed timber posts. Yet this simple house was a luxury compared to sleeping on hard ground beneath a dray, lulled to sleep by the lowing of bullocks and the pungent scent of their dung.

After they had crossed the Glenelg River at Gray's Crossing, their route to the goldfields had wound from one pastoral holding to another. Lewis avoided the towns and settlements – and therefore the police – where the Chinamen might be arrested for evading the poll tax if they were discovered. Naturally, some of the more venal pastoralists demanded payment for their silence. And with much of their workforce run off to the goldfields, the arrival of two hundred and sixty Celestials upon their doorstep was indeed a gift from heaven.

For Violet, the one blessing of an enforced stay upon this property was that the mistress had taken pity on the poor bedraggled governess who landed on her doorstep and lodged her in the homestead. Clearly, the gossip from South Australia was yet to reach the Glenelg shire or her welcome may not have been so warm. For a week, Violet had slept beneath cool white sheets and amused her hostess with tales of London society, while the Chinamen laboured to build a dam. With few tools, they dug enough clay earth to build an embankment across the creek. Their only payment was the pastoralist's silence and a few old ewes, which they promptly plunged into scalding water, plucking the wool like feathers from a duck.

She should have been glad for the respite. She should have been grateful for the woman's kind and cheerful company, especially after her previous humiliations. Yet she jumped at the scratch of a branch against the window. The hairs on her neck pricked at the sound of a man's voice on the veranda. She waited. She watched. She listened. She pined.

It would not do.

For the first few days she told herself that Lewis did not venture to her door in the wee hours for fear of being caught by their hosts and ruining her reputation. But he took to avoiding her even during daylight hours, refusing their hosts' invitation to luncheon at the homestead, pleading the need to keep an eye upon his charges. It did not escape her eyes that the girl, Strong Arm, was rarely from his side. While her countrymen laboured at digging and hauling earth, Lewis kept the girl close.

This afternoon Violet decided that the time had come to remedy the situation. From the homestead, she set off down the hill towards the creekside encampment, intending to remind him of her existence. She defied any man to ignore her when she stood before him in all her glory, as limited as that might be in this primitive land. She had arranged her hair into a neat bun at the nape of her neck, allowing a few tendrils to frame her heart-shaped face and draw attention to her cheekbones, yet nothing so elaborate that she might appear frivolous. Her sprigged muslin had tempted, but in the end she had donned a dull nankeen dress, with a calico apron borrowed from her hostess, and a smile as her only decoration. Against all inclination, she intended to look sturdy and capable – since that was what Lewis so clearly admired – no matter how greatly the costume offended her finer senses.

As she skipped over clumps of dry grass and scattered sheep droppings, the ocean of sheep parted before her. A single sheep veering from her path set the entire flock to stampeding, leaving in its wake a cloud of the nasty March flies she had learned to fear for their vicious bite. Something or other in this godforsaken land was always seeking to dine upon Violet's tender flesh, whether it was flies or mosquitoes, ants or spiders, fishes or snakes. She had soon learned that anything with more than four legs, or fewer than two, was to be avoided at all costs.

She spotted Lewis from a distance, despite his blue flannel shirt, not unlike that of John Chinaman. However, his broader, taller figure singled him out, as did the way his brown moleskin trousers fitted his sturdy thighs. He was standing shoulder to shoulder with one of the Celestials as they leaned over some business they were about in the dray, the rear of which had been propped upon a log. He appeared to sense her presence, for he lifted his head like an animal sniffing the wind, and turned to gaze up at the slope where she walked. Her heart lifted a trifle and she raised a hand in greeting, hurrying towards him.

As she drew closer, Violet recognised his companion as Strong Arm, and that slight lift of the heart slumped. What in this world drew him to the girl? She had few charms that Violet could discern. Her breasts were no more than cherries. Her eyes were bright, and their leaf shape was not unattractive, but her face was browned from the sun and her head, shaved bare at the crown, was as handsome as a boiled egg. She was strong, it was true – and her athleticism would not be out of place in Sanger's Circus – but she possessed few womanly charms. And it could not be denied that she hailed from the Middle Flowery Kingdom. Her appeal to a strapping, handsome man such as Lewis was a mystery. Violet comforted herself with the thought that perhaps he only looked to employ the girl as a shepherd on his pastoral lease, since labour was in such short supply. For what man would choose a child like Strong Arm when he was offered a woman like Violet?

'Halloo there, Lewis,' she called as she glided between the drooping branches of she-oak, trying to ignore the cloud of midges that swarmed around the creek.

'Good day, Miss Hartley,' he said, striding towards her. A milder woman would have taken this distant courtesy as insult. To Violet it came as a challenge.

'I've been missing our dinners of aged mutton and burnt damper.'

'Ha! I wager there'll be more before we reach our journey's end. So don't worry yourself.'

'I feared you'd tired of my poor culinary efforts.'

'Not at all. I thought you might enjoy a few comforts while you can.' Despite whatever promises he had made himself, he cast a surreptitious glance at her figure that she did not fail to catch. 'Unfortunately, the life of a bullocky isn't suited to a lady.'

What was he telling her? That there was no room in his life for a woman?

'Some ladies have no trouble with it,' she said, with a pointed look at the girl who had clambered up onto the dray and was bending over something there. He followed her gaze with a frown.

'Strong Arm tends a patient. One of the Chinamen is ill. Too ill to walk. He may not make it.'

Thus far they had lost five men upon their journey. Two had run off after the attack on Strong Arm at the Glenelg River, no doubt the perpetrator and a companion. Two had proved unequal to the long trek and fetched up at one of the pastoral leases to work as gardeners. And one unhappy fellow had strung a rope over a branch and hanged himself just outside Casterton. There had also been sickness and injury, but nothing life-threatening until now.

'I can help.' She wondered why he had not called upon her skills earlier. Why he kept her at such a distance.

Lewis pushed back his hat and rubbed at his forehead. Was she such a conundrum too?

'The man suffers dysentery.'

She gave him a quizzical look in return. 'I think I can handle it. Robetown was nothing if not an education into men's bodily functions,' she said with a light laugh.

'As you will. But Violet...'

'Yes?'

'Take care. I wouldn't want you to fall ill too.'

'Oh, I am as tough as... new boots,' she said. 'Embroidered blue silk damask with pearl buttons.'

She slid her arm though his, as if they set forth upon a walk through Hyde Park, strolling by the Serpentine, with its mild-mannered ducks and toy boats, rather than the dusty banks of this parched creek, where pink and grey parrots erupted screeching from trees and deadly snakes sunned themselves upon granite boulders. But she noticed none of this. She felt his nearness like a flutter in her belly and when his arm brushed against hers, her breath quickened.

'I'm glad I did not wear my Sunday best,' she said, trying to still her thoughts.

'Not the most practical for tending a man with dysentery.'

'You might have had to strip me down to my petticoats.'

'Violet, I'm sorry. I should never have compromised you... I...'

He closed his eyes against whatever he was thinking. When he opened them again, he drew her closer with a soft groan, so that their thighs touched and she felt the haze of lazy afternoon heat welling up inside her.

'I can't...'

Whatever he was going to say, he was interrupted by the voice of the girl calling out to him. 'Mr Thomas! Mr Thomas! Fever more bad. More blood.'

He pulled away, leaving her bereft. 'Duty calls.'

Ah yes, duty. An anathema to any sensible woman.

'Are you coming?' he asked, a nod of his head indicating the bullock dray settled beneath the shade of a spreading red gum.

Hesitating for the space of a single breath, she followed.

The smell of shit was overpowering. Poor Ah Hong's buttocks were slippery with it, and his forehead was slick with the sweat of his fever as he groaned and thrashed about in a delirium. Strong Arm tried her best to keep him clean and trickle as much water down his throat as possible but she wasn't practised in tending to the sick and felt inadequate to the task. There was no denying her squeamishness when it came to wiping the sick man's arse and the vomit from his chin. She knew that his sickness might be contagious and feared coming down with it. Not just for fear of illness, but also for fear that the entire camp would discover her secret.

To add to her anxiety, the Hartley woman had reappeared in the camp and was even now heading towards the dray with Thomas, a determined spring in her step. She had linked her arm through his as if to claim him, causing Strong Arm to blink in surprise. She had never imagined that a woman might pursue a man so openly. In her world, a woman must wait upon the decision of others when it came to marriage. The foreign woman behaved more like a man than a woman in her desires, yet she usually adorned herself as gaudily as any pampered warlord's concubine.

'How is he?' asked Thomas, appearing beside the bullock dray, the Hartley woman clinging to his arm. Since spending many days in his company, listening to his conversations with Big Nose, Strong Arm's understanding of the foreigner's tongue was growing daily.

'Ah Hong not good. He have blood.' She pointed to the faeces-stained rag. She may not have much medical knowledge but she knew blood in the faeces was a bad sign. The headman had a store of herbal remedies, from which she had made up a potion of dried anemone root to clear the damp heat from his organs, but the medicine was yet to have any effect. In the meantime, all she could do was keep the patient clean, try to replenish his fluids, and bathe his limbs to keep him as cool as possible. Her arms were tired and sore from carrying water, for not only did she have to tend her patient, she was washing her hands continually.

'Miss Hartley has offered to help you.'

She heard the woman's name and the word for 'help' and stared blankly. Perhaps she had misunderstood. Hartley doused herself daily with perfumed water. She did not deal in shit.

'Me,' said Hartley, tapping her own chest, 'help you.' She gestured rudely to Strong Arm with a pointing finger.

'Not need help,' Strong Arm said with a shake of her head. Hartley did not like her, of this fact she was sure. Sometimes she caught the woman staring at her as if she were an insect to be crushed beneath her shoe, although she did not know why. On a mere whim Hartley might denounce her to the entire company at any moment. When she discovered the woman was to stay in the house on the hill her spirits had lightened. And the past few days without her constant presence had been a relief for both her and Big Nose.

But that relief was clearly at an end. Thomas lifted both his shoulders in the gesture she had learned to read, like the saying 'the grass above the wall bends in whatever direction the wind blows'. Hartley was the wind and neither she nor Thomas could do much about where she would blow next. With her pale hair and milky skin, she might look as weak as any lotus-footed, indoor girl, but Hartley followed no law but her own. All Strong Arm could do was hope she blew herself out before she caused too much damage.

37

The light had gone out of Ah Hong's eyes hours before but he continued breathing, wandering in an opium-infused dream for his pain. Violet did not know where the poor man found the strength to keep going. In the four days since she had begun nursing him, he had lost so much weight that his flesh seemed to be melting from his bones and his face was little more than a skin-shrouded skull. He was too lethargic to eat, so the girl boiled up a watery rice porridge that they dripped into his mouth from a spoon. Soon enough, he could not swallow even that. His skin took on a yellow colour, and when he stopped passing water altogether they both knew that there was little more they could do. For four days she mopped his brow and wiped the filth from his body. Sometimes the smell was so bad that she used the last precious drops of her cologne to keep from vomiting. And after all that, he was going to die. She took it as a personal affront.

For the fifth time that day she was washing soiled

linen in a bucket far from the creek bank. Perhaps Ah Hong's illness had been caused by a miasma in the air or some tainted food, but Violet didn't wish to risk making the rest of their party sick by poisoning the creek with Ah Hong's bloody faeces so she busied herself hauling buckets of water with which to wash.

'You make a good nurse.' She heard Lewis's rich baritone behind her and turned to find him considering her perplexedly, as if this fact had taken him by surprise. What did he think she had been doing in Robetown all those months? Writing the men's letters home to China?

'Is that so strange?' she asked, looking down at her filthy apron.

'Oh, I don't doubt your compassion, Miss Hartley, but this,' he indicated the soiled rags in the bucket, 'is beyond the call of duty for any lady.'

'I thought I was Violet.'

'And how is our invalid?' he asked, ignoring her comment.

'It will not be long, I think.'

And so it wasn't. By the time the sun rose the next day, the poor man gave up his struggle while the rest of his countrymen were filling their bellies with their morning rice. Big Nose and Thomas dug a shallow grave on a rise overlooking the creek, for they needed to get him into the ground quickly in the heat. His tent mates bundled him into several layers of clothing and carried him up the hill upon a bier made of branches, the rest of the party following. Each of the mourners had tied a scrap of white cloth about their hat. Violet stood to one side watching as they set fire to a pile of thin white paper printed with their strange writing, and set out bowls of food and flickering candles beneath a sheltering tree. The girl, Strong Arm, bowed her head and did not try to hide the tears that streaked her face. Violet watched as Lewis put aside his shovel to exchange several words with her. She watched as he placed a comforting hand upon the girl's shoulder and whispered in her ear, their heads so close together that they might have been lovers.

They struck camp the following morning. Violet arrived from the homestead with her baggage to find Lewis yoking up the bullock team, Strong Arm working at his side. The bullock's yokes suffered so much wear and tear that Lewis had to replace them regularly, carving them from a log of stringybark. The yokes and chains had been laid out in a line the previous evening ready for departure and Lewis was calling each pair of bullocks forward to prepare them for the journey ahead.

'Come on in there, Bruiser. Come on, Taffy,' he coaxed the first pair forward with running patter. 'Easy there, Sailor... In you go, Dusty.'

As Lewis called each pair in with his deep, soothing voice, Strong Arm helped lay the yoke across their necks, before he fastened the bullock's bow beneath their throats and bolted it to the yoke, the two humans working together as seamlessly as the bullocks.

Once upon a time, on the other side of the world, Violet had little contact with animals, other than her employer's peevish lapdog, but after a month of travel through the Australian bush, she had become so intimate with the bullocks that they were on first name terms. Bruiser and Taffy were the responsible leaders who could be depended upon to follow Lewis's commands without too much grumbling. Clipper and Smoky, on the other hand, were the two 'polers' yoked closest to the dray. Older and heavier, they were strong enough to slow the load if it looked like running amok downhill. Sailor and Dusty were the temperamental, younger bullocks yoked in the middle of the team. These two would go for you, given half a chance, and Violet kept them at a polite distance.

'Good day, Lewis. Lovely day for a walk.'

He appeared to take her literally, turning his gaze briefly to the skies and saying, 'Looks like rain to me. You might want to wear a macintosh.'

Determined not to lose her smile at his less than enthusiastic greeting, she offered, 'May I be of assistance with the animals?'

'Oh, I think we have matters in hand here,' he answered.

38

Creswick, Victoria, 1857

All loans must be repaid in good faith.

Countrymen must be helped and protected.

Waterholes and creeks must be treated with care.

Camps must be kept clean.

Conveniences must be screened and maintained.

Claims may not be left unattended for more than one day.

Do not attract the attention of the Europeans.

Therefore:

Do not go without trousers.

Do not go bareheaded or barefooted.

Do not shout or cry out in anger.

Do not point or clench fists.

Do not fight or brawl.

The headman finished explaining the rules devised by the Sam Yap *kongsi* and regarded the assembled miners sternly. 'These rules are for all our benefit. The earth is blessed. The gods are generous.'

It was early and the usual cloud of opium did not yet haze the man's eyes. He coughed twice for emphasis, as if daring them to question the wisdom of their benefactor. Strong Arm took these new rules in her stride. She was accustomed to rules. When she thought back to her life in China, she realised she had been naive to think she could ever be free of rules. She could not evade the duties and obligations expected of her even if she combed up her hair and refused to marry. A self-combed woman might escape the rules of a mother-in-law, but she would still be bound by obligations to family, ancestors and clan. Not to mention the Emperor, his prefects and magistrates. If her life had been ruled by edict and custom in the Middle Kingdom, little had changed here in this wild and uncivilised land. They were just different rules.

Once she thought that if she could fight like a man, she might have a man's freedom. But these were the thoughts of a child. Men weren't free. They merely followed different rules to women. They still had to bow to the wishes of parents, clan and Emperor. They still had to live their lives bound by the expectations of others. Perhaps the only way to be truly free was to be alone in the wilderness, unfettered by duty and obligation. But if she were alone, with no one to talk to, no one to care for, that would be its own kind of prison. If there had been a brief moment by the ocean's shore when she had felt free, that feeling had quickly disappeared once she set out for the goldfields. Now the most she could hope for was the strength to do what she must.

The headman had switched to a more fatherly tone. 'The Sam Yap *kongsi* loves and protects all men from the three counties. It is your duty to love and protect one another in the name of the *kongsi*. Ours is a noble cause and happiness will be our reward.'

The Sam Yap *kongsi* represented all miners from the three counties of Nam Hoi, Poon Yue and her own county of Sun Dak. It ensured that the men from these three counties looked out for one another. But it also made the rules, tallied the gold, apportioned the spoils, collected the debts and issued fines. Until she could win enough gold to repay her debts, the Sam Yap *kongsi* essentially owned her. Even then, it would have a *lien* on her soul.

'Now, there is work to be done. May you find much gold for the benefit of China and all righteous men.' The headman waved the assembled men from Sam Yap back to their claims down in the valley.

When they first arrived, he had assigned each working group a patch of ground on which to pitch their tent. The tents were organised in squares of forty or fifty, with a space between each tent, and wide lanes between each square. The tent villages were pitched upon the higher ground, with the mining taking place around the gullies. She and Big Nose shared their tent with six other men, the same men they had eaten and slept with aboard ship, until Thomas had taken them under his protection. They were fortunate that the others welcomed them back, and for the most part they all got along – since not getting along would be troublesome – plus an English speaker like Big Nose was always useful in dealing with the foreigners.

Once the tents were established, the headman had sorted them into pairs and pointed each pair to another patch of earth that was to be their claim. This was where they were to dig for gold. To Strong Arm, the two patches of earth, for living and digging, had appeared little different. How did the headman know beneath which patch the river of gold ran? Did he have the ear of the gods? She could only take it on faith and hope that at least a tiny tributary of that river flowed beneath the claim allotted to her and Big Nose.

As the men drifted back to their claims after the headman's reading of the rules, she and Big Nose headed for the temple. It couldn't hurt to make an offering to bring them luck. It seemed like an auspicious moment. The Sam Yap temple was situated in the Black Lead Chinese Camp along with the temple of the neighbouring four counties, the See Yap. Temples, restaurants, a teashop, a herbalist, a scribe and several gambling and opium dens clung to each other in the small strip of buildings that made up the Black Lead camp, not far from the centre of Creswick town. The Sam Yap temple wasn't imposing, a small wooden structure, little more than a hut with a roof of bark shingles, and without even the tiniest sky well or courtyard. The poorest farmer in Sandy Bottom Village would be embarrassed to worship here, yet at least the builders had tried to embellish the roofline with carvings of dragons and phoenixes, and several brightly coloured banners fluttered from a flagpole outside.

Once inside, the familiar scent of incense assailed her nostrils, filling the cramped interior with smoke. She placed a simple offering of cooked rice and three cups of rice wine on the table set before the gods. Guan Di, Cai Shen and Guan Yin all looked down at her from their places upon the altar. But something in the way the trickle of light from the doorway lit their faces suggested that the deities were turning up their noses at the poor offerings placed before them. Strong Arm felt a pang of regret. Perhaps she should have sacrificed her share of breakfast too. Food was sparse and the miners made do with a little rice and whatever vegetables they could purchase from the Chinese market gardeners who had set up on the outskirts of the town. There was little left over for the gods.

Big Nose stepped over the wooden board that served as a doorsill and ducked inside. 'I gave Tu Di Gong the last of our salted duck,' he said, rubbing his stomach with regret. The shrine to Tu Di, the earth god, was situated under a straggling tree beside the temple, where the deity could watch over the diggings and protect the miners from misadventure. Mining, she had discovered soon after arriving, was a dangerous business. When it rained, the hapless miners might fall and drown in flooded shafts. When it didn't rain, they might die suffocated by falling earth. They might wander dazed or drunk into one of the many dams or water races that had been dug to bring water to the diggings. They might wander into the path of a stray bullet. And then there was the danger of foul air if they tunnelled deep enough into the earth.

She and Big Nose lit several sticks of incense, bowing three times before placing the smoking joss sticks in the brazier. Perhaps the gods would look kindly on them, despite their poor offerings, for they would need all the luck and protection they could get if they were to make their fortunes in this crowded, noisy camp, with its confusing list of rules. Presumably the rule against fighting also included killing, which happened to be exactly what Strong Arm had in mind as she knelt on the beaten earth floor of the temple prostrating herself before Guan Di. Surely the god of war would understand her need to defend herself. Surely he would forgive her. In his mortal life he had once been a great general. As a young man he had killed a magistrate to rescue a young girl. Surely Guan Di would understand her need to protect herself from Young Wu. If she didn't kill him, sooner or later he would kill her. This fact was as clear as the harsh and brilliant sky in this southern land.

'Are you all right?' Big Nose was looking at her strangely and she realised that her eyes had filled with tears. She rubbed them away with the sleeve of her tunic. 'I am your friend. I wouldn't share your secrets with anyone,' he added.

So... she had not shared her secrets but he suspected that she had them. 'It is safer for you if you don't know,' she said.

'What use is safety without trust, Strong Arm?' he asked with a hurt expression. 'I know there is something important that you aren't telling me.'

She wanted to tell him. She wanted to unburden herself. But if he looked hurt at her secrets, how much more disappointed would he be if he knew the truth? If he knew how great was her deception? She could not face his disappointment. Not yet. One day, perhaps.

She sighed, saying, 'We are far from home. Do you think the gods can find us so far from the Middle Kingdom?' She could not admit the real reason for her tears, not even to herself – for that way lay weakness – but she could admit to homesickness. They all understood this. They had all left parents, wives, or children to seek their fortunes on New Gold Mountain.

'The gods can find us anywhere, if they want. That does not mean they will,' he said. That the gods were fickle was well known. Even the most splendid offerings did not guarantee their benevolence, and splendid offerings were scarce around here. 'You are worried that your attacker will return,' Big Nose added, reading her mind.

She counted herself lucky to have him as a friend and hoped he would not be hurt by what she planned to do. She had already hurt Second Brother. How would she forgive herself if she ruined her friend's life too? But if she didn't act, she might never have the chance to repay her family. Elder Brother and Siu Wan would not be able to marry. Her parents might lose their livelihood. And

Second Brother would never be free to follow his dreams.

'It would not be difficult to track a team of bullocks and two hundred and sixty men through the wilderness. They do not go quietly,' she said, remembering the way the beasts crashed through scrub, and heaved through heavy mud.

'He cannot murder you in the midst of all these people. As long as you stay with the group you will be safe. And perhaps in time the situation will resolve itself.'

'Perhaps. If the gods will.' She borrowed a gesture from Thomas, that lift of the shoulders signifying acceptance of whatever might come. Except she knew that it was a lie. She could never be a woman of *wu wei* as the sages advised. She could never wait to see how things turned out and then adjust for them, nor let life's current take her where it willed. She would always be striving. Fighting. Forcing her way. This was her burden and her gift.

'Come. We'd better return before we are missed,' she said.

She followed Big Nose as he wound his way across the pockmarked earth to their claim. Rank after rank of tents lined the ridges, while the slopes of the Creswick Creek valley and the lesser gullies radiating from it resembled a battlefield. Wherever she turned, the ground was piled up in heaps of yellow clay, excavated from a thousand narrow shafts. Massive tree trunks lay scattered about. The trees had been felled for fuel, or to prevent them crashing down when the diggers undermined their roots. And as the diggers marched further along the valley, more trees disappeared, until the distant woodland stood like a grey-green wall at the far edge of the diggings.

Strong Arm and Big Nose's shaft was round, as broad as two men's shoulders, with precarious toeholds cleft into its walls. Somewhere below, the gold ran in the bed of an ancient underground stream. Some of the deeper shafts were fitted with windlasses to help lug the valuable earth to the surface, but theirs was too shallow yet to necessitate a windlass. She had soon learned that the object of this mining business was to dig until the seam of gold bottomed out. If your claim was large, you could then tunnel where the gold led. If, like most of her countrymen, your claim was shoulder to shoulder with another, you abandoned the depleted shaft to dig elsewhere once you had sieved through the excavated earth. All the dirt must be sluiced with water to separate the gold, from the tiniest grains, to the small pellets... to the greatest nuggets.

Today, Big Nose was digging while she took her turn hauling dirt to the nearest waterhole, where she washed it in a cradle; a wooden box that rocked the gold like a number-one son. Her shoulders ached as she carried the buckets on either end of her *ta'am* down to the banks of the muddy waterhole. If the journey from Robe had left her footsore, and the death of Ah Hong had left her heartsore, mining for gold caused her muscles to scream in protest. But she supposed this torture was small punishment for her crimes.

Stopping halfway down the slope, she set her burden

to the ground to rest her neck and shoulders. Here the diggings spread before her in all their chaos, so different to the green and ordered groves of her homeland. Strewn with fallen trees, pitted with craters and buckled by ridges of earth, the ground stretched out in a scarred and tumultuous landscape. A place to be wary of traps and pitfalls. A place where danger lay but a step away. A place where anything might happen and no one would ever be the wiser.

39

The *Ballarat Star* – Friday, April 4, 1857

Requirements:

A Lady, recently arrived from London, and formerly employed as governess to the Earl of Chetwynd's grandchildren, seeks position as governess to respectable family in the Creswick Creek area.

Apply in writing to V., at Anthony's American Hotel, Creswick.

The advertisement was positioned on the last page of the newspaper, squeezed between a notice proclaiming 'good bricks for sale at Frewin and Miller's Brick Yard, Ballarat', and an announcement that the 'very best position in the Township of Creswick' was to be let. It was small and discreet, as befitted a young woman of good family, and several pence cheaper than a front-page position. Violet was not displeased, but so far it had yielded little response, other than a single enquiry from one Mr T, asking if she was willing to work under canvas, and instruct a family of eleven.

She thought not.

Replacing the newspaper upon a table in the modest salon of Anthony's Hotel, she reassured herself that it had been less than a fortnight since her advertisement first appeared, and there were many outlying farms and settlements whose residents probably rode to town but once a week. Something was sure to come along. And if it didn't, she could always follow the example of the Misses Crowther of Ballarat, and open a small day and boarding school, if she could find money for the premises. Her small store of sovereigns was becoming rapidly depleted, with even the least salubrious premises setting an extortionate sum for board.

The accommodations at Mr Anthony's hotel and boarding house were somewhat primitive, but then so was the entire township. But at least she no longer slept in a tent or under a bullock dray. Scattered timber buildings lined a broad and dusty street, and the surrounding settlement of tents and bark shanties sprawled over rolling country that had been largely denuded of trees. The more comfortable of these temporary dwellings were distinguished by the addition of a mud-brick chimney, while others made do with a ring of stones for a fireplace. Many of the tents and shanties had set up as businesses selling tea, coffee, sugar, tobacco and other necessities, while others operated as 'sly grog' shops masquerading as coffee tents and lemonade stalls, to escape the government prohibition of alcohol amongst the diggings. Their proprietors sold watered-down brandy and gin, and from what Violet had seen of all the broken bottles lying about, the goldfields were largely populated by the inebriated.

With little else to do on this fine and pleasant day, she donned her favourite dress and bonnet, buttoned her jacket, opened her parasol, and proceeded up the main street, intent on attracting notice. Her presence might be a more effective form of advertisement than a few dry words in a newspaper. Indeed, it had not escaped her notice that men outnumbered women in the town by a factor of at least three to every one, with most of these women being plump matrons with a brood of children and very little dress sense, or more enterprising females of dubious respectability. For the most part they were garbed in hues of indigo and dun, so that Violet felt obligated to present the prettiest picture possible in this brown and dusty town.

Beyond the main street and the diggers' encampments, the land rolled away in a series of wooded hills and gullies. The Chinese Camp at the Black Lead was situated a short distance from town, on the south side of the creek, where the Chinamen had established a large pool for sluicing the gold dirt. From what she had seen, the Celestials comprised half the population of the town, their numbers so great that she no longer attempted to differentiate between one blue-clad Celestial and another.

Besides, after more than a month of overland travel,

she was not sorry to see the last of them, especially after the unfortunate death of Ah Hong. For four days and nights she had wiped the sweat from his brow, the vomit from his chin and other more putrid excrescences from his nether parts, only to have the ungrateful fellow die on her. It was enough to bring tears to her eyes.

It did not take long to happen upon a team of twelve bullocks and their Welsh driver outside Roger's Hotel. The township was not large, and after a few polite enquiries she soon learned that Lewis had returned with a load of beer from the Phoenix brewery near Ballarat and was unloading barrels outside the hotel. Coincidentally, on the very route of her stroll, which was not difficult since the town consisted of a single main street and a couple of dusty lanes crossing it.

More than a fortnight had passed since their arrival and Lewis was still here. He could have returned to the other side of the Grampians, tending to his pastures and his sheep. He could have returned to Robetown for another party of Chinamen. But he hadn't. Perhaps she was deceived by his courtesy. Perhaps there remained a stronger attraction in Creswick. Perhaps she might win him yet.

The bullocks stood placidly as the man in question hoisted a barrel from the wagon and rolled it through the hotel door, handling the heavy barrel with ease. She had heard that he would depart soon with a load of wheat and oats for the port of Geelong, before travelling onward to the Western district and home. She might never see him again. The thought made her furious. She had expected a gentle wooing. Followed most probably by a proposal. She had thought him a gentleman. But instead he had cast her aside. Something she had vowed never to allow again. If nothing else, he owed her an explanation. And if she could get him alone, he owed her so much more.

She approached the lead bullocks and removed one of her lace gloves. She scratched the nearest furry white forehead, while avoiding the animal's long curving horns. It dipped its head obligingly to make the scratching easier, nudging her side with its nose.

'Easy there, Taffy, my glove isn't luncheon,' she said, swatting away the inquisitive bullock's nose.

'Getting reacquainted?' said Lewis, returning from the murky interior of the hotel. There were patches under his arms and the bright handkerchief tied at his neck was damp with sweat. He smelled of the road.

'I think he likes me.' Taffy's partner Bruiser sidled towards her, nudging Taffy closer. 'Easy there, Bruiser,' she laughed. She did not back away.

He leaned a hand upon the veranda post of the hotel and considered her with his head on one side. 'It seems Taffy's not your only admirer.'

'I could be forgiven for thinking so.' She challenged him with her eyes and the lift of her chin. How dare he ignore her for so long?

'When we set out upon our journey, I never imagined you might take a liking to the beasts,' he said, ignoring the challenge.

'Beasts have their uses.'

'Now there's the Violet Hartley I know,' he said, tipping back his head and laughing, exposing the smooth brown skin of his throat and the bump of his Adam's apple. She wanted to smother his throat with kisses, or slash it. She wasn't sure which yet.

'But then you know very little about me, Lewis Thomas. You only think you know.' He might think he knew her mind, because he had known her body, but like all her acquaintance, he only knew the face she chose to show him. He did not know her secret self. That would be far too dangerous for both of them. He did not know that she sometimes woke shivering in the night, wondering if this was to be her life forever. Exiled from her home, hanging onto the last threads of respectability by a fingernail. Retaining the last shreds of gentility with a pitiful few sovereigns.

'I should have been born a man. Then I would not have to apologise for love.' The words emerged in a low growl, slipping from her tongue before she could call them back. For a solitary breath, she was so shocked at what she had revealed that she stood with her lips still parted in an 'o' of surprise. But she quickly righted herself with a derisive laugh, saying, 'We all have our fantasies, I expect. Even you.'

He was silent for a moment, as if reading the truth of her life on her face. 'You deserve more, Violet.' She did. She deserved so much more. She had been fighting for more all her life.

'I deserve an explanation, certainly.'

He sighed. 'You do. But not here in front of the entire town. It will only cause talk if we're seen to be arguing.'

Arguing? Is that how he described a conversation about love?

'And for "a Lady recently arrived from London", that could prove unhelpful.' He smiled and she had to stop herself from taking a step towards him, stop herself from reaching up to caress his cheek... or slap it. Both had their appeal.

'You saw my notice then.'

'I did. I mentioned it to Mr Randall, who owns several public houses in Ballarat. He and his wife have two children and another on the way, plus a home and a pastoral lease on the Creek Road. A man with a business on the up and a growing family has to be in need of a governess. I thought it might suit.'

'Perhaps.' She concentrated on stroking the bullock's forehead. 'And my explanation?'

'Tomorrow night, once the diggers are fully occupied getting drunk, I'll meet you outside your hotel after sundown and we'll take a stroll in the fresh night air.'

40

Fat Lu was looking a little fatter than he had the last time Young Wu saw him. Despite the long overland trek and his exertions with pick and shovel, he had gained an extra chin in the weeks since they had last met face to face, most probably courtesy of Young Wu's cash. His tunic now strained at the shoulders and he was panting heavily from the short walk out to Slaty Creek from the town.

'Why'd we have to meet so far from the Black Lead?' he said, wiping the sweat from his brow with his sleeve. 'You could have saved me the walk.'

Young Wu hesitated before he replied. So... it seemed that neither the girl nor the bullock driver had spread news of his attack at the river, otherwise his reason for meeting here would be self-evident. 'I don't want to make it easy for the boy or his friend. If they knew my uncle and I were here in New Gold Mountain, they would be more vigilant. That's why I paid a messenger to find you. The boy knows both our faces.'

'We are on important business for the Wu clan,' said his 'uncle', puffing out his old-man chest. 'We cannot afford to risk failure.'

His 'uncle' always had to stick his nose in where it wasn't wanted. If the old man hadn't got himself so well known, Young Wu might have been able to slip through the Chinese camp unnoticed. But in the short time they had been on the road with Little Cat, he had made himself acquainted with everyone in their party. Even now, he had befriended most of the Chinese diggers out along Slaty Creek, and not a few of the Europeans. To make matters worse, he had learned to speak some of the foreigners' tongue and loved nothing better than to practise his new-found skill over a bottle of their fiery gin.

'What kind of business?' Fat Lu narrowed his eyes and jutted his lower lip.

'Nothing you need concern yourself with,' Young Wu replied, placing his hands upon his hips and raising his chin in a gesture he had learned from his father. Fat Lu wasn't the only one who could display belligerence. 'You will be paid well for any information you bring us. That is your only concern.' He nodded to the old man, who opened the pouch at his waist and dropped a coin onto the other man's palm, as a sign of more to come.

'Well, he knows you are here now,' said Fat Lu, closing his fist over the coins. 'He asked me to bring you a message.'

'How did he know to ask you?' asked Young Wu. For

a moment he was shocked. Despite all his care, Little Cat had spotted him again. Then again, she would expect that he follow her. He had vowed to follow her to the death. But how could she know that Fat Lu was his associate?

'Perhaps Strong Arm is smarter than he looks,' said the old man, glancing conspiratorially at his nephew. 'He must have guessed we paid Fat Lu to start the fight with the mixed-egg boy.'

'And perhaps you talk too much, old man! You are always blowing wind up a cow. It is your tattle that has alerted the boy.' Young Wu regretted his words as soon as they were uttered but he could not take them back. Even if he could, he wouldn't. That way lay weakness, the quality his father most despised. He was thousands of *li* from his father's house, yet he still felt his presence.

Your father is dead, he reminded himself.

'I may be dead but I will be with you always,' said his father's *po*, so that he was tempted to put his fingers in his ears. Except that would be futile, since the voice was inside his head. In his head his father was always watching. Judging.

He shook off his father's voice to find Fat Lu regarding him with a shocked expression that he should speak thus to his elder. The other diggers remained under the impression that the old man was indeed his uncle, rather than a distant and lowly cousin. No nephew should speak with such disrespect. Meanwhile, that same uncle's shoulders slumped and his face drooped.

'It's just as well that my father is headman of our

village and clan elder. And that I am his first-born son. It's just as well that you were second-born,' he said.

Except his father was dead, and the gatekeeper was not. His father despised him, and the gatekeeper treated him with kindness and affection. 'It's just as well that you did not father children, for what could you hope to give them?'

The old man bowed his head in shame so that Young Wu saw the deep-etched creases in the back of his neck, creases earned through many decades of hard toil.

'I'm sorry, nephew. You are correct. This old man talks too much.'

Fat Lu did not bother to chase an answer to his question about their business. One foot had taken to tapping restlessly as if he could not wait to be gone from their presence and he stole a nervous sideways look at Young Wu.

'Enough of this talk. What was the boy's message?' Young Wu folded his arms across his chest, looking down his nose at the fisherman and his uncle.

'He wants to talk. He says there must be another way to conclude your business. One that is mutually satisfying.'

'Hmmmph!' scoffed Young Wu. 'There is only one way to conclude my father's business with the Mo boy.' His father's *po* and the ancestors would accept nothing less than a life for the life taken. 'But perhaps I could meet with him.'

'He says he'll be waiting for you at the fork where Slaty Creek meets Creswick Creek tomorrow night at dusk.

Now I must go or those greedy bastards will have eaten all the rice.' His chins wobbled as he nodded his head to the old man. To Young Wu he offered no farewell.

Young Wu watched him thread his way through the sparse trees lining the creek bank, as he headed back towards the township. Beside him, the old man did not lift his eyes from the ground. For all his sixty or more years, he usually vibrated with energy. He was always ready for the next task, the next challenge. He took life as an adventure. He never complained that he was tired. Now, in the space of a few moments, Young Wu saw that he had grown old. His tunic hung from his shoulders like washing from a line. And his wrists poked out from his sleeves bony and frail. Young Wu's harsh words had stolen all his *qi*.

He knew that the old man had only been trying to help. Everything he did was in an effort to help, even all his talking and gossiping. Young Wu was surprised to find himself saddened at his retainer's shame and his own behaviour. When had he become so proud and unforgiving? How could he be a man of *yee*, a righteous man, if he wasn't also a man of *ren*? The great sage taught that to be righteous, one must also be benevolent and loving. When had he turned into his father? It struck him then that his father was not a loving man. Was he also then unrighteous?

But this thought was too much for him to process. It went against eighteen years of duty and respect. He turned to his uncle saying, 'We had better get some rice into our bellies too.'

'I will set a fire, Master,' said the old man, his voice flat with acceptance. Harsh words were his lot in life, after all. When had he begun caring how he was treated? At the house of Recommended Man Wu, he had been called much worse and did not blink.

Young Wu realised that he had become attached to the gatekeeper. He realised that if he died tomorrow, the only person who would truly mourn him was his lowly dependant, the gatekeeper Wu. His mother and sisters might mourn the loss of a first-born son and brother to carry on the family name, and keep the relatives from the door, but they would not mourn his passing. Once upon a time, his friend Ah Yong would have mourned his death, and even Little Cat might have shed a tear. Now Ah Yong hated him, and Little Cat lived in fear of him.

The old man had become more of a father to him than Big Wu had ever been. Advising him, challenging him, sharing his hardships and helping him to achieve what he must without complaint.

'I'm sorry, Uncle,' he said, dropping to his knees. Above his head a passing wind rustled the leaves of a tree and tickled his bare scalp.

'No need for that,' said the old man, waving him to his feet with a shake of his head.

'Forgive me. I'm the one who talks too much. I'm the one who speaks out of turn. A thousand pardons. I'm a worthless son and an ungrateful nephew.' He bowed his head to the stony ground.

'We are tired. We have travelled far to finish your father's business.'

He felt a light touch to his shoulder, and then a hand under his elbow as his uncle urged him to stand. He looked up into the old man's face, expecting to find sorrow or resignation. Instead he found a gap-toothed smile. *'Jat Jai.'*

Brother's son, the old man called him.

'I think we may be more than tired before this business is finished, *Suk Suk*.'

41

Violet paced the confines of the cramped room with its narrow iron cot and bare timber walls like a nervous mare, thanking providence that she was not yet reduced to sleeping in one of the tented boarding houses that had sprung up on the goldfields. In these salubrious accommodations, the boarders slept on log couches no more than a foot and a half wide, paying the outrageous sum of five shillings a week for the privilege. But if her luck did not change soon... well, she preferred not to think about that. Better to escape the room and her thoughts. Both were making her anxious. Wrapping a paisley shawl about her shoulders against the cooler autumn night, she stepped out of Mr Anthony's boarding house into the long shadows of dusk. She would walk off her agitation before Lewis arrived. She intended to be in complete possession of her emotions when they met. Her head must rule her heart, because her treacherous heart could not be trusted.

Up and down Albert Street candlelight flickered behind windows and the street bustled with miners heading for the legal drinking establishments of the township and the more questionable establishments of the camps. Most of them gave her a second and third look as she set off down the street towards the creek, but she ignored them. Even one man's polite 'good evening' was rewarded with barely a smile. She did not have the heart to be charming this evening. Something was wrong with her. Her limbs tingled. Her skin prickled. Her body fairly twitched with impatience, no matter how sternly she told herself to remain calm. Lewis Thomas was just a bullocky with a struggling sheep farm somewhere out in the wilderness. No doubt he lived in a bark humpy like the rest of the poor dirt farmers. He should not be provoking this reaction. He had got her to the goldfields. Now she could be done with him. Thoughts of the bullocky were only distracting her from securing her future. And she did not have the luxury of walking off that precipice.

That was what she told herself as she set off down the street, avoiding the swaying miners who had imbibed too much, too early. Avoiding the glances of women who sashayed openly about the town soliciting business.

'Looking for business, love?' one insolent woman with brassy blonde hair and rouged cheeks called as she passed by, and her colleague burst into gales of laughter. Violet crossed to the other side of the street, determined not to think about how they had come to their occupations. Their business was none of hers.

She continued along the road, each of her senses on high alert, which was perhaps why she recognised some familiarity about one of the many Celestials hurrying past her. He looked little different to hundreds of his countrymen, with his long black queue and shaved crown, rough tunic and baggy trousers, the straw slippers slapping upon his feet, but there was some fineness about the curve of his chin, some delicacy about the ankles that begged her notice, hinting that he was in fact a she.

Violet wasn't surprised to see the girl hurrying down Albert Street. There were Chinese stores here as well as in the Black Lead camp. What surprised her was that Strong Arm was heading away from the town, in the opposite direction to the Black Lead, and she did not have her big-nosed friend as chaperone. The two were always together, and yet she had ventured from the camp alone.

Picking up her pace, Violet followed.

The girl continued along the road for a short way, keeping her head down so that she did not have to engage with any passer-by. There was nothing casual about her walk. Her pace was brisk, her direction sure. She knew where she was going. All alone, risking discovery. Or worse. Especially after her previous close call at the river. She must have a very good reason. Leaving the last of the straggling settlement, the girl abandoned the path, taking to rough ground. What was she up to out here alone in the burgeoning night? Violet had always suspected her of harbouring more secrets than she would admit to. She suspected that Lewis knew more of those secrets than he divulged as well. On the road they were so often together, their heads bent over some business or other. Despite their lack of a common language they seemed to understand one another. They seemed to have a common compact.

Violet's skin twitched in sudden realisation and she cursed herself for a fool. The bullocky was camped out along Slaty Creek, somewhere in this direction. The bullocky who, for his own mysterious reasons, had shown such care for her. Well, that mystery was now plain as day to Violet. To think that she had tried to be a friend to that duplicitous girl.

Following fifty yards behind, she picked her way around shafts and puddles, until the girl came to a halt at the confluence of two creeks. Their waters were muddied by the army of miners who had been at work here. What had once been a picturesque meeting of two meandering creeks now resembled a battlefield, with hummocks of earth and shell holes pitting the nearby ground. Not unlike the hostilities that raged inside Violet at this very moment.

The girl stopped to scan her surroundings. Searching for someone, someone who awaited her. The diggings were mostly deserted by this time of the day. After the hum of the town it was strangely silent, without even the usual bush night noises, for the ground had been cleared of vegetation. There was no rustling of small animals or screeching of birds. There was little tree cover either, apart from a few straggling she-oaks and an enormous grandfather red gum that would have taken ten men to chop down. Its trunk and lower branches were gnarled and burred and its roots snaked crookedly towards the polluted waters of the creek.

But the diggings weren't completely deserted. Someone waited for the girl beneath the red gum's sprawling branches. The man was facing away from the town and the approaching girl, looking up to the darkening sky as if searching for something in its vastness. At first, Violet thought that the man was Lewis Thomas. But this was her fear talking. For, in fact, the man beneath the ancient tree was another Chinaman, taller than the girl and most of his countrymen, with the bearing of a soldier.

Violet ducked behind a hummock of earth, hoping that she would not be seen in the deepening shadows. She peered out across the muddy creek to the man, who had now turned at the sound of the girl's footsteps as she crossed the plank of wood laid over the creek. Even from this distance she could see the tension in his body as Strong Arm approached. He stiffened, pulling back his shoulders, almost imperceptibly thrusting out his chest and lifting his chin, and Violet had to stifle a giggle. The pose was subtle but she had an instinct for these matters. And the Chinaman, it seemed, wasn't so different to any other man she knew, preening like a peacock for his hen. Whatever he intended, and whatever the girl was doing here... this John Chinaman wanted her.

The girl stopped a few feet from the man and they

exchanged words. Even if Violet had been able to understand their sing-song language, they were too far away to hear clearly. The conversation drifted to her like the murmur of distant music. After some discussion, the man turned and headed out along the banks of Slaty Creek towards Cabbage Tree Hill. The girl followed at his side, keeping him at arm's length. Between them lay a thick blanket of subterfuge, and they both glanced about them, not wanting to be seen, searching for somewhere hidden from the view of others.

Each step pressed cold hard steel against the warm skin of her stomach. She was so conscious of the knife tucked beneath the waistband of her trousers that she felt sure Young Wu must notice her awkwardness. The cold metal was a reminder of her deceit. Yet steel might prove the only way forward. What if her twin was right and she could not beat him in a fair fight? She had bested the fishermen but they were untrained bullies. Young Wu and her brothers had practised kung fu from childhood, and he was bigger and stronger than her. She remembered the feel of his long muscular legs entwined with hers at the river, the crush of his chest against hers. The memory was ingrained upon her flesh. A woman's flesh garbed as a man.

Her life, and her family's future, depended upon tonight's outcome. She may have no choice but to resort to trickery and let the gods be her judge, for she was damned already. What difference would one more death make?

He walked beside and slightly ahead of her, sure-footed through the scarred landscape. He did not glance back, confident that she followed, trusting that she would not attack precipitously but wait for the proper moment. He swaggered with all the arrogance of the Wus, instinctively avoiding the gaping shafts that pitted the earth. He seemed to know where he was heading, somewhere distant from the view of other diggers. To their right the ground was higher and she could see the outline of the foreigners' tents silhouetted against the dying sun, tents cobbled together from whatever they could scrounge. The more organised had procured canvas, while others made do with sheets of bark, bits of tin and raw bullock-hides. Soon they would be far enough away to bring an end to things. For by silent agreement they both knew that a reckoning must be had. Their destinies were entwined.

'There is a place nearby where we will not be seen,' he said, indicating the way ahead with a nod.

She followed as he turned his back on the creek and distant tents to climb a slight rise that flattened out to a narrow ridge. Here he stopped and faced her.

'I did not want this to happen, Little Cat. Or should I call you Strong Arm?' Despite the power in his body, she saw that his hands trembled.

'You are very confident you will defeat me,' she said.

'I have the gods and ancestors of the Wu lineage on my side. And you are only a girl.'

'Once I was a girl but I am a woman now.' A strong and resourceful woman who had survived a treacherous journey amidst two hundred men. 'I am not so easily defeated. You would do better to go away from here and let matters lie.'

'What kind of son does not avenge his father's death?'

'Then you must accept the consequences.'

She had already placed her feet in a fighting stance, slightly side-on to Young Wu. Now she brought her arms to the ready, bent loosely at her sides, hands open. With a brisk nod, he copied her action and so it began, their limbs following each other in a complicated dance. Their arms circled the other, extending and retreating. She let her senses feel for an opening in his defences as he sought the gap in hers. When he took the first opportunity to strike, punching straight for her, she blocked him with fingers thrust out. When she struck, he blocked her blow with his forearm. But they were merely feeling each other out, testing each other's strength and speed for the real fight to come.

She tried to calm her mind and let instinct take over. All those years of training with Second Brother had taught her the necessary movements but she had had little practice of late. She needed to reach deep within herself so that her body could find its centre once more.

Slowing the movement of her arms, she allowed Young Wu to strike, then at the last moment turned her wrist so that his blow slid away. Taken by surprise, he adjusted his weight to control his momentum, giving her a tiny window of opportunity in which to kick out at his knee with her leg. But it did not hold him for long. Righting himself, he flew towards her, surprising her with his speed so that his punch connected with her chin before she could block it. Reeling backwards, she spun in a circle and kicked out at his chest but he ducked beneath her leg and returned her kick with a front kick to the groin.

They had fought their way down the slope now, spinning and twisting, kicking and punching, neither able to land a blow hard enough to inflict serious damage. In skill they were evenly matched, but Strong Arm knew that her opponent's greater strength would eventually wear her down. Her breath coming in gasps, she tried to slow the fight but Young Wu responded by speeding up his attack, sensing her fatigue.

'Why did it have to be this way?' he groaned as he panted with exertion, and in his voice she heard the rasp of pain and sorrow.

'Because your father attacked me. Because he violated me. Because he...' a sob caught in her throat, '... forced his penis inside me and took away my power.' She could finally admit it. 'He stole the only thing that was truly mine. How could I not kill him for that?' How could she not bludgeon him over and over with the stone seal that bore his name, until he lay in a creeping puddle of his own blood? How could she not be glad that he was dead after he had defiled her?

She could not stop Young Wu with her kicks but her words halted him. He stood facing her, breathing hard, an expression of disbelief upon his face.

'It isn't true! He would not do that!'

'Why? Why else would I kill him? Why can't you believe me?'

'Because I asked him to arrange a match between us, because I begged him to let us marry... My father would not violate the girl I loved!'

His words emerged as a howl and in that moment Strong Arm saw his vulnerability. He had opened himself to her attack and instinct responded. Drawing the knife from her waistband, she lunged towards him. He was her brother's friend. He was her childhood companion. In another life, he might have been her lover. In another life, she too might have loved him.

The realisation stole her breath away and she hesitated. At the moment her knife should have plunged between his ribs and slid into his heart, she relaxed her fingers and let the blade drop to the ground. She could not kill him, not even to save her life or repay her debt to her family.

In that same instant when she realised that she too loved him, he must have caught the gleam of metal in her hand. Grabbing her wrist, he pulled her towards him so that she felt the length of his body pressed against her. She felt the beating of his heart, hammering out his grief. Then with all the power of his anguish, he spun her out and around, releasing her when their arms were stretched to their full extent. The momentum carried her backwards, flailing for control, as she felt her feet leave the earth. Then all she knew was the sensation of falling and the hard smack of her back and head landing at the bottom of a shaft, as all breath and sense was knocked out of her.

It had all happened so fast that Young Wu did not have time to think. He could only act. When he spotted the knife in Little Cat's hand, his fighter's reflexes took over, performing a movement he had practised a hundred times. Snatching her wrist, he used her forward momentum to propel her out and around, then released her to fly backwards, giving him time to position himself for a renewed attack as she regained her balance. He did not mean to kill her. Despite his vow to avenge his father, he realised now that he could never kill her. He would rather die.

But by the time he saw her drop the knife it was too late. By the time his brain registered her open hand, she was already falling.

Young Wu had never moved more quickly in his life, yet he wasn't quick enough to save her. As he reached out to grab her arm, her leg, her trousers, any part of her, she was already disappearing over the lip of the shaft. If it had been one of his countrymen's shafts she might have been saved by its small circumference, but she fell into one of the large rectangular holes dug by the European miners. The thud of her landing was echoed by the thud of his heart as he realised what had happened. He stood at the edge of the shaft peering down to the shadowy bottom. He could just make out the shape of her, lying motionless about twenty *chi* down.

'Little Cat!' he called into the silence. 'Little Cat!'

There was no answer and no movement. He waited a short while and called again. 'Little Cat.'

She was brave. Annoyingly so, it was true, yet she could never be anything else. That was her nature. Difficult and disobedient and a terrible dancer, yet he wanted to hold her close and never let her down again. His father had violated her and now he might have finished what his father began. It was a long way to fall and she lay so still. What if she were dead?

Never in his life had he felt such a torrent of emotion, not even when he found his father's lifeless body lying in a pool of congealing blood. His body shook with it. His mind whirled with it. His heart ached with it. Dropping to his knees at the edge of the shaft, he leaned out into the dark hole, trembling with anger at his father's betrayal. He had come to accept that his father wasn't the righteous man he had once believed him to be. He realised that Big Wu might well abuse his power over a vulnerable girl. Yet how could his father have defiled the girl his son wished to marry? How could he steal love from his son? He accepted the truth of his father's actions now. That day by the river when Little Cat first told him, he had refused to see it. But nothing else made any sense.

Little Cat wasn't a killer. She was a fighter. She would fight to save herself or those she cared about but she would not kill unprovoked. And she had dropped the knife. She did not want to kill him, just as he could not bring himself to kill her that day by the river.

Perhaps, despite all that had happened, she too might love him.

'Little Cat.' He breathed her name. He wanted to shout and rage and rend his clothes but he could not give into fear and grief now. Not while there was a chance that she might yet live.

42

When Violet arrived back at the American Hotel a smile played unconsciously at the corner of her mouth. She had been wrong about Strong Arm meeting the bullocky. She was meeting someone entirely other, someone with whom Violet did not need to be concerned. The girl had seemed uneasy, it was true, but Violet suspected from the tension in the two Celestials' manner that she was also in love. It was clear that they knew each other well. Perhaps the man was a friend from her village. Could it be that she had followed him here? What other reason would a girl from the Middle Kingdom have for disguising herself as a boy and exposing herself to the dangers of journeying so far alone, in the midst of thousands of men? Look what happened to her at the Glenelg River. One error of judgement and she had almost been killed, or at the very least, ravished.

But love often called more stridently than good judgement, as Violet knew to her shame. She had vowed never to heed it again and yet... here she was, breathless with anticipation before her rendezvous with a Welsh bullocky. But that was different. He was different. This time she would speak of love like one man of business to another. And then they would arrive at a satisfactory arrangement. She would not be taken for a fool again.

'Back again, love?' the yellow-haired woman cawed as she hurried down the street towards Anthony's Hotel. 'Where's your man then?'

Her man would be waiting for her. Just as Strong Arm's man had waited. Violet supposed that a woman might find the Celestial attractive. From what she could observe in the fading light, his features were broad and regular with high cheekbones and a solid neck. He had a certain swagger about him if you could overlook his odd hair. But then all the Celestials wore their hair in a long plait with a shaved crown. Strong Arm might well find him acceptable.

She wondered if Lewis would say the same about the situation. He had an annoying concern for the girl. Sometimes she wondered if that concern bordered on attraction. But what red-blooded Welshman would hanker after a skinny Chinese girl garbed in shapeless blue rags when Violet was to hand? No, his concern was no doubt of the fatherly variety. There was nothing fatherly about his concern for Violet. At least, that was what she told herself as she spotted the man leaning against the veranda post outside her hotel.

'Am I late?' she asked. She noted that he had changed

his moleskins for the occasion and wore a blue serge coat against the cooler night air. Damn, the man. Why did he have to look so handsome?

'A lady's prerogative.'

'Prerogative? That's a fancy word for a simple bullock driver,' she said.

'Ah well, I wasn't always a bullock driver.' He offered her his arm. 'It's a beautiful evening. Shall we walk?'

They strolled arm in arm down the wide main street. Lewis was courteous but oddly distant. He wore the air of a man who had ordered a new suit because he could not pay his tailor. But Violet was not about to be dunned.

'I hear you return to the Glenelg shire soon. I had thought you may have formed attachments here.'

'It's past time. I've been gone too long. I can't be sure my shepherds haven't up and left for the goldfields. Though they're good men and have been with me for years.'

'And you were going to leave without saying goodbye.' She stared up at him with a smile that didn't quite reach her eyes.

He shook his head. 'I'm not a good prospect, Violet,' he said. Like her, he ignored polite convention and got straight to the point. Then again, their friendship had been hardly conventional. She had travelled across country with him for five weeks, two hundred and sixty Chinamen as chaperone. She had tended a dying man to impress him. She had wrapped her legs about his hips and let him love her.

'I'm not prospecting,' she said.

No, she had done with that, she realised. She wanted to find a sure thing before it was too late. Before she exhausted her finest attributes. She did not want to find herself poor and alone at five and fifty, making over her gowns year after year until they were threadbare, little boys chasing after her in the street hurling unkind words or worse. She did not want to be the joke of the parish. She wanted a roof over her head and a man who had the gumption to go places and take her with him. Lewis could be that man. He might not be rich but he was ambitious. More importantly he was here, with no evidence of a wife.

In return she would give him her love, her loyalty and all that remained of her youth. It wasn't a bad bargain. Moreover, there was something that neither could ignore, a heat that radiated between them. Violet knew when a man wanted her. Lewis might crook his arm through hers and hold her at a discreet distance, but she could not miss the tension in his body that betrayed the effort it took not to pull her close.

'To be frank, Violet, I have to find £640 to buy my homestead outright or I'll lose it to someone else. The remainder of the run is leased from the government and if I don't make some improvements I may lose that too. Wool alone isn't going to pay my costs. Every penny I scrape together driving bullocks goes towards that purchase, and making the necessary enhancements,' he said, his mouth set in a hard line. 'I will not lose my land again.'

Clearly, there was more to the story than he was telling her, some history that had nothing to do with her. Some wound from his past.

'What do you mean, you will not lose it again?'

He heaved a sigh in answer.

'You made love to me, Lewis. I won't pretend that I was an innocent, but you took advantage of my vulnerable situation. I trusted you. I think you owe me an explanation, at least.'

'Ah, it's an old story...'

'But it's your story.'

'Well, if you insist. My brother and I had a farm once. More a manor than a farm, with considerable landholdings in the Welsh vales. After my father died, my brother and I inherited. But my brother, being the elder, inherited the greater share, and also control over the management. And he lost it.' He paused in the telling, and she nodded encouragement.

'Gambled most of it away, squandered the remainder on fine clothes, fancy carriages and fancier women. I had to sell my last holdings to save him from the debtors' prison.' She could feel his arm rigid as it held hers, the muscles taut with the memory.

'I don't see what that has to do with you and me,' she said, turning to look up into his eyes. 'I don't expect a manor in Wales.' Although it would be nice, she would be content to make do for the moment.

They had reached the edge of town now, where an ancient gum tree threw its shade over the street during the hottest part of the day. With the dusk, it loomed over the ramshackle town like a protective giant. Drawing her behind the tree, he released her arm and swung around to face her.

'You're a beautiful woman, Violet. Any man would be proud to have you as his wife. But I can't provide you with the comforts you deserve.'

'But you were happy for me to comfort you.'

'What can I say? I can only apologise and assure you that it won't happen again.' His voice rasped the words. 'But I can't promise to make a life with you.'

She didn't have to pretend anger or tears. They fell freely, rolling down her cheeks, fat and glistening and dripping onto her collarbone. She had given him her body but he had stolen her heart. And now she required payment.

He made to comfort her, taking her by the shoulders and drawing her towards him. But she shook him off. 'No. You're all the same.'

'If you need money—'

'Not everything is about money! Sometimes it's about self-preservation. And sometimes it may even be about love.'

'And this time?' he asked.

This time? For the blink of an eye, the flutter of an eyelash, the beat of a heart, she had thought this time might be different.

'The last thing I want is to hurt you.'

'It would take a more callous man than you to hurt me.'

Her shoulders shook with shame remembered, disappointments suffered. Her entire adult life she had walked a tightrope between respectability and shame, until that day when she had fallen. Fallen so far that she might never have risen again. Even now she heard the shrill screech of the earl's daughter calling her 'whore' as her husband buttoned his trousers and escaped the room. She felt the cold stone of the steps through the thin muslin of her gown where the footman had deposited her like unwanted baggage. She saw the scandalised glances of neighbours and passers-by as she avoided their eyes.

She had come to this land to pick herself up. To make herself anew. She had thought Lewis might be the one to help her but she should have known better. She could only rely upon herself. She stood, hugging her quaking shoulders, half hoping she was wrong, that he would change his mind. But she had been too strong in fending him off. This time, when she needed him to hold her, he stood back.

'I'm sorry, Violet.'

'I'm the one who is sorry.'

'You're a strong woman, difficult and demanding, but more resilient than I would have guessed. I wish I could be the man for you, but I can't give you a fine house, a carriage and servants. I can't give you the life you want, the life you deserve. If I take a wife I will need a woman to help me build a life from nothing.'

'I could have been that woman.'

'I don't think so. You would tire of the life. Tire of being a bullocky's wife.'

So... he needed a woman to help him build. A woman accustomed to hardship. A woman with a strong arm and a fierce will. A woman like... Suddenly, it occurred to her that the reason he had lingered in Creswick wasn't for her. She had let love blind her to a truth she should have seen upon their journey. She should have listened to instinct, but she let love blind her to a slim girl with leaf-shaped brown eyes, black hair and trousers.

'If it's the China girl you want, you're too late.'

'What do you mean?'

She looked away with a toss of her curls.

'What do you mean?' he asked, taking her chin in his hand and turning her to face him.

'You're hurting me.'

'I would never hurt you. I...'

'You've already hurt me. More than once.'

'Do you know something about Strong Arm?' She hated the expression of fear in his eyes, his open lips waiting upon her answer when they should have been waiting for her kiss.

'With her lover, I presume. I saw them meet at sundown. From the way they looked at each other there was little doubt what they had in mind.' She cast the words at him like a stone.

'What did he look like, this man you saw her meet?' He brought his other hand up to her face now. The grip on her chin was firm, cradled by his hands, and she hated him for his concern.

'He was tall for a Celestial,' she said with a shrug, 'taller than her. With a broad face and the build of a soldier.'

'Oh, Violet, what have you done? Why didn't you tell me this before?' He dropped his hands to his sides, staring at her with a mixture of fear and disappointment. 'If I'm not mistaken, this is the same man who tried to strangle her at the river. The same man who has followed her all the way from China. This man isn't her lover. He's her killer.'

'No. That can't be true.' She had seen the way they looked at each other. She had seen the man preen for the girl. She couldn't have been mistaken.

'Where did you see them?'

'Out along Slaty Creek, beneath the old red gum where the two creeks meet. Then they walked in the direction of Cabbage Tree Hill. I thought they were seeking somewhere secluded to…'

'Somewhere secluded for him to finish what he started. Strong Arm killed his father after the old man attacked her. He has hunted her across half the globe. This man won't rest until he has his vengeance.'

She thought of the way the two had walked side by side yet apart. Had the man forced the girl to go with him? Did he have a weapon? Had Violet seen a pair of lovers because that was what she wanted to see?

Lewis snatched up her wrist, holding it in a tight grip. 'You're coming with me.'

'Where are we going?'

'I'm going to find her,' he said, patting the breast pocket where she knew he carried his revolver. 'And you're going to show me the way.'

Violet heaved a great sigh and rolled her eyes. 'If I must.'

43

'Little Cat has fallen down a shaft and isn't moving.'

He got the words out so quickly that he wasn't sure that his uncle had heard him at first. The old man looked up from his place by the campfire, where he squatted on his haunches cooking up some vegetables. The flames cast his face into a moving picture of ridges and furrows. When Young Wu spoke, the furrows on his forehead seemed to writhe in incomprehension.

'She may be dead.'

The old man nodded, making a small noise in his throat. Young Wu wasn't sure whether it was a noise of approbation or sorrow. 'We had better move her then. If the white ghosts find her they will start asking questions. The headmen will not like that. I will get the handcart.'

'Is that all you have to say, Uncle?' His heart still pounded, as much from fear as his wild run through the diggings.

'If she is dead, we must bury her where no one will find the body.'

Young Wu realised he was waiting. 'Don't you have an opinion? You have opinions on everything else.'

The old man bowed his head, staring into his pan of vegetables. 'I no longer know, *Jat Jai*. I no longer know if the Wus are worthy of this killing.' He removed the vegetables from the fire, setting the pan on a flat rock. 'It is easier to have opinions on simple matters. In important matters, perhaps we must trust the *tao* to show us the way.'

Young Wu took a deep breath. The old man was right, in his roundabout way. This was a time to follow instinct, to follow what the universe was telling him. Despite everything, he loved Little Cat. And she had dropped the knife. She couldn't bring herself to kill him. His father had betrayed both of them. And now the woman he loved lay at the bottom of a deep hole in need of his help.

'Perhaps this too is a simple matter,' he said, turning back towards the creek and Little Cat's resting place beyond. 'Go fetch the doctor and bring him to our tent, Uncle.'

'Where are you going?'

'To the other side of the creek. I will pull Little Cat from the shaft. If she lives I will carry her here. If she is dead, we will say the doctor is for me.'

Strong Arm opened her eyes to darkness and the smell of earth. When her vision adjusted, she realised that a small patch of that darkness was lit by distant pinpricks of light. At the same moment she became aware that every part of her body was hurting. Her head thumped as if it had been hit by a rock. Every muscle in her back was rigid with pain. And apart from the faraway lights, the blackness was so thick she could almost feel it pressing down upon her. She moved her head. A mistake, as needles of pain shot up her neck. She twitched her sides, a safer option. Both arms lay close to her sides. She reached out with her left arm, feeling rough grit beneath her fingers as it slid away from her body. It did not get far before touching a wall of earth. She tried the right arm with the same result.

She was in a hole of some kind, perhaps a well. A square well. Gazing up into the darkness, she realised that those distant pinpricks were stars. Perhaps if she called out, Second Brother's face would appear at the lip of the well, laughing at her predicament. He would call her '*fai mui*' and then he would find a way to get her out. She held onto this thought for a few moments, enjoying the feel of it, the warm notion of home and safety. But instinctively she knew that it wasn't true. Unlike the well at home in Sandy Bottom Village, this one was empty of water and it lacked the mossy smell of wet bricks. It was wider, too, and square, where her well was round.

She gasped involuntarily as she recalled the truth, sending another shooting pain through her ribs. Her head hadn't been hit by a rock; the rock had been hit by her head. Now she lay at the bottom of a mineshaft on the diggings at New Gold Mountain. She had been in a fight with Young Wu. They had tried to kill each other and he had pushed her into this hole. He might return at any time to finish what he had started.

But he said he loved her. He asked Big Wu to speak to her father about marriage. How could he kill her if he loved her?

Except that he was the swaggering son of the headman and she was a lowly silk reeler in his clan's silk filature. He had always treated her like a troublesome child who needed to be a taught a lesson. And then she had gone and killed his father. How could he love her?

She tried to recall his face as he confessed his feelings for her. There had been so much pain at his father's actions that she might almost have missed the yearning that lit his eyes, if she hadn't recognised it for the same feeling locked away in a hidden corner of her heart. He wanted her, as she had denied wanting him to herself. It was possible that he might love her. Was it also possible that she might love him?

She rolled these thoughts around in her mind like a dried plum on her tongue. Sweet, salty and sour, all at the same time. She no longer knew what to believe. So she must prepare for anything.

He barely noticed the weight of the handcart as it skipped over the uneven ground. His *qi* fizzed through his body, giving wings to his feet. They had pitched their tent far from the Slaty Creek camp, on a ridge at the very edge of the diggings. Yet he covered the distance between the tent and the shaft where Little Cat lay in the time it took to boil water for tea. The bare earth, the blanket of stars above, and the rhythm of the turning wheel felt so like a dream that he might have imagined the battle with the girl he loved. He might have imagined that she lay like the dead in a deep dark hole. But when he arrived at the shaft and looked down, she was still there. He could just make out the dim outline of a body, lying motionless at the bottom. The woman he loved was merely a subtle alteration in the depth of blackness.

Setting down the handcart close to the edge, he unreeled a length of rope that was attached to the windlass and dropped it into the hole. Then he crouched down, searching for the toeholds that were carved into the side. When he had found them, he knelt facing away from the shaft and shifted one leg over the brink and down, placing his foot in the first of the toeholds. It was a slow climb down in the dark, feeling for each precarious shelf with hands and feet, conscious that they might crumble at any moment and deposit him and a deluge of earth on top of Little Cat. Perhaps burying them both forever.

He did not mind so much for himself. If Little Cat died, there would be nothing left to live for anyway. He would have to face his father in Hell, or the next life, sooner or later. That reckoning could be postponed but not denied. But he would rather face that battle than see Little Cat die, either by his hand or by misadventure. He could not lose her. He didn't want to live in a world without her, even if she despised him. Whether he lived or died, his love for her had made him a man. Her strength had given him strength to become his own man, rather than his father's son.

One foot touched earth rather than air, and he realised that he had reached the bottom of the shaft. He lowered his other foot carefully, not wishing to stand on Little Cat. Then, kneeling at her side, he placed a tentative hand upon her chest. She lay so still that he feared it might already be too late. Yet despite her long fall and hard landing, he was relieved to detect the slow rise and fall of her chest. She may have broken bones, or worse, but she was alive. He must trust to the gods now.

He searched the darkness for the rope, which dangled against one wall of the shaft. Lifting her upper body gently, he wrapped the rope beneath her arms twice and tied it securely. Her journey to the top would not be comfortable, but hopefully it would be safe. He scaled the wall of the shaft once more, pulling himself over the edge and leaping to his feet. The windlass groaned in protest as he tried to turn the handle. He leaned all his weight into it, breathing a sigh of relief when it began to turn, the rope creaking as it slowly hoisted up Little Cat's body. His muscles strained with the effort, but he ignored the pain. When she reached the top, he gripped the handle with his left hand and reached out over the abyss to gather her to him with the other, hooking a leg around the pole of the windlass to anchor himself.

For a moment, he wondered if he would be able to hold her weight with a single arm, but he knew that he must for there was no one else to help him. He alone was responsible for her life.

Releasing the handle, he took her full weight with his right arm, hugging her to his body, then levered them both to safety using the power of legs and torso. Standing upright at the brink once more, he wrapped her in both arms and held her close, nestling his head upon her shoulder in a brief respite. During all his exertions, she had not moved nor made a sound. To all intents, she was as lifeless as a puppet. Yet he felt the soft breeze of her breath against his cheek and her heart danced against his chest.

He lifted her onto the handcart to lie curled up like a sleeping child. Then he grasped the handles and prepared to carry her to the tent where he hoped the doctor would be waiting. Her weight was distributed awkwardly, but he couldn't do anything about that now. He put his back into the task and heaved, pushing off with a grunt of effort. Once it got going, the handcart bumped and wobbled around the mullock heaps, skirting gaping holes, as he headed in the direction of the creek where his tent lay up a rise on the other side. Steadying the cart, he braced for the descent into a gully. In the distance campfires flickered like fireflies, while ahead the bush beckoned. Dark. Silent. Secluded enough to hide a secret forever.

The gully's banks were ridged with erosion where the miners had been at work. A makeshift plank bridge spanned the trickle of water at the bottom. The gully wasn't deep but its banks were steep. If he faltered, the cart would escape, hurtling over the uneven ground to fling Little Cat into the creek. He paused for a moment to catch his breath, looking up into the night. But the skies of this southern land did not offer any comfort. He would have to count on himself.

He started down the slope cautiously, taking small steps. But the cart dragged him forward, intent on yanking him from his feet. Gathering speed, it rumbled over a ridge of earth before becoming briefly airborne so that Little Cat slid sideways, threatening to topple them both. Straining his entire body to stop her from sliding off, he twisted his forearms, battling her weight and the cart's momentum. Then, in a semi-crouch, he used the power of his legs to halt the runaway cart.

Breathing hard, he rested halfway down the gully's bank, the cart stable for the moment. But one of Little Cat's legs now dangled over the edge, the foot bare and covered with scratches. He took her leg by the ankle to place it back where it belonged and its heat sent a jolt through his arm.

Cradling her leg, he felt a dense mass fill his throat, as if everything that had happened in the past year was rising up to choke him. His eyes were drawn to her figure – arms crossed haphazardly over her chest, a single braid draped about her neck – and he felt hot tears well. How had it come to this? How had they found themselves so far from the ordered groves and rice paddies of the mighty Pearl River? Why had the gods of the Celestial Kingdom abandoned them?

'How did it come to this, Little Cat? Why didn't we trust each other?'

They had been friends of a sort once.

She heard the tears in his voice and flicked open an eyelid. It had been difficult to remain silent as her body was jolted across the uneven terrain, but she had done so, despite the agony wrought by every bump. Even more difficult when he cradled her foot in his hand. Now at the sound of his pain she could no longer resist opening her eyes to spy him standing vague and shadowy against the starlit sky. His shoulders were hunched, his head buried in his hands. His voice, as he spoke her name, was gruff with sadness.

Yet intuition warned her again that he was a Wu, and not to be trusted.

'Why did I listen to my father?' he pleaded with the sky.

Despite her misgivings, she couldn't ignore the lure of his physical presence. She had matched him blow for blow. She had felt her naked body held tight against him. She had felt his hands crushing her throat. There were some urges more powerful than intuition. Despite their history, despite her pain and her doubts, she wanted to reach out and touch the smooth brown skin of his cheek and tell him that everything would be all right. She wanted to feel him hold her close. She did not want to fight him.

'Everybody listened to Big Wu,' she whispered.

'Little Cat! You are awake.' He crouched by the side of the handcart, caressing her face, searching her eyes in the darkness. 'Where do you hurt?'

'Everywhere. I think I have broken a rib. But I will live. If you let me.'

'I didn't mean for you to fall. I only wanted to stop you from killing me...'

She raised an arm to put her finger to his lips, but thought better of it when her entire body protested. 'I know.' Her mouth was the only part of her that did not hurt.

'My family will disown me. My father's *po* will haunt me. But I can't kill you.'

'I can't kill you either,' she said. She thought of Elder Brother with his shy glances at Siu Wan, and realised there were many ways to love. Not killing each other was simply one of them. 'But if I have to spend another moment in this handcart I might change my mind.'

'If I lift you out, can you walk?'

'If I can lean on you.'

She slid her other leg over the edge of the handcart as he moved his arms beneath her upper body and slowly sat her up. She winced, watching as he mirrored her pain.

'This might hurt,' he said, preparing to stand her up.

'I will put my arms around your neck.' She placed her hands around the back of his neck and felt him loosen his hold on her ribs. Then he stood, all her weight hanging from his neck so that she felt the muscles straining with the effort. He had become even stronger since she had seen him last. He was more man than boy now.

When they were both standing, she let her hands slide from his neck and down over his back so that their arms locked around each other's waists. The pain in her ribs faded, replaced by a dull ache in her deepest valley.

So this was the feeling the older girls described when they talked about playing at clouds and rain. She moved closer, pressing herself against his jade stem and he moaned as if in pain.

'Now I have hurt you,' she said.

'I could bear this agony every day of my life.' He ran his hands down over her hips, pulling her hard against him. Ignoring the pain, she clung to him.

'We cannot be together,' she murmured in his ear, letting her tongue lap the salt on his skin.

'I will tell my family that you are dead.'

'Then you will have to return home.'

'I will tell them I plan to stay and dig for gold. Grow the family prosperity to honour my father,' he said, touching his lips to hers.

It was a nice thought, but futile. She leaned back, so that she could see his handsome face. She might not have many more chances. 'You are Big Wu's only son. They will send someone to find you... and then they will find me,' she whispered, shaking her head as she spoke.

'We will go away. We will...' He took her face in his hands, caressing the fine bones of her neck.

She kissed his lips to silence him. She felt as if every

sensation in her body was focused on her lips touching his. She wanted to glue her body to his so that they would never be parted. So that she could hold this feeling forever.

She also knew that they could not fight the future. It was larger than both of them. The Wus would never let him go. They would never forgive. And she and Young Wu could never wed. Not in this lifetime.

But at least they could have this moment.

He crushed her against him and she cried out once more. In pain and pleasure and the bitterness of their fate.

44

For the second time that night Violet headed out along Slaty Creek where it trickled slow and brown through the diggings. She was conscious of Lewis glowering at her side as they hurried along the creek bank but he did not engage her in conversation. All his attention was focused on finding Strong Arm. Every so often he spared a few words to check the direction that she had taken, but he did not slow his pace until they reached the lone red gum standing sentinel by the creek about a mile from town. Then he relented, allowing her a brief respite to catch her breath.

She held her hand to her ribcage as her breathing slowed, wishing she could quell the turbulence in her heart so easily. Above her, the night sky was bright with a river of stars, giving the barren landscape an unearthly appearance, and the quiet was eerie. But she would not be the one to break the silence. She was too angry, with Lewis, with Strong Arm, but most of all with herself. She thought she had done with this pain. She thought she was done with betrayal. And yet she had allowed herself to be fooled again.

'Is this the tree where they met?' said Lewis, once she had caught her breath.

She was tempted not to reply, since if she could not get her due, there was still a certain sweetness to petty vengeance, but the urgency in his voice stayed her. Perhaps Strong Arm really was in danger. She might wish a disfiguring pox upon the girl, or an unpleasant bout of diarrhoea, but she did not wish her dead.

'Yes. But I did not follow them further. They continued along the creek that way.' She pointed towards the distant bushland, beyond which the moon was rising above Cabbage Tree Hill. 'How will you find them in the dark?'

'There is light enough.'

He set off once more along the gully, following the course of the creek by the light of stars and a rising half moon. She could have returned to town now that she was no longer of use in showing him the way, yet something held her to this course. A spark of determination, a tiny flame of… hope. He owed her. And perhaps she might win him yet. She was as much a warrior as Strong Arm in her way. *Her* father had been a sailor, an adventurer, not a farmer of silkworms. Oh yes, if necessary, Miss Violet Hartley could fight as hard as anyone. She would not let pride prevent her from getting what she wanted.

Campfires glowed on distant slopes nearer town but as they travelled further the diggings became sparser.

Lewis's sure stride took him easily across the uneven ground, while Violet scrabbled to clamber around holes and hummocks. She did not fancy being swallowed up by one of these dark and dirty holes, and her breath came in ragged gasps, but she did not turn back. It felt like they had been walking for hours, but was probably only a quarter-hour, when a sharp cry pierced the night up ahead. Lewis took off immediately at a run. Violet picked up her skirts and followed. There was more vegetation this far from town, so that patches of scrub and the occasional eucalypt, which had escaped the digger's axe, interrupted her view of the path ahead. She veered around some bushes to emerge on the banks of the gully several yards distant from Lewis. He had ceased running and was staring across the gully to the other side, where two figures were silhouetted by starlight. To Violet, they appeared to be locked in an embrace, standing so close that they might have been one person. The taller figure caressed the smaller one's neck as if to bring her mouth to his, while she encircled his waist with her arms.

But she also knew that love could resemble a struggle as much as an embrace. It all depended upon one's perspective. And Lewis, it seemed, was determined to see death where she saw love.

Another cry. Muffled this time.

She watched as Lewis removed his revolver from his breast pocket and held the gun in front of him, his arms rigid with intention. He hesitated for an instant, as if weighing the time and distance between himself and the embracing couple and Violet hesitated with him. Instinctively, she knew that Strong Arm faced her lover rather than her killer. 'No…' she said quietly.

Lewis cocked the revolver and aimed.

'No!' she shouted, taking herself by surprise. Despite her cry, Lewis was not disposed to listen. He did not lower his arm. He did not waver in his intention. Yet what could she do to stop him? And what should it matter to her if some stranger from the tea land died? What should it matter to her if the girl lost someone who she loved? One way or another Violet had lost everyone she had ever risked loving. At least it had taught her resilience. It had taught her to survive. One might even say that she would be doing the girl a favour by not intervening. That was what she told herself in those brief moments before Lewis fired. And yet…

With a speed she didn't know she possessed, Violet sprinted the last few yards that separated her from Lewis. 'No!' she screamed. But she was too late. With an explosion of sound and saltpetre, he fired the gun just as she reached him. She felt a savage jolt, and reeled with the impact. Pain scorched her upper arm like a hot needle as she crumpled to her knees, whimpering.

Lewis sprang to her side, catching her before she could collapse to the ground. 'Violet! What have I done?'

'You have shot me,' she croaked, staring in shock at the blood already staining the sleeve of her jacket. 'I'm bleeding.' She had had her jacket copied from the latest Paris fashion plate, and now it was ruined.

'Let me look.' Gently, he undid the buttons and slid the jacket from her shoulders. She winced as he pulled the sleeves down over her arms. Then he unfastened the bodice of her dress, loosening it enough to bare her upper arm. Taking a neat handkerchief from his pocket, he dabbed at the blood seeping from the wound. 'I believe it's merely a flesh wound.'

'You would not say that if it were your flesh.'

'There doesn't appear to be any bullet lodged here, Violet.'

She heard the relief in his voice and was placated. A little. So... he did care. No doubt, he could be encouraged to care a deal more with the right incentives. And without that girl around.

'I think you'll live. But we need to get the wound cleaned up properly.' He was staring at her with a puzzled frown. 'I could have lost you.'

'But you haven't.'

He could have lost her. That meant that he wanted her. That he needed her. She felt a swell of happiness at his words and allowed herself to swoon towards him, but just as she was about to surrender to his arms, she remembered.

'Strong Arm.'

That troublesome girl was getting in her way yet again.

One minute she was lost in a heady sweep of sensation and the next the air shattered into a million pieces of sound, the noise reverberating along the gully before escaping into the night. At the same time she was knocked to the ground by the weight of Young Wu's falling body. Bone and flesh were buffeted by the impact. And for the second time that night her head hit the ground with a thud.

After the first shock passed, she lay quietly beneath him, trying to shake her thoughts into some semblance of order. What had happened, and was it likely to happen again? She listened to the night for clues, hearing nothing other than the rustle of small things, the murmur of the creek and a shuffle of sound from the far bank. Above her she saw nothing but stars. Perhaps they had been caught by a random shot from a drunken digger. That had happened before on the diggings, where so many of the foreign devils carried guns. Some nights the air was peppered with the sound of gunfire.

When nothing further occurred, she decided that they were safe for the moment. If they weren't, she could do little about it, stranded as she was beneath the body of Young Wu.

'Are you all right?' she asked, unwrapping her arms from around his waist to touch his face, which lay against her chest. 'Wu. Speak to me.'

He was heavy, unmoving, and silent; the weight of his inert body crushing her injured ribs.

'Wake up.' She shook his shoulders, expecting him to protest. He could not be dead. The gods could not be so unkind. He was simply resting after the shock of whatever had happened. In a moment he would raise his head from her chest with his usual disdainful expression, invoke Second Brother's name, and tell her not to behave like a child.

She counted to ten and shook him again. 'Wu. Wake up. You have to wake up.' When he didn't answer she waited another ten breaths before trying a different tack. 'You're too heavy. You're hurting me.'

If his head hadn't been pressed against her chest she might have missed the faint moan that hummed through the fabric of her tunic and into her heart. He lived.

'I need to move.' She could not help him while she lay trapped, but his *qi* seemed so fragile that she feared any violent movement might stifle it altogether. She began counting another ten breaths to give her time to think, but soon realised that the faint sounds issuing from the far bank had resolved into footsteps, the heavy-footed gait of a European man and another lighter tread. Perhaps it would be safest to play dead. Wu wasn't going anywhere. She closed her eyes.

'Strong Arm!' She recognised the voice immediately but that recognition did not allay her fears. Someone had shot at them. And here was Thomas. Had it been him? How could she trust these enigmatic foreigners whose ways were so different from her own. Who seemed to owe allegiance to neither clan nor *kongsi*.

'They're not moving.' She recognised this voice too, although the fear she detected in it was unexpected.

A moment later, she sensed that Thomas and Hartley were standing above her. She caught the whiff of gunpowder and knew that one of them had fired the gun that shot her beloved. Then she felt a disturbance in the air as Thomas knelt beside her to place his hand upon Young Wu's back.

'He's still breathing,' he said.

'Perhaps there's time. If we can get him to a doctor,' said the Hartley woman.

'He had his hands around her throat, Violet. I thought he was going to kill her. I thought I wouldn't have time to stop him.'

She couldn't understand the bullock man's words but she heard the anguish in his voice.

'He wasn't killing her. He was embracing her. Don't you know the difference?'

By contrast, the Hartley woman's voice was sharp with anger. Was she angry with Thomas or with Strong Arm and Young Wu? And which of the two foreigners had shot him? Strong Arm could not be certain.

She felt a knee nudge her as Thomas lifted Wu's body from her chest and she breathed more easily. The scent of perfume and a rustle of silk told her that Hartley now knelt at her side. She probed Strong Arm's body with gentle hands from shoulder to waist.

'I don't think she has been hit.'

Then Strong Arm had the strangest sensation of a soft cheek pressed against hers, and words whispered in her ear. 'Open your eyes. We need your help.'

Help. She understood this word. But could she believe it? One of them had shot Wu. One of them had wanted him dead or wounded. Why would they now help him?

Yet what choice did she have?

'Help Wu.' The words emerged from her throat thin and parched. She opened her eyes to find Hartley's face hovering like a ghost in front of her eyes, large and pale in the silvery light. 'Help Wu,' she repeated.

'We'll try,' said Hartley, grasping her by the shoulders.

With her help, Strong Arm sat up, trying not to wince with the pain. Beside her, Wu rested in the bullock man's arms. Thomas sat with his legs stretched apart, Wu leaning against him. A dark flower of blood seeped through her beloved's tunic over his heart. It appeared to grow as she watched.

'Wuuuu…' His name was a wail of loss.

'He lives…' said Thomas. She knew these words. Yet she heard other missing words in the silence that followed them. He lived… but for how long?

She went to him on her hands and knees, leaning as close as possible, to await the brush of air against her cheek which would confirm that he lived. His breath was fast, as if he had been running. And beneath his tan his face was pale, his skin clammy. Sitting back on her heels, she took one of his hands in both hers. His beautiful hand was so cold, his *qi* sluggish.

'Don't leave me, Wu.'

They had only just found each other. He could not leave her. Not yet.

He parted his lips and she held her breath, waiting for him to speak, waiting for him to tell her that he would live. There was a strangled gurgling in his throat as he searched for the strength.

'*Yuen fen…*' The words were barely audible.

'Wu…' She squeezed his hands, before lowering her lips to his. She would force the life back into him. She would win the battle that waged between them, if it killed her. For if they could not be together in this life, then at least she would know that somewhere in the world Wu Hoi Sing lived. Somewhere in the world he might think of her, that troublesome girl from Sandy Bottom Village, and he would say her name. One day when he was father to eight children, grandfather to many more, he would remember her and he would smile.

She didn't know how long she held her lips to his, but as Hartley pulled her free the words he had whispered next to her ear reverberated into the night. *Yuen fen.* Now was not their time. They were separated by something greater than an ocean, greater than a river of stars, greater even than death. They were separated by fate.

'It takes a hundred rebirths to ride in the same boat, a thousand to share the same pillow.' So it was said. One day it would be their time. Even if it took ten thousand thousand years, one day they would find each other again.

One day they would be lovers.

But Strong Arm did not believe in fate. And she did not want to wait.

45

The girl's howl of grief was pitiful as she clung to her lover's inert body. Tugging gently at her quivering shoulders, Violet prised her away, to hold her tightly against her chest. She felt each shivering breath send tremors through her thin frame, as she muttered the same phrase over and over in her incomprehensible tongue.

'*Yen fen... yen fen... yen fen.*'

Violet patted her on the back, not knowing what else to do. She still had not found a remedy for grief.

'Is he gone?' she asked Lewis, looking over the smaller girl's shoulder. Lewis sat with his back against a hummock of earth, cradling the man in his lap as if he might wake at any moment, complaining of the stony ground.

'Not yet, but his pulse is weak and he's losing a great deal of blood. At this rate it won't be long.' He ran a hand through his hair. 'I didn't want to kill him. Only stop him from killing Strong Arm.' It was a plea for understanding as much as anything. 'He was hunting her.'

'I know. You were merely protecting her,' Violet sighed. She could not give him absolution, if that was what he sought, and now was not the time for soul-searching. They had to try and stop the bleeding. Already, the man's blood smeared Lewis's hands and stained his clothing.

'We need a doctor. Perhaps the sound of gunshot will bring help.'

He shook his head. 'Every second digger shoots off his pistol at bedtime to warn thieves he is armed.'

So... if he were to be saved it was up to her and Lewis... and quickly. Even in the dim light she could see the flood of crimson soaking the man's tunic above his heart. At least she thought it was above his heart. If it wasn't, well... there was nothing to be done. If it had missed that organ, then there was only bone, sinew and muscle to contend with, and these might be healed with a little luck and a few prayers.

'Can you place him on the ground and mind the girl so that I can tend his wound?'

Lewis nodded, lifting the man's body to the ground and sliding out from beneath him to relieve Violet. But her charge was having none of it. She opened her mouth, hesitating, as if caught between a scream and a sob, then closing it again she hammered her fists against Lewis's chest in a silent tattoo of rage and sorrow. Lewis stood motionless as a tree, accepting the barrage as his due.

'Strong Arm. We help,' said Violet, tugging at her arm and pointing to the injured man. 'We help.'

She lifted her skirt to reveal a petticoat made from

the finest Swiss eyelet cotton. 'Only the best will do, I suppose,' she said with a shrug before tearing at the fabric with her teeth and ripping a wide strip from the hem. She repeated this action until she had several yards of cloth to work with. Then kneeling in the dirt, she began unfastening the loops of the man's tunic. The girl seemed to understand her purpose because she wriggled from Lewis's grasp and knelt at her lover's other side, easing the tunic up his body, until she had it bunched under his arms. Lewis joined them, manoeuvring the man's upper body so that the two women could slide the tunic gently over his head. When his torso was bare Violet folded a length of bandage into a thick wad and applied pressure to the wound.

'Hold this while I bandage it,' she said, taking the girl's hands and pressing them to the wad of cotton. With Lewis's help she wrapped the bandage beneath his arm and across his opposite shoulder again and again before tying it at the neck. Throughout these ministrations the wounded man did not make a sound. If not for the whisper of his breath upon her cheek as she wrapped him in cotton, and the blood that continued to seep from his wound, she might have thought him dead.

'Let's get him to the doctor in this handcart,' said Lewis.

'What will you tell him?'

'The truth. That I thought he was attacking Strong Arm and intervened.'

'But if he should die the doctor will notify the police.'

Violet realised she must think quickly before he became set in his resolve. Men could be so selfish sometimes, especially when facing a crisis of conscience. Conscience seemed to set them on a path where other people got dragged into martyrdom along with them. What good could come of involving the police? *If* they could find one in this godforsaken country. Mostly the miners seemed to deal out a rough justice of their own. If the man should die, Lewis would be thrown into jail. Strong Arm would be exposed as a woman. The dead man's family would send someone else to hunt her down. And Violet would be required to secure her future afresh. And all to pander to one man's conscience.

'Then her identity will surely become known. Wu's family will hunt her down. And the poor child will never be free. Perhaps it would be better to say he caught a stray bullet.'

He considered her words for a few moments, before accepting their good sense with a nod. 'You are a wise woman, Violet Hartley.'

She heard a rumble behind her and realised that the girl was trundling the handcart towards them, tears glistening on her cheeks in the moonlight. And that was how the newcomers found them, as they clambered up the side of the gully, surprising Strong Arm so that she halted, her eyes darting from one stranger to the other.

'*Jat Jai. Jat Jai.*'

One of the newcomers fell to his knees alongside the wounded man, moaning in despair. He was just another old Chinaman with his straggling grey pigtail and weathered face, and yet he seemed vaguely familiar. Perhaps it was his one roving eye that singled him out. He was certainly familiar to Strong Arm. She seemed ready to pounce on the old man like a cornered cat, spitting a stream of words at his face. The old man backed away from the body on his knees, his hands held out before him, open-palmed. He looked from Lewis to Violet saying, 'My nephew. What happen?'

'It was me, Mr Wu,' said Lewis. 'I did it to protect Strong Arm. Your nephew attacked her once before on the journey here. She told us the story of his father's death. He would have killed her.'

'He not hurt girl.'

'She killed his father. He came for vengeance.'

The old man dropped his head. 'Young Wu not kill this girl. He love this girl.' When he looked up, Violet saw that his face was shiny with tears.

The girl in question remained poised to attack even as she wheeled the handcart closer. 'Need doctor,' she said.

'He doctor.' The old man pointed at his companion, a man of middle years dressed in a long black robe. He approached the injured man to kneel at his shoulder. 'Nephew say wait but Uncle worry. Bring doctor... for girl.'

The doctor was bent close over Wu's chest, listening to his patient's breathing as he inspected the wound. Then taking Wu's wrist in his hand he felt for the pulse, all the while listening and watching. Meanwhile, the old man stared at his nephew's blood-soaked body as if mesmerised. Then after the exchange of some rapid conversation, the old man indicated that they were to lift the body into the handcart.

'We take Wu to doctor tent. He give herbs. He make plaster,' he said. 'He do his best.' He shuffled forward on his knees to lift his nephew's head and shoulders from the clump of grass where he lay. 'Look,' he said with a nod, his voice strangely flat.

They all turned to look where he indicated, at the ground beneath Wu's head.

'It must have been washed up here when the creek last flooded,' said Lewis, staring at the clump of grass.

'*Gum*,' said Strong Arm, glaring at the ground with dislike.

'My goodness,' said Violet.

For peeking out between the blades of grass, glinting brightly in the starlit night, was a lump of gold the size of her fist.

46

Western District, Victoria, 1859

Some days, when the wind was up, simply hanging out laundry was a struggle. As well as the normal business of contending with heavy, dripping washing, Violet had to wrestle flapping sheets and flyaway shirts and grapple with the leaning timber props. Lewis couldn't understand that she wasn't built for such skirmishes. He couldn't comprehend that she belonged in the drawing room not the laundry room. At times she suspected he was more interested in the welfare of his sheep than his wife. When her feet became blistered from wearing worn-out boots, he suggested she line them with straw. But if his sheep developed foot rot it kept him up all night.

She heard a gurgle issue from the laundry basket and could not suppress a smile, despite her ill mood. Baby Lewis delighted in the snap and pop of laundry flapping above him. He crowed with joy at the fluffy white clouds drifting overhead. He must take after his father in his sunny nature. She lifted him from the basket and kissed the top of his head before placing him on the grass at her feet. Then she unpegged a dry sheet from the line and stowed it in the basket before replacing her baby atop the mound of fresh washing. Cooing with pleasure, he plucked at the cloth with his plump little fingers. Unless it was raining, Baby Lewis always rode in the laundry basket, making the entire endeavour unnecessarily complicated, but a great deal more pleasurable for them both. Living out here on their sheep station, she had to take her pleasures where she found them. At least for the moment.

The sun was warm upon the back of her neck, as the afternoon shadows grew longer. She should take Baby Lewis inside for his nap, but it was such a lovely afternoon that she could not resist standing in the sun a while longer, dreaming of the future. With the last of the drying laundry flapping behind her, she eyed the low bluestone cottage critically. Four small rooms. Kitchen, scullery, parlour and a single bedroom. Soon they would need a nursery or she and Lewis might be sleeping in the scullery, if the signs of her body could be relied upon.

She imagined the additions Lewis had promised her. A second storey and a separate outbuilding to accommodate the kitchen, scullery, laundry and maid's quarters. For Violet was determined to get herself a maid as soon as one could be enticed away from the goldfields. With all this manual labour she was growing old before her time. Why, she had recently developed a plague of freckles upon her nose, and on Thursday a faint line had manifested upon her forehead where none had been evident a week earlier.

Yes, a maid could not come soon enough. The gold nugget they had discovered the night Wu was shot had been welcome, but divided amongst them it did not make for a fortune. Especially given Lewis's ridiculous pangs of guilt. He was too warm-hearted for his own good.

Sighing, she picked up basket and baby, balancing them upon her hip. She took one last look out over their sprawling domain of kangaroo grass, to the mountains beyond. Somewhere out there, five thousand head of sheep grazed upon the sea of native grass, sheltered beneath the spreading branches of giant red gums, drank from the gentle waters of creek and river. And it was all hers. Well, hers and Lewis's. She should be pleased. She had acquired a husband. She had acquired a manor of sorts. Soon she would acquire a suitable house and servants. She should be happy.

Strong Arm leaned her weight upon the shovel and dug manure around the sapling. She smiled to herself as the earth turned freely. It had taken many months of toil but the soil was improving at last. Unlike her home in Kwangtung, where summer brought the monsoon, the summers here were so hot and dry that all moisture was sucked from her body. The rain was sparse, the rivers parched, the land thirsty. Despite the Wannon River, which bordered the property, and the narrow creek, which flowed through it, water was precious. But they had laboured to build a dam. They had dug canals to channel the water. And now the plants flourished even in high summer.

The garden rolled out before her in a carpet of green. She had worked the hard earth to a fine grain, woven windbreaks from she-oak branches and planted the soil with a profusion of vegetables. Potatoes, carrots, cabbages, turnips, beans and onions to suit European tastes and *bok choy*, *gai larn* and *choi sum* to suit her own. She had even created a small pond to raise ducks, giving their manure back to the earth to add to the soil's goodness. Yet despite her efforts, the country here was so different from home, where the Mo, Wu and Yee ancestors had devoted centuries to taming land and river. Here, she was only just beginning.

In the east, the Grampians snaked like a purple shadow upon the horizon. To the west, perched on a slight rise overlooking the creek, was the dark smudge of a low bluestone cottage. While behind her sat a small slab hut. These were the only buildings within sight. The hut was hers. Thomas had helped with the heaviest work of constructing it, but for the most part she had brought it into being with her own hands. First she had sawn the four sturdy posts of blue gum that stood at the corners to hold up the roof. Then she had attached beams at ground and roof levels, fitted saplings as roof struts, and split slabs of timber for the walls, before filling the chinks with clay. The roof was made from bark shingles.

The floor was of pounded earth. And the chimney and fireplace were of stacked bluestone.

She had formed it of this earth. And now it was part of her.

The first of the beans were ready to be picked. They hung in clusters of bright green from vines, which twined around two neat rows of frames. Tomorrow she would rise before dawn to harvest them while the dew was still fresh on their skins. She would cut some cabbages, pull up a good number of carrots and turnips, and fill her baskets. Then she would take up her *ta'am* and walk five miles into the village to sell her produce from door to door. On Tuesdays, the townspeople had come to expect her arrival. They opened their doors with coins in hand for the woman with the long black braid and blue trousers. She had let her shaved scalp grow out until it was once more long enough to be plaited into her braid.

This was the pattern of her days. Tending her garden, selling her produce, practising her writing so that she could send word back home to Second Brother. One day, if she sold enough beans, she might even have enough coin for his passage to New Gold Mountain. As for Elder Brother, with her share of the money from the nugget, their father had finally come to an arrangement with Mr Yee and soon she hoped to receive news of a new arrival. Elder Brother and Siu Wan's first child.

Every couple of months, she borrowed a horse from Thomas and rode into Creswick to visit with Big Nose and stock up on rice, tea and other goods from home. He and Uncle Wu were doing well with their store, although she suspected that many of their customers came to gossip with Uncle Wu rather than spend money. Big Nose had recently purchased a plot of land in the main street and was now a respected member of the community. He had even petitioned the government for better drainage on behalf of his countrymen.

Soon the bullock dray would return from its latest journey carrying wool and wheat to the port and returning with supplies for the settlers, since her countrymen no longer landed at Robetown. She caught her breath at the thought that he would be home any day now. Often he was gone for weeks at a time and she felt his absence like an empty chamber in her heart. She worried for him driving the team across vast swathes of country with only Ruby's pup for company. But Thomas had taught him well. The road kept him away from anyone who might recognise him, anyone who might be sent to look for them.

Thomas always said that Wu was lucky the bullet only shattered his left shoulder, not his whip arm. Wu always said that he was lucky Thomas repaid his debt by bequeathing him the bullock team and freedom. But Strong Arm believed they were luckiest of all to have this chance of a life together. Lucky they did not have to wait a thousand lifetimes. Lucky… and determined.

Placing the shovel in the ground, she stood back to take stock of that morning's toil. The sapling had almost doubled in height since she planted it, shooting up tall and straight under her care. She thought of the brilliant green cloak of mulberry that draped the fields of Sandy Bottom Village. From a distance the bushes appeared lush and verdant. Their leaves sparkled in the sunlight. But each year the villagers cut and pruned the bushes, keeping them shrunken and truncated, to more easily harvest their leaves for the silkworms. The mulberries of Sandy Bottom Village would never grow tall. They would never bear fruit. They would never reach their potential.

Strong Arm did not have a grove of mulberry plants. She had only the one. But she would feed it and nourish it, so that it grew tall as its nature allowed. And one day, a few years hence, when the time was ripe, it would bear fruit.

Acknowledgements

In researching this book I made my own trek from Robe – albeit on four wheels rather than two feet – and I would like to thank the many people who helped me along the way. Many thanks to the staff at the Customs House Museum, Robe, Evelynne Bowden at The John Riddoch Centre, Penola, Anne-Marie Matuschka and Margaret Hanel at Mary MacKillop Penola Centre, Ian Black at the Hamilton History Centre and the staff of the Gum San Chinese Heritage Centre in Ararat. Heather Funk at the Dunkeld and District Museum went out of her way to open up the museum for me and find and send on material, as did Joy and Henry Gunstone of Ararat. This on-the-ground research helped bring the book to life.

A book is a collaborative project and *The Boy with Blue Trousers* wouldn't exist without the enthusiastic team at Head of Zeus. My wonderful editor Rosie de Courcy helped me make it into a much more subtle and dare I say, likeable beast. Thanks go to Sophie Robinson, Clare Gordon, Christina Ryan and the entire team at

Head of Zeus for their continued support for my books. I also appreciate the fantastic efforts of Samantha Teo and Jinli Tang at Pansing who helped get the word out in Singapore and Malaysia. Thanks also go to the international publishing team at HarperCollins Australia.

I continue to be grateful for the ongoing support and encouragement from my agent Judith Murdoch, who can be counted on to tell it like it is.

A big thank you to family and friends who gave me such lovely compliments about the first book and encouraged me to continue.

And as always, lots of hugs to my husband Vincent Kwok – who keeps me company on research trips and can be counted upon to help with all things Cantonese – and to my children Ru and Kit Kwok, two of my biggest supporters.